SO MUCH OWED

JEAN GRAINGER

So Much Owed

By Jean Grainger

Copyright © 2022 Gold Harp Media

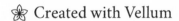 Created with Vellum

For Betty and Hilda

PROLOGUE

1 *2th December 1918*

From the outside, it was barely recognisable. Gaping holes in the walls and piles of smoking rubble had irrevocably altered the once imposing facade of *l'Hôpital Saint Germain*. The Allied propaganda machine had claimed the Battle of Amiens as a great victory – a turning point, spelling an end to the horrific futility of trench warfare. It was here in Amiens, the victors crowed, that the Germans had stumbled their first steps towards surrender. Yet as Dr Richard Buckley picked his way through the decimated city, he saw nothing about Amiens to suggest a city basking in the glory of victory. Instead, he found himself thinking: *So this is what winning looks like.*

He climbed what was left of the marble steps leading to the ornate entrance. Everything was so different from when he was last here four months ago. Gone was the officious Reverend Mother, who had vetted all entrants to the hospital with her suspicious eye. Gone too, the all-pervasive smell of beeswax and disinfectant that had permeated the quiet, ordered corridors of the past. Now the smell reminded him of Willy McCarthy's butcher shop in Skibbereen, where he and his school friends had gone one day to see the farmyard animals being slaughtered. The sickly scent of their dying had haunted him for years. Now the same mingled odour of blood, flesh, bone and fear again assailed his nostrils. It no longer made him physically sick – one can get used to anything, it seemed – yet as he strode through the foyer and up the stairs, he found it a struggle to endure the anguished cries of the wounded all around him. Two years spent treating the casualties of war had done nothing to desensitise him to the suffering of others.

'*Excusez-moi.*' He tried to seize the attention of a passing nun. Like everyone else here, she looked exhausted; her once-white uniform was spattered with bloodstains, some brown with age. '*Vous connaissez Solange Allingham...*'

'*Non, Monsieur.*' She shook off his arm and hurried on.

He had been moved further up the line last August, to where his services were in even greater demand. It seemed the turnover of hospital staff in his absence had been so rapid that there was no one left here who knew him. Perhaps he should have worn his uniform, but he had taken it off the day the armistice was declared and had vowed never to put it on again. He wanted nothing to do with the sense of triumph expounded by the top brass. Not because he was Irish and, therefore, it was not his country's glory, but because he was sickened by the whole bloody thing. He'd endured their congratulations at his decision to do the right thing, despite his nationality, with gritted teeth. It was pointless trying to explain his motivation had nothing to do with patriotism or a desire to defeat anyone, and everything to do with trying to alleviate suffering. Anyway, those men who aired such views were usually patients, and so he treated them as best he could and avoided any discussions on the subject.

HE TRIED AGAIN, THIS time approaching a

young nurse with red hair who just might be Irish.

'Excuse me – do you know Madame Solange Allingham?'

She stared at him as if amazed to see a fully intact man and answered him in a west of Ireland accent, 'Yes, she's in the theatre, but I think she's due a break sometime soon. Whether or not she'll get it is another thing. We've both been on duty,' she glanced at the watch pinned to the front of her uniform, 'twenty-nine hours now. If you want to wait, she'll come out this way. *If* she comes out. Now, please excuse me. If I don't lie down, I'll fall down.'

Richard sat on a wooden bench and leaned his tall frame against the dark-brown wainscoting. He also was exhausted. He thought he should probably go to a ward, offer to help, but he simply couldn't. He'd worked more or less constantly for two years, only going home on leave twice during that time, and apart from those brief visits, never taking a day off. He had treated the wounded day and night and only stopped when he felt his exhaustion was a danger to the patients. He would then sleep dreamlessly for a few hours and begin the whole bloody process again. The waves of battered and broken young men in front of him, many of them begging to die, never subsided. Some survived, a great many more didn't, and thousands were left with injuries so horrific that perhaps death would have been preferable to life.

His tiredness was playing tricks on his mind. Every time a doctor came round the corner, he found himself thinking it was Jeremy. Even though he had seen so many young men die, Richard still found it hard to accept that his best friend had joined the rest. He had been so vital, so much larger than life – smiling and joking and keeping everyone's spirits up. Yet it had turned out he was mortal like everyone else; apparently, he'd been killed in a bomb blast on his way to the hospital after a much-needed sleep. Even the nurse who had written to him with the news, herself so used to sudden death, had sounded shocked. Such a beloved doctor gone and so close to the end too – another week and it would have been all over.

Now Richard had nothing left to do but to collect Solange and bring her home with him. Jeremy should have been the one to take care of her after the war, but that was not to be. Solange Allingham had no one else to protect her now – her parents were dead, her brothers both killed at

Verdun. Jeremy and Richard had talked about this – if either of them was killed. Somehow, Richard had assumed that if either of them died, it would be him. He was so dull and uninteresting, compared to his friend. Yet in the end, it had been the lively, ever-smiling Jeremy who had died. And now it was down to Richard to take care of his best friend's sad, young widow.

CHAPTER 1

2 0th January 1919

Solange Allingham gazed out the window of the black Morris Oxford at the sodden fields. The endless journey through England by train and the choppy crossing to Ireland had barely registered with her. She could feel nothing except a dragging despair, deep within her. Even the rhythmic slosh of the car's wipers seemed to beat out the mantra, 'Jeremy is dead, Jeremy is dead.' They had been planning to buy a vineyard in the Dordogne after the war; they were going to have a huge family – three boys, three girls. *'Jeremy is dead, Jeremy is dead.'*

Gradually, the green rolling hills of the south-eastern counties of Wexford and Waterford gave way to rugged stone-filled fields. She kept on catching distant glimpses of a grey, cold ocean. Beside her, Richard drove in silence, his vivid green eyes focused on the wet road ahead, his sandy hair neatly cut and combed. How he and Jeremy had been such good friends amazed her. Her Jeremy had always been so bright and funny and full of life. This quiet, shy Irish doctor entirely lacked that sort of charm. When he spoke, it was always slow and deliberate. He was painstakingly methodical in his work, irrespective of any chaos that surrounded him. Yet she had seen injured soldiers stop screaming in agony when Dr Buckley spoke to them or touched them. 'The gentle giant,' Jeremy had dubbed him, and he was indeed big – well over six feet tall, with a deep voice she knew his patients found reassuring.

'Not long now. We'll be in Skibbereen by six, I should think. I hope you aren't too uncomfortable?' His eyes never left the road.

'No, thank you.' She hesitated, seeking the English words. Her mind felt like it was wrapped in wet cotton wool, and all she really wanted to do was sleep. 'I am fine.' In the weeks since Jeremy had died, she had barely spoken, in either her native French or her husband's English. Not that she had learnt much English from Jeremy – he had always said he was too romantic and passionate to be Anglo-Saxon and so spoke in French to her most of the time.

All the nurses had been in love with the young doctor with his thick, wavy hair and warm hazel eyes; he had flirted outrageously with all of them, but they knew there was nothing in it – he only had eyes for Solange Galliard. He had pursued her relentlessly from when he was first assigned to the hospital, ignoring her protests that she was engaged to Armand De La Croix, the son of a local banker. Jeremy saw this as no obstacle whatsoever: she simply had to break off the engagement and marry him instead. It was impossible to do anything else, he'd claimed – she had bewitched him with her deep azure eyes and her black corkscrew curls, forever threatening to liberate themselves from the starched white veil of her nurse's uniform. He told her regularly that she occupied his every thought, waking and sleeping, and, despite herself, she had fallen in love with the incorrigible English doctor. When he talked, he made her laugh till tears flowed down her cheeks, and when he touched her, she tingled with desire. She had married him and was the happiest girl on earth.

Back in 1914, the war had been seen as something to be over by Christmas. The girls had giggled with delight at the vast numbers of handsome soldiers arriving daily. It had all seemed so romantic, the men so gallant – a bit of a lark really, as Jeremy termed it. How wrong they all were. The fun and high spirits of those early days had quickly given way to scenes of unprecedented human misery. Those scenes would haunt all those who witnessed them for the rest of their lives.

Solange wondered if Jeremy would even recognise her if he were to see her now. Grief had taken its toll on the curvaceous body he had loved; her once round cheeks were hollow, and dark shadows circled her blue eyes. At twenty-six, her jet-black hair had become suddenly threaded with silver hairs. The person she had been before the war seemed a distant stranger to her now. She suspected the carefree girl of her youth had died along with that whole generation of young men. All gone now, and Jeremy gone with them.

'There is a rug on the back seat if you're cold.' Richard's voice interrupted her reverie.

'No, thank you. I am fine.' She realised her answer was a repetition of her response to his earlier enquiry so she added, with an attempt at enthusiasm, 'Ireland is a very pretty country. Quite like Brittany in places, I think.' She knew her voice sounded flat and colourless. She couldn't help it.

He nodded thoughtfully. 'Yes, I'm glad you like it. Though, of course, when the sun shines, it's much better. When we were students in England, Jeremy often came here on holidays. He complained that it never stopped raining. I tried to get him to consider moving here after the war, but he said he would rather get a suntan in France than rust in Ireland any day.'

They both smiled at the memory of him; his presence was almost tangible between them in the car.

'Thank you for doing this for me,' Solange began again. 'You have been so kind. I cannot imagine how it would have been if I would have stayed in France. I don't know if I can survive now, but at least here has no memories. I will try to be of service to you and your family.'

Richard drove and sighed deeply as if weighing up how best to phrase what he was going to say next.

'Solange, I'm not bringing you to Dunderrig to be of service to us, I am bringing you to be a member of our family. Please understand that. It's your home for as long as you want it to be. We, Edith and I, don't expect anything from you, but I, we, both hope that coming here will help you. I can't imagine how hard it must be, considering all you have lost. Not just Jeremy, but your parents, your brothers. It's almost too much to bear. We just want to help, in any way that we can. Jeremy would have taken care of Edith had the situation been reversed. We talked about it, you know. What we would do if either one of us didn't make it. I know if it had been me who was killed then you and Jeremy would have helped Edith. So please, you are family as far as we are concerned. You don't owe us a thing.'

In the four years she had known Richard Buckley, this was the longest speech she had ever heard him make. His voice was cracking with emotion and it was clear his offer came from the heart. She hardly knew what to say – she sat in silent gratitude as he drove the narrow, twisty road.

'Down there is Skibbereen, but this is where we turn off,' he said, taking a slow right at a signpost marked 'Dunderrig'. 'I wrote to Edith to let her know we were arriving this evening, so she will be expecting us. Though naturally, she has been very tired of late.'

'Of course. She has only a few more weeks to go?' Solange enquired politely.

'Two weeks, perhaps. No more than three. I would have given anything to have been here to help her. She has suffered badly with sickness throughout this pregnancy. And she had to cope with the loss of my mother and father too, within a few days of each other. Thank God the influenza spared my wife, if not my poor parents. She has had so much to cope with.'

'It will feel strange for you to be home and not to see them. Even as an adult, you are never ready to lose your parents.' She was conscious that her voice had grown heavy with her own pain and made an effort to be stronger for him. 'But you must be very excited to see your wife after all this time.'

'Yes, I am.' A brief smile but nothing more.

She glanced at him, questioningly. Richard very rarely mentioned Edith; Solange had often speculated with Jeremy about what kind of marriage the Buckleys had – practical, passionate, romantic? When she wondered what Mrs Buckley was like, Jeremy told her that he had met Edith only briefly and explained how he had dragged his shy best friend to a dance while they were still at medical college in England. To his surprise, Richard spent his evening talking about Ireland with a cool but beautiful blonde from Dublin. Only weeks later they qualified, and Jeremy signed up for France and met Solange while Richard went to work as a doctor in Ireland and ended up marrying the Dublin girl. Solange's only knowledge of Edith was based on the photo Richard had of her on his desk in the hospital; it showed a tall and elegant woman, beautifully dressed. She also knew that Richard had seen his wife very briefly eight months before, when in Dublin on leave – a leave that had been cut short before he'd been able to travel home to Cork to visit his parents, then still alive and well. Poor Richard. 'And are you also excited to become a Papa?'

'Yes. I am.' The same answer, but this time the smile was warmer.

THE HOUSE WAS SET back from the road and was impressive in its size and architecture. While not a *château* by any standard, it still seemed to be a very large house for a couple to inhabit alone. It was built of a buttery stone with limestone edging, and despite its grand size appeared welcoming, with lights blazing in each window, promising a warm and inviting end to her long, tiring journey. The tree-lined avenue passed through gardens that were beautifully kept, even during their winter sleep. Large sections of the housefront were covered with crimson-and-gold creeping ivy and as they drew level with the large, bottle-green front door – the car's wheels crunching on the gravel – Solange admired the blood-red Poinsettia spilling from pots in wild profusion on either side of the door. Perhaps Edith was a keen gardener. She hoped so because she loved gardens too – it would give them something to talk about.

Richard opened the car door and offered her his arm to assist her out. Standing, she found she was stiff and sore, and suddenly longed for a bath and a good night's sleep. As he opened the front door, a plump, matronly woman with iron-grey hair and a currant-bun face came hurrying from the back section of the house.

'Dr Richard, you're home! You're as welcome as the flowers of May. Let me have a look at you! God in heaven, you're skin and bone! We'll have to feed you up. Oh, 'tis wonderful to have you home, so it is. I can't believe 'tis two years since you set foot in Dunderrig. Wouldn't your mother and father be just delighted to see you, God rest them home safe and sound. They never stopped worrying about you, God be good to them.' Tears filled the woman's eyes.

Solange stood by as Richard put his arms around the grey-haired woman and held her tightly.

'You were so good to them, Mrs Canty. My mother's last letter told how much ye did to ease my poor father's passing, and how skilful ye were at nursing her. I can't believe she won't be in the kitchen or he in his surgery ever again.'

He spoke quietly; their loss was shared. Mrs Canty was clearly much more than a housekeeper – more like one of the family. After a few minutes, he stepped back and indicated Solange.

'Mrs Canty, this is Madame Solange Allingham, Jeremy's wife.'

The woman hurried towards Solange, dabbing her eyes with the corner of her apron.

'I beg your pardon, I didn't see you there. What must you think of us at all? You are very welcome to Dunderrig, pet, and I'm sorry it's only me here to greet ye. We didn't know exactly when to expect you, you see. My Eddie is out and about somewhere, and Mrs Buckley is upstairs having a lie-down. She's been very out of sorts all day.'

She took Solange's hand while sadly shaking her head.

'I remember your husband well – a lovely lad and no mistake. He was like a ray of sunshine around the place when he used to visit. Dr Richard's mother, God rest her soul, used to knock a great kick out of him altogether – the antics and tricks acting out of him! I was so sorry to hear he had been killed, and ye only a young couple starting out in your lives. 'Twas a terrible thing that war. So many grand lads like Jeremy, gone forever.'

The woman spoke so quickly that Solange struggled to understand her – but she could tell enough to be moved by the kind way this woman spoke about her dead husband and warmed to her at once.

'Thank you, Mrs Canty. Yes, my husband often spoke about the happy times he enjoyed in Ireland.' Solange hoped her English was clear enough.

Whether Mrs Canty fully understood her or not, she seemed satisfied with Solange's halting answer. 'You're very welcome here, especially now. God knows, with the new baby arriving any minute, we'll be all up in the air soon. I'll tell you, Dr Richard, she's not great at all today. I've been trying to get her to eat a bit all day long, but she's not having a bar of it. You'd think she'd be all excitement over having you home after all this time! Normally, women get a bit of a boost just before, you know, getting things ready for the baby and all that, but she just lies in bed, the only thing she's interested in is writing letters...'

'Thank you, Mrs Canty, that will be all.'

Both Richard and Mrs Canty turned with a start, and Solange followed their eyes to the top of the stairs from where the cold, sharp voice had come.

'It is perhaps not so inconceivable that I would not wish to eat, given the standard of cuisine in this house. Please attend to your duties.'

The haughty tone brooked no argument. A tall, blonde woman was descending the staircase, which curved elegantly around the walls into the large square entrance hall. She was dressed in an ivory silk gown, over which she wore a contrasting coffee-coloured robe, and she moved remarkably gracefully, given the advanced stage of her pregnancy; despite the large bump, she was slender, almost thin. She looked pale and tired, but also something else. She seemed to exude disdain, not just for the verbose Mrs Canty but for her entire surroundings. She certainly seemed to show no delight at the safe return of her husband.

'Edith, you look wonderful, blooming. Mrs Canty was telling us you haven't been well? It's so good to see you.' Richard crossed to the bottom of the stairs, offering his hand to assist her down the last few steps. She allowed him to take it and turned a powdered cheek for him to kiss, but Solange could see her actions lacked enthusiasm. Richard must have noticed it too – having pecked his wife lightly, he released her limp fingers and retreated a few steps, looking around him, clearly searching for something else to say. His eyes alighted on Solange. 'Edith, this is Solange Allingham, Jeremy's wife.'

Edith Buckley heaved a huge, sarcastic sigh as she approached Solange. 'Yes, Richard, I did gather who this was. You wrote to me several times to tell me she was coming, and it is not as if Dunderrig is such a hive of social activity that I would confuse the guests. Mrs Allingham, what on earth possessed you to leave France for this godforsaken place?'

Uncertain how to respond, Solange silently extended her own hand, but Edith ignored it.

'Oh well, you're here now, so you will have to make the best of it. Presumably, you will either expire from boredom or food poisoning, but if you are determined to take your chances... Oh, Mrs Canty, are you still here?'

Mrs Canty marched off furiously to the kitchen, saying loudly how someone had to pre-pare a 'good, wholesome meal' for the poor trav-ellers. Richard seemed unsure what he should do next. He made to put his hand on his wife's back but the look she gave him was so frosty, he changed his mind.

Solange hurried to lighten the mood. 'Madame Buckley, I must thank you for inviting me into your home. Please believe me, after the past few years in France, a quiet life is something I wholeheartedly desire, so do not be concerned I will be bored. Besides, when the new little one arrives, it will be a very busy household. I hope to be of some service.' She tried to infuse her voice with gratitude and friendliness to bring some much-needed warmth into the situation.

Edith shrugged. 'I suppose so. But I warn you, it will all seem deathly dull. I am sorry about your husband. Still, if countries insist on colonising smaller nations then war must be an inevitable outcome.'

Solange was nonplussed. Was Edith saying that Jeremy deserved to die because of the past decisions of English and French rulers? Surely she could not be so callous. She glanced at Richard, who had coloured with embarrassment.

Nonchalantly changing the subject, Edith addressed her husband, 'Richard, please contact Dr Bateman to come out. I'm not feeling well, and I need to consult him. I'm going back to bed. Welcome home. Please don't disturb me until he arrives.' She turned away.

Richard followed his wife across the hall to the foot of the sweeping stairs. 'Perhaps it's something I can help you with? It is rather a long way for Bateman to come...'

'Richard,' Edith said wearily, without looking back at him. 'While I accept you are a doctor, you are not *my* doctor. You have been conspicuous by your absence throughout my confinement so it would be wholly inappropriate for you to involve yourself in my care at this late stage. Please contact Dr Bateman as soon as possible.' Moving wearily but not slowly, she climbed the stairs.

'Very well. If that's what you want, then of course I'll contact him – and then maybe we could have tea?'

Richard was almost pleading. But Edith had already disappeared into a room on the second floor, and his request was met with the closing of the door behind her. He turned anxiously to Solange.

'She is very tired. And she is so devoted to the cause of Irish independence. She didn't mean anything against poor Jeremy. Her opinions...she is not a supporter of the Allies. But of course, she doesn't support the other side either. I'm afraid I have to leave you a moment to call Dr Bateman. Can you take a seat here, until Mrs Canty returns? She will see you to your room and feed you to within an inch of your life and hopefully you'll start to feel normal again.' Then he backtracked as if worrying that he had sounded as crass as his wife. 'I mean obviously not normal, not after everything, but maybe you can feel just a little better. Welcome to Dunderrig.'

While Solange waited for the housekeeper's re-emergence, she studied her new surroundings. The entrance hall was warm and welcoming, in stark contrast to its mistress. It was as generously proportioned as any reception room and carpeted with a rich-red-and-gold rug. The furniture – a hall stand, a writing table and chair, a loudly ticking grandfather clock, and the upholstered chaise longue on which she had seated herself – were all highly polished. Oil paintings – landscapes and horses, mainly – adorned the silk-covered walls. The cantilevered staircase had a deep pile runner at its centre. A passageway led from the hall towards the back of the house. It was down this that Mrs Canty had disappeared and, based on the aromas of baking, it was connected to the kitchen. To her left and right were four large oak doors, also richly polished and all closed. Richard had gone through one of them into what was clearly a doctor's surgery. Why had Edith insisted Richard call her a different doctor? If she, Solange, had been pregnant with Jeremy's child, her husband would have been the only doctor she would have trusted to attend her.

She glanced up to the second floor. The mahogany banister became a small but ornate balcony for the rooms above, all the doors of which opened out onto the landing. The effect meant the entranceway felt like a stage and the upper gallery the viewing point. Solange felt exposed and wished that Mrs Canty would reappear. She dreaded the possibility of Edith's return.

'Ah Lord, did he leave you here all on your own? Where's he gone to, in the name of God? I don't know what's happening to everyone in this house, honest to God, I don't. God knows, in the mistress's time, Mrs Buckley now, I mean old Mrs Buckley, Dr Richard's mother, no visitor would have been left alone in the hall, but I don't know, things are very different around here these days. Poor Dr Richard, home after that terrible war and you'd think his wife would be happy to see him anyway.'

The housekeeper's voice dropped to a whisper as she pointed theatrically upwards while ushering Solange down the passageway into the kitchen.

'She's a bit of a handful, and she can be very cutting when she wants to be. Poor old Dr Buckley and the mistress, God be good to them, nearly drove themselves cracked trying to please her, but the day young Dr Richard left her here in Dunderrig while he went off to the war was a sad day for this house. At first, he'd taken work in Dublin to please her, but he couldn't rest easy when he heard from your husband about all the terrible goings-on at the front, and in the end, nothing would satisfy him but to follow Jeremy to France. He thought his wife would understand how she would be better off waiting for him in Dunderrig, and maybe look after his parents for him. But she stayed above in her room with a face that'd turn milk sour. Sure, even when the poor doctor got the flu earlier this year and we lost him, and the mistress less than a week later, not a budge out of herself above! And there were never two kinder people, God rest them. They were lovely, lovely people. I know she's from Dublin and not used to life in the country, but she's stuck in something to do with the rising and all that nonsense. Her father was some kind of a bigwig professor in the college up there, and he knew them all, Pearse and Yeats and all of them. We're not fancy enough at all for her, to my way of thinking. Sure, she just writes letters all day and gets letters back, too. I don't know who they're from, but 'tisn't right for a married woman to be going on with that kind of thing. Though I keep my own counsel, because of course, Dr Richard won't hear a word against her. He was forever writing to us to make sure she was all right and what have you, and Mrs Buckley decided he had enough to worry about over there so she told him 'twas all grand, but I'd say he got a bit of a land when he met her above in Dublin. Though she came back expecting, so I suppose they must have worked it out some kind of a way.' She softened, and chuckled.

Solange found herself standing in the middle of a warm, cosy kitchen that looked out onto a cobbled courtyard. The stones shone in the wet twilight of a winter's day.

'Now, you poor misfortune, you must be perished alive after sitting in that car for so long. My husband Eddie – he does the gardens, you see, and a bit of fetching and carrying around the house – he drove it down to the boat yesterday and got the train and bus back so 'twould be there for ye when ye got off the boat, and he said it was cosier on the train by far. Sit down there, let you, and I'll get you a bowl of soup to warm your bones. Were you ever here in Ireland before?'

Mrs Canty's patter was so like a babbling brook – comforting and restful, whatever its content – it took Solange a second to realise she had been asked a question.

'In Ireland? *Jamais...* I mean, no, never. Jeremy always said he would bring me here when the war was over but... Well, that was not meant to be.' Solange tried to recover, but Mrs Canty noticed the break in her voice. Turning from the large range, she crossed the floor and took Solange by surprise by enveloping her in a warm hug.

'Your husband was a grand lad entirely, and I'm sure you brought him great joy in his short life. 'Tis better you had him, even for a short time, and had the happiness of a good marriage than years stretching out without it.' And she nodded knowingly again in the direction of upstairs.

Anxious not to take sides, Solange said, 'Perhaps things will be better after the arrival of the new baby. Madame Buckley is probably just tired. I do not know myself as I have no children, but I imagine the last weeks can be exhausting. So, perhaps, once the baby is born safe and well, Madame Buckley will feel better.'

'Hmm. I don't know about that. I was never blessed with children either, but I know plenty of mothers and none of them are like herself above, I can tell you that.'

Mrs Canty placed a steaming hot bowl of creamy vegetable soup and a slice of brown soda bread thickly spread with butter on the table in front of Solange. After the deprivation in France, the richness of the food was glorious. Realising that she was very hungry, she ate greedily while Mrs Canty continued in the same vein.

'I don't know what to make of her. She arrived here with all her grand notions, but then she didn't change one thing about the place. I mean, even before she was expecting, you'd think a young bride coming into a place, especially a place like Dunderrig, would want to put her own stamp on the house. But 'twas as if she was a guest, and one that mightn't be staying at that. Very vexed she was with Dr Richard, over him joining up, I suppose, but 'twasn't as if she was heartbroken without him. Sure, she has no *meas* on him at all; she treats him no better than an auld stray dog. His parents now, the old doctor and Mrs Buckley, they idolised young Richard. He was their only one, you see. They nearly went out of their minds with worry when he went over there to France, and who could blame them? Sure, what has France to do with us here?'

Suddenly, remembering that Solange was French, Mrs Canty corrected herself hastily, 'Not that we thought the other side should win or any-thing... But it's just they were so worried, and him the only son of the house and all, but when they heard he was going to be with Jeremy, well that made them feel a bit easier in their minds. They were mad about Jeremy. We all were.'

'My husband loved you all, too. And he never wanted Richard to leave his parents. In truth, he was angry when Richard followed him. He didn't want his friend to be in danger, even though when Richard came, Jeremy was so happy to see him and so glad to have the help of such a good doctor.'

Remembering her young husband's concern

for his friend, Solange felt very far from home, and from him. Jeremy had been the essential link between her and Richard; in Amiens, she had only ever met the Irish doctor in Jeremy's company. Richard had never called on her separately or even chatted to her apart from a polite enquiry after her health. Yet here she was in Richard Buckley's house, in this foreign country so far from anything she'd ever known, and without Jeremy. Perhaps this had been a terrible mistake. Yet there was nothing left to which to return. *Maman and Papa both gone, Pierre and Jean-Paul too, and the city in ruins. You can't ever go back, only forward.* She had no choice. Richard had saved her from a life inhabited only by ghosts. At least, here in this strange place, she could be of use – help with the new baby, and begin again. Richard had thrown her a lifeline, and though at the moment drowning seemed like a more appealing option, she knew that she could and would survive.

'NOW PETEEN, WE BETTER get you to bed,' announced Mrs Canty as she ushered Solange upstairs and into a pretty room overlooking the garden. The walls were covered with an exotic bird of paradise wallpaper, in royal blue and gold, and on the teak double bed lay a beautifully embroidered cream bedspread. There were a large matching armoire and chest of drawers and a full-length mirror stood on a stand. The room was pleasantly warm and scented by a bunch of snowdrops arranged in a cut-glass bowl on the dresser. Her bags had been delivered to the room, presumably by the reticent Eddie, whom she still hadn't met.

'*Les fleurs*… The flowers. They are beautiful.'

'Oh that's himself, my Eddie, he grows them. Winter and summer he has flowers growing. He has Latin names for everything; you'd be demented trying to remember them all. There's nothing he can't grow, that husband of mine.' Her voice glowed with pride. 'Now so, let you have a good sleep, and we'll see you tomorrow sometime. Don't be in any rush to get up now, do you hear me?'

Solange slept fitfully, despite the comfortable bed. She tossed and turned and dreamed of France, and of her parents – though never of Jeremy. That often struck her as strange, how his loss was like a large gaping hole of pain in her every waking moment, yet once she slept, he never entered her dreams. The countryside was so quiet; only the crowing of a rooster in the early hours disturbed the peace. Lying awake, she decided to make the best of this situation. She would do her utmost to be a good friend to Richard's wife. Though Mrs Canty seemed a kind person, there was probably not a woman on earth whom the housekeeper would have thought good enough for her precious young master. And although Edith had seemed very cold and even rude to her at first, Solange acknowledged that if Jeremy had brought a young widow into their home, she too would have been cautious at first, however much she trusted her husband.

As dawn crept across the sky, she dozed off into a light sleep. She was disturbed by a piercing shriek from across the hall. Dashing out of bed, she threw on her dressing gown and ran in the direction of the sound. She found herself at the door of Edith's bedroom and hesitated, unsure if Edith was in there alone or if Richard had already joined her. A second later, another loud scream rent the air. This time, tentatively, Solange opened the door. The room was in complete darkness; she moved in the direction of the bed.

'Madame Buckley? Are you well?' The words sounded foolish to her ears, but she didn't know what else to say. Moving towards the curtains, she pulled them half open, allowing in sufficient dawn light to see Richard's wife alone in bed, a terrified expression on her face.

'Something... something is happening,' Edith gasped.

Solange ran to the bed and, gently moving back the covers, discovered Edith's water had broken. Her nightgown was soaking, as was the sheet and presumably the mattress beneath. Despite the pain, Edith was clearly mortified by the mess and was trying to cover it with her hands.

'Please, do not worry, Madame,' Solange said soothingly. 'This is normal. Your baby is now coming. Please stay calm, and I will send for your husband...'

'No!' Edith screamed.

Solange was unsure if the woman's cry related to Richard or to the pain, but Edith was holding her hand so tightly, it would have been impossible for her to move away from the bed anyway.

'No,' repeated Edith, this time as a hiss. 'Not Richard. I don't want him seeing me like this. Not Canty either. Get Dr Bateman back.'

'But Madame, I think there may be no time to send for him. I'm sure your husband will be here any moment.'

Where was he? No one could sleep through these screams. Solange took a deep breath; she must stay calm.

'If you will permit me to examine you, I think

we will find that the baby is almost here. Please do not worry, everything is going to be fine.' Solange was trying to measure the time in between the waves of pain that seemed to grip Edith with such savagery. She'd been present at many deliveries and could tell that this labour was very advanced. Had Edith been having contractions for hours and said nothing until she could bear the pain no longer? Was she that resistant to her husband's presence?

'Please Madame, please try to relax. I know it is difficult but please trust me, it will hurt less if you –' Frustratingly, the English would not come to her. 'Breathe slow and deeply,' she finished, relieved to have recalled the words. 'If you can try to relax, you are doing so well, and then the baby will be here very soon, and all of this will be over, I promise.'

Edith's response was another high-pitched scream. Mrs Canty appeared at the door, in her night-robe and bonnet. 'Oh Lord above! It's time, is it? Dr Richard's gone out on a sick call, tonight of all nights, and he only in the door. I don't even know where he is. What should we do?' Mrs Canty's voice was rising to a crescendo of panic.

'Please, don't worry, everything is perfectly normal. I have delivered many babies before.' A white lie – she'd only ever played a supporting role, and that was when she was still in training – but she had to calm the old housekeeper down. 'So Mrs Canty, if you can just help me by... No, there is no point now trying to get towels under her. I think the baby is coming soon. Please, go and wash your hands and sterilise some scissors in boiling water and bring them back to me. Now, Madame, please just breathe, *oui*, yes, very good, you are doing everything beautifully and very soon you will hold your baby in your arms.'

Edith's breathing became deeper and more even as she locked eyes with Solange. Then she screamed again.

'Now, Madame.' Solange attempted to infuse her voice with both kindness and authority. 'The next time you feel the pain, you must push down very hard. Your baby is almost here. Just a few more minutes and all this will be over, everything will be well. Just keep your energy for delivering your baby. You are doing very well.'

It seemed that Edith was beginning to trust her. As the next contraction came, she gripped Solange's hand tightly and pushed with every ounce of strength she had.

'Now Madame, the next one will be the one to deliver your baby. Try to pant, like this...' Solange demonstrated and Edith followed her instructions. The next contraction began to build. Solange moved to the foot of the bed. Between Edith's legs, the head of the baby was crowning.

'Now, just push very hard, and the little one will be here.' The infant came slipping from Edith's body into Solange's arms. 'Oh, Madame, a little girl, a beautiful little girl!'

She cut the umbilical cord with the scissors and handed the wailing child to a tearful Mrs Canty, who wrapped the tiny body in freshly warmed blankets. Minutes passed as Solange waited for the placenta to follow. Surprisingly, Edith's contractions continued. The pain should have ceased with the delivery of the child, but she seemed to be still in full labour.

'What's happening?' Edith gasped, terror in her eyes. 'Why is it not over? You said it would be over once it was born!'

Solange fought the urge to panic; she looked again between Edith's legs and was astonished to see another head crowning. 'Madame, please do not worry, but there is... Yes, there is another baby. Please, you must push once more.'

With a loud cry from Edith, the second infant slipped out quickly and easily and was also deposited into the waiting arms of Mrs Canty.

'A little boy! Oh, Madame, how wonderful for you!'

The two placentas followed, and finally, Edith lay back on the pillows, exhausted. Solange helped her into a more comfortable position, murmuring soft, soothing words in French. Then she changed the sodden sheets and replaced Edith's nightgown with a fresh one. Throughout this process, the new mother avoided her eyes as if acutely embarrassed by what had just happened. She appeared self-conscious of her body, even in front of the woman who had just assisted her giving birth.

Mrs Canty was busy wrapping up the babies and cooing over them. 'Oh holy mother of God. Oh, missus, ye have a pair of beauties here and no mistake.' She was wiping away tears as the lusty wails of the newborns filled the air. Solange took them from her, wrapped in their warm blankets, and brought them to the head of the bed, preparing to place them in their mother's arms.

'*Félicitations*, congratulations, Madame, they are beautiful. I am sure you and your husband will be very proud of them.'

Edith looked down at her two babies and to Solange's dismay, turned with difficulty onto her side, away from them.

'Please take them away, I need to sleep now.'

'*Oui*, Madame, of course, but perhaps you should feed them first? Then I can take them and bathe them?' Solange suggested.

'No, I shan't be feeding them. Please attend to them and do not disturb me.'

'But Madame, how will I...'

'Canty knows where everything is.' Edith settled down to sleep.

'I wasn't sure she'd go through with it,' Mrs Canty whispered as she and Solange were wrapping up the infants once more, having put napkins on them. 'But by God, it seems she is. She had some bottles and tins sent over from England a few weeks ago. Nestlé, it says on the labels. She told me that's what the baby – well, I suppose it's the babies now – anyway that's what we're to feed them. Not nursing her own babies, did you ever hear the like...'

'Please, just leave.' Edith's voice had regained some of its lost strength.

AN HOUR LATER, AS Solange sat dozing in the rocking chair with both babies asleep in the smart new bassinet beside her, Richard burst into the kitchen. 'Oh Solange, thank God you were here. Eddie only just found me! I was up the mountain at Coakley's farm. I should have left a note, but I thought there was still weeks to go... I'm so sorry you had to manage on your own but thank God you were here. So where is he? Or she?'

The news that there was not one baby but two filled Richard with joy. She had never seen this quiet man so animated and excited. She thought of Jeremy and how he would have loved the children they would never have. So often in bed they had discussed names for their children. She, favouring English names to match their surname, he arguing for French. He had loved France and everything about it. Most of all, he had loved her.

'Did you have no idea?' she asked Richard as he stood gazing down in amazement at his sleeping twins. The babies were sharing the bassinet – there was only one of everything for the moment.

'No. Bateman never spotted it, I suppose. Sometimes it can be difficult, depending on what position the babies are lying in. Edith must have got a real surprise.' He gently stroked their heads.

'Well, *félicitations*, Richard. They are beautiful. Do you know what they are to be called?'

'Yes. We'd like to call the boy James, after Edith's father; that's what we'd decided if it was a boy. And Juliet, after my mother, if it was a girl. I suppose we will just use both.'

He was beaming but seemed hesitant, almost nervous, to pick them up.

'Go on,' she whispered.

'I'm afraid I'll wake them,' he replied.

Solange reached in and gathered the tiny babies up, placing one in each of his arms. They stirred and instantly fell back to sleep. Richard Buckley looked at his children and Solange saw raw emotion on his face for the first time since she'd known him. He gazed at their tiny faces and fingers, amazed at the miracle of life despite all his experience of death.

Eventually he spoke, 'Thank you, Solange, from the bottom of my heart, for delivering them safely and for taking care of them until Edith has had her rest.' He glanced at the bottle and tin of Nestlé powdered milk, still on the table. 'Poor girl, it must have been exhausting for her.'

'Of course,' she replied. 'I'm glad I was able to help. They are healthy little ones. They are enjoying the milk from the tins. I have never seen that before, but they are drinking it happily, so all is well.'

He said, clearly a little embarrassed, 'Well, to nurse twins would have been very difficult for her at first. I'm sure they will do wonderfully on the powdered milk for a day or two. I can't tell you how grateful I... *Edith* and I... are for all your help. Now, if you don't mind taking care of them for just a few more minutes, I've been in these clothes all night so I just need to clean up. I don't want to asphyxiate my children. I won't be long.'

'Of course.'

'Was that Dr Richard I heard?' Mrs Canty came bustling into the kitchen. Outside, the winter morning was brightening up at last. 'He must have been over the moon with the little beauties, God bless them. Anything from herself above? Is she interested in looking at her children? Not a bit of it, I suppose, and you up all night. Here give them to me and let you go for a snooze.'

Solange looked down at the two tiny babies, still in her arms from where Richard had handed them back to her. They slept soundly, their little fists bunched up tight. They were so pure, so innocent; they knew nothing of ugliness or brutality. For the first time since she had heard the news of Jeremy's death, she felt something thaw deep inside her.

All that morning, instead of sleeping as Richard and Mrs Canty insisted she must, she lay in bed thinking of the twins and hoping they were all right. When the quiet of the house was finally shattered by a newborn's cry, she couldn't stay in her room. She went downstairs to help Richard, who was attempting to feed one while the other bawled in the bassinet.

'Mrs Canty is just gone for a few messages; we need a few things from the shop. I told her I could manage but...' Richard was all fingers and thumbs.

As soon as Solange picked up and cuddled Juliet, she stopped crying. She started to suck on her bottle and began drifting off to sleep again. Then she did the same with James, and soon both babies were fast asleep.

'You have the magic touch with them, Solange,' Richard whispered in awe as they slept cuddled up together.

Gazing into the crib, she said, 'I think they like to be near each other. They have been close for all this time and now to be separated – it must be a shock.'

'MADAME?' SOLANGE TENTATIVELY ENTERED the bedroom, having first knocked gently on the door.

Edith was awake and propped up on pillows reading a letter that had arrived that morning.

'Yes, Solange? Did you want something?' she asked, still reading.

'I was wondering if you would like to see the babies. I could bring them to you.' She had contemplated simply walking into the room with the twins but had thought better of it.

'No, thank you, not just now. Are they well?' Edith asked as if enquiring about a distant relative.

'*Oui*, I mean, yes, Madame, they are very well and so beautiful.'

'Yes, I'm sure. I may come down to see them later. Although I'm sure they are better off not being disturbed from their routine.' Edith paused in her reading and looked up. 'Thank you for your assistance with the births. I am in your debt.' Her tone conveyed dismissal.

Still, Solange lingered. 'Madame, I am always happy to help.'

'Well, yes. It was good you were here.' Edith returned to her letter.

'And when you are ready for me to bring the babies to you...'

Edith looked up again with a sigh. 'Solange, not now, please. This is an important letter from an old friend of mine in Dublin. There are going to be changes in this country. Ireland may not remain the calm and peaceful place you imagine it to be. British imperialism will not be tolerated any longer. Now if you'll excuse me...'

This time, the implication that Solange was outstaying her welcome was too obvious to ignore.

CHAPTER 2

The weeks that followed were cold but bright. Solange wrapped up the babies well and took them for walks around the garden in their pram. The crocuses that bloomed in profusion around the trees delighted her. Her life had altered so irreparably and so often in these last months that she had lost all sense of continuity and this garden gave her an anchor to cling to in an ever-changing world. It was a comfort to know that spring had come again as it had always done, irrespective of the turmoil in human lives.

Yet the main distraction from her own sorrows came in caring for James and Juliet. She was deeply grateful that the endless demands of two such healthy infants gave her so little time to brood over all she had lost. The twins seemed never to sleep simultaneously and were always hungry. Richard insisted that it was not expected of her that she care for them, but given the continued lack of interest their mother showed in them, there seemed to be no other option. He was so busy with the practice, and Mrs Canty, although a great help, had the household to run. Besides, Solange wanted to look after them. She could sit for hours just holding them and kissing their downy heads.

After Jeremy's death, she had moved as if in a trance. Presumably, she had slept and ate, but if so, she had no recollection of it. Life had stretched out in front of her as an endless, colourless void of time without him in it until she herself died. Over and over, she thought how things should have been different. He was a doctor, not even on the front line, yet he was dead. She thought of her Maman and Papa, too – so full of life and fun. Her mother's flashing eyes that could make her adoring husband agree to anything she wanted, and her father, who loved his sons and his only daughter with all his heart. But then Maman had got sick and died – a simple cut on her foot that had turned to blood poisoning. Papa was killed a short while later, shot by a

German soldier in reprisal for some imagined slight. Her older brothers had fallen at Verdun, dying side by side as they had lived since early childhood. To be left entirely alone in the world was a terrifying prospect. Yet in those early weeks, all she had thought about was how she could manage to live without Jeremy.

She was by no means over her loss – she doubted she ever would be, but the twins had become her new reality, and she adored them more with each passing day.

Sometimes, she felt guilty for loving them as if she was their mother, yet Edith showed only the most cursory of interest in the babies. Once a day – or, on rare occasions, twice – she would descend into the kitchen to glance into their pram. She would enquire as to their health and whether they were eating or sleeping properly but without any sign of genuine concern. She never picked them up or even looked too closely at them. It really was as if Solange were their mother and Edith a gracious employer enquiring after her housemaid's children – something to be done as a matter of form, rather than stemming from any real desire to know.

Richard loved the twins and often gave them their bottles; occasionally he even changed a napkin – though not with much success. He asked daily if Edith had been down to see them, and if Solange thought that perhaps this was a question he should be putting to his wife, she gave no indication of it.

Time and again, Solange wondered how the Buckleys' marriage survived. Their union could not even be described as one of convenience; the entire household seemed to be a source of annoyance to Edith. Solange had long ceased to imagine that Edith's initial coldness to her had sprung from a natural caution; it was clear to her now that Edith's *ennui* extended to everyone in her life. Time and again, she witnessed Richard trying to get closer to his wife, but each time Edith rebuffed him – avoiding him whenever possible and engaging in brittle conversation with him only when it was necessary. The letters kept on coming – two, sometimes three, a week, from her friends in Dublin, all of whom were, it seemed, involved in the struggle for independence. It was the only subject on which Edith seemed close to animated and, perhaps because her husband showed no interest, she would often explain to Solange certain points regarding Irish politics.

Last week, Edith had summoned Solange to her room.

'Ah Solange, thank you for coming up. I think we need to talk, to clarify some things. Tell me, are you happy here?'

Solange was nonplussed. '*Oui*... I mean, yes, of course, Madame. I am very happy and grateful to you and Richard for...'

'No, I know that, but I think if you are happy to stay, we should formalise the arrangement. You are looking after the twins, no doubt admirably, and, therefore, we should be paying you. It is not reasonable of us to expect you to work for nothing. Now if you don't wish to do it, then of course there is no obligation on you; we will simply hire a nurse to come in. Please don't feel pressured due to some sense that you owe us something. That is simply not the case.'

Solange stood there wondering what to say. The thought of anyone else taking care of the babies was abhorrent to her; she loved them so much. Also, she had very little money. Jeremy was due a pension, but the process of claiming it was taking a very long time. She did need something to live on, but she wondered if Richard knew about this arrangement Edith was proposing. He was always so adamant that she was a member of the family.

'Well, Madame, I do love taking care of James

and Juliet, so I am happy to do it. I don't know what else I would do if I did not do that. So yes, if it is acceptable to you and your husband then I would be glad of the job.'

'Good. That's settled then. Shall we say two hundred pounds per annum? And one and a half days off per week? Mrs Canty can cover your holidays. Of course, should you require more time off, please just ask, and we will arrange it. I think that's fair.'

Solange was impressed – she hadn't expected this cool, indifferent woman to be so generous. A nurse generally earned only one hundred pounds a year, and one day off per month was typical. 'That is most kind, Madame, but please deduct from that my board and lodging.'

'No. That won't be necessary. Ordinarily, that would be factored in, but these circumstances are far from typical. My husband promised your husband that we would be taking care of you and so we will. Now, there are some details we need to discuss.'

As part of her new role, Solange was to list all the items necessary for the raising of two babies. She should not be thrifty, explained Edith – just simply write down whatever she thought they would require over the coming months, and

Richard would see to it that everything was delivered. The babies were to be dressed exclusively from the Munster Arcade in Cork, or Arnott's in Dublin. Under no circumstances were they to be dressed in anything hand-knitted or bought locally. Prams and other paraphernalia were to come from Dublin also.

RICHARD SIGHED OVER HIS newspaper as he ate his breakfast in the kitchen with Solange and the twins.

'I never realised when I offered you a life of peace in Ireland, how things would turn out here. This struggle between the British and the IRA is, I fear, going to get worse. God knows how it will end.' He looked pensive but then seemed to shake himself out of it. 'Still, it's a bright spring morning and hopefully someone will get a bit of sense and end this before it escalates. Now, will we take this pair for a stroll before I face the parish and their ailments?'

He pushed one pram and Solange the other around the path that encircled the house. The April sun warmed the old walls of Dunderrig and the garden had sprung to life. At nearly four months, the twins were thriving and loved to lie without blankets and furiously kick their chubby legs.

'They are so beautiful, *n'est-ce pas?*' Solange smiled. 'I don't know much about this independence war, I don't read the papers though I should I suppose, but it just all seems so...'

'Pointless? Repetitive? Futile?' Richard suggested.

She nodded. 'After France and everything that we saw, war seems to be just waste. Nothing else, just waste. People, property, land, villages. I hope this is not the same fate for your home, Richard.'

Their relationship had become less formal in the past months. Richard would always be reticent, and she spoke as guardedly as he, but they enjoyed a good relationship. He was becoming more accustomed to fatherhood and was taking more and more of an active role in the care of his children. He'd even mastered changing their napkins. Nothing had improved with their mother though she did still visit the kitchen once a day to glance briefly at them.

THE TWINS WERE BAPTISED in the local Catholic parish church and on the morning of the christening, Edith arrived downstairs looking so glamorous that she took Solange's breath away. She had only seen the doctor's wife in nightgowns up to then and was amazed to see how elegant Edith could be with her hair pinned in an elegant chignon and wearing a beautifully tailored dress, cut daringly low at both front and back, with panels of cream sat alongside panels of ivory and white. Solange had never seen anything like it on a real person before, but she had taken to looking over various fashion magazines when Edith had finished with them. So she knew that since the war, when women had learnt to drive cars and wear trousers, they were reluctant to incarcerate themselves once more in torturous corsets and restrictive dresses. The postwar generation was raising hemlines and dropping necklines and, despite living in West Cork, it seemed Edith Buckley was not going to be left behind. For the first time, Solange could see why Richard had married her. She was so beautiful.

The twins were also dressed handsomely – Juliet in the simple christening robe that had been used to baptise at least four generations of Buckleys, and James in an identical robe made for the occasion by Mrs Canty. Both babies were wrapped in elaborately embroidered white blankets.

Mrs Canty told Solange she had overheard Richard and Edith arguing about the christening robes. Edith had wanted to order new ones from some French couturier based in Dublin but for once Richard had put his foot down. Every Buckley baby was baptised in the family gown and the twins were not going to be an exception. Mrs Canty delighted in telling the tale of how 'The One' – as Edith was unflatteringly called by her – got her comeuppance.

Richard made two trips in the car that day: the first, bringing Mrs Canty and her husband and a silent Edith to the church; the next, to collect Solange and the twins. As Solange entered the church with a baby in each arm, she felt the eyes of at least a hundred people upon her. Perhaps she imagined it, but it seemed as if they were more interested in her than in the babies. Edith and Richard sat side by side in the front pew, not touching, and next to them sat Dr Bateman and his wife, who were standing as the children's godparents. Once again, Solange was struck by the peculiar ways of the Irish. These people were offering to be the babies' guardians in the event of their parents' death, yet here in the church on the morning of their christening was the first time they had ever even seen them.

Dr Bateman had called late on the morning of the birth to ensure Edith was well and that she had delivered safely. He had complimented Solange on her professionalism and when she

JEAN GRAINGER

had asked if he'd like to examine the babies, he had stated that he was quite sure they were in excellent hands between her and their father, and promptly left. He had not appeared in Dunderrig since.

The babies were duly baptised and afterwards Richard invited a select group of people – friends and family, Solange assumed – to the Eldon Hotel in Skibbereen for lunch. He'd pleaded with her the night before to come to the lunch, but she had refused. Edith wouldn't want her there – she was staff now, whether Richard liked it or not, and it wouldn't have been appropriate.

CHAPTER 3

*R*ichard sat beside the fire in his study thinking about his wife. She had been bored and disparaging ever since her arrival at Dunderrig. He had hoped that the twins would soften her heart, but it hadn't happened. He tried to pinpoint the time when she had turned into this cold, snobbish person.

She had been such a beautiful, quiet, serene kind of girl. Such a restful person to be around, that he had decided only two weeks after meeting her at that hospital dance in England that she was the girl for him. He wasn't much of a dancer, but Jeremy had convinced him to have a night out. They had almost finished their training in Beauford Hospital, in Bristol, and Jeremy was planning to join up as soon as he qualified. There was a girl that Jeremy had had his eye on all week, and he was determined to have a crack at her. Richard was used to his friend falling for a new girl every few days; he also knew Jeremy would not let him rest until he agreed to accompany him to the dance. It was easier just to give in.

Richard had never had much success with girls. He had always envisaged himself married, but the process of becoming so seemed a bit of a mystery. There were a few girls at home in Dunderrig who were chatty and seemed friendly, but he was painfully shy and clammed up whenever a girl approached him. Since meeting Jeremy, it had become even harder for him to meet anyone – the girls were always dazzled by his handsome and vivacious friend while he himself faded into the background.

He had seen Edith straight away when he walked in. He had plucked up the courage to speak to her after he heard her ordering a cup of tea in an Irish accent. She had been visiting an elderly relative in Bristol and had been convinced to attend the dance by her cousin. They danced several times that night, and Richard was sure he had never seen a girl as beautiful. They had gone to tea the following day and for a walk afterwards. She seemed to be happy to discuss issues of the day but rarely answered a direct question and made very few demands on him emotionally; often they just strolled in comfortable silence.

Yet on their fifth date as they walked through the Clifton area of Bristol, he had inquired about her parents. And after some hesitation, she had told him that her mother had died when she was still a child and that her father had become everything to her. Then, after much prompting, she told him her father's story. He had been a professor of English and History in University College Dublin, who regularly spoke out against the horrendous living conditions endured by the working classes. He had supported Jim Larkin in encouraging the workers' strike of 1913 and had been addressing a rally when a riot erupted between the crowd and the police. Badly injured in the ensuing melee, he had died a week later of his wounds.

The normally serene Edith became visibly upset as she spoke, and he realised then how difficult it was for her to discuss such emotional issues. There had been minimal physical contact between them up to that point but there, in the middle of the street, he had held her in his arms and comforted her. That was the turning point;

she was so vulnerable and beautiful, and he decided he wanted to take care of her, always.

After that initial fortnight in Bristol, they arranged to stay in touch when Edith returned to Dublin. He was working hard in the hospital, gaining experience before deciding his next move. He'd always intended returning to Dunderrig and taking over the practice from his father, but the old doctor wasn't yet ready to retire, and besides, meeting Edith had made him rethink. She seemed very settled in Dublin and so, after a few months of letters and an occasional meeting, he had accepted a locum position in Kingstown. Edith had been so pleased. He had proposed in Stephen's Green, and she had agreed happily. He smiled ruefully at the memory. Nothing he did seemed to please her these days.

Those days in Dublin seemed a lifetime ago now. Edith had been happy and busy then; she had continued her interest in matters political, and he was so absorbed in his work that he was only glad she had a wide circle of friends to keep her occupied. Many of them were well-known literary and political figures – people who had known her father. Occasionally, they came to the house for dinner or drinks; yet while Richard did his best, he found their conversation about the

Irish cause a little wearisome. It wasn't that he didn't care, but these academics and writers seemed so far removed from the common people they purported to represent. He contributed very little to these conversations, and he knew his lack of enthusiasm embarrassed Edith. They never argued, but he remembered one such dinner at a grand house in Ballsbridge when he'd explained to an artist sitting on his left that while Irish independence was of course something to aspire to, it wasn't worth one drop of blood. He said that negotiation and dialogue were the only way and that he hoped a peaceful solution could be found.

He would never forget the looks from their fellow diners; it was as if he'd just said something incredibly rude or vulgar. Edith was furious with him and didn't speak to him all the way home. From then on, he didn't attend those dinners – much to the relief of them both. They rubbed along well together, while not seeing too much of each other.

And that was where everything would have stayed, had he not received that letter from Jeremy describing the conditions in the hospital in Amiens. It was not in the true Jeremy style – his letters were usually about his passion for the gorgeous Solange. Before he'd convinced her to marry him, he had regularly asked Richard's opinion about how to get her to see him as someone serious, rather than a playboy. Richard found the idea of Jeremy asking *him* for advice ridiculous. Jeremy was the one who could talk to women. He himself could barely manage a romantic relationship with his own wife.

This latest letter was in a different vein, however, as Jeremy described the kind of injuries the young men at the front were sustaining and how supplies and staffing levels were woefully inadequate. He wrote of the horrors suffered by so many Irishmen in the bloodbath of the Somme – many of them from the Munster Fusiliers regiment, from Richard's native west Cork. Suddenly, the idea of going to France, making a difference and helping his own countrymen seemed the logical thing to do. He asked his parents if Edith could live with them in Dunderrig while he was in France, and they agreed at once. The idea that his wife would refuse never crossed his mind.

'No,' she said calmly when he had finished.

'No? No to what? To Dunderrig? Look, Edith, I know you have your friends here, but I can't leave you here alone and unprotected.'

'It's true that I do not want to go to Dunderrig. My life is here. I am helping, doing something worthwhile, something my father would be proud of. But nor do I want you putting on a British uniform and fighting for their King.' She spoke slowly but with steeliness to her tone he had never heard before.

'But Edith, my dear, I won't be fighting. I'm a doctor. I will be working in a hospital, tending to the wounded. I don't have any political opinions about it; I simply want to help. Irish boys are out there too, you know, thousands of them. Please try to understand, I love you, but I have to go. And while I'm gone, I want you to be safe.' He was aware he was pleading.

She looked as if she was weighing up whether or not to continue. Her voice held a bitterness he'd never heard from her before. 'Yes, Richard. There are thousands of Irishmen fighting. Thousands of traitors to their own country. If they were so anxious to fight for something, then why not here, on their own soil, for their own people? You know how I feel about the British, and everything they stand for. Their puppet police murdered my father. Murdered him, Richard, for having the courage to speak out. I cannot support you putting that uniform on your back. Frankly, I'm shocked that you would even consider it. The Rising might have ended in disaster, but we are not beaten. Already we are working on getting our men out of British gaols and when they come home, I want to be here, in Dublin. *Here* is where you should be, looking after your own, not risking your life and wasting your skills in a country that has nothing to do with us. I am asking you, as your wife, not to do this.'

Richard felt as if he were seeing her for the first time – he had been so busy with the practice, he hadn't realised how deeply she had become involved with the volunteers. Since the Rising the previous Easter, the city had been on tenterhooks. It seemed to him now that her support of an Irish republic could only get her into trouble, and that it was more important than ever that she relocate to the peaceful backwater of Dunderrig while he was away in France and unable to protect her.

At first, he tried to reason with her, 'Edith, I do understand your loyalty to your father. He was an honourable and brave man, but really, this is no environment for a woman, let alone one whose husband is away. I love you, and I want you to be safe. Please try to understand my reasons for going. I don't agree with war – I hate it, in fact – but medicine is not about ideology. The boys and men who are suffering need me to help them. I'm sorry you are unhappy, but I must insist that you go to Dunderrig. I would be out of my mind with worry were you to stay here.'

She looked at him with disgust, and from that moment on, she rebuffed all efforts he made to be conciliatory. They had driven to Dunderrig in silence a few weeks later and everything he said was greeted with monosyllabic responses. His parents went to great lengths to make their daughter-in-law welcome, yet Edith showed them the same level of disdain she now did Richard. His father had taken him aside and questioned him what was the matter, whether they had done something wrong. Richard didn't wish to explain. He simply said that Edith would need to get used to country living, and that would take time; he was sure they would be a comfort to Edith, and she to them. Then, with a heavy heart, he set sail for England.

FOR RICHARD, THE WAR passed in a haze of noise and blood. There was nothing glorious or noble about it, just the daily and nightly grind of trying to patch together the broken bodies with which he was constantly presented. He tried to get home on leave to see Edith, but he'd only managed it twice. He wrote long letters, but she replied only with short notes – answering all questions he asked her but with absolutely no warmth. Still, she had met with unexpected enthusiasm the news that he was coming home on leave in May of 1918 and announced she was coming to Dublin to meet him off the boat. He half-suspected his wife was more interested in seeing Dublin than in seeing him. He had heard from his mother that she often travelled up to the city, staying with friends overnight. He supposed there was no harm in it. It must be dull for a young woman to be stuck in a house with his elderly parents and no one her own age to befriend. He knew some of his old school friends' wives had made efforts to include her in their social circle, but it seemed she was still very much a Dublin girl. He told himself that when he returned home and the war was over, they would patch up their marriage, hopefully have children, and all would be well. By then, she would have forgiven him.

They arranged to meet at the Bayview Hotel in Kingstown. They had often gone there for dinner in the early days of their marriage, so he hoped the location would rekindle their love. When Richard arrived at the hotel, around seven in the evening, he had expected to find her dressed for a night out. Instead, he was surprised to be greeted by his wife wearing a negligee and even more delighted to find her in an amorous mood. They'd made love quickly and silently. Richard would have liked to remain in bed with her, but she was determined that they go down to dinner. She never asked about his life in France. A group of her friends were waiting for them in the dining room. Hiding his disappointment, he made light conversation; his wife had taken up smoking and kept abandoning him for the terrace of the seafront hotel. Yet he was so happy to see her animated and smiling again that he indulged her and agreed to her suggestion that they stay in the hotel for a few more days before travelling to Dunderrig. Although his leave was suddenly cut short before he could get home to see his parents, he had returned to France with a lighter heart. In her next, very short letter, she had told him she was pregnant. He was overjoyed, although worried that she expressed no pleasure in the news.

THE DEATHS OF HIS parents from influenza came as a shocking blow to him. It happened only weeks after he'd been in Ireland, and he was crushed not just by grief but also by guilt that he had been in the country but hadn't managed to travel down to Dunderrig to see them. If only he hadn't agreed to stay those extra days in

Kingstown. He wrote long letters to Edith, describing his pain as best he could but, while she commiserated, he could tell that the death of the old couple meant much more to their housekeeper Mrs Canty and her husband Eddie than to his own wife. He longed to go home but could not get leave. John and Juliet Buckley were buried in the cemetery in the village without their only child there to say goodbye.

As the war wore on wearyingly to its end, the waves of wounded growing daily, Richard received a second, longer letter from Edith:

Dear Richard,

I hope you are well and that you will be home safely before too long. The house is very quiet without your parents though Mrs Canty does her best to fill it with her relentless prattle. I am well though I have been feeling quite nauseous. Mrs Canty's boiling of cabbage does little to help that situation. I have not been up to Dublin in some time, so I have no news about anything there. I am under the care of Dr Bateman from Cork. The child will be born in January sometime, he thinks. I hope you will have returned by then. I know we have had our differences, Richard, but now that we are to be parents I think we should make the best of it for the sake of our child.

Fond regards,

Your wife,
Edith.

Richard felt great relief. *Fond regards.* Impending motherhood had clearly softened her. The war was in its final stages, he was sure of it, and he would return to Dunderrig, take over the practice and raise his family with Edith. Everything would be all right.

CHAPTER 4

*R*ichard was finishing up in the surgery after a long and trying day. He'd spent the past hour with a woman from a farm a few miles outside of town. She was on her twelfth pregnancy and was in no physical condition to carry it to term. She barely had enough food to feed the other eleven, and she and her husband were good people. He had tried as delicately as possible to explain the concept of the 'safe period' and how she and her husband should abstain from relations at particular times of the month, but he feared his lesson fell on deaf ears. Even if she could understand what he told her – which he very much doubted – she, like so many others, was deeply entrenched in Catholicism, which was vehemently opposed to any intervention in the propagation of the faithful. Richard wondered why God had made so many mouths, yet often not enough food to put into them.

Ireland's War of Independence against the British, which had begun as soon as he'd arrived back in Ireland, had already cost the lives of so many sons, fathers, and husbands that much of the land had been left untended. British reprisals against any Irish rebel activity were swift, arbitrary and brutal, and so many poor women were left to fend for themselves with all these hungry mouths to feed.

When Richard had returned to Ireland in January of 1919, he'd already had more than his fill of war. He had spent so many nights in France listening to the incessant shellfire and trying to transport himself home, to the peace and tranquillity of West Cork. How naïve he had been, to imagine such savagery could never happen on his own doorstep.

Now he refused to engage in the politics of this new war, thus enraging many of his neighbours, who questioned his loyalty to his country. He tried to explain how he had already seen too much waste of life and too many horrific wounds – both to men's bodies and to their souls – and that in his opinion, no matter what the cause, war was never worth it. His sermons against violence were lost on West Cork revolutionaries. Nonetheless, he was determined to treat all patients ethically and honestly, regardless of political affiliation. If called on to treat a bullet wound or some other trauma sustained in fighting, he asked no questions. When the patient or those around him tried to explain or glorify an injury, he only answered that it was better if they told him nothing. That way, if questioned by the British, he would have nothing to tell.

On one particular occasion, he was called to a house near Glandore to treat a young man who'd been shot in the thigh and was losing a lot of blood. The boy lay half-conscious, raving about 'English bastards'. Richard spoke soothingly to him while attempting to remove the bullet and staunch the bleeding. In a moment of clarity, the boy looked up and recognised him.

'Are you that traitor who fought for the British?'

'I know it is difficult but try to hold still... I never fought for or against anyone in my life. I wore a uniform but not so I could kill anyone. I am a doctor, and I spent the war in France treating lads like you.'

The boy screamed and writhed. 'Get away from me, you Sassenach fucker! Get your filthy fuckin' hands off me! Mam, send him away!'

'Ssh, Patrick… Don't mind him, Doctor Buckley,' the boy's mother pleaded. 'He don't know what he's saying, honest to God he don't.'

Richard sighed. 'Listen to me, Patrick. You can call me whatever you wish. My only interest right now is in saving your life. Now, you have to keep still. However much this hurts. If I don't remove the bullet, you will bleed to death within the hour.'

'Lie still, Patrick, lie still for the good doctor.' His mother was weeping now. 'You'll die if you don't let him help you.'

The boy turned his face to the wall, but he lay still. Richard removed the bullet and stopped the bleeding.

As he was leaving the house, a man arrived whom Richard recognised from his school days – and as well, from that long-ago trip to the slaughterhouse in Skibbereen, the smell of which had followed him to France.

'Richard,' the man nodded in greeting. 'Will the lad make it?'

'I wouldn't like to say at this stage. He's lost a

lot of blood and needs a transfusion. If you can get him to the hospital –'

'Hospital isn't an option.' Seamus Corrigan, now a captain in the IRA, was adamant.

Richard didn't argue. 'Try to keep the wound clean to stop any infection and give him plenty of water. The next twenty-four hours will be critical.' And he walked away across the yard of the farmhouse to his car. Opening the door of the Morris Oxford, he realised Seamus had followed him.

'Richard, we appreciate you coming out like this, taking care of our boys. This war is hard on the lads, not to mind their families, and those British bastards are so fuckin' –'

Richard turned to face him, running a hand through his sandy hair. He was too exhausted and demoralised to endure this conversation. 'Seamus, it's been a very long night. My twins are cutting their back teeth. No one in our house is getting too much sleep. I sincerely hope the lad makes it, but I've done the best I can. In the hospital, he would be certain to survive. But if you won't take him, then he is as likely to die as to live.'

Corrigan shook Richard's hand. 'Thanks for everything.'

Richard nodded and drove away.

Colonel Maxwell, the commanding officer of the British Army stationed in Skibbereen, had appeared at his house a week after that incident, demanding to know the name of any man he had recently treated for bullet wounds. Richard explained that he couldn't break patient confidentiality and reminded the colonel that the British soldiers came to him as well, for all their ailments. Many, like he himself, suffered night terrors after their experiences in France; they trusted him to listen to them. He'd removed bullets from their bodies too, patching them up as best he could and sending them on their way. He only desired to be left to his work, unhampered by any allegiance to either side.

'That is a luxury I cannot afford you, I'm afraid,' Maxwell replied in his clipped public school accent. 'You were on our side over there, Doctor. Surely you can see what we're dealing with here. I simply will not have you giving these terrorists *carte blanche*. There must be accountability. From now on, I will require a weekly log of all patients you see, either in or outside of your surgery.'

'I can't do that I'm afraid,' Richard replied calmly.

'Look here, Doctor, you perform a very valuable service. Do not force me to do anything that would jeopardise your practice or your livelihood.'

Richard didn't react to the thinly veiled threat but sat in his chair impassively.

Taking his silence as acquiescence, the colonel nodded, satisfied. 'Jolly good. I'll be in touch in the coming days.'

TWO EVENINGS LATER, Richard sat alone in the kitchen reading the newspaper and enjoying a moment of peace. The twins, now mischievous toddlers, were tucked up in bed, and the rest of the household had retired. To his annoyance, the restful silence was suddenly shattered by loud knocking on the front door. He sighed, setting aside the paper. He hated leaving his family unprotected when he was called out to a patient in the night. The days when he could be sure they would be safe were over because of the tension that now existed between the IRA and the British. When he opened the door, a young private was standing on the top step; a British army car stood with its engine ticking over in the driveway behind him.

'Yes?'

'Dr Buckley, sir, Colonel Maxwell sent me to

fetch you, sir, it's 'is boy, sir, there's somfing up wiv 'im. He says you're to 'urry like. Sir.' The cockney accent reminded Richard of a patient of his, in Amiens. The poor lad had died – his injuries too catastrophic to survive.

Putting his hat and overcoat on while scribbling a quick note for Solange to find if she woke, Richard seized his doctor's bag from his surgery and jumped into the waiting military vehicle.

On his arrival, he was greeted by a staff officer who was standing in the open doorway of the large grey barracks in the middle of the town of Skibbereen. Richard had been inside this cold and functional building once before, with his father, and knew there were living quarters on the upper floor. He also knew that the local policeman had preferred to inhabit the smaller, more comfortable house next door to the barracks for many years. It seemed that the Maxwell family – the colonel, his wife, and their three sons – had moved back into the main building in recent times, clearly fearing for their safety.

As Richard was led up the stairs, he asked the staff officer, 'What age is the boy?'

'I'm not sure exactly, sir. Ten or eleven.'

'His name?'

'Arthur.'

75

'And his symptoms?'

Before the officer could reply, a woman emerged from a room on the second floor of the house. She was dishevelled and clearly frantic with worry.

'Oh thank goodness, please, you have to help him, he can't breathe, my poor Artie...' Her accent was English but soft and rural – perhaps from Devon or Cornwall.

Richard ran past her into the room. Lying on a bed, struggling almost soundlessly for air, was a thin dark-haired boy whose lips were turning blue. His father, wearing only trousers and a vest, knelt by the bed holding his son's hand, his face a mask of fear. It was hard to equate this man with the authoritarian figure who had been issuing commands in Richard's surgery just two days earlier.

Richard bent over the bed. 'Hello Artie, I'm Doctor Buckley. I'm just going to have a little look in your throat.'

The boy was unable to answer, but his eyes were wild with panic as his body bucked and strained with the effort to breathe.

Richard soothed him: "You are a big, brave lad. Now, I need you to help me help you. Open your mouth a little wider...'

The boy's eyes fixed on Richard's; he opened his mouth as wide as he could.

Gently, Richard examined him. 'Now Artie, I see what the problem is, and we'll have you right as rain in just a few minutes. I need to talk to your Mammy and Daddy for a moment and then I'll be back to make you better.'

Pausing only to instruct the officer by the door to fetch him a basin of boiling water, Richard ushered the boy's parents into a corner of the room. He spoke very calmly and methodically to them while selecting the necessary instruments from his bag. 'Your son has epiglottitis. The flap of tissue that sits at the base of the tongue has become infected and inflamed and is obstructing his windpipe. I have no option at this stage but to attempt an emergency airway puncture. I will need to make an incision in your son's throat, through the skin and cricothyroid membrane, to enable him to breath.'

Artie's mother gave a stricken cry, and the colonel straightened his shoulders, attempting to assert his authority. 'Have you done this before? How can we be sure you know what you are doing? You're a country doctor. There's an ambulance on its way from Bandon. We need to take our son to the hospital. If you are right, and he needs this procedure, it should be done by a proper surgeon.'

'Colonel Maxwell...' He lowered his voice further. 'I realise how worried you must be. I'm a father myself. But if I do not attempt this procedure now, your son will certainly die. It is dangerous, and, yes, I have performed a cricothyrotomy before – twice.'

'And...?'

'In one instance, the patient lived. In the second, he did not, because it was too late.'

The couple stared at each other and at their choking son, whose thin little body was in spasm now with the increasingly impossible effort to breathe.

'Do it,' said the colonel grimly.

His wife hurried to comfort her boy. 'The doctor is going to make you better now, Artie. Don't you worry about anything. Daddy and I are here, so don't worry, darling, whatever happens. Everything is going to be fine.'

The officer returned with a basin of boiling water and placed it on the table beside the bed. Richard laid out his instruments beside it. 'Go to the other side and hold his hand,' he instructed the boy's mother. He leant over the trembling boy. 'Now Artie, I want you to think about

Christmas and what Santa Claus is going to bring you. I think you might get something very special this year for being such a big, brave boy.' He placed a rolled-up towel under the child's shoulders, stretching out his neck. Feeling for the hard edge of the thyroid cartilage, he closed his eyes, trusting his fingers. Once he had located the site just below the cartilage, he sterilised his scalpel in the boiling water. Making the incision quickly, he inserted an endotracheal tube into the boy's throat. Instant relief registered on the boy's face; he inhaled noisily, his chest expanded, and the colour flooded back to his lips. Richard secured the tube and turned to Colonel Maxwell.

'He is out of immediate danger, but we must get him to the hospital.'

Mrs Maxwell was weeping with relief, and Colonel Maxwell was hoarse as he replied, 'The ambulance should be here any moment. It will take him to Victoria Military Hospital in Cork. Will he...will he stay well enough for the journey?'

Richard checked his patient's pulse and breathing. Both had stabilised. 'He has an excellent chance.' Gently, he shook the boy's hand. 'You're a great lad, Artie. You're going to be grand. I'll see you kicking a football with your brothers in a few weeks, all right?'

Artie's mother was whispering into her son's ear, reassuring him that all was well. Moments later, two military medics hurried into the room and under Richard's instructions gently loaded Artie onto a stretcher. The colonel's wife insisted on being the one to travel with her youngest, leaving her husband to ensure the safety of her older sons – both still sleeping – from any attack made on the barracks by Irish rebels. She paused before leaving to take Richard's hand. 'Thank you, Doctor Buckley. He's our baby, and... There are no words to convey the fullness of my heart, except to say that we are forever in your debt.'

'You are welcome.' He packed up his instruments and made his way to a bathroom to wash his hands. When he emerged, he was directed by the staff officer to a large room that had been turned into a sitting room of sorts. Despite its imposing size and drab walls and floor, the Maxwell family had endeavoured to make it home. A fire burned merrily in the grate and on either side of the fireplace were large, comfortable-looking sofas. The tables and shelves around the room held books and toys, and stacked in one corner, were cricket bats, fishing rods, and footballs.

Colonel Maxwell stood with a glass in his hand, his back to the fire.

'Drink?' he offered.

'Yes, I think I will.' Richard accepted a large whiskey and stood taking in the room.

Maxwell followed his eyes. 'It's not much, I know. The house was better but just not safe. Dorothy and the boys are better here. I would like to send them back, away from here altogether. But she won't be bossed about, my lady wife. Says if I'm here, then that's where she's staying. Though after this, I don't know.'

Richard said nothing and sipped his drink.

Maxwell poured himself another glass. 'And how are your two children? Twins, I heard. Boys or girls?'

'They're fine. Ruling the roost. A boy and a girl, James and Juliet. They're two and a half now and full of mischief. Sure you know yourself with your own lads.' Richard's tone was light. There was no indication that the men had been at loggerheads just days earlier.

'The time goes so quickly. It seems like only yesterday our boys were babes in arms and now they're growing up. The eldest will be off to Eton soon.' He paused, staring into the flames. 'Look, about that other thing. I need to present a report to my superiors. The local population, you know, providing aid to the rebels – it can't be tolerated. Even if you are a doctor. But I won't be enquiring too deeply if you understand me. It's the best I can do.'

Richard smiled, drained his whiskey and handed the glass to the colonel. Putting on his coat and hat he said, 'Good night. Let me know how Artie fares.'

CHAPTER 5

'The thing is, Mrs Allingham, I know they don't mean a bit of harm, but they are going to get hurt someday. I've told them over and over they're to stay out of my orchard, but they don't take a tack of notice of me. The sooner they go up to the master above in the school the better, if you don't mind me saying so.' Ted Collins was working himself up to a rant about the twins breaking into his orchard again.

'Monsieur Collins, I am *désolée*, so sorry. I spoke to James and Juliet last time, and they promised me that they would no more go in your orchard, but they say your apples are the sweetest in all of Ireland and so... They are little children, and it is hard for them to resist, *n'est-ce pas?*'

Solange's charm had its usual disarming effect on Ted. She watched his face return to a normal colour.

'Ah, sure, don't I know they're only children. But if I let them at it, I'll have every child in the place scaling the walls and not an apple left come September.'

'I understand, Monsieur. It is most frustrating, I know. I will have their father speak to them tonight, I assure you. They have been promised a trip to the mart, but if they go into your garden again, it will be cancelled. Please be assured we will deal with them most strictly, Monsieur Collins.'

'Ted, Mrs Allingham. Ted's the name,' he said with a smile.

'Of course, Ted. And I am Solange. Now would you like a cup of tea before you go? Perhaps some of Mrs Canty's porter cake?'

Solange spotted two pairs of mischievous green eyes looking in through the kitchen window. Behind Ted's back, she gestured to them to keep down. She knew the sight of James and Juliet would start a further diatribe from their neighbour. She'd already had a lecture from Mrs Kelly in the local post office and grocery shop, who said she distinctly saw James trying to lift

Juliet up high enough to reach the sweet jar while she was down at the other end of the counter getting the colouring pencils he had asked her for. Solange defended them, explaining that it was just a game, and they wouldn't have helped themselves, but Mrs Kelly was not convinced. She was a bitter, miserable woman anyway, in Solange's opinion. Luckily, the white-blond heads and sparkling green eyes of the twins could melt even the hardest of hearts; they managed to charm virtually everyone they met. Except, of course, their mother.

Edith had not changed discernibly towards them since the day they were born. The children knew she was their mother. They spoke to her politely if they passed her on the stairs, and they took tea with her every Sunday in the drawing room – they disliked this latter ritual because Edith insisted they were dressed formally and behave impeccably. She never hugged or even touched them, but neither did she speak to them sharply or with the rude malice she reserved for Mrs Canty. She merely treated them as yet another vaguely boring aspect of Dunderrig.

The twins loved their father; he adored them and despite his best efforts to get cross when they did something naughty, they knew they always

had it in their power to make him laugh. Several
nights a week, when he wasn't called out on a
medical emergency, he would read them stories
as they sat on his lap in their pyjamas by the
range, giving all the characters different voices.
Solange loved to watch them.

Edith had insisted the twins should have a
bedroom each from the beginning; she found it
unseemly that a boy and a girl, even ones so
young, should share a room.

Juliet's room was decorated as Edith deemed a
little girl's should be, complete with china dolls
she never played with and embroidery sets she
never used. All the furnishings were sent from
Dublin and were, in Solange's opinion, too fussy
and frilly for a little girl of Juliet's temperament.
The little girl loved music, and Solange was beginning to teach her the piano. She played French
folk songs by ear, and Juliet picked them up very
quickly. She made a note to herself to ask Richard
to teach her some Irish melodies as all she knew
so far were French ones. Richard was a reluctant
but powerful singer, on the few occasions he
could be pressed into performing. Juliet must
have got her musical talent from him.

James's bedroom was decorated with motor
cars and utterly failed to reflect his love of art. He

didn't dare do any painting in there, in case he accidentally got a stain on any of the expensive fabrics. Instead, he spent hours at the big kitchen table alongside Solange, painting with water colours or doing charcoal drawings and leaf rubbings.

Despite their elaborately furnished and decorated rooms, by the morning the young twins usually ended up together in Solange's bed. Richard knew about this but chose not to acknowledge it, as to do so would be to deliberately go against his wife's instructions. Since Edith never went to tuck the twins in or check on them during the night, it was easy not to mention the sleeping arrangements. Besides, he was glad that Solange was willing to show the twins so much affection as, despite his hopes, Edith had never softened towards her children.

As Solange returned to the kitchen, having seen Ted out the front door, she found her charges had sneaked in the back door. Mrs Canty was giving them freshly baked soda bread and homemade blackberry jam – their favourite snack.

Juliet was cross-questioning Mrs Canty as usual. She was always full of questions. James sat beside her, always interested in the answers but choosing to let Juliet lead, as she did in everything.

'Why are you so chatty, and Eddie doesn't say hardly anything?' asked the child, her mouth full and jam on her cheeks.

Mrs Canty pealed with laughter. 'Well, child, sure there couldn't be two of us talking all the time now, could there? So I do the talking for the both of us!'

'Well, our daddy doesn't talk as much as you, but I think you talk more than anyone in the whole wide world, and our mammy doesn't talk much either, and Solange talks but only in French because she has two brains, a French brain and an Irish brain, but the French one is bigger because she lived there for longer.' Juliet delivered the pronouncement with all the certainty of a precocious five-year-old.

'Eddie talks to us, though. He says when we are seven, he'll teach us how to – *Ow!*' Juliet glared at her brother, who had kicked her ankle under the table. He was shaking his head rapidly. Eddie had promised them lessons on how to shoot rabbits, but James knew that Mrs Canty would not approve, so they'd decided to stay quiet about it. Juliet had forgotten the pact.

Changing the subject, Solange tried to look

cross. Launching into rapid French she began to scold them, '*Bah, mes petits, qu'est-ce que vous faites?* What will I do with you? Always Mr Collins comes here to say how you have taken his apples once again! If your papa hears this, he will say there will be no mart for you!'

She plumped down in the big rocking chair, and the twins climbed onto her lap. They were tired after a long day making mischief. Despite her tone, she couldn't resist kissing each of them on their tousled blond heads. They cuddled deeper into her. Their hair was bleached almost white by the sun, and despite Edith's strict instructions that Juliet's be teased and pinned, Solange often 'forgot' and let it fall down her back. James's hair was cut short but in between cuts a riot of blond curls appeared. They were both brown from a summer spent outside and freckles dusted their noses. They had their father's unusual green eyes and drew attention wherever they went. Solange could not have been more proud of her beautiful, creative charges than if they had been her own flesh and blood.

'We're sorry, Solange,' began James.

'*Non, non, en français s'il vous plaît.*'

'*Nous sommes désolés, Solange,*' they chorused.

'*Je peux avoir du chocolat chaud, s'il te plaît?*' Juliet smiled sweetly. 'We promise to be good.'

'*D'accord, chérie*, but you must be *très calme*, very quiet, because Papa is speaking with Maman in the drawing room, and they do not wish to be disturbed. A little glass of *chocolat chaud* before your bath and then to bed *tout de suite, d'accord?*'

'So can we go to the mart tomorrow?' James's eyes were bright with excitement. 'Eddie said we had to ask you, Solange, and if you said yes, then we can go. Please say we can! Please!' they chorused, making elaborate praying gestures at her.

'*Il faut demander à ton père.*'

'He'll say whatever you say, you know that,' James said, wise beyond his years.

It had never been Solange's deliberate intention that the twins be bilingual, but she found herself speaking to them in French when they were alone, which was most of the time. They were very bright children and so picked up both English and French simultaneously. Edith had never heard them speak anything but English, but Mrs Canty had told her beloved Dr Richard how the children were able to babble away in French with Solange and seemed to understand everything she said, though they instinctively reverted to English whenever anyone else came near.

RICHARD LINGERED OUTSIDE THE kitchen window that evening. It was a mild day and Solange was in the kitchen, colouring with the children. To his amazement, his son and daughter, who had never in their short lives been further than Skibbereen, were explaining in detail and in flawless French the exact colour of a wet fox to Solange.

When he entered the kitchen, the conversation seamlessly changed to English mid-sentence. Later, when the children were sleeping, Richard came back to the kitchen again.

'You don't have to stay in here, you know,' he began. 'I could ask Eddie to put a fire down in the drawing room any evening you wish to sit there, to read or whatever you enjoy.'

'*Non merci*, Richard. I am comfortable here. I have this nice big rocking chair and if the children wake, they know where to find me. Would you like some tea or perhaps *chocolat chaud*? I made it earlier for the twins.'

'That would be very nice, *merci*.'

Smiling as she rose, she replied, 'Ah, you are using your French. You should keep it up.'

Sitting in the chair on the other side of the range, he watched her making the hot chocolate. 'Perhaps I could aspire to the linguistic heights of my twins,' he said, then smiled at her surprised expression. 'I confess to eavesdropping on you earlier. It is remarkable how well they can communicate. How on earth did you teach them so well?'

'I hope you do not mind. When I came here for the first time, my English was not so good, so it was natural for me to speak in my language to babies who do not know anyway. Then when they began to speak, I would teach them two words for everything, instead of just one. For example, I would say *window* then *la fenêtre*. They just picked it up that way, I think. If they were to land in France now, they would be taken for little French children.'

'Well, I think it's wonderful. They really are clever, aren't they? Though I hear that the pair of scallywags are up to tricks again. Mrs Kelly gave me chapter and verse while I looked at her corns.' Richard heaved a rueful sigh.

'But Richard, she leaves this big jar of *bonbons* in front of little children's eyes and never offers them one. Of course they will try to get them. It is mean, I think, teasing little ones like that. James and Juliet are so good really. Anyway, Ted Collins called today to say they were in his orchard again. I told him you would deal most strictly with them and there would be no trip to the mart if they are naughty.' Solange kept smiling as she told Richard of all their latest misdemeanours which, as well as Ted and Mrs Kelly, included letting a neighbour's ducks out of their pen because they had decided the poor birds should fly free.

Richard accepted the cup of hot chocolate gratefully. It had been a very long day. The Civil War had finally ended, but feelings still ran high. Many scores had been left unsettled. De Valera might have issued a statement instructing the anti-treaty side to disarm, but not everyone was happy to do that.

In many ways, the past two years had been much worse than the War of Independence. At least the lines of demarcation between the Irish and the British had been clear. The fact that young Artie Maxwell had returned from Victoria Hospital a healthy boy with a very impressive scar on his throat had also given Richard a certain protection from investigation. He'd managed to keep to his plan of helping anyone who needed it.

The years that followed had been much more complicated. Families and communities had split over the treaty signed in 1921 by Michael Collins, which gave a sort of independence to most of the country while maintaining the six counties of Northern Ireland under British rule. They were mostly Unionist up there anyway, but some of the die-hard republicans here weren't happy. Richard had despaired. He had seen enough senseless death and destruction to last several lifetimes and to watch his countrymen tear themselves apart like this was almost too much to bear. A few months before, he had been threatened by Free-Staters in Skibbereen, who had taken over from the British as per the terms of the treaty. They demanded that he not treat any bullet wounds without notifying the local barracks. Once again, Richard had referred them to his Hippocratic oath in which he had promised to use his skills to preserve life and alleviate pain where possible. Nowhere did the oath mention taking sides. He'd had to listen to jibes about how he'd put on a British uniform during the war and what more could they expect, but he rose above it. Luckily, he recognised one of the thugs as being a cousin of a man whose life he had saved after an ambush during the War of Independence. Richard had mildly enquired after the cousin's health, and they had left it at that. Still, it was exhausting.

The house seemed so still now, despite the troubles outside. He looked forward to those moments in the evenings when the children and Mrs Canty had gone to bed. He often sat with Solange, telling her about his day and hearing the latest devilment his twins had got up to. She was so restful and funny, she delighted him with her take on the characters of Dunderrig. When she first arrived, she had been so traumatised by all she'd endured that she had been slow to mix, but now she was part of the community. Her exotic good looks no longer drew too much attention. The men all still admired her as she walked up the aisle at mass on Sundays – her thick jet-black hair hung in corkscrew curls, and Mrs Canty's cooking had restored her curvy figure. The women used to resent her beauty but as the years wore on and Solange showed no interest in leading their husbands astray, they had come to accept her.

Yet things were so uncertain now, with the resentments between the two sides of the Civil War still bubbling beneath the surface – making life, in many ways, more dangerous than ever. He prayed his children, and all children, would be able to grow up in a time of peace. Free to live and love without this endless need to kill each other. Now though, peace seemed a very fragile thing indeed.

CHAPTER 6

*R*ichard hoped things would be calm at home as he turned off the main road. It was the twins' birthday, and they were having a tea party. He had listened to Edith complaining bitterly last night that Solange refused to dress the children as she wished and instead allowed them to roam like ragamuffins all over the village. She said she had spoken to Solange about it, but Solange had insisted that the fine linen and silk outfits she'd had sent from Dublin would be ruined if they played in them, and that's why she allowed them to wear patched and mended clothes. Edith was at a loss to understand why on earth the children could not simply stay inside and stay clean. Why they had to scamper up trees and be driven around by Eddie on the cart was beyond her. She had taken to insisting they take tea in her room with her at four in the afternoon each day, instead of only on Sundays, and she had been most put out to overhear Juliet complaining about having to come home early every day and change into a pretty frock to have tea with her mother.

Edith had caught her daughter declaring in her bright, high-pitched voice, 'No one else has to dress up to see their mammy. Everyone else's mammy is in the kitchen, but our mammy sits in her room all day. Reading letters and writing them. Why can't you be our mammy, Solange?'

Solange had shushed her and explained that she was a very lucky girl to have so many beautiful dresses to wear and that she should be on her best behaviour for her mother. She'd urged her to play the new song she had learned on the piano after tea; surely Edith would approve of piano playing as an activity for her daughter. If she could see how talented Juliet was, then she might offer some praise to her little daughter instead of constant criticism.

Richard contemplated suggesting Edith have a more natural relationship with her children – take them for a walk or bake a cake in the kitchen

– but he knew such ideas would be greeted with disdainful silence. Whenever he tried to improve things between his wife and their children, it came out as criticism. The last time he had suggested she do something vaguely maternal, Edith had sneered, 'Ah yes, like Solange does, do you mean? The saintly French widow. Are you sure you only admire her qualities as a governess? I've seen how you look at her, Richard. You might be fooling yourself but not me.'

Richard was horrified. His feelings for Solange were complex – certainly, she was a beautiful woman, kind and funny, and wonderful with the children, but he was a married man.

It was true that he and his wife had not shared a bed since the birth of the twins. But that was not about him rejecting his wife; it was because Edith disliked physical and emotional intimacy. She always had. Even at the start of their relationship, before his decision to join up, she had only acquiesced to sexual relations stoically, as her duty; she had never been responsive to his touch. He had tried romance, flowers and sweet nothings, but it had been pointless. He'd considered asking Jeremy for advice at one stage but the thought of discussing his sex life with anyone, even his best friend, had made him blush.

Still, he was shocked to think Edith believed him capable of conducting an affair.

Apart from the fact he was married, he was sure Solange was involved in some small way with someone else. About a year ago, she had started asking for two days off together once a month, and staying away overnight. Of course, he had agreed. Mrs Canty and he were well able to manage on their own. She had never said where she went, nor did he ask. It wasn't something he liked to think about, but Solange was a free agent. At first, he had feared that whoever she had met might whisk her away from them all; the thought filled him with dread. Though he might not admit it even to himself, the idea of Dunderrig without Solange was unthinkable. Yet time had passed and no mention was made of her leaving. He asked no questions and hoped she would stay. He knew Jeremy had been the love of her life and trusted this unknown man was only a form of consolation, a way of Solange reminding herself she was still a woman.

The children once asked him where she went, and he had truthfully told them that he didn't know, but that Solange was entitled to her own life and her own friends. She gave his family the lion's share of her life as it was; she was allowed her privacy.

He did try, for the twins' sake mainly, to keep the lines of communication open with his wife, and he went to her in her sitting room most evenings. Yet he found these visits something to be endured rather than enjoyed.

Last night's conversation had ended when Edith demanded once again that he speak to Solange, complaining that the French woman clearly didn't understand the type of upbringing that was appropriate for the heirs of Dunderrig. It was almost as if she wanted to set Richard and Solange at loggerheads. She could easily have complained to Solange herself but chose instead to have him do it. By agreeing with her and giving in on trivial matters, Richard managed to maintain the equilibrium. And so he had gently asked Solange to make sure the children were dressed in all their finery for their birthday party.

As he parked the car and ran up the steps into the hallway, he discovered an atmosphere of gloom in the house not at all suited to a children's birthday party. Mrs Canty was in the hall and jerked her head disapprovingly in the direction of the hardly-ever-used dining room, where the moss-green carpet and ivory-flock wallpaper had

remained unchanged as long as he could remember – there had never seemed much point in
redecoration as it was used only once or twice a
year. Edith took all of her meals in her private sitting room, and Solange and Mrs Canty always ate
in the kitchen with the children. Richard either
ate in the kitchen or if he had missed the children's dinner, in his study.

Now, trying to look enthusiastic, he walked
into the formal, forbidding room.

James and Juliet were perched on either side
of the long mahogany table. They were dressed in
all the finery Edith had insisted on buying, and
his wife looked like she had stepped out of the
pages of a fashion magazine. Her hair and
makeup were immaculate, and she was wearing a
dress he'd not seen before. Of Solange, there was
no sign. The place at the head of the table had
been laid for him.

There were dainty little sandwiches and a
cake laid out. The fine bone china his mother had
collected but never used had been pressed into
commission. As Richard took his seat, he noticed
how clean and yet how miserable his children
looked. Quite unlike when they ran to him across
the cobbled courtyard each evening when he returned from the surgery, with their wild hair and

smudged hands and faces. Normally, they were full of chat about that day's activities, and he could barely keep up with the seemingly endless cast of dogs and pups and ponies and tadpoles and ducks that seemed to populate his children's busy lives. This sedate and stilted scene was in no way in keeping with their exuberant personalities.

'Greet your father, children,' Edith instructed.

'Hello Daddy... Father,' they chorused quietly.

'Well, hello James and Juliet.' He wondered why he had gone from being Daddy to Father all of a sudden. Trying not to fall into this trap of forced decorum, he attempted to be more lively than his usual self. 'My goodness, don't you two look just smashing! What beautiful outfits!'

'Mammy... I mean *Mother* bought them for us,' James said, ever the peacemaker.

Richard raised his eyebrows at Edith.

'I just think it will be better from now on if they called us mother and father. It's what all the other children will call their parents when they go to school next September, and we don't want them seen as country bumpkins,' Edith explained as she poured tea.

'But Tommy O'Driscoll calls his mammy,

Mammy, and so do the Murphys – they say mammy and daddy, too.' Juliet was very put out.

'That will do, Juliet. Please do not be impertinent. It is entirely irrelevant how the village children address their parents as you will not be mixing with them. You will not be going to the village school. You will be going to a convent boarding school in Dublin, and James will be going to the Jesuits in Kildare. At good schools, people don't use those terms for their parents. They call them mother and father.'

The twins turned their stricken faces towards their father. What was their mother talking about? Dublin and Kildare? Where were they? All summer they'd been talking about the fun they would have at 'big school'. Surely Daddy wasn't in on this plan.

Richard had never discussed the children's education with his wife; he discussed very little with her. He had assumed they would attend the local national school as he had done himself. He'd had to board when he went to secondary school but by then, he had been thirteen. The idea that his children would be sent away to school at their age was news to him and seemed ridiculous. Yet he knew that this would have to be handled delicately as once Edith had made up her mind she was impossible to sway.

'Well, we can talk about this later. How about a nice slice of this lovely cake? I think Mrs Canty spent a long time making it so it will be just perfect for the big birthday of James and Juliet Buckley.' Richard did his best to inject some cheer into his voice and into the sad little faces in front of him but knew he was failing miserably. He also knew they would have loved to have jam sandwiches and cake and lemonade with some of the village children in the kitchen surrounded by the Cantys and Solange and himself. This cold, musty-smelling room and those ridiculous-looking frilly outfits made his children look tiny and sad.

CHAPTER 7

'Daddy, I'm not going away to a school in Dublin, am I? And James doesn't like sleeping anywhere except Dunderrig. He wouldn't like to go away, either. We have to stay here with you and Solange and Mrs Canty and Eddie...' Richard looked down at his little daughter, so small in her big bed.

Her face was so innocent and trusting, and all he wanted to do was to reassure her that her mother had not meant what she said about boarding school. Yet he knew he could not issue promises that he was not guaranteed to keep. Edith seemed set on sending the twins away to school, and he was reluctant to go against her.

Solange was standing at the door, and she

caught Richard's eye. She'd obviously had a similar conversation with James as she tucked him in.

Juliet searched Solange's face for the reassurance she craved. 'Solange, tell him, we can't leave Dunderrig, we would cry every day and every night, and we would be sad all the time...' Her voice was growing in strength. 'It's not fair, it's just mean old Mammy making us go away. She wants...'

Solange approached the bed, hiding her frustration at Richard's inability to stand up to Edith. The notion of these two babies being sent away from home horrified her, but she tried to settle the little girl who loved and trusted her so much.

'*Ma petite, écoute*, listen now. You must sleep, tomorrow we will talk about this, and we will solve it all, but *maintenant tu dois dormir, d'accord?*' She rubbed Juliet's hair gently and felt the child relax.

'You won't let her send us away, Solange, sure you won't?' the little girl mumbled as she drifted off to sleep.

Solange tried as much as was possible to stay out of any decisions about the children. In the beginning, she had found it very puzzling. She'd had no intention of replacing their mother; she was content to be their nanny. Yet as time wore on, and Edith remained significantly absent from her children's lives, Solange had found herself doing more and more for the twins. She knew they saw her as their mother, but while she loved them with every fibre of her being, she still tried to remind them, and herself, that Edith was their real mother.

Richard did love them undoubtedly, but he seemed reluctant to challenge his wife. When she insisted they be dressed like fashion models, he 'oohed' and 'aahed' over them. When she banned local children from playing in the garden, he upheld her ruling. Yet as far as Solange could tell, they had no relationship at all. They spent as little time together as possible and when they did speak, Edith took the opportunity to insist Richard deal with some annoyance or source of irritation to her. He acquiesced in all things, as far as Solange could see, without argument or debate but without any affection either. He got no pleasure in making her happy if indeed Edith was capable of such an emotion. Sometimes, when the children did something that should have garnered their mother's attention, like when they found a baby bird and nursed it back to health, Solange could have shaken Edith for her lack of enthusiasm. Edith looked at the little bird with a barely concealed shudder and said she hoped they had washed their hands as who knew what kind of germs a thing like that was carrying.

SOLANGE BUSIED HERSELF IN the kitchen making coffee, listening to Richard's footsteps crossing the landing above, then coming down the stairs. As he entered the kitchen, she thought he looked old and weary.

'Coffee?' she asked.

'Yes, thank you,' Richard replied with a deep sigh. The clock ticked loudly in the hall. The normally easy silence between them was now taut with tension. Eventually, Richard spoke.

'I know you probably think sending the twins away to school is a bad idea,' he began, 'and I agree to a certain extent. But perhaps Edith is right. Maybe it's for the best. They do run a bit wild here.'

Solange had remained silent regarding decisions about the twins for five years. She went quietly about her business and unobtrusively gave the children everything they needed, but she felt the anger rise up inside her now. Jeremy had often said that the Galliard temper was hard to rile but once it had been unleashed, woe betide whoever felt its terrifying force.

She breathed deeply. She had never confronted Richard on anything before. They got along well and were friends, but they were both conscious of how too much closeness might appear to the ever-watchful eyes in Dunderrig, and so they had avoided it. He had mentioned their past lives from time to time but only in the context of reminiscences about Jeremy; he made an occasional kind enquiry after her health, but apart from that, their chats were light-hearted. Despite how she felt about James and Juliet, she knew they were not her children and that she had no say in how Richard and Edith raised them, but the thought of them being separated from her, and from each other, was breaking her heart. This time, she couldn't remain silent.

'Richard.' She tried to keep her tone measured despite her frustration and feeling of helplessness. 'I must say, I cannot see what reason you would have to make them leave their home. They are only five years old and Dunderrig is all they know. They are happy here. Please reconsider. They do not have a warm relationship with their mother; she does not seem to show any interest in them at all. They wait all day for you to come home to read to them or to tell you of their little adventures. Mrs Canty and I do our best with them, and no, they do not run wild – they are full of mischief and fun like all little children should be. We saw enough misery in France, you and I, when babies were torn from their families by war. Your children live in a time of peace, thank God. You have the chance to be their father, to love them and hold them and be proud of them, and if you let them go to some fancy school, who will do that? Tell me Richard, who will kiss them and cuddle them when they have bad dreams? Who will bandage their cut knees? A teacher? A nun?'

Solange was shaking. Her hands were white with rage as she gripped the tea cloth she was holding. Richard looked shocked. He usually exuded such logical serenity that even the most hysterical of patients became calm and reasonable in Dr Buckley's presence. Solange doubted anyone had ever spoken to him in the way she had spoken to him just now. It was his composed attitude in the face of inflicting such misery on his children that had infuriated her. She wanted to shake him, kick him, slap him – make him respond with something other than this *sangfroid*.

Though she knew she shouldn't, Solange continued, 'She is their mother, I'm not denying that, but she does not know what is best for them. She does not know them, their little ways, the funny things they say. She simply tells them what to wear and how to sit correctly at the table. She doesn't know that Juliet only has to hear a tune once before she can play it on the piano and that she sings beautifully, or that James can paint landscapes and portraits better than most adults. They would die of loneliness in a place like that! Without you, the Cantys, Dunderrig, and everything they love around them. They are only babies, Richard! Surely you can see that. It would break their spirit to send them away, and they have done nothing to deserve that. You and I, we saw such terrible waste – young lives cut down for no reason, other young men so broken they will never be the same again. And now, you think that to send your children away to be raised by an institution is a good idea? You know this is wrong, you must not allow this. You must say no. Please, Richard, please...' Her voice tapered off, and she knew if she allowed herself to continue speaking, she would break down; so she stopped.

The clock ticked loudly on the wall. Richard fixed his gaze on Solange. He sighed deeply as the seconds ticked by; the silence between them was deafening.

'You are right, of course. I will speak to her. I just... I'm trying to keep everything going,

Solange. You see it with your own eyes. We don't have a marriage, Edith and I, we just both live here. I thought when I came back that things would improve, but you can see how things are. I tried, I really did. We did love each other once you know, but she never forgave me for wearing a British uniform, and I don't think that she ever will. We can't send them away, this is their home, where they belong with me and you and the Cantys. She will just have to accept it.'

He straightened his shoulders and left the kitchen, leaving Solange wiping away tears of relief.

CHAPTER 8

'*A*re they up?' Richard asked as he entered the sunny kitchen on the first Monday of September.

'Up?' Mrs Canty exclaimed. 'They've been up since dawn, so excited they are to be going to school at last. Though what the Master will make of that pair of scallywags, I don't know! They have the lunch packed and the two satchels out by the door, and they've gone out with Solange to feed the hens. The poor birds shouldn't be fed till mid-morning, but if she didn't find them something to do, they'd wake the parish with the yakking out of them. Honest to God, you'd swear 'twas to the circus they were going and not to school.' She paused for a moment, then said, 'I hope they'll be all right, Dr Richard.' The normally assured Mrs Canty had a hint of worry in her voice.

'Of course they will, Mrs Canty. Sure, Master Cotter and his wife are lovely, kind people, who'll look after them fine for us. 'Twill be a quiet house now with them gone all day though, won't it?'

Mrs Canty wiped her eyes.

'Sure, 'tis only till two in the afternoon, I know, but we're so used to them in and out all day long, driving me cracked, that we'll miss them something desperate, myself and Solange. I'll tell you one thing for nothing, Doctor Richard, and it's this. 'Twas a lucky day you brought Solange Allingham to this house. She's been a mother to those twins, and she loves them as if they were her own. And they love her, too. I don't know what we'd have done only for her and that's the truth.'

Richard knew Mrs Canty had no time whatsoever for Edith, and even if Edith had made any effort to be a mother, Mrs Canty would have criticised her. Yet he couldn't help but agree with her.

'I know. She's been a godsend. I just wish it was happier circumstances that brought her to us. I sometimes think that she should marry again. She is still such a young woman, and I hate to think she is trapped here.'

It had been troubling him for a while that maybe Solange was keeping her secret lover at arm's length because she felt she could not leave Dunderrig and the children. Not that he wanted her to leave – selfishly, he had already offered her the position of medical secretary, just in case she got it into her head that she was no longer needed once the children had gone to school.

Mrs Canty had obviously not grasped the obvious reason for Solange's monthly overnight absences.

'Well, I'd say she hasn't much interest in that kind of thing. 'Tisn't like she doesn't catch their eye, anyway. Sure half the parish is in and out here offering to help her do this or that, but she gives them no quarter. Ted Collins is mad for her, but sure he's way too old, and I told him so the last night he called. Sniffing around a lovely young woman like Solange and he in his dotage. "'Tis down on your knees praying for a happy death you should be, boyo!" says I to him. He didn't like it a bit.' Mrs Canty chuckled. 'But sure, all the Collinses have notions of themselves. Always did. No, James and Juliet are all she cares about. I know 'tis a long time since poor Jeremy died, but she's not ready yet. Maybe she never will be. Love like that, Dr Richard, you can't just wipe it away and start again.' The implication was clear – in her opinion, poor Dr Richard had never known such love.

'Daddy!' Juliet squealed as she raced through the double doors from the courtyard. *'C'est aujourd' hui! Finalement! Solange m'a dit que...'* Remembering she was speaking in French she stopped, then continued, 'That we can go to big school, and James is going to sit beside me 'cause he's not able to open his sandwiches on his own.'

'I am, Daddy, I am able to. Solange wrapped them up for us in an easy way. She is only saying that so everyone will know she is older, but she's only six minutes older and that's nothing, sure it isn't, Daddy?' James yelled, drowning out his sister.

Richard pulled his twins onto his lap, one on each knee.

'Now, listen here to me, the two of ye. I want the best behaviour, is that clear? No blackguarding or we'll cancel school altogether and you won't be going at all.' The tickling that resulted in gales of giggles softened his words.

'Careful, Richard,' laughed Solange. 'Knowing

this pair, they could use that against you as soon as the novelty wears off.'

'We'll be the best in the class, and we won't fight or say bad words or do nothing bad,' Juliet promised while James nodded sincerely. Richard looked into the tanned faces of his children, so happy and carefree from a summer spent climbing trees and riding the old donkey Eddie kept in the bottom field.

Solange had been so right to resist the boarding school. Edith had, of course, been furious and hadn't spoken to him in months, but in a way, this made for an easier existence. She spent her evenings alone, still reading and writing those endless letters. He was fairly sure she was in correspondence with another man; things had died down politically after the Civil War, yet still the missives kept coming. He contemplated asking the man's name, just to let her know he was not completely unaware of what was going on in his own house. But in the end, he decided against it. Their love – if there ever had been any love for him on her side – was dead, and so who she corresponded with was her own business. Clearly, Edith didn't want the scandal of separation. He didn't like to think about the future, how he would end his days in his childhood home with a malevolent stranger. But for now, while the children were small, they filled up the empty space in his heart left by his failed marriage.

'Now, are we ready?' he asked, breaking out of his reverie. 'Have you got your lunch?'

'Yes, Daddy,' they chorused.

'Well, say goodbye to Mrs Canty and Solange and let's go.'

The twins ran into Mrs Canty's outstretched arms.

'I'll have the buns ready when ye get home, with currants in some and none in the others, all right?' she whispered to them, trying not to cry. James loved currants, but Juliet hated them. As she released them from her embrace, they came to stand in front of Solange. Richard observed that though they were boisterous and loved horseplay with anyone, they were always gentle around her.

She crouched down to be at their level. Holding a hand of each twin she spoke softly, *'Alors, mes petits. J'espère que tout va bien à l'école. N'ayez pas peur, je sais que vous allez beaucoup vous amuser. Bon courage. Je vous aime fort.'* Kissing them each on the cheek, she rose and went out to the yard. Richard knew she would miss them to-day, but she would never let them see that.

As he shepherded them out of the main door towards the car, he chanced to look up. Edith stood at her window, looking down imperiously. She made no gesture to her children, no wave or a blown kiss. Luckily, the twins didn't see her, nor did it occur to them to ask for her. As far as they were concerned, home was Daddy, the Cantys, and Solange.

CHAPTER 9

The daily routine of Dunderrig continued to bend around the lives of its two noisiest inhabitants. Only their mother remained aloof, keeping to her rooms apart from a daily walk around the garden; there she might stop and speak to Eddie for a moment – just a few words about some plant or bush to which he was attending. He seemed to be the only person in Dunderrig whom she could tolerate near her, perhaps because he was so unobtrusive and quiet.

James and Juliet loved Eddie as a grandfather. They would rush in with tales of how he'd shown them how to do this or that; they regarded him as an authority on virtually everything. Richard knew he took them shooting rabbits as he'd done with Richard himself as a boy, and while he now had a hatred of guns, he trusted Eddie Canty implicitly. Richard suspected Eddie said more to the twins than he did to any other human being.

One Sunday towards the end of September, James and Juliet begged Richard and Solange to take them fishing in the river. Mrs Canty packed sandwiches and cake; they had a lovely day. The children caught two trout, which they insisted were twins, just like themselves; they named them Jimmy and Julie and released them back into the water. Richard lay back on the grass, listening to the gentle lapping of the river and the ceaseless chatter of the little pair as Solange showed them how to make daisy chains. He felt how perfect life would be if all he ever had to do was while away the time with nature and little children all around him.

They returned tired and happy, and with the twins badly in need of a bath. As always, Edith insisted the children dress for tea in the drawing room. They were exhausted but dutifully the little family of four sat down in the austere room with the large table. The twins were different in here, Richard thought, much more subdued.

'Did you have a nice afternoon?' Edith asked.

'Yes, Mother,' they chorused but were unforthcoming with any further details. When they'd arrived in earlier, they had regaled Mrs Canty with stories of fish and flowers and a squirrel they saw, and how Daddy accidentally put his foot in the water and had to take off his shoes and socks because they were all wet. They giggled, chatted, and finished each other's sentences.

Now, James was scratching his neck where the collar of his shirt was irritating his skin.

'Stop scratching, James,' his mother said. 'It looks awful. I hope you haven't caught fleas. I told you not to pick up those cats from the barn. Though, given the children he mixes with in school, God knows what kinds of things he is exposed to,' she added pointedly to her husband.

'Mary Sweeney had creepy crawlies in her hair, and the Mistress had to make her go home to get them combed out and when she came back the next day, she smelled yucky,' piped up Juliet.

Edith glared at Richard.

'Head lice,' Richard explained, 'like to live on clean hair, so anyone can get them. I suppose they are just like rabbits or cats or humans, just trying to live their lives. They wouldn't hurt you at all, but they just make your head a bit itchy so that's why you have to use a special soap to get rid of them. That's why she smelled a bit funny, but it could just as easily have been you or James. Lice are happy to live on anyone's head.'

James giggled, 'Imagine if you had rabbits in your hair. Going boing, boing!' Juliet joined in, making funny noises. Soon both twins were in fits of laughter.

'For goodness sake!' Edith exclaimed. 'You've had a whole afternoon running wild like animals, is it too much to ask that you sit and have a meal like civilised people?'

Immediately, the children stopped laughing and resumed eating their tiny sandwiches.

The meal continued interminably in silence and after what seemed like an hour to Richard, Edith addressed the children once more.

'You may go.'

Relieved, they scrambled off the high-backed upholstered chairs and escaped to the kitchen, where they knew Solange and Mrs Canty would be waiting with hot chocolate and their pyjamas warming near the range.

Richard made to leave also.

'Please wait, Richard,' Edith spoke. 'I wish to speak to you.'

Richard sat down again, dreading what was sure to be more criticism of Solange or Mrs

Canty or the children. Since she hadn't spoken to him in months unless the children were present, it seemed unlikely to be anything good. 'Yes? What is it?'

'Well...' For once, Edith did not seem to be delivering a prepared speech. She cleared her throat. 'I'm sorry to say this to you, although I suppose it won't come as a shock. In fact, you'll probably be quite relieved. I'm going away. I'm going to London.' She stared at the linen napkin in her hands.

'London? What are you going to London for? Shopping? Because really, Edith, the children have enough clothes and so on, and you are constantly annoyed that they don't wear the things you buy them, and now if you are suggesting you come back with more...'

'No, Richard. I'm not coming back. I'm leaving Dunderrig. I'm leaving you.'

Richard was stunned. He knew she was unhappy, but he had never thought she would leave him. He had assumed she was too afraid of scandal.

'Why?' he asked. 'Why now?'

Edith gave an exasperated sigh. 'Why? Why? For goodness sake, Richard, I'm leaving you because if I don't, I'll go insane – stuck here in this bloody house all day with Solange and that fat peasant Canty. You arriving in the evenings, looking like you are having a tooth pulled! You have nothing to say, you don't know anyone – well, anyone that matters – you are a mediocre country doctor whose idea of fun is... Well, I don't know, actually... What is your idea of fun, Richard? I doubt you know the meaning of the word. Life with you is suffocating; it's so boring, so tediously, deathly *dull!*' Her voice had risen to a scream.

'Why did you agree to marry me, Edith?' Richard asked quietly. 'I never claimed to be fun, as you put it.'

'I really don't know.' Edith was dismissive. 'I've had plenty of time to reconsider though, have I not? Stuck first with your aged, decrepit parents and then you, back from playing soldiers for the British. The same British Army that was butchering your own people, incidentally, not that such things ever occurred to noble Doctor Buckley, oh no, just saving lives and not taking sides, how honourable.' She spat the last words in disgust.

'There's someone else, isn't there?' Richard looked straight at her.

'That's irrelevant,' she snapped.

He felt cold, inside and out. 'I would think it's highly relevant, Edith.'

She twisted the napkin fiercely. 'Yes, there is someone. I suppose you are going to find that out, anyway. But he's not the reason. It's just because I can't...'

'Yes, yes, you can't stand us anymore, so you've said. So, do I know this someone? Let me guess, some suave Gaelic revivalist or politician, probably one of your parlour room Republican friends, pouring forth about the cause from the comfort of some hotel bar?'

'Look, Richard, this is hardly helpful. I am going, and I just...well. That is it. I'm leaving, and I won't be coming back. Whom I am going to is not your concern.'

He clenched his hands beneath the tabletop. 'There are two small details you haven't mentioned, Edith. Perhaps you feel they are, as you are so fond of saying, irrelevant, but you do have two children – or had you forgotten them as usual?'

'Of course I have not forgotten them,' she snapped. 'Caring for them both will be difficult until I am settled, so I only plan to take James for now – he's more manageable than Juliet. Then when I can, I will send for her, as well. Though how long that will be, I'm not sure.'

'Over my dead body.' He tried to keep his voice low. Rising from his chair, he walked around the table. He looked into Edith's eyes; he knew she was frightened. Crouching down in front of her, their eyes were level. He was physically closer to her than he had been in years.

'You can do what you like, go where you like, with whoever you like, but you will *not* be taking my children. Either of them. Is that absolutely clear? Solange, Mrs Canty and I have taken care of them and loved them since they were born, without any input whatsoever from you, their so-called mother. They don't love you. They don't even like you – do you know that? They hate these stupid tea parties and they love Solange. Do you know why, Edith? Do you? Because Solange knows what love is. She is not afraid to hug them and kiss them and tickle them – things a normal mother would do. She's known a life of pain and loss, and you've had nothing but privilege and what did it make you? A spoiled, selfish bitch.' His face was inches from Edith's. He hated the sound of his own voice as he spoke – cold and threatening – but she had driven him to speak like this.

'Your children? *Yours?*' Edith's eyes glinted hatred as she shouted at him. 'You're so sure of that, are you? You stupid man! I only slept with you in Dublin because I was afraid I was pregnant by another man. A *real* man. Your precious twins? They don't even *look* like you!' She stormed out of the room, pushing past Solange and Mrs Canty, who had come running when the shouting first began. 'I hope you heard that, you eavesdropper!' she screamed into Solange's face before she rushed upstairs. 'They're not yours, they're not even his – they are *mine*, both of them, and if I wish to take my son with me now, none of you can stop me!'

Richard felt as if he was going to be sick. They were his children; they had to be his children. He loved them so much. Everyone always said they were the image of him. Solange ran to his side.

'Where are they?' Richard croaked, leaning on the table for support.

'Eddie took them out when the shouting began, they heard nothing. They are down with the donkey,' she comforted him.

'I have to find them, stop her from taking them…' His eyes were frantic.

Edith reappeared down the stairs, carrying a small valise.

'I will send for the rest of my things later.

Solange, pack some things for James immediately. Canty, have your husband bring the car round, we are going to the station.'

'Do you hear her, Dr Richard?' Mrs Canty puffed up like a balloon. Grabbing the valise from Edith, she threw it out on the gravel outside the open front door and, rounding on the taller woman, she gave vent to all the fury she'd been bottling up inside her for years.

'Now, you listen here to me, you tramp! Do you think we don't know what's been going on with your fancy man above in Dublin, and you a married woman writing love letters like an auld hoor? You'll get your scrawny carcass out of this house, and we never want to see you again, do you hear me? Those are our twins, they are Buckleys through and through, sure little James is the living head cut off his father when he was that size. There's nobody for three counties around has those same green eyes so whatever you were up to with some auld tom cat above in Dublin, it did not result in our twins, d'you hear me? Dr Richard did nothing but be a good decent husband to you, you hussy, and this is how you repay him? You are no better than you should be, with all your airs and graces. You think you are so high and mighty with your bigwig friends and relations? Pah! This house and this family are too good for the likes of you, not the other way round! Now, my husband will leave you to the train because 'tis the way we'll be sure to be rid of you and let me tell you something...' Mrs Canty now had a fistful of the front of Edith's dress, pulling her towards her, 'You are a cold, unnatural woman, and those children, or us, never want the misfortune to clap eyes on you again. If we do, 'tis more than a slap on that pointy, miserable face you'll get! Now you sit in there, in the drawing room and keep your filthy mouth shut while I fetch my husband and don't even think of speaking to James and Juliet. We'll explain everything to them when you're gone. Don't worry, they won't miss you a jot, and by next week, they'll have forgotten you completely.' Shoving a shocked Edith into the drawing room, she turned the key, locking her in.

Solange was trembling. She'd never seen such a display, and she thanked God the children hadn't been there to hear any of it.

'Solange,' she heard Mrs Canty saying. 'Go with Dr Richard and find the children and Eddie. Send him back with the car to take that baggage to the station, and you take the children up the fuchsia wood for a walk till all this is over.'

She did as she was told. Her instinct was only to keep James and Juliet safe. Edith could not have been serious, surely, about taking her son? How could she? She knew Edith always preferred James, and she knew that Juliet noticed it – making her even more sullen around her mother than she might otherwise be. Nevertheless, for Edith to want to take James and leave her daughter behind was unfathomable. Solange vowed that Juliet would never know.

'Richard, I think they are still down in the low field where Eddie took them with some carrots for the old donkey. Let's go and fetch them and talk to Eddie about the car.'

Richard seemed dazed. 'No need to get Eddie, sure I can drive her...'

Solange spoke gently, 'I think, perhaps, it is better for you if Eddie takes her. We can take the children for a walk, pick some flowers, and try to behave normally. We can talk about this later if you wish when they are in bed.'

'Yes.' Richard replied, glad Solange was taking charge. Edith's words were still ringing in his ears: *You stupid man. They don't even look like you.*

Solange and Richard walked through the fields leading to the river. On the still autumn evening, the children's high little voices rang clearly in the distance.

'There they are,' Solange said, relieved. Though she knew there was no way Edith could take them now, she still felt on edge; she needed them close. Realising she would have to do most of the talking, she said as brightly as she could, 'Ah *mes petits*, Papa and I are going to take you for a walk, to pick some fuchsia for the table. Mrs Canty is making shepherd's pie because she knows it's your favourite dinner, so we'll get her some of her favourite flowers. *Quelle bonne idée!*'

The children were delighted at the prospect of an impromptu outing with Solange and their Daddy.

'Yay!' Juliet squealed, 'and we can show you the tree with the shape of a dog's head on the bark, Daddy!'

'I'm showing him,' James said. 'I found it.'

Bending down and wrapping his arms around them, Richard held them close.

'You can both show me,' he said, not wanting to let them go.

'Daddy, you're squishing us,' James giggled, wriggling free.

Solange, meanwhile, was having a quiet word with Eddie, outlining the events in the house. He seemed to understand perfectly and was not in the least surprised. He smiled when Solange told him how Mrs Canty had given Edith what for.

The children scampered happily through the fuchsia wood as the late September sunshine flooded through the trees, dappling the path in front of Solange and Richard as they walked.

'Did you know?' Richard asked.

'Know what?'

'All of it, any of it. That there was someone else. About the twins. That she was planning to leave?' He spoke quietly so the children couldn't hear him, even though they were far ahead on the track.

'Of course I didn't know. How could I have known that, Richard? Edith never spoke to me except to tell me how to dress the children or what they should not be doing. I knew she received and wrote a lot of letters, and Mrs Canty said she had spent a lot of time in Dublin when you were in France, but apart from that, no, I knew nothing.'

Solange wondered whether she should offer some comfort to him, touch him or try to console him in some way. She tried to imagine what Jeremy would have done. She often spoke to her husband when she lay in bed alone at night, telling him of the events of her day. She could hear him in her mind reacting to Edith's departure, outraged that someone could treat his dearest friend so callously. Jeremy had always been fiercely loyal to those he loved. *'Good riddance, old chap, she was a cold, old fish, anyhow. What you need is a passionate Frenchwoman to take your breath away; it's all that sunshine you see, warm blood!'* She could hear his infectious laugh and see him clapping Richard on the back, lifting him out of this black humour that had descended on him.

She wished there was something she could say, but she struggled to find the words. They walked silently together, following the course set by James and Juliet.

'They are your children, Richard, it's as plain as anything. They are so like you, and those eyes of theirs are exactly yours – very unusual. You know, I thought all Irish people had those bright green eyes until I got here. You were the first Irish person I met. And even if you were not their biological father – and believe me, you are – then what would that matter? It is you who has loved them, played with them, read stories to them since they were born. We both know how life can take sudden turns for the worse but what matters is love. Nothing else. You love James and Juliet more than anyone in the world, and now you will have to love them even more.'

Solange hoped she was saying the right thing. Richard sat down on a mossy rock and watched the children as they climbed a large beech tree.

'What if she wants them? Tries to take them from me? If you and Mrs Canty hadn't been there today, to stand up to her... I never thought that she'd try to do that. I never even realised she might leave.'

The normally capable and stoic Richard Buckley seemed broken and unsure of himself.

'I did love her, you know. She was so pleasant when we met, so calm and restful, not demanding like some other girls. I was never very good with women, I suppose, not having had sisters maybe. I always wished I could have been more like Jeremy. He would enter a room and light it up. Everyone wanted to talk to him, all the girls flirted with him, and he was so cheery, so confident, but I just wasn't like that. I've learned to be confident in my job. I know what I'm doing most of the time, but socially I'm still hopeless. I know I am. Edith was a city girl, lots of friends and social engagements. She mixed with a very sophisticated group in Dublin. Of course Dunderrig suffocated her. She never understood about my joining up, you know. She hated me for that. She thought I was betraying her father, whom she adored. He was a real Irish patriot, she said; he died for Ireland. She never understood that I didn't join up because I wanted to fight with the British. I just wanted to help our own poor Irish lads in France. And I think I went because I missed Jeremy, too. When I was around him, I felt a little less dull, I suppose. Without him...' Richard smiled sadly. 'I really miss him, you know.'

'I miss him, too,' Solange replied. 'As we walked along there, I was trying to imagine what he would have said to you if he were here now. He cared so much for you, Richard, you know that. You were the first person he told me about when we met, and when you said you were coming to France, he was so angry. Not because he didn't want to see you, but because he loved you and the war was no place for someone you loved. I must admit, I found you a little strange at first. You and he had such very different personalities; I was puzzled you were friends. I remember once, Jeremy telling me that you were all the bits of him that he wished were better: a better doctor, a better friend. I think he would have told you that Edith was wrong for you, that you needed someone fun and lively. And he would have loved the twins. Sometimes, I can see him laughing at their tricks. They are naughty and lovable and brave, just as he was.'

Richard smiled, idly scraping moss from the rock. 'They would have been mad about him, too. Can you imagine what he would have let them do? I think they'd need a doctor each if Jeremy was left in charge. He never saw danger, even over there, where every day survival seemed unlikely.'

A pensive silence descended between them. Eventually, Richard spoke again, 'So what now, Solange? What do I do now?'

'You carry on. You tell people that Edith has left and won't be coming back. Don't explain any further.' She gave a small chuckle. 'You'll be good at that part. You don't ever feel the need to explain yourself, anyway. Most importantly, we must tell James and Juliet.'

Richard looked up; the twins were coming slowly towards them, bearing huge armfuls of the red and purple fuchsia that grew in such profusion around West Cork. 'I suppose you're right. Will we tell them now?'

'Would you like to tell them on your own? Explain without me being there?'

'No, Solange, it would frighten them. They know if you're there everything is going to be all right. It would be better coming from you. I'm not great at this kind of thing. I wouldn't know what to say to them...' His voice betrayed his panic.

She soothed him, 'They are your children, they trust you. Just tell them the truth, gently. Obviously, not anything about Edith questioning their parentage, just that she has gone away and you don't know when she will be back. Children are resilient, but those two are clever. They'll know if you lie to them, so a simple version of the truth is best.'

She stood and went to meet the twins. '*Mon dieu!* What a big bunch of flowers! You are so strong to be able to carry so much!'

She shepherded the children towards their father.

'James, Juliet, I want to tell you something,' said Richard, taking the fuchsia from them and then holding their hands. 'Today, Mammy decided she was going to go away for... Well, for a while... I don't know how long...' He searched Solange's face for the right words. She smiled encouragingly. He went on, 'Well, maybe for a long time. But Solange and Mrs Canty, and Eddie and

I will be staying in Dunderrig with you to take care of you, so you mustn't worry.'

The children looked questioningly at their father. Then the braver of the two, Juliet, piped up, 'Does that mean we don't have to wear those scratchy dresses anymore?'

Richard suppressed a smile and drew both his children to him, enveloping them in a hug. 'No, pet, you don't.'

James, taking in this new and exciting information, asked excitedly, 'Can we have our tea in the barn, with the new kittens?'

Solange decided it was time to intervene. 'Well, perhaps not in the barn. But you can have it at the kitchen table with Mrs Canty and me, and of course, with your Daddy. And after tea, perhaps, we can bring the kittens inside for a little while, and you can both play with them.'

The twins' eyes lit up with excitement; this was a wonderful development.

'And what about the bedrooms? Can we stay in your room, Solange, and not have to pretend to sleep in our own rooms?' Juliet asked with wide innocent eyes.

Solange had not realised that the children knew they were supposed to sleep all night in the fancy rooms Edith had decorated for them.

It seemed they were aware all along of the conflict.

'Yes, you can both sleep in my room all the time until you are seven years old – that is a very long time away.' Solange was laughing as she ruffled Juliet's curls.

'Will Mammy be back when we are seven?' James enquired.

Richard caught Solange's eye. Her look told him it was better to be honest now rather than face endless questions later. Also, the little pair seemed not remotely upset by a life without her.

'I don't think so, James. I think Mammy might not come back for years and years.'

James and Juliet struggled home under the weight of the huge branches of fuchsia that they had insisted on bringing with them for Mrs Canty. Richard and Solange walked behind them, listening to their animated chatter. It confirmed what they'd always suspected – no one in Dunderrig was going to miss Edith.

CHAPTER 10

June 1937

'Solange! Solange! We're home! *Nous sommes rentrés!* Solange? *Où es-tu?* Solange!'

Solange looked out the bedroom window of Dunderrig to see James and Juliet tumble out of their father's car amid a sea of tennis racquets, violins, hurleys, and bags. They'd made better time than she'd thought they would.

Solange and the Cantys had been counting down the days. Having the twins home after their final summer term was an event the entire household had awaited with growing excitement.

It had been so hard to see them grow up and go off to boarding school – Juliet to the Ursuline

Convent and James to Farranferris College, both in Cork city – but now the six years were over. Mrs Canty had been baking and cooking all week in honour of the grand homecoming, so they would have a happy family dinner in the kitchen and – as at the beginning of every holiday – everyone would be regaled with the stories of the antics the twins had got up to in school.

James was a model student. Always completing homework in full and on time; he never cheeked the teachers and had two close friends who remained unchanged throughout his six years at the school. He was the captain of the school hurling team and always returned home proudly brandishing his medals.

Juliet, on the other hand, had been quite a handful, as the nuns had told Richard on more than one occasion. The only area she excelled in was music; after years of playing by ear, a sweet octogenarian teacher convinced her to read music, and whenever she came home, she delighted her father and Solange with her recitals. Otherwise, she displayed a slapdash attitude to her work; she was inclined to be a little too vocal with her opinions, leading to several sanctions, which seemed to enrage her and lead to even more unacceptable behaviour. In October of their last year, in desperation and with the threat of expulsion looming, Richard had begged Solange to speak to her.

Solange had refused Richard's offer of a lift and had caught the bus to the city, where she had arranged to meet Juliet. The warm hug that enveloped her as she entered the steamy café quickly dispelled any firm words she had intended to say. Poor Juliet was high-spirited, funny, and brave as a lion – qualities the nuns did not seem to rate very highly.

Juliet had poured her heart out – in flawless French, much to Solange's pride, lest she be overheard by what she called spies from the school – about the horrible regime she was being subjected to. She hated pinning her hair up, she couldn't help talking in the corridors, she couldn't get up in time for morning mass – the list was endless. Solange soothed and calmed her and managed to convince her that if she managed to behave until after the final exams, she would be free of the nuns forever. She confided to Solange that she wanted to study medicine, but that she believed her father wouldn't agree. Nursing, perhaps – but a doctor? Never. Her father was too old-fashioned. The role of doctor was reserved for his son, James. James, however, had no interest whatsoever in medicine and wanted to be an artist, something he too was dreading to reveal to his father.

Solange told Juliet that she was underestimating their father and that her and James's happiness was all that mattered to him. She assured her that Richard would support them in whatever career they chose when they finished school. She hoped she was right. It was difficult to know with him.

Richard loved his children, but he was also sure he knew what was best for them. She knew he did indeed assume that Juliet would stay at home, presumably until she found an eligible young man to marry her, and that James would follow in his footsteps and train as a doctor. If Solange knew her twins, they would make up their own minds about their futures.

James and Juliet loved their father, of that there was no doubt, but in general, they confided only in her. It was she who was given the role of go-between whenever they wanted to ask something big of their father. Over the years, she sometimes wished that he could have been different, more open; but Richard had remained pleasant and calm, and a bit of a mystery. He showed no interest in any other women; clearly, as far as he was concerned, he was still married. Edith, to the best of Solange's knowledge, had never resurfaced. No letters, either from her or anyone representing her, had ever landed on the rug inside the front door of Dunderrig. She had never once enquired after the health or happiness of her children and after the first few weeks following her abrupt departure, they had stopped asking about her. It was as if she had never existed.

She and Richard had rubbed along together quite well over the years. At his suggestion, her role as a nanny had evolved into medical secretary for the practice, and everything ran smoothly. She still spent two consecutive days away from Dunderrig every month, and she would not be drawn on where or with whom she spent them despite Mrs Canty's less than subtle questioning.

She and Richard had never become closer though she knew that, secretly, Mrs Canty had high hopes that they might. She was surprised at the older woman's attitude, given that she was such a devout Catholic, but it seemed the old woman's values went out the window when it came to Dr Richard's happiness. She still held the long-departed Edith in the lowest of contempt and was even heard to say that the church should, in very special circumstances, allow people to re-marry. Mrs Canty's rather ham-fisted attempts at matchmaking thankfully seemed to go unnoticed by Richard. It was as if that aspect of his life had simply ceased to be.

She was contented with her life; it was certainly not the one she had envisaged as a young girl in France, but it was a nice life, and she was happy. The twins had suffered no ill-effects from the loss of their mother all those years ago and had grown up to be wonderful people whom she adored with every fibre of her being. Very rarely, Juliet and James wondered whatever became of Edith. They had imagined all sorts of amazing tales when they were younger, reducing each other into fits of giggles, imagining their mother as a lion tamer or as a magician's assistant. Yet they spoke of her as if she were a character in a story rather than their mother. Though Solange never encouraged them to verbalise it for fear of confusing them, she knew that to all intents and purposes she was their real mother.

Now she ran down the stairs to greet them.

'*Me voilà mes petits chous! Bienvenue!* Oh, how we have missed you.' She embraced both twins, simultaneously. 'How are you? *Bien?* James! My goodness how grown up you look! *Et si beau!'* She squeezed his face playfully. 'My darling Juliet, you are so pretty but so thin! Are those nuns feeding you at all?'

Her greeting was interrupted by a familiar voice emerging from the kitchen.

'Well, if it isn't trouble in the house back again! Come here to me ye pair of divils till I get a proper look at ye!' The twins ran to Mrs Canty as they always had done. 'Aisy, aisy, let ye! I'm an old woman and ye are two fine big people to be launching ye'rselves on top of me! Juliet Buckley! I don't know if 'tis the fashion up in Cork now, but there isn't a pick on you! Come in to me till I feed you up, God almighty girl, you're like a twig, you're so skinny! James, there isn't a fear of you then, growing up to be a fine handsome man like your father and grandfather before you, God rest his soul. Come in let ye, come in, come in...'

Dinner was a loud affair with James and Juliet both bursting to tell their stories. Solange and Richard gazed at them proudly. Juliet was exceptionally beautiful. The blond hair of her childhood had never darkened or faded, and she had all the poise and grace of her mother but with a warm, engaging presence. Her flashing green eyes were always full of fun and her petite frame made her look like a mischievous fairy. James, on the other hand, had grown up more like his father, physically and in temperament. Solange had been worried when they were children that he would always be as petite as his sister, but he was much taller and broader than Juliet now – a fine, strong young man bulked out from playing so much hurling and football in school. Their personalities, as always, were polar opposites: Juliet, bubbly and headstrong while her brother was quieter and more sensitive. The bond between them was as strong as ever, even with the term-time separation; they still finished each other's sentences and seemed happiest when left to their own conversations.

Over dinner, the discussion turned to political matters.

'It seems things are really heating up in Europe,' James began. 'We listen to the wireless at school and one of the lads' fathers is in the Department of External Affairs. He's fairly sure that there's going to be another war. The priests were telling us that Hitler had a hundred and fifty Catholic youth workers shot for treason and that now he's looking greedily at Austria.'

'Oh, it's kind of exciting though, isn't it?' Juliet squealed. 'I know war is terrible and all that, but all those soldiers going off to fight nasty Mr Hitler is kind of glamorous. Don't you think?'

Her father interrupted her, uncharacteristically harsh. 'Don't be so stupid, Juliet. There is nothing exciting or glamorous about war. It's just bloody and destructive and destroys lives and property. I can't believe you would say something so silly, especially given what happened to Jeremy. Anyway, we are a neutral country, so even if there is a war, it won't be anything to do with us, thank God.' Richard's face was white with rage.

Everyone was looking at him in dismay. He never spoke in this tone to anyone, even the most irritating of his patients.

Juliet just stammered, 'Solange, *je suis désolée*, I should not have said that, I'm sorry Daddy...' Her voice trailed off.

Richard looked at his stricken daughter and guilt flooded through him. He took her hand across the table, instantly contrite for upsetting her.

'No pet, I'm sorry. It's just I saw so many young people the last time thinking it was going to be all medals and victory dances and it was...it was... There are no words.' He couldn't finish. Though Richard encouraged his war veteran patients to deal psychologically with what they'd seen and experienced, he did the complete opposite himself; he simply never spoke about it and, in as much as it was possible, tried not to think about it. Seeing it all happen again, watching the conflict in Europe build with every passing week, was bringing it all back to him. Thank God, de Valera was keeping Ireland neutral. He couldn't bear the thought of James joining up. He was beginning to understand the terror his parents had felt when he had decided to go to France in 1916. With the thoughtlessness of youth, he had not concerned himself with their fears, thinking them old and fussy. Now, as a father himself, he couldn't even consider the prospect of his children being involved in any kind of war, suffering the deprivation that conflict brings, having someone point a gun at them, trying to kill them. Killing them. It gave him a pain in his chest even thinking about it.

Solange broke the silence, 'Ah, Juliet, my darling girl, I am so happy you think this way, maybe that is how I thought when I was a young girl like you, too. Your papa and I, we have seen too much in the last war. They were terrible times, and if you had been there, you would never be the same again. We are not angry with you, you are young and only see the good in things, and this is how it should be. I pray you never have to find out what war is really like. I hope that they will find a way of dealing with this Hitler. Maybe it was not right to blame Germany for everything in the last war. They have been left with nothing, and this is dangerous. But they were so cruel; I find it hard to forgive them, even now. Jeremy always said he liked the Germans before the last time. War makes people do things they would not ordinarily do. You and he went there on a holiday once, didn't you, Richard? He said it was a walking holiday, but I think it might have been more of a beer-drinking holiday! I wish so much that you could have known Jeremy, he would have been delighted with you both, would he not, Richard?'

Effortlessly, Solange lifted the mood and did as she always did – made everything all right.

'Oh, he really would, he was so much livelier than me, ye would have had great fun with him,' Richard agreed.

'Ah, you're not so bad.' James gave him a playful punch on the shoulder. 'Did you really go to Germany? You never told us.'

'Yes, it was in 1913, in the summer. Of course, it was Jeremy's idea, but we had a great time. It's a beautiful country, Germany, you know? And really friendly, too. It was so hard for me to believe they were the same people capable of such savagery. I don't mean on the battlefield, that was just war, but in the way they treated the French in the villages and towns they occupied. It was hard to comprehend how men – fathers, brothers, sons – how they could be so unfeeling.'

Juliet was uncharacteristically quiet during the meal, and Richard looked at his daughter, feeling ashamed that his words had deflated her so much. Wanting to restore the buoyant mood of earlier, he asked brightly, 'So, what's the plan for the next few weeks? Seamus Hickey has been watching the swallows and all indications are telling him there's a fine warm spell coming. I met Mrs Dalton in the shop by the way – she asked when you were coming home.'

Juliet obliged with a knowing smile. 'Daddy, you know well the only reason she was asking was so that big lump of an eejit Danny Dalton can waltz up here, thinking that he's God's gift to women and whisk me away to the dance in Skibb.'

'Would that be so bad?' her father asked, a hint of an answering smile playing on his lips.

'Are you serious? Danny Dalton is a spoiled

mammy's boy and I've no more interest in him than in the man on the moon.'

Mrs Canty piped up from the stove, 'Dead right too, Juliet. All them Daltons are a bit cracked. Sure, his Uncle Connie, his father's brother, is above in the county home, convinced the Blessed Virgin is living in the snug of Sheehan's pub in the village. I'll tell you this for nothing, there was never yet a Dalton that was the full shilling as the years went on. You'd be landed with him then, Juliet, and he rambling and doddery. Sure anyway, every young lad in the parish will be up now that they know you're back.'

'Will ye all lay off her,' James said, ever ready to defend his twin. 'Juliet has no interest in any of those fellas. She is setting her sights much higher, imagining all the lads she'll meet up in the university.'

Juliet glared at her brother.

They'd talked on the train to Skibbereen about their plans and had both agreed that telling their father straight out what they wanted to do was the best way. They knew Solange would back them up and that even if their father was against their chosen careers, then it was better to be open and honest about their dreams. Still, this wasn't the best way to approach it, especially on their first night back and everyone so pleased to see them. Things had gone badly when the subject of war came up, so best leave anything contentious alone for the moment. She had intended to wait a few days, to get her father on his own and explain quietly, in private. This was not the plan, blurting it out like this.

James, however, seemed determined. 'Yes, we were talking on the way down. She'll make a wonderful doctor, don't you think, Dad?' he asked, his face a picture of innocence.

Richard glanced at Solange for advice on how to handle this. She was, however, paying very close attention to spoon out the last traces of the delicious apple crumble and custard Mrs Canty had made.

'Well...mhmm... It's...it's not really a suitable career for a lady, is it really? Lots of blood and infected toenails and that sort of thing. I'm sure Juliet has no interest in spending a life paring corns or examining varicose veins.' He finished with a laugh.

Juliet stared intently at him. When she spoke, it was with the steely determination he remembered so vividly from her childhood.

'I don't see why not, Daddy. If it's a good enough career for you, why not for me? I want to study to be a doctor. I thought you'd be pleased. Proud of me, even. Obviously I was wrong. Perhaps the height of your ambition for me is marriage to the likes of Danny Dalton and a big brood of kids and never leaving the parish so I'll look after you in your old age. Was that your plan, Daddy? Well, I'm sorry to disappoint you but that won't be happening.'

Juliet's voice was shaking with emotion. She pushed her chair back from the table and made for the door. Before exiting the kitchen, she turned.

'And by the way, James doesn't want to do medicine; he's going to study art. So now, nothing is working out as you planned, is it?' She slammed the door behind her.

Silence descended on the room, the clock ticking loudly on the mantle. After what seemed to Solange to be an interminable delay, Richard spoke.

'Is this true?' he asked his son quietly.

James hesitated, less confident about his own talents than his sister's. 'I think so. I've always loved art, even since I was little and the brother that taught it at school, Brother Jerome, said I was good enough to earn a living from it.'

'And what kind of income do you expect to

earn from drawing pictures? James, for God's sake, be reasonable. Art is all well and fine for the aristocracy or for women whose husbands will provide for them but do you intend to marry, have a family someday? Because let me tell you something, rearing children doesn't come cheap and painting pictures won't put food on the table or shoes on their feet.'

James's reaction was typical of him and the opposite of his sister's. Calmly, he said, 'Dad, you know that good doctors are born not made. You were born that way, everyone says it, with that need to fix people in you – you had it from you father. From what Solange has told me about Jeremy, he had it too, in spades. The thing is, Dad, I don't. I could do the work at college, and maybe pass the exams, but I wouldn't make a good doctor, I just wouldn't. I'd spend all my time painting in my head. Juliet is fiery and a bit wild sometimes, we all know that, but she longs to help people and make everything right. She would make a great doctor if you just gave her the chance.'

He kept his voice steady, not pleading, but not belligerent either.

'I want to paint. Will I make any money at it? Who knows? If I don't, I'll get a job doing something else to pay the bills. I won't be asking you for handouts if that's what you're thinking. You wanted to go off and join the Great War, and you told me yourself Nana and Granddad were dead set against it, but you went anyhow because you knew what was right for you. Juliet and I, we're the same. We know what we want, or at least we want the chance to try it, anyway. Is that too much to ask?'

Richard didn't answer, and James quietly got up from the table. 'Thanks for a lovely dinner, Mrs Canty, it was delicious,' he said, kissing her on the cheek. Approaching Solange, he bent to kiss her, too. 'Good night, Solange.'

'*Bonne nuit*, James,' she said, patting his hand.

Mrs Canty used his departure to make her escape too. She'd not seen Richard so miserable-looking since that tinker of a wife of his took off, good riddance to her.

Solange poured two small brandies and placed one in front of Richard.

'No thank you, Solange.'

'Drink it,' she replied. 'It will do you good.'

They sat in silence sipping their drinks, the house going quiet around them.

'Now what?' Richard broke the silence. 'Do I just allow James to throw his life away on some foolish notion? Or send Juliet up to Cork to train as a doctor so she can have a lifetime of examining farmers' prostates and children's snotty noses?'

Solange smiled gently at him. 'You can see why she's upset though, can't you? It was always the plan that your son would take over the practice, and you would have been delighted to see James doing all those things – but it's not suitable for Juliet? James is right; you do know that, don't you? You cannot make a doctor, not really. The good ones are born for it, as you were, as Jeremy was, but James? No.'

'But Solange, that's this week, you know what young people are like. Change their minds as often as their socks. It will probably be some new figarie next week.'

'Perhaps,' Solange agreed, 'but I don't think so. Would it really be so terrible to see Juliet qualify as a doctor? You often said in many cases women might make better doctors, especially for female patients – so why not Juliet? James will be guided by you, but Juliet is stubborn. She might just decide she's going anyway.'

'Not without the money for fees, she won't. No, it's wrong for her. She wouldn't stick it, she's not one for the books, you know that,' Richard said, draining his glass. 'Good night, Solange.'

He made for the door and with his hand on the handle, he turned.

'I know you have their best interests at heart, so please don't encourage these fantasies they are both having. If we stick to our guns, they'll come round and see sense.'

Solange looked at the closed door and wondered what she should do. Richard was so distant sometimes that trying to talk to him was very difficult. Juliet didn't lick her stubbornness off a stone, as Mrs Canty said. Moreover, he had a point. She was sure his objections to her studying medicine didn't stem from the old-fashioned belief that women shouldn't be doctors, but more from his correct perception that Juliet wasn't particularly academic. The nuns had had great difficulty getting her to study anything except music and French. Also, Solange wondered if he was afraid of history repeating itself if Juliet did manage to qualify. Wars needed doctors. Yet he'd been happy to let James study medicine. Perhaps he believed James was steady, and would stay in Dunderrig and not go seeking adventure. Some solution would have to be found.

CHAPTER 11

The following morning dawned bright and sunny and both twins woke early. Meeting on the stairs, they decided to get a quick breakfast and head out for the fields to discuss the events of last night out of earshot.

James knew Juliet had been crying, but he didn't mention it. He knew she liked the world to think she was tougher than she really was. Besides, he had something he wanted to talk to her about.

Luckily, their father had morning surgery and had finished his breakfast before they arrived into the kitchen. Mrs Canty was baking bread as they entered.

'Well, if it isn't the greatest pair of cafflers God

ever put in shoes. Your Daddy is in wicked form this morning with the shenanigans of the pair of ye. Juliet, you have his heart broken. And James, a painter no less! Well, I don't know, but I hope for yeer sakes Solange is able to talk him around because he went out to surgery this morning like a divil. I'm glad 'tisn't my corns he's looking at today, I can tell you!'

Despite her words of admonishment, they knew Mrs Canty was only half serious. She, like Solange, would always defend them to their father as she had done since they were babies.

'Now what'll ye have? A few rashers and an egg maybe?'

Both twins were anxious to get away and so refused the offer of a cooked breakfast, wolfing down soda bread slathered with hand-churned butter and Mrs Canty's own blackberry jam and large mugs of tea.

'See you later, Mrs C,' they chorused as they left by the double doors that led into the stone courtyard.

Neither of them spoke until they'd climbed the fence into the long field. Instinctively, they made their way to the large copper beech that dominated the emerald green landscape surrounding it. Often as children, they sat facing each other on a high solid branch from which they could see the azure sea twinkling in the distance.

Agile as ever, they clambered up.

'I just can't stand the way he just issues a decree like some kind of Caesar, and that's that. We all have to bow and scrape, the Master has spoken...' Juliet was still outraged at what she saw as her father high-handedness. 'It's not like he did what Nana and Granddad told him either, it's so hypocritical and...'

'I got a letter from Edith,' James interrupted. 'Did you? It was waiting here for me, but the name and address were typed, I suppose so no one would guess who sent it.'

Juliet's shocked expression answered his question.

'What did she want?' she asked finally.

James pulled the letter from his pocket and handed it to his sister.

'I'm sure she meant it for both of us. I think she just posted it to me because...well, because it saved her the price of a stamp, I suppose.'

'No, because she always preferred you to me, that's why.' Juliet's reply was matter-of-fact. '*Dear James*,' she read aloud, then laughed a little shrilly. 'God, she's got mad writing, hasn't she? For one that was all about neatness. Remember her plaguing us about our clothes?'

She shivered, and continued: *'Dear James, I know it must come as a surprise to hear from me after so long, but I felt that I should stay away while you and your sister were still young, rather than risk upsetting and confusing you. I have no idea what your father has told you about me, but I would like to meet you both, to explain my side of things, as it were. Do either of you ever come to Dublin? If you do, or if you could make the journey without too much trouble, I would like to meet you both for tea, perhaps in the Shelbourne. I look forward to hearing from you. Fondly, your mother, Edith.* Fondly!' She was ready to explode. 'Is she serious? Nothing for years, not since we were small and now this?'

James said nothing.

Juliet squinted at him in the bright sunlight, raking his face for a reaction. His blond hair curled lightly on his neck and his green eyes were as emerald as her own. She knew exactly what was going on in his head.

'You're thinking we should see her, aren't you? Please tell me you're not serious.'

'Well, I think we should talk about it at least. She *is* our mother,' he replied quietly. 'Aren't you even a bit curious as to what happened? Daddy won't say, and Mrs Canty just starts ranting until Solange stops her. Remember when we were about ten and Katie McCarthy told us our mother left because Daddy was in love with Solange and we came home all upset? Solange put us right about that, but she never really explained what actually happened. I just think there is something that we weren't told, and I'd like to know what it is. This is the only way we'll find out.'

'Jesus, James, do we have to? I don't remember much, but what I do remember is all bad. I don't really care why she left, and it's not like we've had a rotten life without her. Solange was a better mother to us than she could ever have been. Why can't we leave well enough alone? Not to mention Daddy would have a fit if we told him we were meeting her. God knows we're in enough trouble as it is without giving him any more reasons to be angry with us.'

Juliet felt in her jacket pocket for her cigarettes and a match. James knew that despite her bravado, she adored their father and hated being on the wrong side of him.

'He'd have a bigger fit if he catches you smoking,' he smiled. 'Well then, what are we going to do? We could just ignore the letter, or write back telling her to get lost, but then we'd always be wondering, wouldn't we? Or I can write back and say we'll come up on the train, but we won't stay over or anything and just meet her, hear what she has to say, and if we don't like it, never see her again. Agreed?'

Juliet sighed, taking a long drag on her cigarette. 'People think I'm the bossy one, you know? But in the end, we always end up doing what you say. Oh well, I suppose I'm a bit curious about what she's like, but I think she is going to be a stuck-up old cow and we're going to hate her.'

'Quite possibly, but we'll never know unless we go. Now, will we tell Solange, or not?'

'Well, definitely not a word to Daddy, and I think it's better to say nothing to Solange either, just in case. She never lied to us about anything, but this is different. There must be a reason she won't talk about Edith, so maybe let's hear what she has to say first and then we can talk to Solange afterwards – when we have some information. We can say I'm going up to Dublin to visit Mary from school. You can come with me. They'll be grand with that. It's probably a good idea to put some distance between us and Daddy at the moment, anyway. Maybe by the time we come back, he'll have calmed down, or maybe Solange will have got him to see sense.'

'Maybe, but you know what he's like. At least Solange thinks you becoming a doctor is a good idea. I'm not sure she's as enthusiastic about my career choice,' James said ruefully. 'Maybe they're right. I mean it's not much of a career, is it?'

'James Buckley!' Juliet admonished. 'Is that how determined you are? The first hurdle and you decide to give up? Sure, why not just sign up for medicine now and be done with it if that's your attitude. Spend the next forty years listening to auld ones going on about their phlegm! I thought you set your heart on being an artist? Well, that doesn't sound very heart-set to me. You'll just have to stand up to him. You know he'll come round in the end.'

James laughed and jumped from the tree, offering his sister a hand to get down. 'Yeah, yeah, you're so brave with all your big talk. Let's see how brave you are when Daddy refuses to pay your fees!'

CHAPTER 12

The train slowly puffed into Kingsbridge station. The twins had booked into a hotel on the quays and felt very grown up when they checked in. Their father and Solange trusted them, so when they said they were visiting Juliet's school friend Mary Sheridan who lived in Rathmines, they simply accepted it.

'I wish we hadn't lied,' James said as he lay on one of the two single beds.

'Telling the truth would have been worse. They would have refused us permission or even worse, have insisted on coming with us. At least this way we get to meet her and make up our own minds. I'm kind of dreading it though. Are you?' Juliet stood at the window with her back to her brother, watching the hustle and bustle on the quays.

'I suppose I am, but I'm looking forward to it a bit, too. I've always wondered about her,' he said. 'Mrs Canty half said there was someone else and that's why she left, but you know Mrs Canty and her yarns. What will we call her? It's going to sound stupid calling her Mammy or Mother or whatever, but I don't know if we should call her Edith either. What do you think?'

Juliet considered for a moment. 'I think we don't call her anything. Just say: hello, how are you, and let her do the talking. I'm damned if I'm making it easy on her. She summoned us up here, she contacted us, so let her do the work.'

'You're probably right. God, I'm starving, will we go and get a bag of chips? I think the funds will stretch to that, but we'd better keep some in case we have to pay for the tea tomorrow. I'd say the Shelbourne will be fierce dear.' James looked worried.

'Go way out of that, you big dope, she'll be paying for the tea. Sure, hasn't she great notions of herself, and she is our long lost Mama after all. If she can't stand us a cup of tea after all these years, then things are very bad altogether,' Juliet laughed. 'C'mon let's go down to Beshoffs, they're supposed to have gorgeous chips, and we might even share a fish.'

Over fish and chips and steaming mugs of tea, they chatted easily.

'Wouldn't it be great to live in Dublin?' Juliet sighed. 'It's so busy and loads of people and no one knowing or caring about your business? When I qualify, I'm going to travel, see the world, London, New York, even. Look at the style here, everyone all done up to the nines. They don't make this much effort in Dunderrig on Christmas Day even. The state of half of them down there, with their good "shtrong" shoes and fine heavy overcoats.'

James laughed at her impersonation of the West Cork accent. 'I think Dunderrig people have the right attitude – they dress for the weather.'

He was always quicker to defend their home. Juliet was the one who was dazzled by the films and the style they saw at the pictures. She was as beautiful as a film star herself – she turned people's heads wherever she went, the girls in envy and the men in admiration. Most of the time, she didn't even notice. Danny Dalton and the rest of them were dreaming if they thought she would look sideways at them. James knew that his sister had much bigger plans than marrying anyone from within fifty miles of Dunderrig.

'I don't know about living here,' he replied. 'I like Dunderrig, the way we know everyone and the way you can see the seasons. In a city, there's no real way of seeing the seasons change. And everyone is in such a rush all the time. I think I'm more suited to country life.'

Juliet gazed at him. Girls at school often asked her if she and James were telepathic – if one was hurt or sad, would the other know, wherever they were? Juliet always laughed and said that she had no clue what was going on her brother's head and that from her limited experience of what boys think about, that was something for which she was eternally grateful. However, when she and James were together, they did seem to know instinctively what the other was thinking. Not in the way the girls at school imagined; it was just that she knew him so well, she could gauge his mood without him saying anything. She recalled Solange telling her that it was the same with her and Jeremy – they just knew each other so profoundly that often words were superfluous. It was like that with James.

'Would it be so bad, being a doctor like Daddy? You love Dunderrig, and you'll probably marry someone who feels that way about it, too. You've a ready-made practice there, waiting for you. God knows, you're miles more intelligent than me so the studying would be no bother to you. Are you sure you're not being too hasty? You could still paint in your spare time.' Juliet's tone was light but her question was serious. 'There's nothing to say we can't both do medicine. We'd have a right laugh, the two of us above in the college.'

James put down his cup. 'I know. You're right. How bad could it be? This is what's been running around in my head for months. Maybe I owe it to him to at least try. Maybe I'll discover that I love it,' he finished miserably.

Disappointing their father weighed much more heavily on James than on Juliet, and she knew that. She also knew that their father loved them and would eventually forgive them whatever they did, but the sadness of not handing on the practice to his son was something he would find hard to accept. Even if her father agreed to her desire to study medicine, which looked doubtful at the moment, she had no intention of going into practice in Dunderrig. She wanted to travel, to experience things. Her father was right when he said looking at farmers' enlarged prostates and ingrown toenails was no job for her. She envisioned herself in a fancy clinic in New York or as a life-saver on some far-flung battlefield, performing surgery under impossible conditions with a success rate that would stagger the medical profession. No, the prostates of West Cork would just have to be admired by someone else. In so many ways, it was a pity James didn't feel it was his calling. Juliet, Solange and Mrs Canty agreed that he was more like his father in temperament than Juliet, while being much less buttoned-up. He would make a wonderful doctor, whatever he thought of his own abilities.

A bunch of girls were giggling in the corner of the café and as Juliet got up to go to the ladies, they wasted no time.

'Is she your twin?' one of them asked James cheekily.

'Yes, she is.' He lowered his eyes – unused to such obvious female attention. 'We're just up from Cork, visiting a friend.' He wished he didn't blush so easily.

'And what friend are you visitin', up from Cork?' another of the group demanded in a thick Dublin accent. 'Your girlfriend, maybe?' This reduced the other two to helpless giggles.

'No...no...' James stuttered, completely embarrassed now.

'Well, girls,' the first one piped up, this time ruffling James's hair as she planted her ample behind on his lap. 'Isn't that great news? Cork's answer to Gary Cooper isn't spoken for. How would you like to take us out, handsome?' James could smell the alcohol on her breath as she leaned in to deliver what she imagined was her seductive invitation.

'We could teach you a few Dublin tricks,' her friend chimed in, taking Juliet's chair and running her red talons up James's thigh.

He was speechless; he felt as if he were a particularly juicy creature and they the circling vultures.

'I don't think so.' Juliet's voice was so cut-glass and haughty that the girls immediately jumped up and backed away. 'We are meeting friends at the Gresham for drinks now, and then lunching at the Shelbourne tomorrow. Do you know it?' Looking them imperiously up and down, she added, 'No, I don't suppose you do. Therefore, I'm afraid my brother and I have other plans. Terribly nice to have met you though. Cheerio!'

James and Juliet beat a rapid retreat up the quays, laughing hysterically.

'You're something else,' James gasped once he'd caught his breath. 'Lunching at the Shelbourne...if you heard yourself! And the tone of you! You'd swear we gave our lives wining and dining in fancy hotels. You're gas, Juliet Buckley. You could pull anything off. 'Tis on the stage you should be, not training to be a doctor. I bet those poor girls are scratching their heads now wondering what such a pair of lah-de-dahs were doing sharing one portion of fish and chips!'

Strolling around the city in the twilight, they stood admiring the displays of beautiful things in Cleary's window. James smiled at his sister in their reflection.

'You're not going to like this, but the way you spoke to those girls back there I'd say you get that from her, from Mammy. You look a lot like her, too.'

Juliet examined her reflection critically. 'Hmm, maybe. Sure, all we have to go on is that one photo taken when we were small. She probably looks totally different now. Anyway, if I look like her, so do you! I hope we'll recognise her now, after all these years. What will she look like now, d'you think?'

'I can't picture her as anything except the photograph. We'll find out tomorrow, I suppose. Juliet?' He turned to face her, his expression serious. 'Give her a chance, will you? Don't be prickly.'

Juliet contemplated rearing up in indignation, but she knew her brother was right; she could be prickly as he called it. 'All right. I'll give her one chance. But if she says anything bad about Daddy or Solange or Mrs Canty, then she'll hear about it.'

CHAPTER 13

The subdued activity of the Lord Mayor's lounge was intimidating. The West Cork Hotel in Skibbereen or the Imperial in Cork for a treat on a shopping day had not prepared the twins in any way for the luxury of the Shelbourne. They had promised each other to look confident even if they were quaking inside, so with a quick squeeze of their hands, they walked purposefully into the sophisticated tea room.

Eyes turned to take in the glamorous couple, obviously twins. Juliet had dressed them both carefully, determined they wouldn't look like country bumpkins. When James objected, she'd asked him if he wanted to give Edith an excuse to criticise Solange and their father. She liked them to be dressed well – Mrs Canty had said it was all she had ever cared about – so by God, they were going to wipe her eye and not have her despairing of the cut of them and they up from the wilds of West Cork.

Juliet wore a fuchsia pink dress with a flared skirt cinched at the waist and a matching jacket, showing off her perfect figure. She'd been up since early morning, pinning her hair into a chignon beneath a black pillbox hat with birdcage netting. Black patent leather high-heeled shoes completed the look. James wondered if it was a bit over the top, but she had researched the fashion magazines on what was appropriate to wear for afternoon tea since they'd decided to come, and she was confident she had got it right. James wore a charcoal double-breasted suit of their father's – luckily they were similar in size. Juliet was sure they cut a fine dash as they scanned the room for someone who looked like their mother.

A liveried waiter approached them before they ventured too far into the room. 'Miss Buckley? Mr Buckley? Please, follow me.'

Glancing at each other in surprise that he

would know them, the twins followed him to a table at the window.

The woman stood to face them, the hint of a smile on her face. Removing her glove, she extended her hand.

'My, how you two have grown,' she said coolly. 'Though, of course, I would have recognised you anywhere. You are both exceptionally beautiful.' She smiled more widely at James. 'Though, of course, you are *handsome*, my dear. Please sit. I've ordered afternoon tea. Have you ever had it here? It's really rather good.'

Juliet was mesmerised. Her mother looked almost as she remembered her. A little older, perhaps, but still trim and beautiful. Her hair was more ash than blond now, but she was made up and styled to perfection. Her dress and coat were shades of cream and gold and her accessories were understated but expensive-looking. Edith clearly had the money and the ability to hold back the tide of time, it seemed. Though she had to be in her forties, she didn't look much older than her children.

'So,' Edith said, graciously indicating that her children should sit and taking a seat herself. 'How have you both been?'

'Very well, thank you.' James, like Juliet, was

trying hard not to stare – it really was remarkable how little Edith had changed in the intervening years.

'Have you finished school? I imagine that you have. It must be pleasant to be out in the world now.'

'Yes, we just did our Leaving Cert in June. We're waiting for the results.'

'And what are your plans? Medicine I suppose?' Edith was still exclusively addressing James.

'Perhaps. I'm not sure. I haven't fully decided yet.' He had no intention of revealing the current disagreement between himself and his father.

'And how is everyone at Dunderrig? Solange, is she still there? Your father? The Cantys?' Edith's tone was polite, interested. To the outside observer, there was nothing in her words or demeanour to suggest that the people she enquired after were those she had abandoned so suddenly years ago.

'Everyone's fine,' James replied. Looking across at Juliet, who was uncharacteristically quiet, he willed her to contribute something. To fill in the silence, he added, 'Dunderrig is looking lovely now. Eddie has done a great job with the fuchsia and the rhododendron. He managed to tame them without cutting them back too much so it all looks very colourful. Daddy got someone in to help him, Joey Flanagan – do you remember him from the village? Because Eddie is getting too old for the heavy lifting...' his voice petered out. He shouldn't have asked if she remembered anyone, he thought.

'No, James, I can't say the name Joey Flanagan means anything to me. I'm glad Dunderrig is so interesting to you, though. And how about you, Juliet? Do you have a plan now that you've finished your education?'

'I haven't.' Noting her mother's look of surprise at her words – or possibly the sharp tone in which she had delivered them – she continued more calmly, 'I haven't finished my education. I'm going to university, to study medicine. I want to be a doctor, like Daddy.'

'How modern of you.' Edith produced a small smile. 'Well, it's a different world than when I was your age. Though looking at things in Europe, perhaps things will be very different again in the not too distant future. We shall have to wait and see.'

'Do you think there's going to be a war?' James asked.

'Oh yes,' Edith said with conviction. 'Un-

doubtedly, there will be a war in Europe, although it's unlikely Ireland will be involved in
any official capacity. De Valera will see to that. I
shouldn't worry, my dear. My husband, on the
other hand, should be concerned, being a German.' The offhand manner in which Edith
dropped her bombshell stunned them both.

Juliet was the first to recover. 'Your husband?
You've remarried? Are you and Daddy divorced?'

Edith glanced up from pouring the tea.

'Divorced? No. The marriage to your father
was a Catholic one and so was indissoluble.
Luckily, Otto is not interested in religion and
neither am I, so we married in a civil ceremony in
Bremen, Germany in 1928. Have you ever been
to Bremen? It really is pretty.'

The twins tried hard to process this news.

'But you are legally married to our father. To
remarry without first divorcing your first husband is bigamy,' said Juliet, bewildered. 'Our father has never even looked at another woman; he
knows he's still married to you...'

'Oh, for goodness sake, Juliet!' Edith spoke as
if dealing with a difficult child. 'That foolish marriage was a lifetime ago. He should consider himself free to do as he pleases, with whomever he
pleases. Europe is changing as we speak. Nothing

is ever going to be the same again. Everything about the past will soon be entirely irrelevant.'

'I'm sure Daddy won't see it that way.' Rage was building up inside Juliet; she was horrified at how this woman could dismiss her father so callously.

'You don't need to tell me that, Juliet. Your father made his position very clear in the past. He is fundamentally opposed to divorce. That was why I had no other option.'

'But to marry another man without even... Well, I just don't know how you could even...' She could hardly get out the words.

'Juliet. Please calm down. People are staring. Conduct yourself.'

While Juliet was still trembling with fury, a tall silver-haired man approached the table.

'Ah, this must be the beautiful *Fräulein* Juliet – and this gallant young man is James?' The stranger with his heavily accented English threw Juliet, and she momentarily forgot her rage at her mother. 'Let me look at you. Yes, you are exactly the beauty your mother said you would be.' The man bent low and kissed her hand.

'Children, this is Otto Hugenberg, my husband. Otto, James and Juliet Buckley. My children.'

The twins stared in astonishment. How should they react?

James, on automatic pilot, shook the German's hand – and immediately felt disloyal to his father.

Otto was fairly tall, almost six feet, heavily built and dressed in a very well-cut suit. The canary-yellow tie suggested someone who didn't take life too seriously. His skin was lightly tanned and the piercing blue of his eyes shone from his face. A full head of blond hair was swept back from his handsome face. His smile was broad and seemed genuine, as if meeting his wife's estranged children was something one did every day of the week. In any other circumstance, James found himself thinking in confusion, he would have liked the look of the man.

Juliet shook the man's proffered hand; she felt rigid with shock. This situation was simply ridiculous. Edith couldn't be married to this Otto Hugenberg. Coming here, part of her had hoped – even assumed – that Edith wished to seek forgiveness for deserting them. Not that she wanted her mother back in her life – far from it – but an acknowledgment that she had done wrong seemed fair. Yet, apparently, Edith was the same as she had always been – expecting the world to revolve entirely around her own needs. Another

aspect of her mother had also gone unchanged –
Edith was still clearly far more interested in her
son's life than in her daughter's. Though Juliet remembered little of life in Dunderrig before her
mother left, she always knew that although Edith
had left them both, she had loved – or at least,
liked – James more.

Juliet mentally shook herself. Why should she
care whether Edith felt any affection for her? The
woman was a deserter, an adulterer, and now a
bigamist. They were all better off without her.
Let Edith live where she wanted and with whom-
soever she chose and stay out of their lives. This
German man seemed pleasant enough, if a little
effusive. Let him be the one to look after Edith.
All Juliet wanted to do now was finish this stupid
meeting and go home, and forget they had ever
seen her.

She turned to her brother – and her heart
dropped. He was gazing in wonder at Edith and
Otto as they extolled the virtues of Germany in
the summertime: the Black Forest, Bavaria, its
beautiful medieval cities. Edith was telling James
that he simply must go, that he would love Germany, and that he would find such inspiration for
his painting. For the first time in her life, Juliet
felt that she was on a completely different wave-

length from her brother, and she hated the sensation. Normally, even if they were in disagreement about some minor issue, they could always easily reach a compromise. Deep in her heart, she felt this time was going to be different. She should have known; she should have insisted that they both refuse to meet with Edith. But James had been fatally tempted by that letter – addressed to him – and now her mother was weaving a terrible spell around him. Juliet feared she would never get her brother back.

Otto's voice interrupted her thoughts. 'What about you *Fräulein* Juliet? How does a trip to Germany sound to you?'

'I have never considered it.' Juliet replied coldly. 'And if your Mr Hitler has his way, perhaps, it is not the best location for a holiday anyway.'

Edith stopped her chat with James. 'You don't approve of the Führer's plans, Juliet? Perhaps, if you visited Germany and saw for yourself how things are there, you would be better informed to discuss it. Hitler is trying to help the German people to recover and emerge from under the huge yoke placed on them by Versailles and the British. The German people were left destitute after the last war. It is entirely understandable that they should try to regain their position. We, the Irish, should understand that better than others – colonised as we were for so long.'

Juliet was about to retort sharply to her mother when Otto, clearly disliking tension, interrupted.

'Come now! A beautiful day and beautiful ladies on our arms. James, let us not spend our time discussing boring politics. I'm sure that sense will prevail and all will be well again. Let us go for a walk in Stephens's Green, shall we? We will ask the waiter for some crusts, and we will feed the ducks. What do you say?' His eyes sparkled with enthusiasm and fun, and it would have been churlish to refuse. Taking a deep breath, Juliet rose to follow them from the table.

Strolling through the beautiful city park in the August sunshine did nothing to lift Juliet's mood. James was talking animatedly with Edith, who had linked his arm. They were discussing the Impressionists, a subject about which Juliet knew nothing, so she couldn't have joined in even if she had wished. Despondently, she threw little pieces of bread into the duck pond. The mother duck paddled over to retrieve them, followed by her ducklings – at least six of them.

'Life is so simple for ducks, no?' Otto spoke to

her. His large body reflected his large personality. In other circumstances, she could have warmed to him. He had crinkly eyes and a broad genuine smile. 'Mother takes care of the little ones until they can take care of themselves. It is the same for all ducks: German ducks, Irish ducks, Spanish ducks, Chinese ducks. Ah, I am glad to see you smile, my dear. You are too beautiful to look sad.'

Juliet turned and gave him a weak smile.

He said, 'It is hard, families. I understand. You are so like her, you know. She is brave, sometimes fiery, as are you, I imagine. But James is different – softer, maybe?'

'Yes. James is the sensitive one, I suppose. People always assumed it would be me, being the girl, but he's the one who understands art and nature and all of that. He's kind and sometimes a little naïve. When we were children, I was the one that got into fights, and our father would scold James for not defending me, his sister. What Daddy never knew was that most of the time, it was me protecting James.'

Turning back and looking over the pond to the verdant trees on the skyline, she added, 'I just wish I could protect him now.'

'Please don't worry, Juliet. James is fine. Your mother is so happy to reunite with you both. She has been planning this for some time. Can you give her a chance?'

Juliet sighed, 'That's exactly what James said. I just can't get around the idea that she married you when she is still married to our father. Didn't you realise she was a bigamist? Didn't you care that your wife was already a married woman? Not to mention the kind of woman who walks out on her husband and children without a backward glance. She's probably told you that my father is an ogre, a terrible husband, or that he was having an affair with Solange. But none of that is true. My father is a good man and was a good husband to her, giving her whatever she wanted. Yet she just upped and left without a word. Do you have any idea what that was like for him? For us?' Juliet's voice was cracking now, betraying her emotions.

Otto led Juliet to a nearby bench and sat facing her. Holding one of her hands in his two big ones, he looked deeply into her eyes. The intimacy of the gesture made her slightly uncomfortable, but she didn't pull away.

'Firstly, I think these are questions you should direct at your mother. You are very angry, and that is your right. Of course, it must seem strange. You and James have been well brought up, by good people I am sure, so you have a strong sense of what is right and what is wrong. So you are...I don't know the word, *verletzen* in German...outraged, I think? Yes, outraged. However, this you must understand. Your mother, she did not love Richard. Never did she tell me he is a bad man, who was unkind, but she did not love him. It was simply impossible for her to stay. You have had a good life, no? Better perhaps than if she had stayed with your father? She is not good with little children, not everyone is, but now that you are grown, she wants to be a mother to you.'

Juliet whipped her hand away, eyes blazing in indignation. 'And that is all she has to do, is it? She just reappears after all these years, no apology, no explanation, and we just welcome her back with open arms? She is not good with children! I never heard such rubbish! Solange is no blood relation of ours but she was, she is, our mother. Not that cold-hearted bitch!'

Years of anger and hurt bubbled over, and Juliet fled from the park, bumping into strollers as tears blinded her. Running down Grafton Street, she reached the quays. They had stored their bag with their train tickets at the station ready to pick up before the six o'clock train to Cork. She would wait in the train station for

James, go home to Dunderrig, and never think about Edith ever again.

She went into Bewley's to freshen up and fix her face after the bout of tears. Composing herself in front of the mirror, she resolved that she would have to convince James to cut Edith from their lives. It would be a difficult task, she knew, but that woman brought nothing but destruction and division wherever she went. Juliet was determined to cut her off completely, in the same way that Edith had cut them off as children.

CHAPTER 14

*J*uliet was sitting in the sunny kitchen reading the *Southern Star* newspaper. Richard stood with his back to her, gazing out at the gardens of Dunderrig in the late summer sunshine, taking a break during morning surgery. The atmosphere in the house since the twins had returned from Dublin was strained.

Richard had remained entrenched in his wishes for his children and so James had enrolled in first-year medicine. Juliet knew her brother's heart wasn't in it even if he pretended to be enthusiastic. He just didn't want to displease his father – especially now, when he was feeling guilty about meeting Edith. Studying medicine seemed to him something he could do to make up to his father for his secret betrayal.

Things had never been like this between Juliet and James. He'd arrived at the station in Dublin in time for the train on that day, but he was furious with her. Without giving her even a second to explain why she was so upset, he had launched a verbal attack that shocked her. She'd never seen him so incensed. He accused her of being selfish and hard-hearted and claimed that she had never intended to give Edith a chance to explain. He said she'd been rude and sullen and he wondered why she'd agreed to meet their mother in the first place if that was all she was going to do.

Juliet recalled the sinking feeling that came with the realisation that she had been right. Their mother had beguiled her brother and sowed division between them – as no doubt had been her plan all along.

That was three weeks ago and though there had been some stilted conversation since, they had lost the closeness that had always defined them. She tried hard to find a way to make James understand what a manipulative woman their mother was, but James would hear none of it. She knew he must be appalled at the bigamy, but whenever she tried to raise the subject, he became so defensive of Edith that any rational argument was impossible. Finally, she realised that his infatuation with their mother was outside her control, though it still hurt her more than she could ever say. Edith had indeed driven a huge wedge between them.

Solange had asked what was wrong and Juliet longed to confide in her, and nearly did on one occasion, but knew she couldn't – to do so would mean admitting that she and her brother had lied and that they'd met Edith. Despite the frostiness between the twins, neither would betray the other by telling the truth. So Juliet had no one to talk to, and her estrangement from James left her feeling dull, dispirited and lonely.

Danny Dalton had been in the shop the other day and had asked her if she'd go to the dance with him. He was less cocky than she remembered and she needed a night out, so she'd agreed. They'd actually had fun, and he wasn't as bad as she remembered him. He clearly adored her, and it made a pleasant change from the heavy silences and gloomy atmosphere that was hanging around Dunderrig these days.

The growing threat from Germany wasn't helping the mood. Every morning over breakfast, her father bemoaned the situation in Europe and the stupidity of allowing it to escalate into another war – a war he was sure would be as pointless as the last.

Juliet knew her father's fierce opposition to violence did not stem from cowardice. Long ago, a college student had come to the house explaining he was researching the history of Irish medics in the military. Richard was out on a call and the young man had passed the time in telling a mesmerised Juliet how her father had been awarded the Meritorious Service Medal with bar, the Distinguished Conduct Medal and a Military Medal, as well as several mentions in dispatches for his services to the wounded in Amiens. Yet when her father arrived, he claimed he didn't know where his medals were, and neither did he care. As he showed the young man to the door, he had told him that all anyone needed to know about the war was that millions of innocent people had been slaughtered needlessly.

Juliet couldn't help but feel the coming war might be different. Despite the animosity between Ireland and England, most people seemed to think the German Führer was a thug and a bully and that something should be done to stop him marching his troops wherever he liked. There were also of course those who subscribed to the theory that 'my enemy's enemy is my friend'. Independence was still a relatively new reality and anti-British feelings ran deep, but even allowing for that, the consensus was that Hitler was bad news. Juliet recalled her mother's insistence that the world they knew was about to change.

She wondered how it would affect Edith and Otto if war did break out – as seemed inevitable now. Maybe it would be the best thing ever. Perhaps they would just take off back to Germany and no one would ever hear from them again. Then she and James could return to their old closeness. If only it could be that simple.

CHAPTER 15

James was miserable at the university. Juliet could see it, despite his cheery tales of student life when he came home. She longed to confront him but those days were gone. They'd reached a level of friendship again – the frostiness had thawed – but they weren't of one mind as they had been before.

Despite her best efforts, her father had refused to allow her to go to college with her brother. She replayed the last conversation repeatedly in her head. They had been sitting in the kitchen, the silence heavy between them, the new term only weeks away. She knew he hated having this strained atmosphere between them as much as she did. She decided to give it one more try.

'Is there any way you'd reconsider about me going to university? It's all I want to do, Daddy.'

Eventually, Richard spoke. 'Juliet, you know I love you, don't you?'

She was taken aback. Of course, she knew he loved her, but it wasn't something he came right out and said very often.

'I do,' she replied, and waited for him to take the lead in the conversation.

'And I want you to be happy, more than anything. However, I just don't think this would make you happy. There isn't room in this practice for two. I know James wasn't too keen on the idea of studying medicine but once he gets going with it, he'll realise it's in his blood. You're different. He's a bit like me, plodding and maybe a bit of an old stick in the mud, but you need something else. I really think you do. You hated studying at school. Didn't you break our hearts with the nuns, in trouble ten times a week? No, medicine is not for you. You'd hate it.'

Juliet tried to stay calm. Hysterics would only prove his point that she was flighty and over-emotional.

'Can't I at least try, Daddy? If I do hate it then so be it, but at least let me try...'

'No, Juliet, and that's my final word on the

matter.' His words were hard, but his tone was gentle. 'I know Danny isn't your choice, though what on earth is wrong with the lad I can't fathom, but there must be some nice lads around the place that have caught your eye? Don't go filling your head with a load of nonsense about careers and the like. You don't need it. You're a beautiful girl, and you could have the pick of the county, so browse around...'

Juliet was trying so hard to control her temper. 'Solange works as your medical secretary. And what about Mrs Canty? And Mrs Kelly in the Post Office, and Molly Sullivan inside in an office in Skibb. Loads of women have jobs now, but no, you just want me to sit around like a brood mare waiting for a stallion to show interest. Is that all you see me as? A burden to be married off to the highest bidder?' Despite herself, her voice was rising to a crescendo.

He sighed heavily. 'Juliet, please calm down. Don't be so dramatic. This is precisely why I don't think you are cut out for medicine. What are you going to do the first time someone is rude or difficult to deal with? Fly off the handle like you're doing now?'

'I'm just trying to explain things from my point of view...'

'Juliet, I genuinely don't think it would suit you to be a doctor. The reality is a far cry from whatever romantic image you've conjured up in that active imagination of yours. It wouldn't be right for you. You'll just have to accept that I know what's best for you in this case. Over in Europe, hundreds of thousands of young men will, in the not too distant future, be wasting their lives doing something pointless and stupid. All because of some imagined glory. I will not have you being equally foolish. They'll need doctors over there, and when things get very bad, which believe me, they will, they'll take anyone who is prepared to go. No, staying here in West Cork where you're safe and protected is the best thing. At least we are away from it.'

'Is that what you're worried about? That I'd want to go over there and join up like you did?' Juliet's voice was accusing.

'I'm sorry to say, that's exactly what I'd be fearful of. That's the truth of it, Juliet. As a doctor – or even as an unqualified medical student – you'd be ideal fodder for the British war effort.'

'Why are you more worried about me than about James? Supposing he wants to go to war?'

'James is sensible. He'll settle down here in Dunderrig and take over from me when the time's right. You, on the other hand, are just flighty and impetuous enough to do something daft.'

'Solange worked as a nurse in the war. You didn't think that was daft.'

'That was different. It was her own country that needed her. That mess in Europe is nothing to do with us. We've had more than enough bloodshed and violence in this country. What I witnessed the last time, there aren't words to describe the horror of it all. I went because it seemed like something interesting. I thought that I could make a difference. In the end, no one could do anything to alleviate the savagery. We just patched them up as best we could. The few we sent home were broken men. Most were sent back to the front and within days a shell or a sniper finished them off. They were the lucky ones in lots of ways. The way they were treated when they got back – by the empire they destroyed their lives to save – was almost worse than the war. I will not have England use my children to fight their war. They are a lying, duplicitous nation who exploit others and then dispose of them once they have sucked them white.'

Juliet had never seen her father so moved in

her life. His usual mild manner was gone as bitterness and raw anger dripped from every word.

'But...but that's not fair!' she stuttered. 'You're
angry with England and because of that I can't
study to be a doctor. That's just ridiculous and if
you thought about it for even one second, you'd
see how hypocritical you are being!'

'Juliet!' Richard was roaring now, his fingers
white as they gripped the kitchen table. 'You are
not going to study medicine and that's all I have
to say on the matter.'

Sobbing, Juliet ran from the room. She
stormed up to her bedroom and slammed the
door. Screaming in frustration into her pillow,
she wept bitter tears at the unfairness of it all.

She ignored the gentle knocking on the door
twenty minutes later. If it was her father, she
couldn't bear to look at him, let alone listen to
another of his stupid reasons why he was killing
her dream. Eventually, she looked up as the door
opened to reveal Solange. The French woman
came in and sat on the edge of the bed.

'*Ma chère*, I know you are angry and upset *mais
s'il te plaît, explique-moi*, why you do want to study
medicine so badly? You must admit you were not
a studious girl in the convent, and you never

wanted to help your Papa in the surgery, so you must understand why we are all a little confused.'

Never, apart from the doomed visit to Dublin, had Juliet lied to Solange. Blowing her nose on the handkerchief Solange offered her, she tried to compose herself and replied in French.

'I just want a life, Solange. I know you all love Dunderrig, and so do I, but I want more. I want to see the world, meet interesting people, have adventures. I don't want to stay here and have babies and be nobody. I want to be somebody and by going to university and studying, I just might have a chance of doing that. Medicine seemed the best choice because all the other courses are for women's jobs – teaching, nursing, librarian – and from where I see it, that's only delaying the inevitable. Marriage, children, the whole, boring pointless lot of it. Daddy as good as said just forget it, find a husband and settle down here. It feels like a death sentence, honestly it does.'

Solange rubbed Juliet's back, smiling that the girl's French never faltered despite her distress.

'My darling,' she began. 'Your papa loves you so much. He is so afraid of something happening to you. We are damaged, he and I, by what we saw when we were just your age. He just wants to protect you.'

'But Solange, don't you see? I can't live my life through the lens of yours or Daddy's life. Can't either of you understand that? I need to live my own life, have my own experiences.'

'Of course I understand that, darling, of course I do. You are special and brave and fiery and you are hungry for the world, and that is how it should be. Please have patience, we can work something out. I know we can. Now, another thing, what is the matter between you and James? Never have I seen this atmosphere between you. And please don't say it is nothing. There is something.' Solange looked deeply into Juliet's eyes.

'I can't tell you,' replied the girl, lowering her gaze. 'I wish I could, but please trust me, I really can't. Don't worry, we aren't in any kind of trouble or anything it's just… We'll work it out, I suppose.'

Solange sighed. It was so unusual that the twins were anything but totally united, and even stranger that Juliet wouldn't tell her what was the cause of the problem. James had been equally reticent when she'd tackled him about it. Richard and Mrs Canty seemed not to know anything.

Solange would never encourage Juliet to defy her father although she could understand her frustration. Her father loved her, but he was allowing his fear that she would end up in Europe as he did, cloud everything. In his eyes, women were gentle creatures that needed protection: in childhood, by their fathers, and as adults by their husbands. It was that kind of thinking that had moved him to bring Solange to Dunderrig in the first place. She would always be grateful to him for giving her a home when her future looked so bleak and empty, but she knew Juliet was not going to be happy with just that. Now she was at a loss; she loved the twins as much as – if not more – any natural mother would have done and she genuinely liked and admired Richard, but she just didn't know how best to proceed with this issue.

Solange believed Juliet was right to fight to live her life in her own way. As she had suspected, the girl was not filled with a burning desire to be a doctor – just to find a way out into the wider world. Perhaps Juliet had imagined that if Richard was likely to let her study anything, it would be medicine, given his genuine dedication to his patients. If so, she had judged wrongly. Richard knew the reality of practicing medicine, both as a country general practitioner and in the theatre of war. Given how things were heating up in Europe, Richard would never in a million years give his consent to anything that could potentially bring either of his children anywhere close to a battlefield. Solange agreed with Richard's perception that James would never volunteer; it wouldn't be in him. James loved Dunderrig and the tranquillity of nature. Juliet, however, was another story. Perhaps Richard was right.

THE MONTHS PASSED AND Juliet found herself spending more and more time with Danny. He was nice, funny, and kind, and it was good to have someone to talk to now that James wasn't around. He was into farming, his uncle was leaving him plenty of land, and she knew that one day he hoped that she would be part of that plan. In the way of Dunderrig, her name was finally up with his and as far as the village was concerned, it was only a matter of time until the ring was produced.

Solange knew that Danny wasn't right for Juliet. He was a nice boy, but he had no spark, no passion. She tried to bring up the subject several times, but it seemed as all the fight was gone out of Juliet – she was listless and didn't want to discuss her future. The resentment Juliet felt towards her father still burned. Yet, Solange couldn't disagree with Richard. Everything he'd said about his daughter studying medicine was right. She wasn't academic, she didn't want to take over the practice, and she was only doing it as a means of escaping from home. Solange had suggested several other options – different courses of study – but Juliet had declined everything, claiming she was happy enough.

The Christmas of 1938 was snowy. James had written to say he was taking the train up from Cork to Dublin to spend it with friends. Richard and Solange were disappointed but at least he had promised to be home for the New Year. As Richard and Solange were discussing it with Mrs Canty, and deciding on two turkeys – one for Christmas and the other for the New Year, Juliet came in the back door with Danny in tow.

'Ah ye smelled the cake, did ye?' Mrs Canty chuckled as they stamped the snow from their boots. She had remained sceptical of the mental strength of the Daltons in general, but she had warmed to Danny, admitting he was a 'pleasant enough' lad and that he was 'cracked' about Juliet and would do anything for her.

'All the way from the gate. Is it ready to eat?' Juliet sniffed the air appreciatively, hovering over Mrs Canty's fresh baking, which was cooling on wire racks.

'Well?' Danny said urgently to Juliet. 'Are you going to tell them or will I?'

'Well, since you're obviously going to explode if you don't get it out, you'd better tell them yourself,' Juliet said dryly.

Solange looked up in surprise, a touch of anxiety in her heart.

'Tell us what?' Richard asked, smiling.

'We're getting married! Juliet has agreed to become my wife! I know I should have asked your permission first, Dr Buckley, but it was a spur of the moment thing. I'll be getting the ring the minute the shops open after Christmas – that is if you agree, of course.'

He looked so eager and hopeful it was impossible for Solange not to feel kind towards him, despite her doubts. Richard was gazing in surprise at his beautiful daughter, seemingly rendered speechless.

'Well, Daddy, aren't you going to congratulate me?' Juliet's voice was resigned – sad, somehow. Unlike Danny, she didn't seem like someone who'd just got engaged to the love of her life.

'If marrying Danny is what you want, then of course I wish you both all the happiness in the world – we all do. Don't we, Solange?'

Solange knew she'd have to tread very carefully. They'd interfered with Juliet's wishes and this is where it had got them, watching their darling girl promise herself to a nice enough boy – just not someone worthy of her. It seemed that they had managed to convince her that this was the best that life had in store for her. Yet to refuse their blessing at this stage would only harden her determination to see it through.

'*Bien sûr, ma petite fille, bien sûr. Félicitations!* When is the big day or have you not decided yet?' Solange asked, deliberately light but praying fervently there was no date set.

'Well, I'll have the hay saved by the middle of August if we get the weather, and then there's a bit of a rest before the harvest in September so maybe, the end of August?' Danny looked at Juliet for confirmation.

'That's fine.' She was smiling. 'We'd better get down to Father O'Brien and get the banns read so, in case Mrs Kelly and the rest of them think it's a shotgun job.'

'Juliet Buckley, you divil! You'll be the death of me so you will with your going on. Come here till I give you a hug – our Juliet, a married woman! Can you believe it, Solange?' Mrs Canty was buoyant.

'No indeed, Mrs Canty, it will be hard to get

used to. Still, we have some time yet before the big day. Lots to prepare. Juliet will be the most beautiful bride Dunderrig has ever seen.' Solange tried to infuse her words with excitement and enthusiasm. A glance from Juliet told her that while the others in the room were fooled by her feigned exuberance, the bride-to-be was not.

Later that evening, after Danny had left to do the milking, Solange tapped gently on Juliet's bedroom door.

'*Ce n'est que moi...*' she spoke gently. Juliet looked up from the book she was reading.

'Oh Solange, please don't start. I know what you're going to say but please don't. I'm going to marry Danny, he's nice and funny and kind and all the things a husband should be. James is gone, off doing his studies though he hates it. You do know that, don't you? So probably Daddy was right about me at least. James was always much better at studying than me, and he can't make head or tail of all those books, so what hope would I have had? And as for chopping up bits of dead people to find out what killed them, can you really see me doing that? I know you think I don't love him, but not everyone gets a big passion like you had with Jeremy. Look at Daddy and Edith, what a disaster that was. Danny is solid and reliable, he's mad about me, and I'll have a good life with him. This way, I get to stay in Dunderrig and be close to you all. I always thought, somehow, I'd end up living out my days with James but of course that was childish nonsense and now we've both grown up and have to find our own companions.'

Solange put her arms around Juliet. Clearly, Juliet's decision to marry Danny had been motivated by James's detachment from his twin. It was going to happen sometime, the twins couldn't live their lives in each others' pockets as they had as children, but Solange wished she could convince Juliet she was making a mistake.

CHAPTER 16

*J*ames doodled a camellia on the corner of his notebook. His fellow second-year medical students were deeply engrossed in the lesson being delivered but as usual he just couldn't concentrate. He was only back at college a week but already he was in deep despair. From the window in the corner of the lecture hall, he could see the sycamores and horse chestnut trees that surrounded the quadrangle of the old university; they were beginning to take on their autumnal colours. The limestone buildings with their leaded glass windows always delighted him for sheer aesthetic beauty. The sky was clear blue and the air was crisp. He thought of how Dunderrig would be looking now.

'Excuse me, Mr Buckley, once again I hate to interrupt your reverie with a trifle – but do you think that you could explain to the class the early indicators of duodenal cancer or are you too busy drawing. What is it today?' The professor picked up James's notebook. 'Ah yes, flowers. You will find an intricate knowledge of all matters floral tremendously beneficial when studying medicine. You can simply say to your patient, oh, I'm sorry, Mrs Murphy, I don't know what on earth is wrong with you but here is a beautiful picture of a lily. Cheerio, now!'

The class tittered nervously. Professor Sheehan's acerbic tongue could land on anyone of them just as easily, though he did seem to have taken rather a dislike to James. Possibly, the boy's complete lack of ability to focus on the professor's terminology-dense monologue was the cause of his aversion.

'It's a camellia, actually,' James muttered, knowing his reaction was childish.

The professor puffed up like a bullfrog. This was not how his classes worked. He talked and if he felt like it, he could ridicule a student, but under no circumstances should that student have the audacity to answer back. The look he gave

James made the boy realise that he had finally sealed his already precarious fate.

JAMES WALKED FORLORNLY out of the college and down towards Cork bus station. A group of young students passed him by, laughing and joking with each other, and he wished he could be as happy and carefree as them. But it was no good. No matter how much he tried, and he felt he really did try, he just couldn't do it. He'd just about scraped through the first year, with disappointingly low grades. He remembered his father's words to him when he returned home with a miserable pass, 'Not to worry, son, a lot of fellows I trained with didn't do wonderfully in their first year. Jeremy barely scraped through, and he turned out to be a magnificent doctor – too busy socialising and entertaining the ladies, no doubt. Just get the head down next year and you'll do fine.'

The thing was, the reason James hadn't done well wasn't because he was having too good a time – he wasn't. It was just that he couldn't stop himself during lectures from drifting off into a world of his own, imagining colours, light and shapes, instead of paying attention to the intrica-cies of science, which bored him rigid. The only thing he was good at was the diagrams and drawings of various body parts. In the practical classes, he struggled not to vomit as his fellow students dissected organs with relish and fascination.

He knew he should tell his father the truth before someone else did. He just didn't have what it took to be a doctor. There was no way that Professor Sheehan was going to let him finish the second year. He had made it clear that James was no doctor, and today's performance had surely confirmed his opinion. There was no point carrying on with this façade.

He hated the idea of disappointing his father – he felt guilty enough already about lying to him about Edith and Otto. He'd tried many times to confess that he was back in touch with his mother, but he could never find the right words. All he'd ever wanted to do was to please everyone: his father, Solange, his mother...Juliet. But in the end, he ended up not pleasing anyone, not even himself.

Perhaps everyone would be so caught up with the arrangements for Juliet's wedding that they wouldn't take the news too badly. He still couldn't believe Juliet was going to marry Danny Dalton. Danny was okay, a good laugh and all that, but for her to marry him...well, that seemed a bit mad. He would have liked to ask her if she was sure she was doing the right thing, ask her what she saw in Danny. But they weren't that close anymore. She'd probably just snap at him to mind his own business. Juliet just couldn't forgive him for having anything to do with Edith, which was so stupid – it wasn't like he was asking *her* to be best friends with their mother. The last conversation they'd had about Edith was over a year ago now. Juliet had accused him of drawing her into his lies. She knew Edith was in James's life, but she couldn't tell anyone and didn't approve. She was so angry and bitter; he had never seen her like that before. Going through all this without her was even more awful. Before, when either of them had a problem, or needed to talk something through, the other was always there with a plan or a distraction to redirect the wrath of Solange or their father. Since before he could remember, he and Juliet had been a team. This time, James felt totally alone.

AS EDDIE PULLED up the car in front of the house, James gasped in awe at the beauty of the gardens. The beds and pots on the terrace exploded in a riot of late summer colours. The lawns looked like an emerald carpet and even the gravel seemed polished.

'Oh Eddie, it looks incredible! You have really surpassed yourself this time.'

'I wanted it nice for her, for her big day,' Eddie replied shyly.

James felt a rush of affection for this quiet man, who was so much a part of Dunderrig. Eddie Canty could never tell Juliet how much she meant to him, so this was his way of doing it – putting all his effort into making the garden beautiful for her wedding. James just hoped Juliet wasn't too excited at the prospect of being married to notice.

As usual, his father was in the surgery writing up patient notes. Taking a deep breath, James decided there was no point in delaying any further. Solange would notice something was wrong anyway, and she'd worm it out of him like she always did. Best get it over with. He knocked on the large oak door.

'James! It's you. Come on in, it's like a madhouse out there with all the wedding preparations. Best stay out of it. I heard you complimenting Eddie on the garden, good man. He's been at it day and night for the last three months. Mrs Canty says he's talking Latin in his sleep!'

Richard noticed his son wasn't smiling and joking along with him.

'What's wrong, James?'

'Dad...' James dreaded saying the next sentence but he had to. 'I've failed.'

Richard rushed to reassure him. 'But sure you passed your first year, and you're only just into the New Year. How can you have failed? Did you just go down in a class test or something? Don't worry about it, you'll be fine...'

'No, Dad, I won't be fine. I haven't a clue and Professor Sheehan hates me. We had a bit of a run-in earlier this week and whatever hope I had before of scraping through, well it's gone now. I know you said when I just barely passed through first year that it would be better this year, but honestly, it's not. I did try, I studied hard, I swear I did, but I'm just useless at it...' James's voice died away. He wished a hole would open in the floor and swallow him up.

Richard sat back in his chair and looked at his son. Long seconds passed.

'First off, don't mind that clown Sheehan, he's an auld windbag, always was. We trained together; he always loved the sound of his own voice. Now, tell me the truth. Did you really do your best?' He kept his voice even.

'I did,' James answered, trying to keep his voice firm. 'Professor Sheehan is only one part of it. If I loved medicine, I'd put up with him. I just don't have the interest in it, I suppose. My mind was always somewhere else. I'd go into each class, determined to pay attention and then I'd just drift off thinking about nature or the shape of the building or whatever. I suppose I'm just not as clever as you. Even if I did manage to qualify, I'd be no good, and especially trying to follow in your footsteps. People just wouldn't trust me as they do you, and they'd probably be right. I know I must be a terrible disappointment to you.'

'Stop that talk right there.' Richard put down his pen. 'You did your best, and you gave it a try. That's all I could have asked for. Maybe I shouldn't have forced you, but I thought you'd like it, I really did. Stop looking so miserable. No one died. We'll just have to think of something else for you to do.'

As James stared at him in disbelief, Richard got up and put his arm around his son's shoulders. 'Now, that madcap sister of yours is going off on Saturday to make Danny Dalton's life hell for the rest of his days – so no more long faces,

all right? We have to put out a good show from
the Buckley side of things. Mrs Canty will never
forgive us if we give the Daltons anything to say.
Listen here to me, I have never been anything except bursting with pride over the two of ye and
that's never going to change. You tried medicine
and it wasn't right for you. Sure if you want to do
art, and see how you get on, I won't stand in your
way. Having said all that, I can't pretend I'm not
worried about it. It's a world I know nothing
about. But we all have our own paths in life to
follow and I did what I wanted with mine, and
you should be able to do what you want with
yours, too. By the way, did I ever tell you the
story of how Jerry Sheehan nearly amputated the
wrong leg on a patient when we were surgical in-
terns? Only that I stopped him and made him
read the notes again, so he's not perfect either, no
matter what he'd like you to think. We never really hit it off, so knowing you were my son
wouldn't have endeared you to him.' Richard
winked at his son, and James felt lighter than he
had in months. 'Now, Mrs Canty is only dying to
see you, and so is Solange. We won't say a bit for
now, we'll tell everyone after the wedding that
you decided against medicine, and we'll leave it at
that. Now then, come on to the kitchen, I think I

smell apple tart.'

Not for the first time, his father had surprised him. With a lighter heart than he'd had since he started university, James took his old seat at the big kitchen table while Mrs Canty and Solange fussed over him.

CHAPTER 17

*J*uliet had hardly slept at all, but she told herself that all brides were this jittery on their wedding day. Apparently, Solange had thrown up four times before meeting Jeremy at the church. Deciding there was no point lying in bed any longer, she pulled on an old jumper of James and a skirt, and went for a walk. The gardens of Dunderrig were beautiful in the bright morning light. She remembered Eddie's face turning pink with embarrassment and pleasure when she'd shown the Daltons around when they came for tea last week. They were astounded at the variety of plants and flowers and said it was like something from a magazine. Juliet had caught Eddie's eye, and giving him an almost imperceptible wink, had proceeded to name all of the shrubs and trees by their Latin names, while giving Eddie full credit for the dazzling display. Eddie had been thrilled; everyone knew Mrs Dalton could be a bit uppity.

Now she let herself out of the garden by the little wooden gate Eddie had put up years ago when she and James were toddlers, and made for the field with the big tree overlooking the sea. Marrying Danny was not what she'd dreamed of but it would be fine. At least he was always going to be there, and she would be able to stay close to Daddy and Solange. She knew Solange wasn't wholeheartedly behind the match, but what did she expect? What else was there? She could go off and do some kind of a course maybe, or get a job teaching, but she didn't really want to. Sure, she would have loved to travel, but that was just a pipe dream. Danny had finally agreed that they should go to Dublin for their honeymoon – she had tried for Rome, but he was worried that war could break out at any moment. She knew that was only an excuse, though – war or no war, Danny wouldn't have left his farm for more than a week. Still, Dublin was better than nothing, she supposed. They would be staying at the Gresham on O'Connell Street – Sackville Street, as it used to be called before independence. Danny had suggested the Shelbourne, but she never wanted to go back there again, after that last time with Edith.

The sun was rising high in the sky though it was only seven thirty, and the tree was bathed in its bright summer glow. It wasn't until she got closer that she realised there was someone already sitting there, on the high, solid branch.

James.

'Good morning, Mrs Dalton!' he called as she scrambled up to meet him, just as she had done a thousand times before.

'Not yet,' she smiled. 'What has you up here so early?' Though they were better friends now, she was still cautious around him.

'Couldn't sleep. You?'

'Same problem – wedding nerves, I suppose.'

''Tis he the one who should be nervous!' James joked, giving her a playful shove.

'I don't know what makes you think that! I'm going to be a model wife, doing exactly as my husband tells me.' Juliet chuckled.

James shielded his eyes from the sun and looked directly at her.

'It's what you want though, isn't it? Really?'

She tried to smile. 'Oh for God's sake, don't

you start too. I already get enough of the looks from Solange, and even Mrs Canty keeps telling me stories about how all belonging to him are half-cracked. You're not a big high-and-mighty doctor yet, you know, thinking you know what's best for everyone.'

'I'm not going to be a doctor at all, neither high nor mighty, I'm afraid. I've made a right dog's dinner of it, fairly spectacularly too as it happens,' James admitted quietly.

'But you are only just back. You passed the first year, didn't you?' Juliet was immediately problem-solving.

James sighed. 'Sorry, even you can't fix this. I'm going to leave before they throw me out. It's just as well really; I was useless at it. I just couldn't tell Dad, you know? I feel bad enough about the other thing...'

'Edith? Look, James, can I just say something? I hate the way things have been with us since she turned up. I know it's your business who you see and everything, but I just can't stand her, really. My blood boils when I think about her and...' Juliet stopped, fearing she was making it worse.

'Look, I hate it, too. Going through all this, I had no one to talk to. Dad and Solange would only have worried, and Edith would say I should never have done medicine in the first place, and Ingrid...'

'Who's Ingrid?' Juliet interrupted.

'Ah, she's a girl I know in Dublin. Otto's niece, actually. I've got to know a lot of their friends, Germans living in Dublin, and some really famous people that Edith knows too...'

'Just a girl you know or a girl you...*know?*' Juliet didn't want to hear about James's life with their mother, but a girlfriend was interesting.

'A girl I wish I...*knew,*' he said, grinning. 'It's complicated. She's incredible, beautiful and funny and everything but...I don't know. Maybe. We'll see. Anyway, what about you and the great passion of Dunderrig, Danny Dalton?'

'Hardly a great passion. He's nice, I like him. It's easy.' Juliet shrugged resignedly.

'Well, that's definitely a reason to marry someone because it's easy or because he's nice. Loads of people are nice; it doesn't mean you should marry them. Since when did you become such a pushover?'

Though his tone was jokey, his words were deadly serious. He was shocked at the idea his sister might be making a huge mistake. He immediately longed to talk her out of it – but he was hardly making wonderful decisions himself these days.

'You know if you want to back out, I'll support you, don't you?' he said seriously. 'And Dad and Solange. Mrs Canty and Eddie. We all love you.'

Her eyes suspiciously bright, she just nodded.

They walked companionably back to the house for breakfast, suddenly as close as they had ever been – complete in each other. Solange spotted them out of her bedroom window: Juliet subdued and James with a comforting arm around her. Suddenly, Solange found herself praying that James had talked his sister out of her wedding.

CHAPTER 18

*R*ichard stood silenced at the bottom of the stairs as Juliet walked out onto the landing in her ivory antique-lace dress. She looked so amazing it took his breath away. He couldn't believe that his little ragamuffin girl, always up to mischief, was this ethereal beauty before him. He'd given her his mother's pearls, and they sat iridescent on her delicate collarbones. Her blond hair was swept up under a veil; diamond earrings, a gift from Solange, glittered in her ears. The house was quiet as everyone else had gone ahead to the church. Eddie sat outside in the car, waiting to deliver the bride and her father.

'Well, Daddy? Will I do?' she smiled.

'You'll do,' he replied, and found himself too choked up to say more.

The years seemed to melt away as he watched her descending the stairs. He saw her as a little baby again, when he could hold her in one hand. Like a series of photographs in his mind, he saw the giggling toddler; the razor-sharp five-year-old, the brightest in her class. He saw her playing piano and singing like a lark when she thought no one was listening; her teenage years, fighting with the nuns or fiercely defending her brother; and now, this beautiful young woman before him. And in every snapshot in his mind there was James, right beside her – and Solange one pace behind.

God knows how he'd have managed without Solange. She always had the best intuition, she was a wonderful mother to them, and she loved them as much as he did. And Solange wasn't happy about this marriage. She'd never said it out loud, but he could tell. He had thought it was a good safe match, and Juliet seemed happy enough. But Solange had been right about James, too; she had never openly interfered, but deep down he'd known all along that in her opinion, his artistic son wasn't cut out for medicine.

Solange was always right. He had been wrong.

And Richard knew at that moment he had to save his little girl from making a huge mistake. He knew only too well the hell of being married to the wrong person, and he wasn't about to allow his daughter to find the same thing out for herself.

He led her to the kitchen, where he sat her down. Taking her hands in his, he crouched down until his eyes were level with hers, their faces only inches apart.

'Juliet, my lovely girl, I'm going to ask you a question, and I want you to answer me honestly.' He paused. 'Do you love Danny with all your heart?'

Juliet's eyes filled with tears. The clock ticked loudly on the mantelpiece, and the sun shone through the big windows on the old terracotta tiles. The familiar smells of Dunderrig – there since his own childhood – of baking and fresh flowers, filled the kitchen.

'Do you, Juliet?'

'No,' she whispered.

Richard straightened up. 'Then in that case, my darling, you won't be marrying him. You will be married one day, I'm sure of it, to a man who adores you as much, if not more, than Danny. And he will be a man you can't live without. But it won't be today, pet, and it won't be to Danny Dalton.'

'But what about everything, the wedding breakfast and the priest and...this dress cost a fortune...' Juliet was distraught; her carefully applied makeup running down her cheeks.

'Don't you worry your head about it. I'll take care of it all. Now go upstairs and take off all your finery. I'll go down and tell them below, and sure, we'll give them a dinner if they want it. You do have to talk to Danny, though. I'll get Eddie to bring him up if he wants to see you. I know you don't want to face him, but it's only fair. That poor lad is innocent in all of this.'

Richard drew his daughter to her feet and held her closely until her sobs subsided. Wiping her eyes of tears with his thumbs, as he'd done since she was small, he smiled at her.

'You'll be the talk of the parish for a bit, but sure, it will give them something other than myself and Solange to speculate about.'

She smiled weakly. 'Is there a you and Solange?'

Richard looked at her. 'Unfortunately not. Because I didn't have anyone to talk me out of marrying the wrong person.'

Juliet took a deep breath and tried to pull herself together. Nodding slowly, she made to leave the kitchen. As she got to the door, she turned. 'Can you get James for me too, please?'

'I'll have Eddie bring him to you straight away.'

'And Daddy...' She paused. 'Thanks.'

'I'm just doing my job.'

CHAPTER 19

Solange poured Richard a large glass of claret as they sat on either side of the blazing fire in the drawing room. The day had turned nasty and there was a late-summer storm blowing outside. They rarely used the room – too many memories of those awkward teas with Edith all those years ago – but it had been aired and dusted and made ready for the wedding festivities. Juliet and Danny were in the kitchen, talking. James had remained in the hall. Danny had every right to be angry and to feel let down, but James was ready to intervene if he heard raised voices and felt his sister needed his support.

'You did well today,' she said.

'If I'd paid attention to you, then it would never have got this far,' he replied. 'I don't know, Solange. I should never have forced James to do medicine. I shouldn't have encouraged her relationship with Danny. I'm hopeless.'

Solange chuckled. 'No, not hopeless, just a parent trying to do the best he can for his children. I don't think there are any parents in the world who always do the right thing. It takes a good person to admit to making mistakes, and an even better one to fix them. Nothing terrible happened. Juliet didn't marry Danny, and that has saved both of them a lot of heartbreak. James won't be a doctor, but that's not a disaster. I think it will all be fine.'

Richard kicked off his shoes and accepted the drink.

'So now what? What does she do now? She'll be the talk of the county after this.'

Solange knew she would have to deal very tentatively with him but if she could just get him to see how much Juliet wanted to go somewhere, to be someone. Perhaps she could convince him to allow his daughter to get away for a while, to spare her the whispering of the village and to give her a broader perspective on life. It was because she thought that Dunderrig was all there was that she had agreed to marry Danny. It was time for her to spread her wings.

She knew Richard had an elderly aunt, his father's sister, Kitty, living in Belfast. She'd married a ship's engineer and so travelled with him wherever the work was. He was offered a position in the Harland and Wolff shipyard in Belfast early in their marriage and had been involved in the construction of the *Titanic*. Solange remembered him as a sweet funny man and an incorrigible flirt. They were regular visitors to Dunderrig on their annual holiday to West Cork. She remembered questioning Pat on the subject of the *Titanic* and him saying to her that the ship had been perfect leaving Belfast, but you couldn't trust the British to do anything right. He had died some years ago, but his widow was by then fully integrated into her life in Belfast and, despite Richard's persistent offers of a place for her at Dunderrig, she had chosen to stay where she was. Solange thought she might be able to convince Richard to let Juliet spend a month or two with Auntie Kitty. As children, Juliet and James had loved it when Kitty and Pat visited, laden down with sweets and treats of all kinds, so she was sure Juliet would agree —especially since it meant getting away from Dunderrig for a while.

She outlined her plan to him as they sat by the fire.

'But I don't understand. Belfast? Now? What on earth would she do up there, Solange?'

Solange was patient. She spoke quietly and calmly. 'I think she feels like she is trapped here, and she's so young. She needs time away from everything to decide what it is she really wants from life, away from me and you and Mrs Canty and James, and all our opinions. It is normal, I think. When you were her age, you lived in another country, having new and interesting experiences. She should have the same.'

Richard took a cigarette out of the case in his jacket pocket. Tapping it on the inlaid ivory box, a twenty-first birthday gift from Jeremy, he shook his head.

'Ah Solange, you can't be serious? New and interesting experiences? And who is going to supervise these new experiences? Would you tell me that? Who is going to keep her safe from harm? From making more daft decisions? Poor old Kitty is barely able to mind herself, let alone a headstrong madam like Juliet. She'd run rings around her, you must know that.' His voice was pleading now.

'So Richard, what is the alternative?' Solange

still spoke quietly, but there was an edge of steel. 'This is 1939, Richard, not 1839. She's had a difficult experience, but it's made her grow up a lot. She would be fine, better than you think maybe. You will decide, of course, but if you want to have my advice then you must let her go. Just a little, bit by bit. If you do not, she will go anyway and maybe never come back. Is that what you want?'

Richard sat beside the fire, gazing into the flames. He spoke without looking at her.

'It was so much easier when they were small, wasn't it? The only problems were a grazed knee or a battle over a toy. Now, I just don't know, Solange, honest to God I don't. I just want the best life possible for them and when I think of my beautiful Juliet up there, with randy young bucks roaming the streets and fast, loose girls painting their faces and shortening their skirts... It makes me shudder. I know I'm a dinosaur and you're right, as usual. I can't keep her prisoner, however much I want to. I suppose Kitty isn't the worst option. And at least Juliet will be spared the martyred faces of the Daltons every time she puts her nose outside the door. A few weeks can't do any harm, I suppose.'

Solange felt a rush of sympathy for her old friend. Everything he did was because he loved his children, but he was terrified of letting them go.

'She loves you and wants you to be proud of her. You have done a good job, Richard. They are fine young people, and you need to trust them now. Let them go, let them spread their wings and soar. They love you, and they will always come home, of this I am certain.'

He smiled at her from his place by the fire. '*We* did a good job, Solange, both of us together. You more than me if we're honest. I could never have managed on my own. I wish more than anything that Jeremy had not died, but you were his last gift to me. The way you took over when they were born and then, when...when Edith left... Well, you are their mother. Your blood may not flow through their veins, but they know, and I know, *you* are their mother. So, if you think letting her go up to Belfast will cheer her up then I'll leave her to the train myself. And I'll let her go with a cheery wave. And be sick with worry until she's back under this roof.' He added, only half-jokingly, 'I suppose you have a master plan for James, as well. Is he off to Paris to wear an artist's smock and live on crusts in a garret in Montmartre?'

Solange was overcome with emotion. She

knew Richard appreciated everything she had done, she didn't want thanks, but that he acknowledged in words what Solange had always felt in her heart was enough. She was their mother, in every way but one. She knew he was joking about James – and it was hard to picture James in Paris, painting away to his heart's content, living like a church mouse and separated from everyone at Dunderrig. Still, boys don't pose the same worries for their fathers as girls, so though Richard would be equally reluctant to let him go, it wouldn't be because he was frightened for his safety. The funny thing was, Solange knew that Juliet was better able to look after herself than her brother in many ways.

Eventually, she found her voice. 'No, no, nothing like that. In fact, he has not spoken to me about his plans at all. Has he asked you what he should do?'

'Well, yes and no,' Richard said. 'He said he wants to leave university and from what he's told me, I don't think the medical faculty will be shedding any tears over him. I told him that he'd given it his best, and we said no more about it. I've even told him to give the art a go if he's heart set on it. I don't know the first thing about it. Sure, maybe he'll make a fortune.'

'I'm proud of you. That wasn't easy. Like Juliet, I think maybe we just have to let him go, too. See where this passion for art takes him. And Richard, while we're on the subject, have you noticed the distance between them this last while? That was never there before. James came to Juliet's support today, but still there is something not quite right. Did you notice it?'

Richard frowned. 'I can't say I did, but then I don't notice things a lot of the time. You and Mrs Canty run this place so well, I just don't open my eyes enough. What do you think it's about? A row over something?'

'I don't know. There is definitely something wrong. Juliet told me that herself, but she also said she couldn't say what it was. She did say that neither of them was in any kind of trouble, and that there was nothing for us to worry about. But I do worry, as you do – I can't help it. He's spending a lot of time in Dublin. I think there is maybe a girl there – perhaps Juliet doesn't approve.'

Richard was pensive. Solange knew so much more about his children than he did.

'Yes, I did wonder what the attraction was with Dublin. Juliet went up with him a year or so ago – do you remember? When she was visiting

239

some school friend. Did she say anything when they came back?'

'Not to me, but I think it was after that trip that things changed between them. I thought maybe it was because James was interested in the school friend. Mary Sheridan, was it? Anyway, since then, he doesn't even speak to me as he once did. I have asked him what is the matter, but he just says that he is fine. There is something though, I'm sure of it.'

A comfortable silence fell between them. The wild summer thunderstorm raged outside. They heard the front door close and someone go upstairs. Danny must have gone.

'Sure, poor lad, he's young and he'll find someone else. It's as well for him she didn't go through with it, even if he doesn't realise it yet. Marriage is hard enough work even when both people love each other.' Richard sighed, then said quietly, 'Do you still miss him, Solange?'

She thought about her answer for a moment.

'Yes, but it was so long ago now. I loved him so much, but it was in another lifetime. I was different then, the world was different then.' Solange's voice was filled with sadness. 'It is hard to imagine the world is about to be plunged into war again, so soon.'

'Just so long as Dev keeps his word and makes sure we stay out of it. There's a piece in the *Southern Star* this week, suggesting he'll stay strong, but Churchill will really put on the pressure. He'll just have to keep saying no, absolutely not, no matter what kind of blackmail they use. That's the most important thing. Saying no to the heartless warlords who send innocent young people out to die terrible deaths, using calculating lies about honour and glory.' His gaze met hers. 'I just hope that when she's up there in Belfast, she's not drawn into anything. She's so young and beautiful and so bloody innocent. I'm afraid for her, Solange.'

'When they are little, you are right, it is so simple. But now, we must let her go and hope. That is all that we can do Richard. I wish, like you, to keep them here, in Dunderrig, but we cannot. We must release her and trust and hope and pray day and night that she remains safe. That is all that we can do, unfortunately. If you let her go now, with an open heart, she will always know she can come and go as she pleases. This way is better. Difficult as it is, it is better.'

'Thank you, Solange. Whatever would have become of us if you hadn't come to Dunderrig? I just don't know.'

CHAPTER 20

*J*uliet stared out the window of the red double-decker bus as it wound its way towards Donegall Square. The beauty of the city in the late autumnal sunshine delighted her. In fact, everything about this vibrant city filled her with excitement. Dunderrig and Danny and all that seemed a lifetime ago. She knew that old people like her Auntie Kitty dreaded another war, but amongst the young people here, there was a definite sense of anticipation. It was so frustrating that despite all the guff and bluster, as Mrs Canty would have put it, nothing of any significance had happened since Chamberlain made his statement telling the British people that they were at war, once again, with Germany. That was a month ago. The 'Phoney War' – as it was being called on the wireless that she and Auntie Kitty listened to each night before bed.

Passing the red pillar boxes and the patriotic flags of the British Empire, it struck Juliet once again how strange it was to be in Ireland but to be at the same time in Britain. It felt very exotic and foreign, with their different money, and no Irish language written on any sign.

She wished Solange and Daddy could see how independent and responsible she had become. She knew that the trip to Belfast was only to get her out of Dunderrig in the wake of the wedding that never was, but she was really enjoying the experience. Danny had written to say that he was taking Fionnula O'Regan to the dance in Skibbereen and he wanted her to hear it from him rather than from the village gossips. Juliet suspected the letter was more to let her know how quickly he had got over her than to spare her the shock of discovering that he had already fallen for another girl; still, he was entitled to regain some lost pride.

Thank God, she was gone from Dunderrig before war had been declared. There would have been no way Daddy would have let her come afterwards. As it was, he was trying to get Kitty to send her home, but fortunately, her aunt was reluctant to let her go and had managed to convince Richard that his daughter was quite safe.

Already two months had passed, and Juliet hoped to extend the stay indefinitely. She was determined not to do anything that might make Auntie Kitty feel like she was getting a bit wild or too used to city life. Instead, she worked on making herself indispensable. She sat in the garden with her aunt every morning, reading the paper aloud as Kitty's eyes weren't what they were. Each afternoon, she took off around the city on the bus, drinking it all in, but making sure to be home promptly at six for tea with her aunt. The only aspect of her new life that made her sad was the number of times during the day that she would turn to share something with James only to realise once again that he wasn't there. Things had been better between them since the failed wedding, but the big issue of Edith still loomed over them.

She wondered what her brother was doing now. James was so determined and stubborn he wouldn't listen to reason where Edith was concerned. Every conversation they'd had about her had ended with a row, and in the end, they had made a mutual decision to avoid the subject. The thoughts of Edith pouring poison into her brother's ear without anyone to offer balance bothered Juliet immensely, but there was nothing she could do. She couldn't betray him by telling their father or Solange, even though she desperately wished she could so that Solange in particular could talk some sense into him. She had tried to write to him several times but every letter ended up in the wastepaper bin in her bedroom overlooking Alexandra Park.

Belfast was full with servicemen and women waiting to be deployed to Europe whenever the war got going. Juliet was becoming good at spotting the different uniforms of the air force, navy, and the army. She couldn't help but find the men in uniform attractive, and with this sense of anticipation all around, it felt like the normal rules of society could be relaxed. She regularly found herself being chatted up on the bus or in a queue by young men, who in civilian life and in civilian clothes would never have had the courage to be so forward.

She really envied the girls in uniform, too. There was a group of them in digs near her aunt's house that she'd struck up a conversation with one day on the bus. They looked so smart and brave in their uniforms, complete with ties like men, their hats jauntily pitched to one side. They told her they were Wrens and when she'd looked bewildered, they'd explained it stood for the Women's Royal Naval Service. One of them, Maureen, was a cook in civilian life, but they were all training as wireless telegraphists, she told a fascinated Juliet. She longed to join them, but she knew if she even suggested it to her aunt, let alone her father or Solange, she'd find herself back in Dunderrig so fast her head would spin.

'Is anyone sitting here?'

Juliet looked up at the tall young man who was gesturing at the seat beside her.

'No,' Juliet answered brightly. 'It's free.'

Sitting down beside her, he was pushed close to her as the bus took a corner rather too sharply.

'Sorry about that.' He was grinning, obviously not in the least bit sorry. 'Since I've nearly sat on top of you, I'd better introduce myself. I'm Ewan McCrae.' His blue eyes danced with mischief as he held out his hand for her to shake. A very definite Scottish accent with pale skin and very dark hair; he was a typical Celt.

'Juliet Buckley, pleased to meet you,' she smiled, shaking his hand.

'Now then, Miss Juliet Buckley, that accent

isn't from around here, so what is a gorgeous girl like yourself doing so very far from home?'

Juliet was flattered, but she heard her grandaunt's voice in her head: *Now Juliet, I want you to remember this. They're all better looking in uniform, but war does funny things to men. It was exactly the same the last time, makes them forget the rules. It's up to us ladies to keep everything under control.*

Auntie Kitty could never bring herself to be more explicit, but both she and her grandniece knew exactly what she was saying. Juliet was fairly sure that no men had untoward intentions towards the octogenarian Kitty, so it was clear her warning was intended for Juliet. Auntie Kitty was getting on in years, but she was no fool.

'I'm visiting from Cork, staying with my aunt for a few weeks.' She was friendly but not flirty. She didn't want this Ewan McCrae getting the wrong impression.

'Well, I'm a visitor here myself after a fashion,' he replied laughing. 'So how about we two tourists go for a cup of tea and discuss our findings on this lovely city?'

Tempted as she was – he really was gorgeous looking – she thought it would seem too fast to agree to go out with him just like that.

'Oh thank you, but I'm afraid I can't. I have another engagement this afternoon.' She hoped she didn't sound haughty or rude. She would normally never use a word like engagement.

'Well, that is a very great pity indeed because I am fascinating company, I can tell you, so you really don't know what you're missing. And I'm a perfect gentleman, ask anyone! My mother raised me to treat ladies with respect and not to bore them with men's talk, but you seem to be a girl who'd like nothing better than an afternoon discussing the best way to tackle a brown trout!'

Juliet pealed with laughter. Not just at what he had said but at his accent as well.

'Well, Mr McCrae,' she laughed, 'I happen to know everything about *"broon troot"* as you call them because there is a trout stream behind our house and my brother and I perfected tickling when we were ten years old. So I'm afraid going for tea with you would be a total waste of my time and yours if that is the extent of your conversation.'

The bus was pulling in at its final stop on Donegall Square as Juliet stood up. Ewan gestured that she should go ahead of him and she realised just how tall he was. At five feet five-and-a-half herself, she wasn't tiny – but beside him, she felt as if she were.

Out on the street, he walked alongside her.

'Okay so, there is nothing I cannae tell you about trout tickling, nor am I so crass as to mention any other kind of tickling in front of a lady such as yourself, but I do have some other really good topics I can discuss at great length. Unicycles, for example? Frog breeding? Hydrangeas? All areas of my expertise, I can assure you. My desire is simply to educate the world. The fact that you really are extraordinarily beautiful is entirely beside the point. Scout's honour.' He skipped alongside her as he was speaking.

He was so funny. She stopped to face him. 'That's a boy scout uniform, is it?'

'Might as well be for all the action I've seen so far,' he grumbled good-naturedly. 'Please come out with me? I'm going out of my mind with boredom, and I just love your accent and your hair and your eyes and your...'

'All right, all right,' Juliet sighed theatrically. 'One cup of tea and a bun and you're paying, then I'm off. I do have things to do, you know, but if you're that bored, I can do it for the war effort I suppose.'

Sitting in the window seat of a Lyons Tea

Room ten minutes later, Juliet observed her new acquaintance as he waited in line for their tea. The RAF uniform fitted him well and now that he'd left his hat on the table, she could see that his dark hair was heavily Brylcreemed.

He placed the teapot and two cups on the table. From his pocket, he removed a piece of paper in which were wrapped two buns. 'So, Miss Juliet, can I be your Romeo?'

Juliet's expression told him she was not one of those silly giggly girls who fell at a man's feet at the first sign of flattery.

'Too much too soon?' he asked, still grinning.

'Much,' she agreed as she poured the tea.

'Okay, truce!' He held his hands up in a gesture of surrender.

Juliet smiled.

'So apart from visiting your aunt, why would a lovely young Irish girl leave her trout-filled home to come to the Black North? I've never been to Southern Ireland, but anyone that has says it's beautiful, and it looks like your Mr de Valera is going to keep you all out of this war, so what brings you here?' He sipped his tea, his gaze intense.

'Well,' she began, 'it's a long story. Anyway,

what makes you think I agree with our Mr de Valera? Maybe, I think we should be in this war.'

He put down his cup and sat back in the chair. 'Do you?'

'Yes, as a matter of fact I do. People at home though are very anti-English still, and in lots of ways, you can't blame them. Independence is still very new for us. For most people, the idea of joining forces with what they see as the old enemy would just be unthinkable. De Valera would only be able to keep us out of it if that's what most people wanted, and unfortunately, I think it is.'

'But not you?' he asked quizzically.

'No, not me. I'm not claiming to be an expert, but what Hitler is doing is just wrong and someone needs to stop him. My father, however, would have a fit if he heard me,' Juliet smiled ruefully.

'He's one of those very anti-English people you mentioned?' Ewan seemed intrigued.

'Not so much that. It's more because he was a doctor in France during the last war, and Solange – she's kind of my step-mother – was a nurse. So they are both very against any kind of war. The minute anything actually happens, I'll be shipped straight home to Dunderrig, no doubt,' she sighed.

'Is it that bad? This Dunderrig place?'

'No, it's lovely. A lovely, friendly house with beautiful gardens, but nothing ever happens there, you see. My brother James, he's my twin actually, is still there, but he's different to me. He likes peace and quiet while I...'

'...Like a bit of excitement?' Ewan finished for her. Noting her look of alarm, he rushed on, 'Not *that* kind of excitement, don't worry. But I know what you mean. I couldn't wait to join up once the war was declared, though I must say I thought something interesting would have happened by now. I'm stationed at Aldergrove RAF base, training and awaiting orders, but honestly it's so dull, I just had to escape today. Anyway, tell me more about you. You're a twin, you said? Are you close?'

'Yes, very.' Juliet felt a pang of regret. She wished that were still true, but she wasn't going to admit anything like that about James to this stranger. She wondered what her brother would make of this Ewan McCrae – would he like him or think he was too cocky. 'So Mr McCrae, what about you?'

'I've got four brothers, all in the services. My dad was killed at Guinchy in 1918, so it's really hard for my mum, her watching us all go. I'm the youngest, by seven minutes.' Laughing at her startled glance, he went on, 'Aye, I got you there, didn't I? You see, we are destined to meet. My twin, his name's Douglas – but everyone calls him Dougie – he's in the RAF too, but he's the steady, sensible one and got snapped up to train as a flying instructor back in England. I've not seen him for a while. No one can tell us apart, though obviously I'm the better-looking one!'

'Are you close?' Juliet asked.

'Y'know yourself. I suppose we are, he knows me better than anyone else, but we don't see eye to eye on everything. I'd have preferred to have been posted with him, though. Still, the lads I'm with are a good bunch, so it's not so bad.'

Juliet much preferred this more thoughtful version of Ewan and wondered if he'd ask her out again.

'So, why did James not come on this adventure?' Ewan asked. Juliet thought about it and decided to confide in this man. Now that he'd stopped the outrageous flirting and flattery, he seemed kind, and, being a twin, perhaps he'd have some ideas about what she should do. She couldn't talk about the situation with anyone else, and it was really upsetting her.

'Well, it's complicated. A long story.' She hesitated.

'I've got, let's see, until Adolf and his mates do something dastardly,' he joked, looking at his watch, 'so if I can help, I'd be happy to try.'

Juliet began the story with the Danny disaster, as she dubbed it, but found herself going back to the night of their birth and telling him about Solange and their parents. She finished up by explaining the atmosphere that now existed between her and James. Ewan sat quietly listening without interrupting.

When she stopped speaking, he leaned over and held her hand. She didn't pull away even though she knew she probably should. Getting the whole story off her chest, left her feeling exhausted and vulnerable.

'Firstly, can I say how happy I am that Danny got the heave-ho? On the other thing, that's a difficult situation to be in. I don't know anything about it apart from what you've told me, and I have to say, from the way you describe your mother, she sounds like a cold fish, but maybe James needs to find that out for himself. It's hard to think why she would love him and not you, but it sounds to me like you have a great mother in Solange, so maybe, let James go his own way for now, and agree not to talk about it. I think that's what I'd do if I were in your shoes. It's not a perfect solution, I know, but I can see you're upset by the way things are between you and James. I'd be the same if it were Dougie. Why don't you write him a nice, long newsy letter and at the end, say something like: "I know you have to do whatever you want where Edith is concerned. It's not something I'm interested in, but I don't want it to get between us, so maybe, we can just agree not to discuss it for now and go back to the way we were." What do you think?'

She smiled ruefully, 'I think it's the most sensible idea yet. I've tried writing to him before, but it's like this big huge thing standing between us, but you're right, I suppose he's entitled to have whatever relationship he wants with her. We're adults now, and we were bound to disagree over something. We'll just decide not to discuss it. I hope he agrees.'

Ewan still held her hand, caressing her palm with his thumb. The gesture was surprisingly comforting. 'He'll agree, I'm sure of it. He's probably as upset about this as you are, but he doesn't have someone holding his hand and solving his problems for him like you do.' He winked at her and squeezed her hand.

They chatted on and on all afternoon and by the time Juliet looked at the clock on the wall of the busy café, she realised it was definitely time to begin the journey home. Somehow, almost three hours had passed.

Standing, she said, 'I really have to go. My aunt is expecting me home for tea.'

'Can I see you tomorrow evening? We could go to the pictures if you liked?' Ewan looked down at her as he helped her with her coat.

'I'd like that,' Juliet found herself replying.

That evening, she debated whether to tell Auntie Kitty she was going out on a date. Her aunt was usually in bed by eight, and she liked to listen to the wireless in her room. Juliet knew that she could feign tiredness and slip out without her being any the wiser, but she decided she'd be honest and hope for the best. At least if Kitty thought she wouldn't lie to her, there was a chance she might not tell her father. If he thought she was getting into a romantic entanglement so soon after Danny, he wouldn't approve.

As she sat companionably with her aunt listening to the BBC, Juliet brought up the subject.

'Auntie Kitty, I was wondering if it would be

all right if I went to the pictures tomorrow evening, with a man?' She had decided the direct approach was best.

Kitty didn't seem shocked, which Juliet took as a good sign. 'Who is this man?' she enquired, taking off her glasses. 'Is he respectable?'

'I think so.' Juliet's voice remained strong. 'I only met him today, on the bus. We started chatting, and he asked me to have a cup of tea with him in a café, so I did. He's Scottish and in the RAF out at Aldergrove, and he's a twin, as well. He's got four brothers, his mother is a widow and his father was killed in the last war. His name's Ewan McCrae.'

Juliet was praying that her aunt would say yes, but she wasn't going to plead. She hoped that being straight with Kitty would mean she'd trust her and let her go.

'I suppose he's nice looking,' Kitty raised one eyebrow.

Juliet blushed. 'Yes, Auntie Kitty, he's very nice looking, but I'm not going to do anything that...' Juliet's aplomb was failing her.

'Well, I should hope not!' her aunt exclaimed. 'Mind how you go with your Scotsman, darling Juliet. Have a nice time and be home on the last bus. Now, I'm done in, so I'll say good night to you. Make sure everything is locked up, won't you? You're a good girl, your father is right to be as proud of you as he is.'

All that night, she lay in bed thinking about Ewan. Even though she'd almost married Danny, she'd never gone on a proper date before. With Danny, she'd just kind of drifted into the relationship. Solange had sat her down years ago, when she got her first period, and explained about sex and babies and all of that. She told her that if she ever wanted to know anything, she should come to her, so she was easily the most knowledgeable on that mysterious subject in school. Before she left for Belfast, Solange brought up the subject again one evening as they walked home from the village, having been in Skibbereen shopping for new clothes for her trip.

'You know, you have grown into a beautiful young woman, Juliet,' Solange began. 'And now you are about to leave home, I think we should have a talk about men.'

Juliet squirmed. 'Solange, there's no need, honestly. You told me everything I needed to know years ago. And I was within a half an hour of being a married woman, you know.'

'Yes, and I did not speak like this before that wedding because I knew you were marrying the wrong man, and so, to discuss what I want to tell you now would have been pointless. I know you did not have sex with Danny. It was one of the reasons I knew you and he were wrong for each other. Now, years ago, I told you how it happens when a woman conceives a child, but we have never spoken about love and passion. I know it is awkward for you, your Irish education makes talking about your body so difficult, but please, there are some things you must understand. I know the nuns told you in school that you must not ever have sex before you are married, and then, only to make a baby, but it is not so. Of course, you must be very careful, and this world, it is not kind to young girls who find themselves pregnant without a husband, but sometimes, especially during something like a war, we need each other. Men need women, and women need men. What I am saying is not you must sleep with all the men who approach you, and believe me, there will be many, but if you do meet someone on your travels, and you fall in love with him and he with you, then just be very careful.'

Juliet couldn't believe her ears. Solange had stopped walking and was taking a bulky envelope out of her purse and handing it to her.

'These are from France; your father gets them

sent over. A man wears them to stop the woman getting pregnant.'

Juliet looked into the envelope in astonishment. 'My father gets these?' She was flabbergasted. 'Why on earth does he need...'

Solange laughed. 'Not for himself, silly girl, but sometimes his patients can't afford any more children, so they ask him if there is any way they can still make love but not have a baby come, and well, he gives them these.' Solange shrugged – the Gallic gesture she had used so frequently throughout Juliet's childhood. Juliet sometimes forgot how very French Solange was, despite all her years in Ireland. Though her English was almost perfect, it was still heavily accented, and her attitude to many things was different to the Irish one; but this was really amazing. Juliet was so shocked she couldn't even feel embarrassed.

'So you're giving me these...these... I can't believe Daddy gives these out. If Father Twomey knew, he'd have a fit! And Daddy goes to mass every Sunday even though the Church expressly forbids the use of...of...'

'Condoms,' Solange interjected. 'Yes I know, but your father is a good, kind-hearted man and a wonderful doctor. He thinks it is easy for the Church to make such rules when it is not the

Church who has to support all these children. He asked me many years ago to have them sent from France and so an old school friend of mine sends them, though they have to be well hidden from the authorities. I'm not telling your father I am giving you these, by the way, but if you find yourself in a situation where you want to make love with a man, at least, you will be prepared. That's all.'

Juliet took the envelope and put it in her bag.

'Solange,' she asked, 'did you and Jeremy, you know...before you were married?'

Solange chuckled. 'Of course we did. How would I have known if I wanted to sleep with him forever if I did not first try? But, and please do not be shocked, Jeremy was not the first. He knew that, and because I was not his first either, we could be certain that we were right for each other.'

Juliet was fascinated. 'So who...?'

'Ah, he was a boy who lived near me in Amiens, so nice this boy. But the first time, it's not so good. It hurts a little, and we were both nervous. Let me give you some advice – if you can, for your first time, be with someone who has a little bit of experience. It makes it better.'

'I always thought that there was just Jeremy, I

never knew...' Juliet struggled to find the right words that would show Solange that she wasn't shocked, just that she had never imagined. She supposed she had never seen Solange in that way, but now that she was older, she could see how very attractive the French woman was. She still had the same figure as always, her dark curly hair remained as black as ever. Women of her age in Dunderrig, wore their hair pinned up under headscarves when they went out, but Solange allowed her shiny locks to cascade down her back. She caused a bit of a stir sometimes, but mostly people liked her – and, anyway, she was foreign – the rules were different. All the old farmers were forever trying to get her attention, and she was unfailingly courteous and polite to them – but never anything more.

Solange sat down on the grassy bank and patted the patch of grass beside her. Juliet sat down.

'Juliet, Jeremy was the love of my life. But there are many reasons for going to bed with someone. Love is just one. My first boy, I burned with desire for. Then there was the man from Paris, who was visiting my father's paper factory.' She giggled at the memory. 'This man, I found so funny, and he cheered me up when I was feeling sad. There are many, many, reasons to make love, and also many ways to do it, and as you grow to love someone and trust them, you will become braver and try new things. But sex should never be about fear or trying to be who you are not. Only do what feels right to you, and then you will be happy. Do not let your education dictate how you live your life, my darling, that's all I wanted to say to you.'

'Can I ask you something?'

'Of course, anything. If I know the answer, I will tell you.'

'Was there anyone after Jeremy? You know, here?'

Solange smiled and rubbed Juliet's back, just as she had done when Juliet was little.

'If you are asking me if I have ever made love with your father then the answer is no. I love him, but not in that way, and I think he feels the same about me. I have had sex since Jeremy died, but before you jump to conclusions, it was not with your Papa and it was not in Dunderrig.'

'What?' Juliet spluttered in amazement. 'I never realised. Does Daddy know about this man?'

'I don't think so. And he is just a friend, really. It will never become more than what it is. I met him years ago on the train to Cork, and we chatted and stayed in touch. He is charming and funny and handsome, and we have a really nice time together. It suits us both, we like each other, but we are not in love. I make no demands on him nor he on me. That's how we both like it. I know to you, I am an old, old woman, but I still have needs, and this way it suits me and him, and everyone is happy!'

Juliet chuckled at what the nuns would have made of Solange's attitude. They would have been horrified. She was always taught to keep her distance from boys; apparently men were incapable of controlling their carnal desires, so it was up to the girls to say no – or better still, avoid any situation where it would be necessary to say no. Sister Bonaventure, her religion teacher, was adamant that if the unfortunate situation occurred where it was absolutely necessary to dance with a boy, like at a family wedding, then at all times the girl should ensure there was 'room for Jesus' between them. Juliet recalled the suppressed giggles in the classroom when she had asked the nun how wide Jesus might be, just so she'd know how much space to leave. That had earned her a whole Saturday detention for being cheeky and blasphemous, but it had been worth it to see the nun's face turn from white to purple instantly. No wonder Solange had always taken Juliet's side against the nuns if this was her attitude to men.

Juliet knew now that she had never felt or even understood the pangs of sexual desire. Of course, Danny always tried for a fumble after the dance or the pictures, but he expected her to resist and she did. That's what well-brought-up girls did; he would have probably died if she'd given in. And it wasn't as if she had found him hard to resist. She had thought he was nice looking, but she had never been so overcome with desire for him that she would have even considered sex with him before marriage. Now, as she tossed and turned in her big bed in Belfast that night, she realised she was beginning to understand what Solange had been talking about. Ewan, just rubbing her palm with his thumb while she poured her heart out about James was comforting, certainly, but it also aroused feelings in her that were new. She wondered what it would be like to feel his arms around her, to have him kiss her. She must remain vigilant, she knew that, but he was the first man that she'd ever found attractive; it was so exciting.

CHAPTER 21

'James, darling, you look simply marvellous!'

James found himself enveloped in his mother's fragrant embrace as Otto took his bag and all three of them emerged from the gloom of Kingsbridge station into the bright sunshine. Together they walked to Otto's Deusenburg.

'It's a beauty!' James gasped at the sight of the car. 'Did you import it from Germany?'

'Of course,' Otto grinned. 'You can try driving it later, if you wish.'

'Can I?'

Edith smiled at the sight of her son in such high excitement. 'Of course you can, darling. Has it only been two weeks since your last visit? It seems much longer. Oh, we have missed you! Now, let's get you home and have some lunch – you must be ravenous after that interminable journey from Dunderrig!'

James laughed. 'Well, it does take a while all right, but imagine what it will be like if they ran out of coal and have to use turf. The ticket inspector was telling me about the changes that will happen if coal rationing comes in here. It would take months to get up from West Cork.'

Over lunch in the garden of their exclusive Ballsbridge home, James questioned Otto about the war.

'Ah, my dear James, it is difficult to know what will happen. Lucky for me, I am here in your charming country because my fellow countrymen and women are not faring so well in England. Most of them are being rounded up and imprisoned as enemy aliens. It is very worrying...' Otto shook his head.

'It's simply outrageous, that's what it is!' Edith exclaimed. 'Firstly, why is England even involved? Herr Hitler is only reclaiming what is rightfully the property of the German people. They were treated so badly after Versailles, typically duplicitous and devious behaviour of the bloody British

Empire. They have always thought themselves superior to every other nation on earth and now, here they are again, butting into something that does not concern them...'

Edith was so adamant that James was reluctant to interrupt her, but his conscience insisted. 'But Mother, Poland is not part of Germany, never was, and some of the things that Hitler has been saying... Well, I'm not sure I'd want to live in a society where his ideals were law.'

Edith tinkled a little laugh. 'Oh my darling, you are so young, it is delightful to see, isn't it Otto? The world can be harsh at times, but one must consider the greater good. Of course, initially, some people in the annexed areas will be a bit disgruntled, they are bound to be, but they are being elevated to the culture of the people of the Third Reich. This Lebensraum is necessary for the further development of Germany, something that has been denied us since 1918. This is the nation that produced Wagner and Dürer and Nietzsche. There will be a period of adjustment, of course, but in the end, the Führer is, in fact, doing these people a favour.'

James looked at his mother and wondered at her use of the word 'us' to describe the German people. He found it peculiar that she expounded such pro-Nazi views, though she was undoubtedly Irish when her husband – if indeed that's what he was – seemed much less vehement. His attitude seemed vague at best, while she was full of opinions. He'd never heard Otto refer to Hitler or the Nazis at all, in fact.

James accepted the glass of wine Otto was offering. Lunches at their home were so convivial, and he felt really listened to. What he wanted, how he felt about things, really interested Edith and Otto. Edith had taken the news that he'd dropped out of college with delight – she'd never thought he should have been a doctor in the first place. His father, on the other hand, while accepting his decision to quit medicine, was clearly still not enamoured with the idea of his son being an artist. He had been true to his word and had presented no obstacles as such, but James knew he wasn't happy about it. He stayed around Dunderrig in the weeks after Juliet's departure but although he was painting all the time, he felt like a dropout. During those first weeks, Solange was so caught up with getting Juliet out of Dunderrig after the Danny fiasco that it felt like she'd barely said two words to him. He'd not heard a word from Juliet, who was having the time of her life, no doubt, in Belfast, and obviously didn't give him a passing thought. She'd been there three months now and might not even come home for Christmas. She'd not written to him, so he'd only heard about her adventures second-hand from Solange, to whom Juliet wrote every week.

'Anyway, that's enough of this war talk.' Otto changed the subject. 'Tell me, what did you think of the National Gallery exhibition last time? Impressive, no? Wait until you see what we have planned for you this time.' Edith and Otto filled his days during his increasingly frequent visits with outings to exhibitions and art galleries, as well as visits to their friends, some of whom had wonderful private collections.

'It was wonderful. I could look at them all day. The whole collection is so impressive. The tragic loss of Hugh Lane will never be forgotten but neither will his legacy. How much of his collection went down with him on the Lusitania will probably never be known. It's so interesting and so vibrant, the whole art scene here in the city. I can almost feel a part of it.' James became embarrassed at his own admission – he didn't normally verbalise his deep feelings about art.

Edith and Otto exchanged a glance.

'What?' James asked, noting the slight smile playing on Otto's lips.

'Well,' Edith began. 'It's only a tentative en-quiry, but a friend of ours – of Otto's, really – is connected to the director of the National College of Art, and we asked him to investigate the possi-bility of you studying there. Now that you've ruled out medicine, we thought you might con-sider it. You could live here with us, study and paint and enjoy everything the city has to offer.' She looked at him hopefully. 'What do you think? Is that something you'd like to do, my darling?'

James was speechless. Was it something he would like? Thoughts raced around his head. Well yes, it was exactly what he wanted to do, he knew that. But living here, moving to Dublin, leaving Dunderrig, telling his father... It all seemed so outlandish. He'd not even found a way to tell him that he and Edith were in contact, let alone broach the subject of moving in with her and actually studying what his father thought of as a hobby and not a real career. It was all too much to take in.

If only Juliet was here, she could advise him... Though, remembering how his sister felt about their mother, he reconsidered. That was how things used to be, him and Juliet, two sides of the same person – but not anymore.

'Say something,' Edith said softly, and reached

for his hand. 'I know it's a big move, but we would love to have you, wouldn't we, Otto? You could follow your dream of being an artist. Nothing would make us happier than to help you make your wishes come true.'

James had noticed early on in his relationship with her that Edith very seldom referred to Juliet and never mentioned his father, Solange, or even Dunderrig. She seemed to live for his visits and while he was in Dublin, everything was for him. She learned his favourite foods and made sure they were on the menu; she took him to plays and concerts as well as exhibitions; she bought him clothes and books. Of course, none of her gifts could be brought back to Dunderrig. Solange and his father thought he was spending time with school friends or possibly even a girlfriend and didn't question him too much. Just last week, he explained his frequent trips to the capital by saying he was interested in cityscapes. His father had looked up in surprise and asked him if he was thinking about architecture. It shocked him how easily he was able to lie to them, and he hated deceiving them in this way. He wished he could tell Solange the truth, but he knew she would make him tell his father, and he just wasn't ready for that yet. Perhaps, if

Richard had ever brought up the subject of their mother, he would have found it easier, but as things stood, that conversation was simply impossible.

'I...I don't know what to say. Of course, it's what I want – more than want, it's what I dream of – but to leave home? I don't know. Dad still hopes I'll do something professional, and Juliet...'

'But James, my love, can't you see, you must do what is right for you, not for your father, not for Juliet. I know it will be difficult for them to accept after everything that has happened, but they love you, as I do, and they will want what's best for you.' Edith was pleading. 'Please consider it. You are my son, I want to help you realise the person you have the potential to become. Down there, you are just the local doctor's son, but here, you are Professor James Carney's grandson, someone to be noticed. With mine and Otto's connections, you really could become someone.'

James studied his mother's eager face. The question that he'd avoided asking came bubbling to the surface, to be ignored no longer. He knew that this conversation would have to happen sometime, but she had shown such kindness and generosity to him since they'd been reunited, he never could find the right time. If he were going to consider such a huge life change though, he would have to know.

'If you love me, why did you leave us? We were only children, and yet you just walked out the door and never came back, never wrote. So much happened, and you should have been there. Like the time Juliet fell out of a tree when we were nine and broke her arm, or when I won an all-Ireland hurling medal at school, or the day we got our Leaving Cert results, where were you? You say you love me but how can you turn love on and off like that?' James's voice cracked with emotion. He'd never intended his tone to be so accusatory, he knew he sounded like Juliet, but now that he'd asked his questions, he needed answers. If he was going to consider allowing Edith to be his mother again, they would need to be on a clear, honest footing.

Silence descended on the room. Edith looked as if someone had struck her. Otto's face was filled with concern as he rushed to her defence.

'James, your mother...' Otto began.

'It's all right, Otto, I should explain myself,' interrupted Edith, recovering her composure. 'Of course, you have questions, my darling. And you deserve answers. Perhaps, I should have written, tried to explain things, but you were so young, and I knew Richard had no desire to ever hear from me again. Several times as you got older, I wanted to make contact, but I was afraid. While you were children, I could only contact you through your father. After I left, perhaps a month later, I received one letter from a solicitor ordering me to stay away from Dunderrig and warning me that if I attempted to make any contact whatsoever with my children, your father would drag my name through the mud. The tone of the letter was as rigid and cold as your father himself, and brooked no argument.'

James tried to consider this new version of his father as a hard, bitter man. Edith would not lie about something so important, of that he was sure, but this portrayal of the man who reared him was entirely at odds with his own experience. Reticent, certainly – frustrating occasionally – but he could not believe his father was capable of such deliberate cruelty.

'If you had wanted to, you could have written to us when we were older. He would surely have allowed that. You knew where we were.'

'Of course, I knew where you were. But I was afraid of what your father might say to you if I tried to contact you – perhaps he would set you against me forever. Even writing to you when I did was incredibly frightening, but I had to see you.'

'Why did you leave in the first place?' James looked deeply into his mother's eyes.

Edith sighed. 'When I met your father, I was in deep grief. My own father was not long dead – murdered by the British for supporting the lock-out. Your grandfather was a wonderful man, James, kind and gentle, yet strong and such a proud Irishman. You would have loved him, and he, you. You get your artistic talent from him. He knew everyone: Yeats, Pearse, Lady Gregory, and the Gore-Booths, and I had such wonderful times with him as a child. I was distraught when he died. Your father was just what I needed at the time – strong, solid, but kind. He seemed not to want too much from me emotionally. I didn't love him if I'm honest, but I felt we could get along. I was wrong. I should have made it clearer to him just how much Irish freedom meant to me. I assumed we stood for the same things but when he put on that British uniform, any feelings I had for him died. I begged him to let me stay in Dublin, but he insisted I go to Dunderrig. I had no choice. The Cantys disliked me from the start – no woman would have been good enough for their precious Richard. Old Dr Buckley was pleasant, but Richard's mother was ridiculous, the way she idolised him. I stuck it out as long as I could, even after Richard came back and you two were born. I really did try, but everything I attempted to do to bring us closer as a couple failed. He was so cold, so unreachable and anyway, I just couldn't forgive him. Maybe he didn't care anymore by then. He had another...he had other things on his mind.'

'Do you mean Solange? Did you imagine that he had feelings for her? Because if you did, then you were utterly wrong. There has never been anything between him and Solange. She stayed in Dunderrig because she was our mother.'

He could see the effect of his words on his mother's face, but he wanted to hurt her, for her to feel the pain of rejection he and his sister had endured on some level since they were five. They did not pine for her – the truth was they barely remembered her – but nonetheless the hurt of having his mother walk straight out of his life without a backward glance still lay buried deep within him.

'Did you not want to take us with you?' He realised he sounded like that hurt little boy again.

'I wanted to take *you*, but Richard wouldn't allow it. It was incredibly difficult to leave you, and Juliet too, of course, but I did what I did because I had no other choice. I knew he and Solange would look after you.'

James realised that Edith had just confirmed what Juliet had always suspected. That their mother had preferred him to his sister. He'd always dismissed that idea as preposterous whenever Juliet raised the subject, arguing that she held both of them in equal disdain. But now he knew it was the truth.

Silence lay heavily in the room. James rose and walked to the window, watching the hustle and bustle of the city below. Eventually, he spoke. 'Why me? Why did you want to take me and not Juliet?'

Edith crossed the room and put her arms around her son. Turning him to face her, putting her hand on his face, she whispered, 'Because I loved you.'

Traffic rumbled outside; a delivery cart rattled over the cobbles. Otto's newspaper rustled. The words left unspoken seemed to suck the life from the room. James wanted to leave, to process this information. She loved him, not Juliet – just him. He looked around the room; Otto smoked his pipe in the large wingback chair beside the fire. Beautiful nature scenes covered the walls and the entire house felt cultured and welcoming. The smell of beeswax polish and apple wood logs burning merrily in the grate was inviting and homely. He loved Dunderrig, of course he did, but here he could be himself, an artist without any of the pressure to conform to what was expected of him. Had his father really been so heartless as to refuse Edith contact with them all those years?

'So now you know the whole truth.' Edith spoke without guilt or sadness. 'What is it to be? Do you stay in Dunderrig and go back to study engineering or architecture, living out a life of boring repetition doing something that doesn't excite or challenge you, something Richard deems suitable, or do you come here and follow your dream?'

James turned to gaze out of the window once more, looking out at the world carrying on as if nothing had happened outside. He could feel the expectant gaze of his mother on his back, willing him to understand, to choose her over his father and Solange. James was under no illusion. If he decided to take up Edith and Otto's offer, his father would be furious and deeply hurt. Even Solange, whom he had always relied upon to take his side, would never understand. He knew he was at a crossroads in his life. He could accept his mother's explanation and allow her into his life, she would provide everything he would ever need in terms of his dream to become an artist, and would love him, it seemed, unconditionally. The alternative was to reject her explanation and return to Dunderrig.

His father would never understand his re-union with his mother, and neither would Solange or the Cantys. Juliet, while supportive of his career choice, had made her feelings quite clear on the subject of Edith.

Whatever he decided, he realised, he was going to hurt someone.

CHAPTER 22

'*Frankly, my dear, I don't give a damn.*'

Juliet tried to stay gazing up at Clark Gable as he dismissed Scarlet O'Hara.

Normally, she became so engrossed in a film that everything else was ignored, but the intensely masculine presence of Ewan McCrae kept distracting her. His dark hair was swept back and cut in the military style; she glanced at him as often as she dared, hoping he didn't catch her. He really was the most handsome man she had ever seen, including on the big screen. His dark blue eyes were like the sea in a storm, and she longed to run her hands down his muscular arm or put her hand on his leg. She smiled in the dark at her audacity – the nuns and Auntie Kitty would be appalled at her carnal instincts – but she knew Solange would be cheering her on if she could see her now. So far, Ewan had been the perfect gentleman – which both pleased and frustrated her. He didn't try to put his arm around her or do anything that would have been unsuitable behaviour for a Sunday afternoon in her aunt's parlour.

As they stood in the foyer of the Astoria Cinema after the film, they watched the crowds dispersing into the night.

'Well?' Ewan asked. 'Leslie Howard or Clark Gable?'

'What about them?' Juliet replied mischievously.

'Which one of them would you choose if you could pick?' Ewan casually offered her his arm as they walked out into the cool night air.

'Hmm. I'm not too sure. Leslie is nicer, more honest and trustworthy, but I think there's a certain element of danger about Clark, which is kind of attractive. But since neither of them are from Cork then I'm afraid I'd have to turn them both down, should they ask me,' she chuckled as they walked along the side of the Lagan towards Belfast Central Station.

'Is that a rule of yours? Any man you might be interested in has to be from Cork? I wish you'd mentioned that earlier,' he replied, mock-indignant.

'Oh, it's not just a rule of mine. It's a rule of all Cork people. We don't believe in inter-county relationships. As for international, well that would be simply unthinkable. Why do you ask?' Juliet's eyes were wide and innocent though her voice was flirtatious.

'I see I've got a tricky one on my hands here. You are fishing, Miss Buckley, don't think I don't know that. But, fair enough, you want me to come out and say it, so I will. I think you are beautiful and funny and interesting and not like anyone I've ever met before, and I would really like to get to know you better. Now how's that for honesty? Though if you prefer the element of danger, I could always...'

He grabbed her playfully by the waist and pretended to push her over the bridge. She screamed and giggled until two elderly ladies passed them and stared disapprovingly at such unseemly antics.

'It's still early; your bus doesn't go for another half an hour. Would you like to go for a cup of tea, or drink, maybe?'

His words were casual, but she knew he was nervous, hoping she'd agree. The more she got to know him the more intrigued she became. On one hand, he was a charming joker, always ready with a quick line to make her smile, but under that flirtatious exterior there was a sincerity that she found appealing. For all his patter, she felt he was to be trusted. She could hear Solange's voice in her head telling her as she always did, *'Fais confiance à tes intuitions.'* And in this instance, she had a good feeling about Ewan McCrae. He'd been honest with her so she decided he deserved the same in return.

'I'd love to go for a drink,' she said, and squeezed his arm.

The pub was busy and the windows were steamed up. Ewan deposited her at a small table in the corner while he got their drinks. He guessed Juliet didn't drink and suggested a soda water while he got himself a pint of beer.

'Would you like to try a sip?' he said, offering her his glass as he sat down. 'It's better in Scotland, of course, but this stuff's not too bad.'

Accepting the glass, she grimaced as she swallowed the dark bitter liquid. 'How on earth can anyone enjoy that?' she spluttered. 'It's disgusting!'

'I suppose alcohol is an acquired taste,' he grinned. 'Don't worry, stick with me, and I'll have you drinking gin for breakfast in no time.'

Juliet didn't want him to think she was a total innocent, so she said, 'Well, I do drink wine, actually. I really like a nice claret.'

'Wine indeed! I can see I've a lady of sophisticated tastes, which does beg the question why you agreed to come out with such a savage as myself?' His crooked smile disarmed her.

'Not really sophisticated, it's just that Solange gave us watered-down wine with our dinner on Sundays. She drinks a glass of claret every evening, always has done, so although Daddy hardly ever drinks, there is always wine in our house.'

Ewan took a long draught of his beer. 'This Solange, she sounds interesting. I just can't imagine a wine-drinking French lady living in deepest rural Ireland. Her arrival must have caused quite a stir.'

'I suppose it did at the time, and no doubt people had an opinion on it. People in Dunderrig have an opinion on everything. But by the time we were old enough to realise that Solange was different to everyone else's mammy, she was part of the community. Our family was always considered a bit odd anyhow, especially after our mother took off. Solange was just part of the peculiarity that is the Buckleys of Dunderrig. They used to love us coming into the shops though; I do remember that, because James and I always speak in French with her, never in English, so the locals were fascinated that we were fluent in the language of a country we had never been to. We still only speak to her in French. She's wonderful. Our mother showed no interest in us and when she finally left, Solange took care of us. In fact, from the moment of our birth she has been our mother in everything but name. She's beautiful, all the local farmers nearly go mad for her, but she's not interested. She was married to our father's best friend, he was killed in the last war, and she never really got over it.'

Ewan seemed to love listening to her talk; her lilting Cork accent always made him smile. 'Go on,' he urged, 'you still haven't explained how she ended up in Cork.'

'Well, Jeremy – that was her husband, he trained with Daddy – was killed a week before the armistice. Poor Solange had lost both her brothers at Verdun and her mother had died and her father had been murdered by the Germans.

Daddy had been moved further along the line but after the armistice, he went looking for her. He knew that Jeremy would have done the same for him, so he offered her a home with us. I can't imagine what it would have been like without her. Our father is nice and kind, but he's not exactly what you'd call emotional. Maybe he never was, but I think the war also affected him very deeply. He doesn't suffer from shell-shock or anything like that, but he just can't really talk about it, even now. He's so against this one, I'm living in fear that he'll summon me home if things really do start. Do you think it will?'

Ewan shrugged. 'Who knows? We're ready to go at a moment's notice, and as it is, there's a lot of surveillance going on. After the sinking of the *Athenia*, they knew the Germans meant business. It all looks peaceful enough, but there are U-boats out there. The navy are coping, but the problem is the air-force. The planes we have are no match for them.'

'What is it like? Flying, I mean?' Juliet's eyes sparkled.

'Och, it's magical. It's all I ever wanted to do. In a way, this war has made my dreams come true. Without it, there'd be no chance of me getting into a cockpit let alone flying. When Dougie and I were wee lads, we used to save up all our pocket money to buy *Flying Aces*. It was an American magazine, but there was this wee shop on Princes Street in Edinburgh – a real old boy ran it, and I've no idea how he got them, but every couple of months, he'd have a few issues in stock and if we had enough money between us, we'd rush to buy one. Things were very tight what with Dad being gone and Mum having us lads eating her out of house and home, so it was a rare treat. We'd cut the pictures out and stick them on the wall of our bedroom. I used to make believe I was a pilot, but I never in a million years imagined it would become a reality. My dad loved planes as well, you know. He was a carpenter, and he'd make wee model planes for us, my brothers and me...' Silence descended between them as they sipped their drinks.

'Do you remember him well, your father?' Juliet's voice was gentle.

'Aye, I do. I remember him going off down our street and us boys running after him. It was well into the war by that stage, the spring of 1918. He'd been rejected at first because he had flat feet, but by the end they would take anyone. We were so excited we couldn't understand why Mum was crying. I must have been four or five, and I never saw him again. I remember the day the telegram came. Everyone on our street had someone at the front, so when the lad from the post office cycled down the street, everyone just stopped and hoped it wasn't for them.'

Juliet reached over the table and put her hand on his. Their eyes locked, and he smiled. 'I suppose I'd better get you home if I ever want to stand a chance of being allowed to take you out again, hadn't I?'

They walked easily, hand in hand, to the bus stop. As her bus approached, he got on behind her. Surprised she turned around. 'You didn't think I was going to let you see yourself home now, did you? Is that what those Cork boys are like?' he joked as he paid the fare.

She argued half-heartedly, delighted he was escorting her but feeling like she should protest. 'But it's in the opposite direction to your base – how will you get back?'

'Och, don't you worry about me, I'll sort something out. There'll be bound to be one or two of our lorries out and about. I'll jump aboard one of them.'

She sat close to him in the seat of the bus as it made its way through the dark Belfast streets. She wished the journey would never end.

He walked her to the gate and as she turned to say good night, she found herself in his arms. He was so much taller than her she had to crane her neck to see his face. His hands rested gently on her hips, and she could feel his body heat. Instinctively, she wound her arms around his neck.

'Ah, my lovely Juliet,' he whispered in her ear. 'Mr Hitler may have a lot to answer for but if he's the reason I met you, then he's done at least one good thing in his life. Can I see you at the weekend? I'm on call for the next forty-eight hours, so I'm confined to the barracks, unfortunately. The Royal Air Force has no compassion for men who need to see their girls.'

'So am I your girl then?' she asked, the smile on her lips belying the seriousness of the question.

'I hope so. I'd love it if you were,' Ewan replied, all traces of joking gone.

'I'd love it, too.'

At her words, Ewan bent his head, hesitantly at first, and touched her lips lightly with his. Juliet closed her eyes as the sensation sent her senses reeling. The feel of his warm breath on her face as he withdrew to gaze at her was like a drug, drawing her into a world where only they existed. His hand travelled up her spine and rested on the back of her neck while he caressed her cheek with his finger, tracing her jaw and down her throat.

She had never felt desire like this. She wanted him to kiss her, deeply and intimately, and never to stop. She pulled his lips to hers once more, this time with more urgency as she moulded her body to his, hungry to have him. As he kissed her, his lips and tongue gently but insistently exploring her mouth, she was glad of the strength of his arms wrapped tightly around her. Their bodies touched and at every point of contact, she felt fused to him as if they were one. She knew she should pull away, she barely knew him, but she just couldn't. She pressed her body against his causing him to moan with pleasure. On and on they kissed, their hands exploring each other's bodies. Juliet would have happily lain down on the grass in her aunt's front garden and made love with Ewan there and then.

Groaning with frustration, he stopped and pulled away from her. 'Stop...stop. If we don't stop now...' His breathing was ragged.

'Then don't stop,' she whispered.

Just then, the garden was flooded in yellow light as curtains opened upstairs. Auntie Kitty had obviously waited up. Terrified that her aunt would see them, Juliet quickly arranged her blouse, which had come undone when Ewan had put his hand up her back. Embarrassed by her own rush of passion, she mumbled a hurried goodbye and tripped up the path to the front door. She let herself in quickly and glanced in the mirror to make sure she didn't look dishevelled. *Oh God*, she thought, *Ewan must think I'm a wanton hussy.* Then giggled, realising her mind had dredged up an old phrase of Mrs Canty's. Solange's words to her had been very different: *Do not let your education dictate how you live your life, my darling.* Glancing out the window as she went up the stairs, she saw he was still standing outside; his back to the house, looking up and down the road – wondering, no doubt, which direction would give him the best chance of finding a passing RAF vehicle to give him a lift back to base. She crept down the stairs again and silently opened the front door. Walking quietly down the path, she came up behind him and stretching up on her tiptoes, placed her hands over his eyes.

'Good night, Ewan,' she whispered. 'I'd love to see you at the weekend.'

Turning to face her, he beamed with delight. 'Good night, my lovely Juliet. I'll pick you up on Friday at six. Now go home before you get me arrested for indecency.' He kissed her on the cheek and was gone.

CHAPTER 23

*D*ear James,

    I'm promising myself that no matter what this letter is not going in the waste-paper basket like all the ones I've tried to write before. I hate this. We will probably never agree on the subject of Edith, but you are my brother and my best friend, and I'm fed up of us being like this. I never said a word to anyone by the way, not even Solange though she pressed me to, about her or Otto or anything, just in case you thought I might have. So apart from this mention obviously, just to say I don't understand it or approve of it, I do accept that you have a right to do what you want and see whom you want, so I propose that we just stay away from the topic of our mother. What do you think?

My news is that I love Belfast. Auntie Kitty is so kind and welcoming, and her house is beautiful. I have a big room overlooking a really lovely park. It's so strange to be in an Irish city, as we see it anyhow, and yet it's very definitely English. All the talk here is about the war, they are worried they will be a target for Hitler because of all the shipbuilding (maybe I'm not supposed to say this in a letter – this place is full of signs warning people against talking with phrases like 'Loose lips sink ships' and 'Be like Dad, Keep Mum). It's gas. It's just as well we in the Free State are neutral if keeping your mouth shut is vital to win a war. Dunderrig would fare very badly I fear with the amount of wagging tongues down there! So, how are things there? Solange writes every week, but I miss hearing your version of events.

Is Daddy still okay about the art thing or is it a bit awkward? What are you going to do? You know what I think, follow your heart, and he'll see it makes you happy and will come round to the idea. That's all he wants for us though he has a funny way of showing it sometimes.

I do have some more news, but I'm a bit shy of telling you. (I know you're smiling at that idea.) Well, the thing is that I've met someone, a boy, well, a man actually. His name's Ewan McCrae and he's from Scotland and he's twenty-five years old. He has the most lovely accent you ever heard, and he is tall and dark and so good-looking I can hardly believe it, and on top of all that, he's great fun too. Don't worry, he's a perfect gentleman; I'm not falling for some cad, Lord knows I've met enough of them up here, too. Even Auntie Kitty loves him; he fixed a leaky pipe in the bathroom last week so he can do no wrong in her eyes. And you'll never guess what his job is... He's a pilot with the RAF! How exciting! And as if that wasn't enough, he is a twin as well! His brother Dougie is stationed somewhere in England, so we are both separated from our other halves. It's nice to be with someone who understands. I talk about you all the time so he says it feels like he knows you. I really hope you can meet him someday. It feels so odd to have someone who has come to mean a great deal to me in the last few months but you don't know him. We go to the pictures or out for tea, and we go for long walks all around the city. Last Sunday, we climbed up Cave Hill and from the top you can see all over Belfast, on a clear day they say you can see all the way to Scotland. He says that when the war is over, he'll take me there, though to be honest, I don't know if this war is ever going to really start, let alone end.

I wonder if I'll ever bring him to Dunderrig. I've told Solange all about him, and I don't know if she's told Daddy. I doubt it, since he hasn't demanded I re-

turn home. He's bad for writing so he usually just adds a scrawl onto the end of Solange's letter. Do they teach them that in doctor school? There's no way Master Cotter in Dunderrig National School would have allowed that awful handwriting!

I've become good friends with a group of girls that live in digs at the end of our road. They are in the Wrens (Women's Royal Naval Service) and they are great fun. We go to dances sometimes, and Ewan brings his pals from the RAF base and it's wild. I'd love to see you. Do you think you could come for a visit? Auntie Kitty wouldn't mind a bit, her house is enormous.

Write back straight away,

Love,

Juliet.

Dear Juliet,

I was just thinking the same thing. I miss you too. I know you said we shouldn't talk about the Edith situation but I am really confused, and I need to talk to someone about it. I can't tell Dad or Solange obviously so you are the only one I can ask for advice. So can you please try to think of this as a question from a friend where you don't know the families involved? A hard thing to do I know, but try. Dad is silent on the subject of my career. He really wants me to do architecture now or something, but I just want to paint, and

I think he is hoping that if he lets me at it I'll get bored and change my mind. I won't.

Edith and Otto have offered to get me a place at the National College of Art in Dublin and to pay for my tuition and put me up and everything. It's an amazing offer, and it's what I want, more than anything, but if I agree, it means leaving Dunderrig and Dad and Solange and everyone, and I know they'll see it as my having chosen Edith over them. It seems that no matter what I do I'll upset someone. I know you don't want to hear this, but she did have her reasons for leaving and for not contacting us. She explained it to me and if you want, I'll explain it to you, but only if you want to hear it. Please tell me what to do.

This Ewan McCrae had better treat you well, or he'll have me to deal with, you tell him I said that too! Unless he's bigger than me then say nothing ha-ha! Seriously though, I'm glad you're happy. Since we're on the subject, remember I told you about Ingrid? Well, when I knew her before. she was living in London and just visiting Dublin occasionally but now she had to leave England altogether or risk being locked up for the duration as they say, since she's a foreign alien, so Otto brought her over to Dublin. She and I are together now, I can't believe it really, she's amazingly beautiful and confident and everything. I can't really talk to her about this though, she wouldn't understand.

She just thinks I'd be mad not to take Edith up on her offer.

Write back and tell me what to do.

I know you don't like Edith and all that but try to leave your personal feelings out of your decision.

Why don't you come down to Dublin, you don't have to see Edith or Otto but you could meet me and Ingrid. Maybe even bring Ewan? Ingrid can't go to Belfast for the same reason she had to leave England.

Love,

James.

CHAPTER 24

*D*espite the war and the deprivations caused by the ever more stringent rationing, Juliet and Ewan were enjoying being young and in love. Auntie Kitty insisted on paying her grandniece an allowance as her companion, arguing that she would have had to employ someone if Juliet had not arrived. Though Ewan tried to pay for everything, it was lovely to finally feel grown up and independent. She never felt happier in her life. They went to dances, the pictures, and drank endless cups of weak tea in the cafés of the city. Auntie Kitty really liked Ewan and often on a Sunday, if he was off, the three of them went for a stroll in Alexandra Park.

Coming out of central station one evening

after a lovely day trip to the coast, Juliet was chattering happily. Suddenly, she stopped mid-sentence by the scene on the platform. A matronly woman was trying in exasperated tones to organise a group of children who were standing huddled together; some were crying while others were sullen and dry-eyed. Each child had a card around his or her neck with their name on it and a number and each carried a small bag or suitcase. They looked such a sad and lonely collection that Juliet was appalled.

'Who are they?' she whispered to Ewan.

'Refugees – Jews, most likely. Hitler allowed some children out at the start; he's closed the borders now, of course. There's a farm out on the Ards peninsula where they're putting them up, though it's a bit rough and ready by all accounts. Still, a better life here than wherever the poor misfortunes have come from I'd say. Some of the Jewish fellows on our base visit there and help out. We give them whatever we can spare whenever they go.'

Juliet's eyes filled with tears, they looked so sad and alone. 'Do you think it's true, Ewan? What they are saying about how he's treating the Jews? It must be, mustn't it, if people are willing to let their little ones go off to a country miles away where they don't even speak the language. Look at them, some of them are so small and lost-looking.'

They went to a bar beside the station and when they were seated, Juliet was still blazing with anger.

'At least Northern Ireland is accepting refugees. It's as if the south is deaf to what's happening. I can't believe they are so unfeeling. It makes me so angry; I'm ashamed of my government and even of the people. They should speak out. We think of ourselves as kind and generous, but the way we're turning our backs on these people just because they're Jews is disgusting. If Hitler had decided to persecute Catholics, then I bet it would be a different story. I can understand our position on neutrality – I mean, I don't agree with it, but I can see how it would be difficult to ally ourselves with the old enemy and all of that. But these are just people – families, children, for God's sake. Why can't we let them in and protect them until this madness is over?'

Ewan put his arm around her shoulders. 'I know. It's difficult for us to understand too, why Ireland won't help out, but I suppose the scars of the past run deep. England was the enemy for so long and did such awful things that the people just can't consider joining sides with them, I suppose. But you're right about the refugees. They're pouring into London every day with horror stories – why would they make them up? It seems unbelievable to us because we can't imagine having that kind of hatred for anyone, but it would be a mistake to underestimate anything about the Nazis.'

'We have to stop him, don't we? Otherwise, what kind of a world are we facing?' Juliet looked deeply into Ewan's eyes.

He just nodded. 'Juliet, there's something I have to tell you. I was going to wait till tonight, I didn't want to spoil our day out, but anyway, I'm being moved.'

'But what do you mean, moved?' Juliet was stricken.

'I'm being redeployed to RAF Ansty, in Coventry. Now that France has fallen, we are the last man standing. There was no way they were going to leave trained pilots here when we are needed over there. We just go where we're sent and that's that.' Ewan was rueful.

'But what does that mean, redeployed? I mean, are you going for a few weeks or months or forever, what do they mean?' Juliet was trying to hide her distress. Ewan had become so much a part of her life that she just couldn't imagine any other life than the one they shared in Belfast. The sun shone gloriously outside. It should have been a perfect day.

'Juliet,' Ewan held both her hands as they sat in the snug of the cosy pub. He thought his heart would break at the idea of leaving her; she was so young and beautiful, so clever and articulate. Over the last nine months, everything about his life had changed. She wasn't like anyone he'd ever met before. She was outspoken and opinionated and never let him away with anything. Girls back home in Scotland had been interested in him – he and Dougie were known as the terrible twins of Green Street – but until meeting Juliet, he'd never taken any relationship too seriously. This time it was different. He'd never met anyone like her and couldn't bear to let her go.

Yet he'd always known there was no chance he would be left in Belfast now that things were really getting under way. Winston Churchill had announced that the Battle of France was over, and the Battle of Britain was about to begin. In lots of ways, he was dying to go and get stuck in but leaving this girl behind filled him with desolation.

He knew she had no idea of what he did as a

member of the RAF Coastal Command. He had never told her of the missions over the channel and the North Sea, looking for enemy activity. The Battle of the Atlantic had begun on the first day of the war and had continued relentlessly ever since. It was deeply frustrating. Despite their efforts, the U-boats had sunk forty-one ships so far. The equipment they had was simply not good enough. Now he wanted to be someplace, where he could actually make a difference.

His guess was he was going to be redeployed to Bomber Command, running bombing missions deep into German-held Europe. Dougie was already at RAF Ansty, and it would be good to see him again. They had joined up at the same time, but Dougie was less impetuous than his twin and so had been selected as an instructor and moved to the flight training unit at the base. The last time Ewan had seen him, they both had a few days leave at Christmas; he was no longer training regular RAF. In fact, his twin had been very cagey about his recent activities. Ewan knew enough not to ask – clearly, Dougie was involved in something hush-hush.

He suspected that Juliet was only staying in Belfast for him. What had started out as a few weeks' holiday was rapidly becoming a year. He wished there was some way he could bring her with him to England but couldn't see how, even if her father would allow it – which was doubtful based on what he'd heard about him. Anyway, English cities were too dangerous these days. She needed to return to Dunderrig, where she would be safe. He'd thought again and again of proposing to her, yet knew it would be unfair to ask her to wait for him until the war ended. He was realistic about his chances of making it, and it would be a crime for her to waste her youth waiting for a dead man.

He realised he had no choice but to say goodbye.

'You know how I feel about you, don't you?' he began, unsure he would be able to get the words out. 'I love you, Juliet Buckley. I really do, but...'

'But what?' her voice was a whisper.

'I don't know what's going to happen, where I'm being sent or what I'll have to do when I get there. I can't take you with me, and I don't have the right to ask you to wait for me.'

He took a deep breath.

'I'm going to let you go, my darling wee girl. I'm not going to hold you to anything. It's breaking my heart, but it's the best way. Maybe this war will end quickly and if it does, and I'm alive to see it, and you're still free, then I'll come to look for you, I promise, but for now, this is the only way.'

Juliet's green eyes filled with tears despite her efforts to control them. 'I understand why you have to go, especially now, after seeing those children. Someone's got to stand up to him. I wish that someone wasn't you, but women all over the country are probably thinking the same thing. It has to be you, and thousands like you, but I won't pretend I'm not broken-hearted or terrified something will happen to you. I love you, Ewan, and I want to wait for you. Or am I making a fool of myself over an airman who'll find a new girl with every move? Because if that's what this is, I'd rather you told me now.'

His face turned stony, and he stared at her for a long moment.

'How could you say that?' he demanded at last. 'Is that how you really see me? I love you, you stupid girl, I do, more than anything, but Christ only knows what I'm facing now, and I'm scared, all right? There, I've said it. I'm scared I'm going to be blown to bits, but I'll do it anyway. Not because I think I'm some kind of hero, but because I want to defend my country so that we – or maybe not us, maybe we'll be dead – but so people like us can meet and fall in love and get married and live happily ever after in a world where people are allowed to live and love and be whatever religion they want to be.'

He grabbed her by both arms, and she thought for a moment he was going to shake her; she'd never seen him so angry.

'Now, I know you're not going to like this but if I'm to have any chance of concentrating on that job and stopping that bastard Hitler in his tracks, then I don't need to be worried that every bloody Luftwaffe plane has a bomb aboard with your name on it. If you really mean to wait for me, then I want you to go home, to Dunderrig, where you'll be safe. Then if I'm still here when this mayhem is over, and if you still want me, then we'll get married, all right?'

Juliet dissolved into tears and clung to him. The buttons of his tunic stuck into her cheek, but she held him close and cried at the unfairness of it all. He kissed her hair and when her sobs subsided, he wiped her eyes with his thumbs. The gesture reminded Juliet of her father.

'Was that a proposal?' she giggled through the tears. 'Because if it was, then I'd always hoped it would be a bit more romantic.'

'I can see your point. I never imagined that if I

ever got to the point where I'd want to marry someone, I'd ask her by yelling at her. Sorry!' He smiled his crooked smile, the one that always melted her.

'I'll tell you what, Mr McCrae. I will wait for you, but when you come home to me, and I know that you will, safe and sound, how about you ask me properly? Do we have a deal, as the Yanks say?' She was laughing through her tears as she extended her hand to shake on it. He took it and kissed her palm.

'When do you have to go?' she whispered.

'Soon. Tomorrow maybe.'

They held hands in loving, grieving silence.

'THERE IS ONE OTHER thing I need you to do before you go,' she said later as they strolled through the park in the warm sunshine.

'So long as it can be done in the next twenty-four hours then consider it done,' he said. 'Oh hang on, it's not that bloody *21 Days* again, we've seen it four times! I cannae honestly look at Laurence Olivier another time…anything else, I promise!'

'Take me to a hotel,' she said clearly and without any coquettishness.

Ewan stopped and looked quizzically at her.

'What? Why?' Realisation dawning on him, he blinked at her in amazement.

'Don't you want to?' she asked.

'Of course I want to, Jesus, I think of very little else...but Juliet, we aren't married, and we might never see each other again after today... Anything could happen and then you'd be... well...' He couldn't finish.

'All the more reason, surely?' Her voice was steady. 'Look, you might die, I might die, we might find each other again, we might not, but surely what matters is now, right this minute. I love you, you love me, and we want to make love. It would be wrong to part and never do what we've both been craving for months, don't you think?'

'You're serious, aren't you?' He ran his hand through his hair. 'I don't know what to say...'

'How about you and I walk over to the Grand Hotel, arm in arm like an old married couple – I even have a ring, in case they look. James bought it for me for our eighteenth, but if I turn it round, it looks just like a wedding band. Anyway, I'm sure they're used to it by now. The Wrens are forever sloping off to hotels in the afternoons with all sorts.'

They confidently approached the counter together. The fact that they had no luggage seemed not to perturb the receptionist a bit and calling the porter to escort Mr and Mrs McCrae to their room, she bid them a pleasant stay. Hand in hand they followed a balding, slightly stooped man up the stairs.

The porter showed them to the room with a knowing smirk. 'Will Miss, I mean Madam, be requiring anything else?' he sneered suggestively.

Ewan towered over the man, 'No, I think she has everything she needs, isn't that right, darling?'

'Oh, absolutely everything I could possibly want or need,' she replied in a mock sultry voice.

They collapsed on the bed in gales of laughter as soon as the ferrety man left them alone.

Propping himself up one elbow, Ewan gazed down into Juliet's face.

'So, here we are,' he said, running his fingers through her blond hair. 'We don't have to do anything if you don't want to.' He was unusually hesitant.

'Have you done this before?' Juliet asked.

Ewan smiled guiltily.

'Yes, a few times. I'm older than you, remember? But never with anyone I loved before now and that's the God's honest truth.'

She remembered Solange's advice to be with

someone experienced the first time, and she was glad. She wondered if she'd tell Solange about this – she probably would, but definitely in French. Imagine if Mrs Canty read the letter. The idea made her laugh.

'What's so funny?' he asked.

She told him about Solange and her advice, and he seemed relieved that she wasn't flying in the face of all that she believed.

'If I don't come back for you, I'll have to come back to meet this Solange. She sounds like one of a kind.'

They began kissing, and she surprised herself by how bold she had become. She unbuttoned his shirt and ran her hands over his tightly muscled torso. She had felt his skin before but never seen him naked and the sight of his broad smooth chest aroused her. Despite the throbbing longing in her own body, she wanted to enjoy him before he undressed her, so she could give her full attention to his perfect body. She kissed his chest and gently sucked and bit his nipples while he moaned in pleasure. She raked her nails gently on his skin, and she felt him shudder. Every time he made to remove her blouse or unbutton her skirt, she moved his hands away whispering, 'Later.' She removed his shoes and socks and glanced upwards to see him staring intensely at her as she undressed him. His dark blue eyes were fixed on her as she ran her hands up his long, muscled legs. She could see the shape of his erection through his clothes and her heart thumped with longing and anticipation as she opened his trousers. She heard him take a sharp intake of breath as her hand brushed against him. When he was naked, she sat back and just looked at him. She wanted to remember this image of him, knowing it would have to sustain her in the stretching emptiness of months, years, without him – maybe forever.

Unable to remain passive any longer, Ewan took her in his arms and undressed her quickly, his urgency taking over. She clung to him, digging her nails into his back as she felt him enter her body. She felt a little pain but only for a second, and then waves of pleasure building – building to a crashing orgasm. She moaned and wrapped her arms and legs around his body as they rocked together, clinging to each other, whispering each other's names over and over.

CHAPTER 25

'Solange, Dad, Mrs Canty, this is Ingrid!'

Solange embraced Ingrid warmly, and Richard shook his son's girlfriend's hand. 'You are very welcome to Dunderrig, Ingrid. I hope you enjoy your visit.'

Mrs Canty was effusive, delighted to meet the mysterious Ingrid at last. 'Well, you are very welcome, so you are. We've put you in the green room, James did the painting over the bed and there's a lovely view over the harbour. Though 'tis the guest room, James and Juliet used to sit in the window when they were children watching for ships. And you brought the fine weather with you; if only ye could have brought Juliet too then

314

everything would be grand.' Mrs Canty's eyes welled up at the mention of Juliet's name.

Ingrid looked a little overwhelmed at Mrs Canty's emotional outburst.

'Don't mind me, Ingrid love, I'm just a mad old woman, but we haven't seen her in so long. I get desperate lonely for her then, sure what she's doing up in that place and them bloody Leftwaffles blowing them to bits whenever the notion takes them. Sure, we are demented with worry over her, still, Dr Richard is right, and he says bad news travels faster than good news, so we'd have heard if anything happened to her, but what in the name of God she's doing up there at all I just don't know.'

At the mention of the Luftwaffe, or the 'Leftwaffles' as Mrs Canty called them, James glanced at Solange. The last thing they needed was an anti-German diatribe from Mrs Canty. James had explained the situation to Ingrid that no one in Dunderrig had the faintest idea that he was back in touch with Edith, and certainly nobody knew anything about Otto. Ingrid suggested at first that it might be better to tell the truth, but James had argued that it wasn't that simple. He had to decide about his future first and then he would sit them down, if that was what was called for, and tell them the whole story.

'So Ingrid, James tells us your family are still in Germany? You must be worried,' Solange said kindly as they ate lunch.

'Yes, my father is in business and my mother is dead. My brother, he is seventeen, lives with him near Frankfurt, in a town called Bernkastel Keus on the Mozelle River. It is very beautiful there. Many vineyards, good for Riesling, I don't know what is the English word for this.'

'I think it's just *Riesling*,' Solange answered. 'I remember when I first came here, I tried very hard to think of the English words for *encore* or *finesse* only to realise that this is the same word from French. Your English is very good, Ingrid, though I don't suppose English is being taught in school in Germany these days? When I was a girl, all the German holidaymakers to Brittany could speak so many languages we were amazed, but I think Hitler has put a stop to that.'

Ingrid smiled but carried on as if Solange had not spoken.

'James and I are lucky, I think, to both grow up in beautiful places. I am so excited to explore this area, especially the ocean. I live far from the ocean so always I like just to look at it.'

Solange and Richard exchanged glances. They had both noticed that Ingrid chose to ignore the fact that her country was occupying most of Europe and at war with the rest of it. Her tone, while friendly, indicated that she had no wish to discuss anything to do with Hitler. James had warned them in advance that Ingrid said she found the subject boring and would rather talk about almost anything else; he personally took her at her word and avoided the subject altogether.

This self-assured girl was very beautiful and certainly had James enthralled. He was gazing adoringly at her as she spoke and never lost an opportunity to touch her, leading her to the table, passing her bowls of food. Solange hoped she would be gentle with him; he'd never been in love before and without the watchful eye of his savvier sister, she feared he risked being made a fool of.

EARLY THE NEXT MORNING, James was loading the picnic basket into his father's Wolseley. 'Mrs Canty, there are only two of us, and it's just a day trip. I think you've packed enough food to feed the whole village,' James was protesting good-naturedly.

'Sure, the weight is mostly the booze herself is

after putting in,' Mrs Canty said, nodding in Solange's direction. 'I told her that ye young people had no interest in her fancy French vinegar, but she said it's roman-teak if you don't mind!'

Solange threw her eyes to heaven at Mrs Canty's good-humoured teasing. They had become very firm friends over the years.

Ingrid emerged from the house out onto the gravelled driveway. She looked stunning, her hair plaited down her back. Her olive skin radiated health against the white of her sundress. Solange recognised her as a girl who put a lot of effort into looking naturally beautiful.

'James! Oh how wonderful, you are so, so, kind. A picnic is just the perfect thing! Can we go to the beach? I have brought my costume.' She indicated the white tote bag slung easily over her shoulder.

Mrs Canty and Solange both noticed James's look of embarrassment at the mention of swimming costumes and grinned.

'Mrs Canty got it all ready, I didn't do much,' James said, anxious that Ingrid should like and appreciate the old housekeeper.

'Then, *Frau* Canty, as we say in Germany, *Herzlichen dank*!' And with that she kissed Mrs Canty

soundly on both cheeks. '*Auf wiedersein,* Solange!
Auf Wiedersein, Frau Canty!'

James held the door open for her, and she got
into the front seat.

'We won't be late back, thanks for the picnic
and the wine,' he winked at Solange.

Richard opened the window of his surgery
and called out, 'Be careful and take it slowly,
those roads are very dangerous out towards
Barleycove. And don't drink too much of that
wine!'

'Don't worry,' James called back. 'I'll be very
careful. Thanks for the loan of the car; I'll bring it
back in one piece.'

'Try to bring the two of yourselves back in
one piece while you're at it,' Richard called after
him drily before closing the window to the
laughter of those outside.

Richard Buckley still wasn't very happy about
the fact that his son didn't seem to want to go to
college or pursue a proper career but – presumably at Solange's suggestion – he was keeping his
opinions to himself. James had spent the past year
painting, in between travelling up to Dublin to
visit Ingrid. Even his father had admitted the
work he was producing was very good. After his
son's miserable time at the university in Cork,

Richard clearly found it a relief to have the old, happy James back again.

JAMES CLOSED HIS EYES and listened to the sounds of the waves crashing and the seagulls arguing as he lay on the beach beside Ingrid. She had changed into her bathing costume, a black and cream one-piece that accentuated her perfect body. Most other women on the beach wore skirts and blouses, so Ingrid was drawing a lot of attention. He would have loved to sit behind her and have her lean back against him, but the beach was full of families and it wouldn't do to have the doctor's son behaving improperly in public with a young lady, particularly one dressed so provocatively. In private, he'd held her hand and kissed her, but he was too shy to go further. He knew if Juliet was around, she'd have quizzed him about that side of things, but he was so mad about Ingrid that he was happy to take things slowly. She seemed to really like him, though she was better travelled and more sophisticated than he was.

She'd had many boyfriends before they'd met – both Otto and Edith had mentioned it – and he was not surprised, given how beautiful she was. In fact, Otto had chuckled how Ingrid was her own woman and had never seen the need to limit herself to one male companion at a time. Mrs Canty might have called that wanton behaviour, but he wanted everyone in Dunderrig to like her so much that he kept some aspects of her life secret. Like the number of her friends, and how a lot of them were boys. And the fact that she, like Otto and Edith, thought Hitler was doing a good job.

Ingrid didn't like to talk about the war he'd discovered, not because she was ashamed of her country's treatment of other nations but because she didn't feel it needed defending. Mind you, Dev was doing a good job at keeping Ireland out of the war so far, and maybe Ingrid had a point about the British. They hadn't treated the Irish very humanely during their occupation so perhaps it was time to stop them. What Germany was doing to Poland and France and all the other countries was only what England had done all over the world itself. He knew Solange saw it very differently, but then she would – being French and having been so involved the last time. And his father just ranted about how all war, no matter what it was for, was immoral and wrong.

The full realisation of Ingrid's attitude had only come to him a few weeks earlier when one night after a dinner in Dublin where she and his mother had giggled like schoolgirls about a very good-looking German politician, he had asked her how she really felt about the war.

'I don't feel anything about it really, except that I wish we'd hurry up and win so things can go back to normal. I like Ireland, of course, and I even liked England, but I want to be able to go home whenever I want. I know National Socialism is painted to be a terrible thing over here, and certainly in England, but it's because people don't really understand it. Hitler just wants a strong Germany, and just as a good gardener has to cull some plants so that the strong ones survive and bear good fruit, so does he have to cull some undesirables. It's not personal, I don't think, but as my father says, who is the villain is decided by the one telling the story. If you are a farmer, the fox is bad. If you are a wildlife enthusiast, the fox is a beautiful creature. So, it depends.'

'But the bombing of all those cities in England, and just marching in and taking over countries just because you are militarily stronger, you can't agree with that, surely?' James didn't want to push her away but his conscience needed to understand. It would be nice just to accept it and see things as she did, but he just couldn't. 'I mean, my sister is in Belfast and a German bomber could drop his explosives on her and kill her any day – how can that be right?'

'Yes James, and also my brother could be going over the bridge in Bernkastel-Kues one day and a British bomb land on him. That's not right either, but in order for the world to progress and improve, then changes have to be made and sometimes, at times of great change, bad things happen. It's a fact of life.'

She made it all sound so logical and simple.

'Besides,' she added, 'England is not the poor innocent little country you seem to think it is. Look at how they treated your country not so very long ago. I'm surprised the Irish have not joined us to rid the world of British Imperialism once and for all. Anyway, what will happen will happen, and there is nothing, my darling James, we can do about it, so let's forget the topic.'

Since then, he had realised that if he wanted Ingrid in his life then he would have to accept that she held pro-Nazi views – even if he wasn't at all convinced she was right. *Stop worrying about it all*, he admonished himself. *Here you are on the beach with a beautiful girl who seems to like you and all you can do is think about politics.* He dragged himself back to the present. Fearing she could read his thoughts, he decided to lighten the mood.

'What's Germany like? Is it like here?' he asked.

'Well, it's bigger than Ireland, much bigger, so there are lots of different regions. Where I live, there are lots of vineyards and castles, and in other parts, lots of forests, and then there are the mountains – so yes, lots of different landscapes. But the people are very similar. Germans are a bit more direct that you Irish, sometimes you are all so full of wit and chat that it is difficult to know what is true and what is not. That doesn't happen in Germany, but the people are welcoming and friendly, just like here. I think you would like it there; there are lots of beautiful landscapes to paint and draw.'

James smiled and then sighed at the delicious prospect of a life spent painting.

Ingrid said calmly, 'The only one stopping you following your dreams is yourself. You know that, do you not?'

She knew of his dilemma but failed to see why it was such a problem.

'I know you say it's not that simple, but I think it is. Just tell your father that you have met your mother and you want to build a relationship with her, so you are going to spend some time with her and Otto in Dublin and accept their offer to put you through art college. It's not like you are asking *him* to spend time with his ex-wife.'

'But that's half the problem, Ingrid,' James explained, 'she isn't his ex-wife. Such a term doesn't exist in this country. She *is* his wife. I know they haven't seen each other in years and years, but it doesn't make them unmarried. How is he – and Solange for that matter – going to react to me bringing her back into their lives?'

He drew in the sand with a short stick he'd found while they talked.

'Well, I do not see what on earth this has to do with Solange. She is your nanny, yes? Then she stayed on to help your father with his practice once you and Juliet had grown up. She is staff, why does what she thinks about it matter in the least?'

The way Ingrid was so black and white about issues sometimes took James by surprise. It must be that German directness she spoke of.

'Well, yes, technically that's true, but Solange means so much more to us than that. She has been like a mother to me and Juliet all our lives. It does matter what she thinks, very much.' James spoke quietly. If he and Ingrid were to have a future together then it was vital she understood how much Dunderrig and everyone in it meant to him.

'But Edith is your mother and she dotes on you. When you go back to Cork after a visit, she is so sad, and she talks about you all the time. It's "James said this" or "James likes that". Even before she was reunited with you, when I met her first, in Germany, she talked about you. It is not as if you will have no family if your father and Solange disapprove of your plan. You will have Edith and Uncle Otto. He is very well-connected, you know. He doesn't let on, but everyone knows him and he is, as you have probably gathered, extremely wealthy. He adores Edith and could never refuse her anything. When they used to come to visit us when I was a girl, he would bring me the most amazing gifts, and Edith was always dressed in the best *couture*. Why, even when he was in Berlin over Christmas, he brought her the most exquisite diamond necklace. If you lived with them, you would want for nothing.'

'Otto went back to Berlin at Christmas? He told me he's not been back since before the war. I thought he was restricted from travel.' James was confused. Otto was a most affable and easygoing man, and he didn't understand why he would lie like that.

'Oh, maybe not Berlin, on business, anyway, I'm not sure where.' Ingrid was dismissive.

'But where could he have gone if not to Germany? He can't go to England and everywhere else is occupied, so it would be difficult to obtain the necessary papers even if you were a German citizen. What business is he in, anyway? I've asked him a few times, but he always says import and export and then gets distracted.'

'Uncle Otto?' Ingrid acted perplexed, then vague. 'I think he's something to do with the trade office or something like that. He had large premises in Frankfurt and another in Heidelberg, I do know that. Oh James, you really must see Heidelberg, it is like a fairytale land. Especially at Christmas, there are skating rinks and *gluhwein* stalls and a huge *schloss*... What is the English word...castle, yes, a castle at the end of the main street. It really is magical.'

Noting she had changed the subject once again, but unwilling to dampen the mood, James decided to leave it.

'It sounds beautiful. Maybe we'll go there together when this is all over.' He swept a strand of her hair from her face and tucked it behind her ear.

She smiled and said, 'Maybe. But now I want to swim! Are you coming?' She jumped up and brushed the sand from her long tanned legs. Running down the beach, she called back to him, 'Come on, James, I thought you Irish boys were supposed to be fit.'

Laughing, she allowed him to catch her and hand in hand they ran into the crashing surf.

CHAPTER 26

The Battle of Britain raged with the RAF suffering horrific losses. Despite that, Churchill assured his people that they were winning. Juliet listened frantically to the news and devoured newspapers because all she could think about was Ewan and the danger he was facing. Last night, she had listened to Churchill's speech crackling over the BBC, explaining just how valiantly the RAF was fighting. She and Kitty had tears in their eyes as they heard his gravelly voice.

THE GRATITUDE of every home in our Island, in our Empire, and indeed throughout the world, except in the abodes of the guilty, goes out to the British airmen who, undaunted by odds, unwearied in their constant challenge and mortal danger, are turning the tide of the World War by their prowess and by their devotion. Never in the field of human conflict was so much owed by so many to so few. All hearts go out to the fighter pilots, whose brilliant actions we see with our own eyes day after day, but we must never forget that all the time, night after night, month after month, our bomber squadrons travel far into Germany, find their targets in the darkness by the highest navigational skill, aim their attacks, often under the heaviest fire, often with serious loss, with deliberate, careful discrimination, and inflict shattering blows upon the whole of the technical and war-making structure of the Nazi power. On no part of the Royal Air Force does the weight of the war fall more heavily than on the daylight bombers, who will play an invaluable part in the case of invasion and whose unflinching zeal has been necessary in the meanwhile on numerous occasions to restrain.

SHE FELT terror and pride in equal measure. Maureen and the others insisted she go out after the speech. They all had friends, boyfriends and brothers in the services too, and they knew what it was like. She didn't feel like going, but Maureen had given her a stern pep talk when she called to Kitty's door to find her in her old skirt and no makeup.

'He's fighting for you, for all of us to have good, normal lives. What's it all for if Hitler is going to make us hide under the bed in fear? Or sit at home crying over our boys. If your Brylcreem boy can be as brave as that, surely he'd want you to go on living. Now then, Paddy, pop your frock and lippy on and let's have some fun!'

Despite her worry, she actually enjoyed the night. They were approached by a group of soldiers, who did their best to chat them up. One of them, a boy with red hair who was very drunk, had been making lewd gestures at women as they walked past on the way to the ladies. Deciding Juliet was tonight's lucky girl, he approached their table. Pushing in to sit beside her, though there really wasn't room, he began by telling her that he was, in fact, French, and so lonely that she would be doing both her country and his great service by allowing him to take her home. Juliet was used to being the object of young squaddies' attention and usually dismissed them gently but firmly, but this one seemed so cocksure of himself she thought she might take him down a peg or two. Winking at her friends, she spoke enthusiastically to him.

'Oh, you're French, are you? I love the French. Especially their language, it's so romantic,' she said, fluttering her eyelashes theatrically.

'Oh yes, I mean wee, wee, mon French ay trez bon,' he said with a flourish, in horribly accented French.

'Oh, your accent is gorgeous. Say something else, I could listen to it all night,' she breathed seductively. The girls were, by now, struggling to remain serious.

'Voullay voo aller to, eh eh, to mon mayson? Voo ay...' Gestures took over as he indicated what exact moves he planned if she agreed to accompany him. He was revelling in the jeers and applause from his comrades at the bar. Cheekily, he put his hand on her leg.

The girls at the table giggled, knowing that Juliet was only playing with him like a cat plays with a mouse, but he was beginning to think his luck was in.

'Jer m'apple Joe,' he said, elaborately pointing at his chest for further clarification of his identity. 'That means my name is Joe.' He brought his mouth to her ear. 'I can teach you some more

French back at mine if you want.' And he flicked her earlobe with his tongue.

Enough was enough. Juliet stood up and lowered her face to inches from his. In a voice loud enough for the entire pub to hear, she let rip, '*Généralement, les gens qui savent peu parlent beaucoup, et les gens qui savent beaucoup, parlent peu. Vous, monsieur, vous parlez beaucoup. A cet égard, je voudrais vous assurer Monsieur, que vous me dégoutez. Il est bien clair que vous êtes bête comme vos pieds, vous êtes un imbécile. Ecoutez-moi bien, je ne sortirai jamais avec un homme de votre espèce, je préfère mourir!*'

Everyone stared at this beautiful blonde girl with the flashing green eyes pouring forth in flawless French. Smiling sweetly at his dumbfounded expression, she then slowly emptied what was left of his beer over his head. As the amber liquid dripped from his hair, nose and chin onto his uniform, the girls and squaddies alike descended into fits of hysterics. Nodding her acceptance at their raucous applause, Juliet stood up and walked to the ladies.

THREE DAYS AFTER THE events in the pub, a man appeared unexpectedly at Auntie Kitty's house asking if Juliet was interested in a possible job with the Home Office. He said his name was Mr Jones, and he was very vague about why he'd called to her at home to offer her employment. She got the impression the job was a clerical one since he asked her if she could type or take shorthand. Though she had learned at school, she had never paid much attention to it, so she told him she had a little experience but not enough to be of any use. He said she'd soon pick it up. Over a cup of tea in Auntie Kitty's front room, he asked about her background and seemed very interested to know she came from Dunderrig and that her father was the local doctor who had been decorated in the last war. He was even interested to hear about Solange and how she had taught Juliet her perfect French.

After that preliminary conversation, he had asked her to present herself at an address in the city centre for further discussions on the subject of her possible employment. Writing down the date and time of her interview, he left.

So here she was. A woman seated at a desk surrounded by panels of opaque glass had checked her name against a list. Gazing impassively at her through horn-rimmed spectacles, she had asked her to take a seat.

While she waited, Juliet reread the latest letter from Solange.

Ma chère Juliet,

I am going to write in English because even though I speak this language every day now, still I cannot write it so very well so please, I must practice on you. Of course, when we speak, it will always be in French!

I am so sad to hear about Ewan being posted to England, but in a war, nobody's life is his own. Soldiers must do what they are told and go where they are instructed to go. I do not show your letters to anyone else and nobody opens my post but me, so it is quite safe for you to write what you wish, especially in French. I am glad that you have no regrets, that you took my advice, I think I understand what it is that you mean.

So what now, my darling? Will you come home to us? We miss you so much.

James is at home for a few weeks and his girlfriend Ingrid is visiting. She is very pretty and she is German. We do not hold that against her though. Well, perhaps a little (just joking) but this mess is not her fault. Mrs Canty calls her In-gridge; it reminds me of all the years she called me So-long! She seems nice, and James is very in love with her (I don't think that is right – very in love?) anyway he loves her. I don't know how she feels about him; she is very independent and seems to be the commander of that relationship. I hope she doesn't break his heart. She doesn't speak very much about herself. Her father is in business in Germany, but she doesn't say anything about the war or anything like that. I do like her, I think.

Your Papa is well, very busy as usual. I told him he should take a holiday. Maybe go to Belfast to see you, but he says he has nobody to take over the surgery. He would love so much to see you though, he really does miss you so much. It has been a whole year since you were home. You know he is not good at saying how he feels, but he does tell me how lonely Dunderrig is without you. James is in Dublin a lot these days, more now that he is seeing Ingrid. I'm not sure how they met, through an old school friend, I think. He said he was hoping you might travel down to Dublin to meet them soon. If so, perhaps I could convince your father to make the trip too, and we could all meet up. I am going to visit my friend (I can see your face – yes, that friend!) next week, but that will just be for a day or two. I am celebrating my birthday there; imagine, I am an old lady now, forty-eight years old!

Mrs Canty is here in the kitchen as I write, and she says to tell you to be sure to eat properly and don't be coming home 'like a pull through for a rifle'. I don't know what that is, but I am being dictated to here. I think she means don't get too thin.

I won't say do not worry about Ewan, or that I am sure nothing bad will happen to him. I am not at all

*sure of that, and I have never lied to you, my sweet
Juliet. I will pray to God, if there is a God, I am not
sure of that either, that he will be safe, and he will return to you. But in the meantime, carpe diem, my love.
Do not stop your life, live it.*

Goodbye for now, my brave sweet girl,
I love you,
Solange.

Juliet folded the letter and placed it in her bag
as she sat and waited on the long wooden bench.
There were three doors on the corridor, each
with opaque glass panels so it was impossible to
tell what was going on inside. From the outside, it
had looked like every other office building. There
had been an old brass plaque on the wall, tar-
nished with age, saying Bell & Co. Eventually, she
looked up as a middle-aged woman addressed her
in clipped tones, 'Miss Juliet Buckley?'

The woman was dressed in a grey suit and indicated Juliet should follow her. Walking obedi-
ently behind her through the maze of corridors,
she noted how nondescript everything was, including her guide. They passed down a flight of
stairs and along several identical hallways – all
painted in a dull beige colour – before eventually
stopping at a door exactly like all the rest. The
woman opened the door to reveal a sparsely dec-

orated office, which smelled musty. Dust mites danced in the shaft of sunlight that came in through the high windows. The floor was covered in brown linoleum, and the walls were painted the same beige as the rest of the building. There was nothing on the walls and no furniture except for a large battered desk with a utilitarian chair on either side.

'Please take a seat.' She spoke briskly, indicating the smaller of the two chairs. 'Someone will be with you shortly.'

While Juliet waited, she considered that perhaps she was making a huge mistake. The more she thought about the manner in which she had been approached, the more suspicious it seemed. The whole thing was most peculiar. Still, she was intrigued, and it was something to do. Perhaps, joining up in some capacity – even as a clerical worker in an office – might help to pass the days. If she was honest, her main motivation was finding a way of feeling close to Ewan. At least if they were both in the services, then maybe there was a chance that they could meet up, somewhere, sometime. A foolish hope probably. There were millions of servicemen and women all over the world hoping the same thing, and she doubted very much that the British Military took

romance into the equation when arranging post-
ings. Still, it was a preferable option to returning
to Dunderrig and waiting for God knows how
long. At least here, she felt part of it, as if she and
Ewan were on the same side.

If she went home, she didn't know how she
would cope with listening to how wonderful Dev
was for keeping Ireland neutral. She doubted if
she could keep her opinions to herself.

'Ah, Miss Buckley, thank you for coming. I
trust you found us easily enough?' The small ro-
tund man with a florid complexion moved with
surprising speed across the room and eagerly
pumped her hand. His tweed suit was tight on his
shoulders and his shoes clicked peculiarly.

'Em, yes, thank you,' Juliet stammered. She
had been so deep in thought that his arrival had
caught her off guard. She didn't know what she
had expected, but it certainly wasn't this. He was
almost entirely bald except for a rim of brown
hair that circled his head, rather like a monk. As
he sat opposite her, her eyes were drawn to the
vivid mustard colour of his shirt and his red
check tie. *This man has no wife,* she decided. *No
woman would let her husband out dressed so oddly.*

'Shall we begin?' he asked brightly, and
without giving her a chance to reply, he contin-

ued, 'You are from Southern Ireland, I take it? Yes. Cork? Yes. Fine. And at what standard would you say you speak French?'

His pale grey eyes penetrated hers. His face was strangely still despite the rather frantic pace of his delivery. He really was most disconcerting. Surely he knew the answers to all of these questions already. She'd told Mr Jones everything when he came to Auntie Kitty's house.

'I think I'm fluent, though I've never actually been to France.' She knew her tone was a little resentful. She was not at all sure that she wanted to go into any more detail with him. She didn't even know his name, yet he just rattled off questions to her as if he had an absolute right to know everything about her.

'Fluent. Hmm. We shall see.' Scribbling on a notepad, he went on. 'Your father is Dr Richard Buckley of the Royal Army Medical Corps, decorated for his services in the last war, is that correct?'

'Yes. My father served in France as a doctor.' Juliet answered as shortly as she dared. Though this man looked rather comedic, there was something deadly serious about him. It was an odd combination, and it made her feel very uncomfortable. He stopped writing and scrutinised her.

She was used to the admiring glances of men but this was different, it was as if he were assessing her, judging. His gaze was neither appreciative nor lewd – he was simply gathering information.

She had used precious ration coupons to buy Miners liquid foundation, her lips were reddened by cochineal from the larder, as lipstick was almost impossible to get, and she had learned from the Wrens how to make mascara from burned coke. Rationing had made the women of Belfast very resourceful. The result was striking, and she knew it. Her blond hair was neatly pinned back from her face with tendrils of curls escaping from her French plait. Her outfit, a bottle-green skirt and jacket with a buttermilk blouse beneath, was an old one of Auntie Kitty's, which she had shortened and adjusted using a *Vogue* pattern. It was an aspect of war that caused Juliet great joy that hemlines were getting shorter and clothes getting more figure-hugging. It was, of course, because of the severe shortage of virtually everything, but she loved experimenting with fashion, and the wartime deprivations made almost everything acceptable.

'And your mother? Is she Irish also?' the man continued, having fully appraised her face and figure.

'Yes, she is. We are estranged, however.' Juliet didn't want to discuss Edith with anyone, least of all this peculiar man.

'Ah, yes. She is remarried in Dublin, I understand?'

Juliet was nonplussed. How on earth did he know that? 'Yes. I believe so.'

'Now, you were reared by your father and a French woman. Please tell me about her.' Again, he fixed her with the bland stare and the soulless grey eyes.

'My father's friend's widow, Solange Allingham, was left homeless and without a family after the last war. My father offered her a home with us. She was our nanny, my brother's and mine, but she was, is, more than that. She is more like our mother.'

'And where in France is she from?' Returning to his scribbled notes.

'Amiens. She lived in the city and worked as a nurse in the *Hôpital Saint Germain*. As did my father and Solange's late husband, Jeremy.'

'And it was from her that you learned to speak French?'

'Yes. Solange always spoke to my brother and me in French, since we were babies.'

Changing the subject he went on, 'And you

had a relationship with a member of the RAF, a Flight Lieutenant Ewan McCrae, which is now ended?'

'He's been posted elsewhere, but we hope to marry when the war is over.' The pain of Ewan's departure was still raw.

'Really? I see.' His tone indicated that such an outcome was unlikely to say the least. 'How do your family feel about you living here in Belfast? Would they not rather you were safe in Southern Ireland?'

Juliet bristled. It was the way he said the word 'safe' as if the Irish were in some way shirking their responsibility.

'I am staying with my elderly aunt as her companion. They are happy someone is taking care of her.'

'And how do they feel about the war effort? About you offering your services, should you be deemed acceptable.'

The tone was pleasant enough, but Juliet could feel the familiar temper rising up within her. Who did this man think he was? Summoning her here without a word of explanation and then asking her questions about her family, about Edith and Ewan? How dare he?

'Well, to the best of my knowledge I have *not*

offered my services,' she said frostily. 'I am an Irish citizen, and we are a neutral country, so I think you are getting ahead of yourself if I may say so. I have not agreed to help you in any capacity. So whether you deem me *acceptable* or not at this juncture is beside the point.'

She removed her gloves from her bag and began to put them on. She wasn't going to listen to this for another minute. She had not felt the same indignation since she was at school, being interrogated by the nuns for playing jazz music on the school piano. She was an adult and in no way answerable to this insufferable little man, who didn't even have the decency to introduce himself properly or explain what on earth she was doing here.

Standing up to leave, she said, 'I don't feel there is anything further to discuss. Good day to you.'

The man seemed unperturbed and remained seated. Sitting back in his chair, he ran his hand over his shiny bald head. Eventually, as she reached for the door handle, he spoke.

'Please forgive me if my questions seem intrusive, Miss Buckley, but it is vital that we know all about you if you are to be offered a position with us. The fact that you came here today suggests you do have an interest in joining the war effort and if that has changed, then I'm sorry to have wasted your time.'

She waited, still with her hand on the door.

He went on. 'However, I suspect you have a unique set of skills that, with the appropriate training, may make your contribution to the defeat of Hitler very important indeed. If you would like to hear more, please have a seat.'

Juliet's mind was racing. Her anger subsided and was replaced with curiosity.

'What do you mean by a unique set of skills? I don't have any qualifications.'

'Not traditional skills, that is true. Simply put, Miss Buckley, Mr Churchill has instructed a specific department within the defence forces to, shall we say, use slightly more creative methods of gaining the upper hand over the enemy. I'm afraid I can't be more specific than that at this stage but suffice to say you might just be the sort of thing he had in mind. Your ability to converse fluently in French could be very useful, and I suspect that you can do that.' Gone was all trace of the efficient arrogance. 'Britain is facing an occupied continent. Despite the success of our military response, there is a very real danger of occupation on the island itself, possibly even here in Ireland. With that in mind, it is imperative that we do everything possible to disrupt Hitler's plans. In order to do that effectively, we must know what those plans are. That's how I imagine you come in.'

He stopped and waited for her reaction.

Juliet struggled to process what he was telling her. Long seconds passed.

'You want me to be a spy?'

Smiling a genuine smile for the first time since they'd met, the man sat back in his chair and said, 'Precisely.'

CHAPTER 27

*J*ames sat quietly at the dinner party. His mother had gone to such trouble to organise an elegant and elaborate dinner to celebrate his and Ingrid's return from West Cork, but the food tasted like sawdust, and he felt wretched. No one would have guessed from the light-hearted chat and clinking of glasses going on around him that these were Germans, at war with the entire world. Fortunately, most of the animated banter was in German, a language of which he had no knowledge – at least that meant he wasn't expected to join in.

Ingrid was sitting across from him, deep in conversation with Francis Stuart, the Irish writer who seemed to travel to and from Germany with impunity. James had been baffled at how all those in his mother's circle seemed to be able to travel effortlessly when such restrictions were in place but when he'd questioned her, she had simply shrugged and said if one had the right connections than anything was possible.

At intervals, loud guffaws of laughter emanated from the other side of the long dining table. Ingrid was flirting outrageously with Stuart and James's heart wrenched. He was old enough to be her father. Stuart's wife, Iseult Gonne, seated at the end, seemed oblivious to her husband's rakish behaviour. There was something otherworldly about her. James had been mesmerised by the ethereal Iseult when he first met her and as he looked at her now, she seemed a million miles away from the dining room. James had read that Isuelt had been conceived in the mausoleum of her dead little brother. Maud Gonne, Iseult's mother, was the muse of Yeats who had died in France in 1939, and apparently the poet had proposed to both mother and daughter. He remembered Mrs Canty saying how all those gentry Protestants had a bit of a want in them, too closely bred in her opinion. He smiled at the thought of the old housekeeper, and it struck James once more how strange life was.

He'd read Yeats at school and now here he was having dinner with some of his closest associates.

When Edith first reappeared in his life, he had been impressed by her cosmopolitan circle of friends and associates. She knew a lot of people in Dublin's artistic scene, from writers to poets and painters. Some contacts were her father's but many more were Otto's, which James found perplexing. How would a German businessman have such a varied circle of influential friends?

Since then, the war had started, and now he felt less and less comfortable socialising so often with the German community. He just couldn't reconcile the situation in his own conscience. Often he'd heard some of Edith's friends complain how the Gardaí were taking an undue interest in their activities, and while the assembled company always shared their sense of outrage, James himself kept quiet. If they were doing nothing wrong, then surely the Irish police wouldn't be bothering them.

At the beginning, before the war, though of course there were rumours about the Jews, he'd believed Edith and Otto when they'd claimed it was all just Allied propaganda; but increasingly the facts couldn't be ignored. Thousands of refugees were flooding into London, many more trying to get to America or Australia – anywhere to escape the Nazis. It couldn't be propaganda – why would people flee like that, break up families, leave their homes and businesses without a very good reason? No, the longer it went on, the more evidence there was that Hitler was a despicable man and that his Nazi followers were no better. The world was facing real evil and James found sitting in his mother's house, listening to these smug Germans laughing at the rest of them, sickening. They were residents in a neutral country and entitled to say what they liked, but James just didn't want to listen to it anymore.

He knew if he raised the issue of the progress of war at home, his father would defend de Valera's position on neutrality, agreeing with the Taoiseach that remaining neutral was the best way to show our independence. In principal, James thought so too, but still, when he heard about all those Jewish people fleeing with their families from this malevolent regime... Well, it was disturbing.

He loved Ingrid and his mother, but he wished he didn't have to be part of their world in order to be close to them. It was sometimes exciting to meet these well-known people, but when they talked like this, laughing so loudly and acting as if they hadn't a care in the world, James wished fervently that he was back in Dunderrig drinking *chocolat chaud* beside the range in the kitchen with Solange, his father, and Mrs Canty. He fought the urge to stand up and ask them straight out why Hitler was treating the people of Europe with such cruelty. Why did they support a man who seemed to want to have his own way, no matter what the consequences, destroying anyone or anything that came in his path? Did they really believe that one person was worth less than another? Yet he knew that to do so would effectively end his relationship with Ingrid – these were her people after all, and she would probably never forgive him.

A loud booming voice was holding court at the top of the table. Helmut Clissman was regaling Otto, Edith, and Dr Hempel, the German ambassador to Ireland, with a story of their latest intake of students. James had met Helmut and his wife Elizabeth several times over the past two years as they were a regular feature of evenings at his mother's house. Edith and Elizabeth, both Irish women married to Germans, had a lot in common and were good friends. Helmut ran an educational exchange programme between Ireland and Germany, and it was by using these connections that Otto was able to secure Ingrid's papers for residence in Ireland. Ostensibly she was a student, though James had yet to see her attend a class. Her English was virtually perfect, anyway, so she didn't need tuition. She'd told him yesterday, on the train up from Cork, that she was going to take up a position next week working for Helmut in his school. James was glad because it would give her something to do. At least if she were busy working, he could return to Dunderrig and not spend every waking moment worried that she was being swept off her feet by some artist or writer.

He longed to be at home, painting the landscape of the ever-changing colours. He had two sets of equipment, one here in Dublin, the finest money could buy, given to him as gifts by his mother. He regularly went to the Phoenix Park or St Stephen's Green and set up his easel, but his passion was for the wild countryside around Skibbereen.

At home, his paints and brushes were old and well-used, built up over the years. There was the easel he'd received as a gift from Solange for his tenth birthday, the brushes he'd got when he went to secondary school, and paints bought one at a time because of the cost from the art supply shop in Cork. His oils were decanted into old medicine bottles, and he often wore a misshapen garment that Juliet had stitched long ago in her domestic economy class. It had been meant to be a fashionable dress, but since she was terrible at sewing, it served as a huge and shapeless smock and was perfect to wear to save his clothes. It struck him that this was representative of his whole life – the Dublin part, all shiny and expensive and glamorous; the Dunderrig part, old and a bit worn but deeply loved and cherished.

Dublin was fine, but a lot of the gloss had gone from the early days. His heart was in Dunderrig, always would be. Ingrid had teased him, asking how he was going to become famous if he spent all his time in West Cork and she was right, he supposed. Dublin was where it was all happening. His mother knew everyone in the art scene, and he knew he needed to be part of it. He was so torn. He loved Dunderrig and everyone in it, but he really burned to be an artist, and increasingly, he couldn't bear to be away from Ingrid. It wasn't that he didn't trust her; it was just that she was so beautiful and confident that she attracted men effortlessly. The same rules didn't seem to apply to her group of friends. He regularly had to hide his disapproval when she told him of their promiscuous antics. In so many ways, this life would suit Juliet so much better than him. She always longed for excitement, meeting new people, experiencing new things. The irony of the situation was not lost on him that Edith may have chosen to favour the wrong twin.

'James, darling?' Edith's voice interrupted his thoughts.

'Sorry...pardon?' James stuttered.

'Dr Hempel was asking you a question, dear.'

James turned to face the man sitting beside him. His well-built physique belied his age. He must have been in his fifties, but he looked a decade younger. His downturned eyes and wide smile gave him a benign appearance. It was hard to believe that he was an employee of the Third Reich, Hitler's man in Dublin. When he'd been introduced earlier as the German ambassador, James had felt very uneasy. Though his father obviously knew nothing about his Dublin life, James knew he would be horrified to discover his son happily eating dinner with anyone so closely associated with Hitler and the Nazis. They had been welcoming to Ingrid, seeing her as an innocent bystander in a war not of her making, but James knew if they realised her connections and, vicariously, his, they would be appalled.

'Please don't worry, James.' Eduard Hempel spoke in accented English. 'You must be tired after the long journey. I was simply asking how the weather had been for your holiday.'

'Fine. Thank you. Then West Cork is always beautiful at any time of year.' He realised he sounded belligerent but, inexplicably, he felt he needed to defend his home.

'Of course.' Dr Hempel smiled. 'I hope to make a visit there. I enjoy sea angling, and I hear there are wonderful opportunities down there.'

James said nothing and continued to eat his dinner. He knew he was being rude and this man was pleasant and polite, but he could feel his father's disapproval even though he was two hundred miles away. When his mother had raised the subject of the ambassador's attendance earlier that evening, she'd explained that Otto was very closely connected to the embassy through business and it was very helpful to him to be on cordial terms with the ambassador. Edith seemed to be delighting in her high society connections. It was an aspect of his mother he didn't really like. Richard treated everyone equally and saw no difference between the widow with seven children, barely surviving, and the landed gentry. He'd instilled that in his children, so James was unsettled by his mother's constant name-dropping and social climbing.

When the evening finally ended and the last guest was waved off, Otto announced he was going to bed. Ingrid had gone into town to meet a few friends but James had declined to accompany her, knowing he would have to endure more of the same: men monopolising her, tripping over each other to buy her drinks. For once, he just hadn't the energy. When they'd been in Dunderrig, it had been wonderful. She was fascinated by the sea because she had been brought up inland. They brought picnics to all the little coves and inlets along the rugged West Cork coast. Sometimes they found little deserted beaches, and he knew that if he'd pushed it, she would have let him make love to her. He wanted to, badly, but he knew that if she was going to consider him as her future husband, which he really hoped she would, he would have to show her that he was not like all the others, who only had one thing on their minds. He respected her and would wait until they were married.

Making for the stairs to go to bed, he heard his mother call him into the sitting room. Wearily he responded, wishing for nothing more than a long sleep in his big cosy bed.

'James, darling, sit with me. Would you like a nightcap?' Edith was pouring a small whiskey into a crystal tumbler.

'No, thanks. I'm exhausted. I think I'll just go up if you don't mind.'

'It's so busy here all the time with people coming and going constantly. I feel like we never just get time to talk, you and I. Please sit with me, just for a few minutes? I want to talk to you about something.'

Resigned, James sat on the gold-upholstered wingback chair beside the fire. His mother sat on the identical one, the other side of the hearth. The lights were low and the embers of the fire glowed. Though it was summertime, the evenings were chilly and a fire was always lit in the sitting room.

'You seemed upset tonight, my dear. Is anything bothering you?' she began.

'No...well, yes I suppose, there is.' James needed to talk to someone. Once, Juliet would have been there to help him but in this instance, he was on his own. The frustration that had been building all night burst free from him.

'It's just, I hate knowing those people, sitting around eating and talking as if we're friends. They're not my friends, and I'm ashamed that I even know them. What Hitler and the Nazis are doing to the people of the occupied countries is wrong – I know it, they know it, everyone knows it. Not to mention the Jews. Is he insane? But still, you and your friends sit there and laugh and joke and drink wine as if Germany wasn't behaving in the most appalling way imaginable, as if destroying lives was nothing. I hate it, I really do, and I don't think I can keep going with it. On top of that, I hate living this lie, not telling Dad and Solange where I am and what I'm doing up here. I've changed. I never used to be like this, telling lies and pretending to be someone I'm not. I don't like myself anymore. Dad and Solange would be disgusted if they thought that I was wining and dining with the likes of the Clissmans or Hempel, and they'd be right.' James stopped, registering his mother's stricken face. He felt so guilty about what he'd said, though it was true, all she'd ever been was generous and supportive. Edith composed herself and spoke quietly and with absolute conviction.

'James. You are young and when we are young, everything seems so clear-cut, so absolute. You've lived such a sheltered life down there in Dunderrig. You are sorry for the Jews, but have you ever even met a Jew? What Hitler is doing might seem harsh, and sometimes the methods used to clean up German society could seem a bit unfeeling, but trust me, the world will be a better place for everyone if he is supported. The Jews are a drain on any society – they think only of themselves and if you really understood how things were in Europe, you'd know that if you look at the heart of most European problems, you will find there the Jews. They are not like us, darling. They just aren't, it's as simple as that. Please don't throw away your future for the sake of a race of people you have never met who care nothing for you. You were always too sensitive, even as a little boy. You don't see Juliet getting all upset over the fate of the Jews, do you? Or your father, or Solange? And your dreams, your art? Are you willing to walk away from all the opportunities we are offering you simply because you don't approve of our friends?' Edith spoke calmly, totally recovered from her son's outburst.

'I don't want to. I really don't. But I just can't see how...' James struggled to find the right words.

'You only have one life, James. Who knows what the future holds for any of us? You are, of course, entitled to your opinion on the war. There are two sides to everything, and you are an intelligent and compassionate young man, I wouldn't dream of trying to influence you. I simply wanted to offer you the chance to do something wonderful, something few people get the chance to do, to follow what is in their hearts. You must make decisions that make you happy, not anyone else. I could have stayed in Dunderrig, with your father, and been miserable; but I didn't, I left and found a better life for myself. The choice is yours entirely.'

It struck James how like Ingrid his mother was. Like her, she saw the whole thing only in black and white. *If you want something then just take it. Don't consider the impact your decisions have on anyone else.* It was so different to the ideals with which he'd been brought up. He loved Edith but sometimes he found her attitudes too hard-line.

'Good night,' he said, getting up to go to bed and wishing for the hundredth time that night that he was at home in Dunderrig. He kissed her proffered cheek. As he went out of the door, his mother spoke again.

'Oh, James, another thing. Ingrid is a lovely girl. You should do everything you can to keep her. She's been brought up differently to you, I should imagine. The Germans are much more open than we Irish are, more free in lots of ways, so don't let your old-fashioned ideas about things stop you having what you want. She won't see it like you do.'

James walked slowly up the stairs. Surely Ingrid had not discussed their relationship with his mother. Yet Edith seemed to be referring to the physical side of things... No, he thought, he must be overtired and reading too much into things as usual.

THE NEXT FEW DAYS, James spent quietly painting. He had considered returning to Dunderrig, confessing everything to his father and breaking all contact with Edith but to do so would also mean leaving Ingrid. She was busy with Helmut Clissman and his school, so they only saw each other in the evenings. Instead, he poured his turmoil and frustration onto the canvas. He was developing a unique style; his work was flourishing. Canvasses piled up in his room at various stages of development.

The work he produced in Dunderrig was different in style as well as in subject from his Dublin art. James knew that how he felt at the time of painting had a significant effect on the finished piece, so he was interested to see how each painting emerged. He'd been prolific in the past month, producing several sketches and watercolours as well as one small oil. He loved how he could submerge himself in the work, nothing infiltrating his mind but the paint and the effects he could create. As he sat on his stool in his sunny bedroom, putting the finishing touches to a painting of the gates of Dublin Zoo, a gift for Solange's birthday, he felt hands cover his eyes.

'Guess who?' whispered Ingrid's voice in his ear.

'Would it happen to be the most beautiful girl on earth?' he asked, turning around to face her.

'Exactly,' she laughed. 'How did you know? Or perhaps, you say that to all the girls.'

'No, and you well know I don't.' James was serious now. 'You are my girl, and I only have eyes for you. I'd never look at anyone else.'

'I know that, silly boy.' She smiled, kissing him.

She stood by the open window. It was unseasonably hot for late September.

'The city is so sticky; I wish we could go back to Dunderrig. I bet it is still warm enough to swim in the sea.'

This was music to James's ears.

'You really want to? I'd love to go home for a bit. If you're serious, we could go tomorrow.' He was trying to keep the excitement out of his voice. Juliet had written, telling him how worried she was about Ewan and for some reason that she wouldn't go into, she said she couldn't come to Dublin to visit him at the moment. He suspected that she still hadn't forgiven him for maintaining contact with Edith; maybe she was afraid it was a trap to get them together. He must write and explain he had no such intentions. He'd not seen her in over a year, and he missed her terribly. He'd thought about going up to visit her, but he didn't want to leave Ingrid and she couldn't enter the United Kingdom. She frequently wrote to him now, addressing the letters to Dunderrig, but it wasn't the same.

'Yes, let's just go. You could paint, I could just read and relax and be your inspiration,' she chuckled.

'What about your job? Won't Helmut be annoyed if you just take off? You've only just started.'

She shrugged. 'He won't mind. The students have all arrived for this term already, and they're settled in. Most of the work is done for now, so he'll be happy for me to take a break.'

'I've been thinking the last few days it's time to tell my family, about Dublin and Edith and everything. This constant lying has to stop. I want to be honest with them, with Juliet, with everyone.'

'You really are unusual, James Buckley – you know that, don't you?'

She sat astride his lap looking into his face. Her fingers played with his hair at the nape of his neck. The sensation sent shivers down his spine. He could feel his body reacting to her, and he wrapped his arms tighter around her.

'All the other boys are all charm and flattery, but you are different. Good, I suppose. Honest. I like that about you.'

She nuzzled his neck, kissing and nibbling his earlobe. How easy it would be just to go ahead, to make love to her, here in his room. Otto and Edith were out; they had the house to themselves. Ingrid put her hands inside his new paint-spattered shirt and traced the muscles on his back and chest.

Standing up, she put her hand out to him, an enquiring look on her face. James so desperately wanted her, but everything he had been taught crowded into his mind. It was wrong, nice boys didn't do that, nice girls certainly didn't – sex was for the procreation of children within the confines of marriage.

'Ingrid. You know how much I want to, I really do, but we mustn't, not until we're married, it would ruin everything. I love you, more than any girl I've ever met, and I want to marry you. Will you?'

Ingrid sighed in frustration. 'James, there's no need. You know what I want. You don't have to propose to me. I'm so tired of waiting, always we go so far and then you say no. What is wrong with you? I thought you said I was beautiful...' Ingrid pouted.

'You are. Incredibly so. Don't you want to marry me?' James was quiet. He'd expected his proposal to be greeted with more enthusiasm.

'Sometime, of course, maybe, but not now.' Her voice became pleading. 'Now we are young, and you are so handsome, and I just want to go to bed with you. Is that so awful?'

'Do you love me?' James asked. He regularly told her that he loved her and while she often repeated it in a joking way, and was forever telling him how attractive he was, she'd never looked him in the eye when they were alone and said, from her own heart, that she loved him. Now he felt it was time for honesty in every aspect of his life.

'Yes, James. Of course, I love you. You are so

old-fashioned; I love that about you, that you're such a gentleman. But in this instance, I just want you to go with your instincts. I can't believe I have to talk you into this. Lots of men would jump at the chance, but you're supposed to be my boyfriend, and it seems it's the furthest thing from your mind!'

She lit a cigarette and gazed out the window. Even with her standing with her back to him, he could sense her frustration. Her slim silhouette was framed in the big bay window; her hair fell down her back, sleek and silky. It was now or never, he realised. Edith was right – Ingrid was brought up differently from him. It wasn't that he couldn't ignore the teachings of the Church and the brothers who'd taught him for so long that sex before marriage was wrong on every level. It was more that he was afraid. What if they made love and then she decided she'd had enough? He couldn't bear to lose her. If they went to bed to-gether, it had to mean more than just the physical act. Yet he feared that if he tried to explain how he felt, she wouldn't understand.

Walking up behind her, he put his arms around her and kissed her neck. 'I want you to be my wife, Ingrid,' he whispered. 'I know we're both young and there are so many things we need to sort out but let's make a pact, you and I, that when the time is right, we'll get married.'

'Does this mean...?' He could sense her body relaxing and the playful tone had reappeared in her voice.

'Yes.' James's voice was husky with desire. He unbuttoned her cotton top and removed it to reveal her golden skin. Picking her up easily in his arms, James carried her to the bed, where he removed her skirt and underwear. He'd never seen a naked woman before in real life and the sight of her body took his breath away. He quickly removed his own clothes.

'You are beautiful,' she whispered to him.

Her choice of words made him smile.

'I know,' she smiled back, 'that beautiful is for women, but it is what you are, strong and golden and...' She giggled, running her hands over his chest. 'Like a Greek god.'

They made love all afternoon until neither of them had an ounce of energy left.

'You're incredible,' he said. 'I never knew women could enjoy it the same way men do.' Feeling a little foolish at his admission, he blushed. She stretched luxuriously, like a cat.

'I never have done. It was never like this with anyone else.' Her voice was sleepy.

He should have known that he wasn't the first man she had slept with, yet her easy admission filled him with pain. She must know she was the first for him. How many had there been for her?

Trying to hide his dread at the answer, he asked, 'So, is this what you usually do on a Saturday afternoon?'

She leaned over him and kissed him on the nose playfully. 'My darling James, I won't lie to you. You are not the first man I've been with, but Germany is not like Ireland. For Irish girls, to sleep with someone before they get married is a terrible shame, I know that, though I don't understand it. You are very special to me, and I want to be with you, only you. So you must trust me now. I am your girl and that is all there is to it. Now, let's get up, maybe we're not too late for dinner. I'm starving.'

He knew he would have to be happy with that explanation. Ingrid had a definite way of closing down conversations and that was as much as he was going to get.

'Let's go down and see what we can find in the kitchen. Edith and Otto are still out.'

'No, they are here. I heard them come in about an hour ago. I think you were busy at the time, so you must not have heard the door close.' She chuckled.

Panic gripped James. If they were back, they must know that he and Ingrid were upstairs, together. Remembering his mother's advice however, he wondered if they did know and chose to ignore it. The thought of sitting down to dinner with them, everyone knowing how he and Ingrid had spent the afternoon, was less than appealing.

'Let's go out instead,' he suggested. 'Let's just go and get fish and chips and sit in Stephen's Green. It's still warm enough.'

Ingrid smiled, knowing why James wanted to leave the house. 'Very well, lover boy, let's go.'

CHAPTER 28

*A*fter the strange meeting with the man in the mismatched clothes who'd eventually introduced himself as Mr Bell, Juliet lay in bed wide awake, wracked with indecision. The prospect of joining up had crossed her mind in recent months, especially since she began her relationship with Ewan and made friends with Maureen and the others, but she knew how her father would feel about it, so she'd always dismissed it. If she had decided to get involved, she had envisaged herself as a driver or a secretary with the Wrens, or in her more passionate moments as some kind of assistant on an RAF base, preferably, in her fantasies, the one where Ewan was stationed.

But a spy...spying was the stuff of novels and films, not something real people did – especially not real young girls from West Cork. It was preposterous for lots of reasons. Yet the prospect of doing something to help, refused to be dispelled. She had twenty-four hours to make up her mind.

Mr Bell had stipulated that no matter how difficult the decision, she could discuss it with no one. There was no one in Belfast she wished to discuss it with, anyway. Auntie Kitty would be horrified, and her girlfriends were too busy with their work and boyfriends to worry too much about 'Paddy' as they called her. Though they were friends socially, she, as a civilian, was in many ways outside of their circle. They did find her non-involvement in the war effort a bit mysterious and once or twice she'd overheard some anti-Southern sentiment from others in the group, but she'd chosen to ignore it. They just didn't seem to understand that Ireland, the Free State, was a separate country in the same way France or China was, and not involved in their war. She sometimes tried to explain, but her arguments fell on deaf ears.

If she were honest, she thought Ireland should pitch in – not for reasons of loyalty to Britain, God no, in spite of Britain, if anything. It was about seeing the World War in a broader perspective, putting aside individual arguments in the face of the greater good. She just thought that Hitler and the Nazis were a new and all-pervasive kind of evil, and that they would have to be stopped. She wondered if the Irish really believed that if England was invaded, Germany would stop there and leave Ireland alone. Anyone who thought that, was, in her opinion, very naïve indeed. After all, what was Ireland if not an easy back door into Britain? One that Hitler would not hesitate to use should the need arise. The notion that he would respect Ireland's neutrality was preposterous. Just look at how he'd behaved so far. The defeat of Hitler was as important for Ireland as for England if the Irish wanted to retain the hard-won peace they now enjoyed.

It would have been much harder for her to keep her own counsel if she'd been in Dunderrig – she would have been so tempted to ask Solange what to do. Or James, her usual sounding board, although he was so caught up in his romance these days, he was probably in Dublin. She knew exactly what her father would say, of course. If he knew she was even considering joining the war effort, she would be on the next train back home.

If she said yes, however, she would have to tell

her family something because, if she agreed, she was to be sent to England for preliminary training. The details of what she would be trained in were frustratingly sketchy, nor was she advised how she might explain her move from Belfast. She was simply to decide if she was in or out. Mr Bell had given her the impression that, while she might have fluent French, they were by no means desperate to have her. Even if she agreed to embark on a training course for subversive agents, acceptance was by no means guaranteed. In fact, he told her, far more potential agents were rejected than progressed through the system. She left the meeting feeling like they, and she was by no means sure who 'they' even were, were ambivalent at best about her decision.

In the end, she came to her decision at the last possible moment. The wind was biting as she worked her way down James Street towards the nondescript building once more. It was a week to Christmas and the shops were doing their best to provide some warmth and good cheer despite the rationing. Presents were being discouraged and those with any spare money were being urged to invest in war bonds, to raise funds for the war effort. The BBC had announced there was to be an address from the ruins of Coventry Cathedral, which had been all but destroyed when that city was flattened a few weeks previously. The images of burnt homes and businesses, shattered lives, haunted her. Each day, she read about the damage done to English cities and the countless thousands dead or injured. Coventry had affected her more deeply than any other bombing. At the time, Juliet had felt so worried and afraid for Ewan's safety, knowing he was stationed near there. She remembered now the overwhelming feeling of helplessness. He'd written to her after the Battle of Britain in October, so she knew he'd survived, but still every day brought new waves of worry. Letters were usually so censored it was difficult to make sense of what he was telling her, but she could understand the most important bits. That he loved her and was counting the days until they'd be together again.

The headline outside the newsagents read: 'We are not victims. We will fight back.'

She decided there and then that she too would be part of that fight. She wanted to stop those people in English cities being killed in their beds, she wanted those bewildered little children she saw on the railway platform returned to their parents, she wanted to make sure no Nazi flags ever flew in Dunderrig. But above all, she wanted Ewan home safely.

Mr Bell was in the room waiting when she arrived.

'Ah, Miss Buckley, thank you for coming.' The same detached tone and peculiar outfit. He stopped writing and looked enquiringly at her.

'I'll do it,' Juliet said, feeling quite calm.

'Good. Yes, good.' His voice betrayed no emotion. 'Here are your tickets, a passport, and directions to where you will begin your training. You leave on January thirtieth at...' he leafed through the sheaf of papers, '...ah yes. Here we are, leaving Belfast Central on the earliest train. All the details are there. You will be met at Wanborough and driven to your final destination. Please do not discuss your plans with anyone or ask anyone's advice while travelling. Good luck, Miss Buckley. We shan't meet again.'

He stood up, handed her the bulky envelope and with a gesture of his arm indicated she should leave.

'What should I tell my family, my aunt here in Belfast?' she asked, utterly panicked. How had they known she would agree? He couldn't just give her a passport and tickets and send her off without any further explanation or discussion. She had so many questions.

He seemed nonplussed.

'I'm sure you'll know best. I suggest you stick close to the truth. Say you've joined up and you are being sent to England for training, but please remember what I said. It is of vital importance that no one is told of your specific plans. Perhaps discontinuing your relationship with your RAF man would be a good idea. Fewer explanations needed, perhaps?' he added, as if speaking to a small child. 'Now, if you'll excuse me, I have another appointment.'

Christmas passed uneventfully. She wrote to a disappointed Solange and her father to say she wouldn't be home for Christmas as with the fuel shortages it was impossible to get train tickets. The truth of the matter was that if she went back to Dunderrig, she wouldn't be able to keep her future plans secret.

At least James was going home, and bringing Ingrid once more. These days the pair seemed to spend their time equally between Dublin and Dunderrig. She knew James was now selling enough paintings to support himself, and that her father had become not only resigned to his son's career but was actually rather proud of the fact that James was already making a name for himself. He'd even hung the painting James had given him of Galley Head in his surgery.

Juliet had not seen Solange or her father since the summer of 1939, and as 1941 loomed without any indication the war was coming to a close she wondered when, or if, she'd ever see them again. She was lonely for them, but the fear that she wouldn't be able to leave them again had stopped her from going home up to now. And now it was too risky. Solange would guess her plans, she knew she would, and the prospect of being kept safe in Dunderrig filled her with dread. So she wrote and explained that, as well as the fuel crisis, Auntie Kitty really did need full-time care now.

It was true that the old lady had fallen on some ice in November and had twisted her ankle badly. Her mobility was, as a result, very restricted. Juliet filled her days taking care of her aunt, shopping, queuing up for miniscule rations, and keeping the house in order. Kitty was very glad of the company; if Juliet hadn't been there, she often said, she would have to go into an old folks' home. Hopefully, she would be mobile again by the end of January. Juliet felt terrible for planning to leave her aunt, especially as Kitty had been so kind to her, but she had to go. The destruction the Germans were wreaking nightly in England made her blood boil. How dare they just destroy people like that? The reports brought by refugees from the Nazi terror were blood-curdling. She thought every day of Ewan. Anything she could do to end this horrible bloody war sooner and to get Ewan home safely, she would do it.

Her letter to him was difficult. Mr Bell had suggested she break off the romance to avoid awkward questions but that wasn't going to happen. Instead, she made a vague reference to having taken a secretarial post with the Home Office and made sure the rest of her letter was full of life and love. It had been weeks since his last communication but often his letters got delayed and arrived in batches. She tried not to fear the worst. She knew he had left her address with his mother, with instructions to let Juliet know if the unthinkable happened. So, no news was surely good news.

She wished she could have gone down to Dublin to see James. Her last letter to him contained the same story she had given Daddy and Solange, but she hated lying to her brother more than to anyone else. Throughout their lives, they told each other the truth, no matter what. This was the first lie she'd ever told him, and she hated it. They had patched things up as much as they could by letter, but the Edith situation was always there, unmentioned but looming. He seemed really happy with his life and mad about this Ingrid. She wondered what the girl was like. Solange seemed a little unsure of her, reading between the lines. Perhaps that's just because she feared for James's heart. James admitted to her that Ingrid was Otto's niece; no one in Dunderrig knew anything about Edith or Otto, so there, she was just a friend of a friend. Poor Daddy and Solange did not deserve all these lies. She worried about what would happen when James did confess that Edith was back in his life. She knew that the longer he left it, the worse it would be, but she also knew why he didn't want to say anything.

The thought of leaving Ireland without saying a proper goodbye to James was horrible. What if she was killed, and they never saw each other again? She longed to confide in him, but she was certain he would try to talk her out of it; he might even break their golden rule and tell Daddy, so she couldn't risk it.

She had never discussed her brother's relationship with their birth mother and her new husband when she was being questioned about her family by Mr Jones or Mr Bell. She felt it had nothing to do with her. They never asked her either. If they had done their homework as thoroughly as they seemed to have done, then they already knew that James spent time with Edith and Otto and had a relationship with Otto's niece. If they knew that, they must also know that she had nothing to do with any of them, which was just as well for her. If she had been in any sort of regular contact with a German citizen – even one as benign as Otto appeared to be – she was sure they would never have recruited her. She knew that the fact she was from Eire – as the British called it – was already enough of a question mark over her loyalty as far as the powers-that-be were concerned.

Not knowing how long she was going to be away, she told her aunt – now back on her feet – that she was going down to Dublin to see James, and then to Dunderrig to see her father and Solange. By the time her subterfuge was discovered, she would be in England, out of their anxious reach.

'BIENVENUE, MADEMOISELLE GALLIARD – VENEZ avec moi.'

Juliet made her way up the large curved staircase of Wanborough Manor. The trip over from

Belfast had been choppy, and the endless train journey from Liverpool to Surrey had left her feeling a hundred years old. She longed for a long soak and a good night's sleep.

When the taxi had dropped her at the door of this huge, sprawling house, she was sure there'd been a mistake. This vast stone edifice, with wings stretching off to either side of the main part of the building, looked more like a country house than a military base. She hadn't known what to expect, but it certainly wasn't this.

The enormity of what possibly lay ahead struck her as she walked down the ornately-decorated corridor. She had to put it to the back of her mind and take it one step at a time. Her shoes were silent on the deep-pile scarlet carpet, and the view of the sweeping driveway from the huge windows was obscured by the gold velvet drapes, held back by heavily tasselled swags. Alabaster busts and dark, brooding oil paintings lined the walls. She felt intimidated and very much out of place. She wanted to run home and tell Solange everything, but she stiffened her resolve. She was just at the preliminary stage, she told herself. They might deem her unsuitable and throw her out after a week and then she'd have made a big fuss over nothing.

The house, unlike the one in Belfast, was a hive of activity with people walking purposefully up and down stairs, and in and out of the many doors leading off the corridors. Juliet doubted if she would ever get the hang of how to find her way around. The whole house was a warren. The woman walking briskly ahead of her made no further effort to communicate until, after ushering Juliet into a room on the first floor, she instructed her, again in French, to wait.

The room was carpeted and had a large leather couch, a sideboard, and some easy chairs. There were dark patches on the walls where some of the paintings were now gone – she presumed in storage. This was clearly the house of an earl or a lord or something like that. He must have given it up for use by the defence forces. Rather incongruous with the other sumptuous furnishings, there was a plain wooden desk and some functional office chairs between the two windows which overlooked the lawn outside, looking totally out of place in what was a beautiful drawing room. Far off in the distance, telephones rang, car doors slammed and conversations were had, though it was impossible to make out the words spoken. She felt nervous about her French. Solange had always assured her that her French was perfect, but she'd never spoken to anyone else in that language. She couldn't stand the nun at school who got cross with her for not being able to explain the *passé composé*. Sister Xavier had nearly had a fit when Juliet had refused to learn French grammar – she spoke perfectly already, she'd explained to the nun. Juliet smiled at the memory. That stunt had earned her Saturday evening detention for a month for insubordination.

A woman in her forties entered the room and greeted Juliet with a smile. Asking her to sit, she explained the rules of the house. She was at no time to communicate in any language other than French, whoever spoke to her. Nor was she to reveal anything about her life before coming here, nor was she to ask any such questions of her fellow students or instructors. For the purposes of this training, she was to be known as 'Marine' and would respond only to that name. Instruction would begin at eight in the morning and would take place every day. She had from now until then to rest and prepare. Her room was on the top floor second last on the left, number 131. Dinner was served in the dining room at seven.

She missed dinner due to exhaustion but was wide awake at five the next morning. After a solitary breakfast – the dining room was empty so she helped herself – she stood in the large hallway of the house along with several more people whom she assumed were new recruits like her. She tried to catch the eye of one of the other girls – there were only three altogether, among about fifteen men – but nobody seemed to want to make eye contact or any effort to communicate.

'Right, you lot. Let's get started.' A man with a broad Yorkshire accent emerged from a room to the right of the front door and addressed them loudly in English. The French rule only applied to the students it seemed. 'Now then. 'Ow many of you 'ave ever fired a gun before?'

The uniformed officer, who Juliet judged to be in his fifties, had a florid complexion hidden for the most part by a huge moustache; his uniform with rows of glistening medals and gold braiding, combined with his huge physique made him a formidable character.

One or two of the men raised their hands, and Juliet did too. She was a good enough shot after years of shooting rabbits in Dunderrig with Eddie. In fact, she was a better shot than James.

Looking at her with a smirk and a raised

bushy eyebrow, the Yorkshire man said, "Appen we shall soon see, shan't we?'

They were led to a barn, which had been converted into a shooting gallery. She was chosen first, and the rest of the class waited while she was given a pair of earmuffs and a rifle by a younger officer. She was glad it wasn't a handgun as she'd never fired one of those. The cut-out figure of a man, already riddled with holes, was placed at the other end of the barn.

'*Quelle partie du corps?*' she asked.

The younger officer looked at her quizzically and said in a Cockney accent, 'Let's just see if you can 'it him at all first, shall we? We'll worry about the logistics of anatomy later.'

Juliet stood squarely and took aim as Eddie had taught her since she was seven years old. Taking a deep breath, she focused on her target. Eddie used to say: 'Breathe in deeply, draw a line between your eye and the target, let out the breath, and fire along that line.' It worked almost every time on the lightning-quick rabbits of Dunderrig. Surely, it would do the same on a static target. Juliet exhaled and squeezed the trigger. The recoil wasn't as severe as the old service rifle at home. She saw with relief that she'd hit the target directly in the heart.

'All right, duck,' the officer was clearly taken aback. "Appen you can shoot right enough. Now aim for 'is 'ead.'

Juliet repeated the motion and shot the target in the middle of the forehead. She returned to her class and noted their looks of admiration. That was one test over with anyhow.

They spent the rest of the day learning about different weapons – how to assemble and disassemble them quickly and how to clean them 'without shooting yer bloody toes off'. No contact was made between any of the students, each focused on the task at hand. Juliet was, along with one of the men, the only student that could shoot with accuracy.

They were taught the two-shot rule, which meant that while they were not to waste ammunition nor draw attention to themselves with excessive gunshot noise, they should always shoot their victim twice. Even if they were sure he or she was dead. The second shot breaks the nervous system down completely. The sudden realisation that they were being taught these skills to use on real people was sobering.

'Ow d'ya learn that then?' the Cockney officer asked her as he fell into step beside her on the walk back to the manor.

'Oh, we live in the country, in West Cork, and when I was younger, the man who looks after the grounds, Eddie, used to let my brother and me shoot rabbits.' She was glad to have someone to talk to. Instead of responding, he simply looked at her, and she realised she'd broken the first rule. She'd spoken in English, and she had just revealed her entire family situation. As she sat down to dinner in the large dining room, having washed up, a young woman touched her elbow and asked her to follow her. The other students glanced at her but continued eating and making polite meaningless conversation in French. Juliet walked down the warren of corridors behind the woman. She stopped at a large oak-panelled door, knocked and walked away.

'*Entrez.*' A male voice came from within. Juliet opened the door meekly. An attractive older man in a tweed suit with swept-back grey hair sat at a desk, writing.

'*Asseyez-vous.*'

Juliet did as she was told, her heart thumping. This was so much worse than being called to Sister Gertrude's office at school. He was writing something and only looked up briefly.

'*Je vous remercie pour le temps que vous avez con-sacré à cette formation. On n'a plus besoin de vos ser-*

vices. Un taxi vous attend devant pour aller à la gare. Bonne soirée, Mademoiselle.' Without waiting for a reaction, he returned to his document.

This couldn't be happening. It was only the first day.

'*Monsieur, tout d'abord, j'ai commis une grave erreur et je m'en excuse. Je comprends bien qu'il est interdit de parler en anglais et de révéler des renseignements personnels. Je n'ai pas réalisé les conséquences de mes actes et je vous implore de me laisser rester ici.'*

He stopped writing and sat back in the chair examining her. His craggy face was impassive. She knew he was the officer in charge though he wasn't in uniform, but none of the normal rules seemed to apply here. He stared at her for a long time before he eventually spoke.

'*Convainquez-moi.'*

His voice was quiet, his eyes never moving from hers. Juliet was unsure if he was just a lecherous old man or if it was a test; either way, she was probably being sent home, so it was worth a shot. She returned his stare and allowed a small smile to play on her lips. She stood up and walked as seductively as she could to the grand piano, which sat in the large bay window of the room. Lifting the lid, she was relieved it wasn't locked –

that would have made her look simply foolish. Sitting on the stool, she ran her fingers expertly over the ivory keys.

The opening notes of the famous French folk song '*Les Temps Des Cerises*' filled the empty space in the room. Juliet began to sing in a deep, husky voice. She noted the slight look of surprise on his face. She knew her singing voice was nothing like her speaking one. In fact, she had been asked to leave the school choir because the nun who taught singing didn't approve of her low alto. Throughout the song, she maintained eye contact with him, the playful smile never leaving her lips. As she struck the last note, she simply sat, awaiting judgement, though she tried to suffuse her being with stillness. She knew instinctively that shows of hysteria or begging to be allowed to stay would achieve nothing.

'*Tout á fait charmant, Mademoiselle*,' he said eventually as the last note hung in the air. His words were complimentary but his expression remained impassive. Juliet was unsure whether he really found her charming or just a foolish girl making a last ditch effort to be forgiven. She sat at the piano, determined not to speak, waiting for him to pass judgement.

'*Bon. Ma décision est prise. Vous avez de la chance.*

Vous pouvez rester, mais attention, Mademoiselle, je ne supporterai plus ce genre de transgression. Ce sera tout.'

She heard the tone of dismissal in his tone. Hiding her relief, she got up to leave.

'*Merci.'*

Back at the dinner table, she joined in the light conversation of her fellow students. They discussed the weather and the latest films but nothing of any significance. She noticed variations in their French accents but since she was only familiar with one dialect, that of Amiens, she could not have placed them. She realised that her narrow experience of France would surely be a tremendous disadvantage and resolved there and then to work hard to overcome it.

The weeks flew by in a blur of daily classes. The students rose at seven each morning and spent until six in the evening learning things Juliet never could have imagined herself doing. The instructors did not mince their words when it came to the more gruesome aspects of the course.

Lieutenant Llewellyn from Cardiff had been most specific as he demonstrated a double-edged knife. 'The knife is a silent and deadly weapon that is easily concealed and against which, in the hands of an expert, there is no sure defence, except firearms or running like hell. Here you will learn how to hold a knife, how to pass it from one hand to the other, how to thrust, and how to then use the disengaged hand to feint and parry.'

Juliet tried not to wince as he demonstrated the vulnerable points on the human body, emphasising the importance of getting at the abdominal region. She learned how to make an opening for a thrust to the stomach by slashing across the face, hands, wrists, and forearms, by flinging gravel, a stone, a hat or even a handkerchief in the opponent's face. She couldn't picture herself ever doing it but as the training went on, she became more determined than ever to do whatever it took to defeat the enemy. She did better than she imagined she would in the 'killing without a weapon' section of the course, quickly learning that with the right technique any sentry could be eliminated from behind. In practice classes, she consistently managed to disable her opponents, despite the fact that she was so much smaller than most of them.

After tea each day, there was further instruction in forgery and how to lie convincingly. She enjoyed identifying military insignia, though map reading was something she found difficult to master. She was better at explosives and paid close attention as the instructors taught them how to assemble incendiaries of various capabilities for a range of potential targets. She learned how to blow out a door lock and blow up a bridge. During the day, she had no time to think about the real possibility of needing to employ her new skills but at night as she lay in bed, she thought deeply about what awaited her. The instructors at Wanborough never underplayed the level of danger they might face, though they never clarified exactly what that might entail. The only time she had heard the word spy mentioned was at that second meeting in Belfast.

She wondered how everyone was in Dunderrig. Once she was in England, she had written to tell her family she'd joined up. She had been instructed to say she had joined the WAAF and to give them the address of an RAF base near Brighton so that they could contact her by post. She was also to warn them that wartime communications were patchy at best, so they were not to expect any further letters for a while but that the RAF had their address in the event that they needed to be contacted. These letters were the hardest she had ever written. Poor Auntie Kitty – she was going to be so lonely without her. James would be so worried. And she felt sadness every time she thought of her father and Solange. Every time she pictured them reading her letter together in the kitchen in Dunderrig, she experienced a stab of guilt – not only had she done the one thing her father had begged her not to do, but she had lied about it. She could just hear Solange trying to calm her father down while all the time being heartbroken herself.

She wondered when she would be allowed to write again. She longed to write again, to ease their pain, but she knew that was forbidden.

CHAPTER 29

James was painting the little inlet harbour at Castletownshend, trying to replicate the luminescence of the water on his canvas. The sunshine danced on the surface, and the clear water reflected the blue sky. Ingrid had gone for a walk along the rocks. She loved walking along the seashore and could just do it for hours, especially now she had a camera. Helmut and Elizabeth had given it to her for her twentieth birthday, and she snapped constantly. James had no interest in photography, it was so rigid, whereas with painting, you could add or subtract from an image as you pleased. Still, he was delighted such simple pleasures kept her happy.

At first, he'd worried that Dunderrig would be boring for her – she was so lively and outgoing and had so many friends in Dublin. Yet she seemed more anxious, even than he was, to get back to West Cork whenever they'd been any length of time in Dublin. He still hadn't told his father or Solange about Edith, and he had definitely decided not to take up the place in the National College of Art. Not only did he not wish to be away from Dunderrig and his father, he had also been further put off by the fact that his mother's contact in the college was the head of sculpture, Dr Gurther, a vocal member of the Nazi party. James had met him once at a gallery with Otto, and the man was insufferable.

Though he wanted his mother in his life, and Ingrid was fundamental to his happiness, he was finding spending time in Dublin with Edith and Otto increasingly trying. After the horrible dinner party, after which he'd lashed out at Edith, he had distanced himself from the social occasions in their house. He just couldn't stand the endless evenings where the conversation invariably led to the war and how Hitler was doing such a wonderful job. He wished once again he could just meet with Edith and Ingrid and forget he'd ever met the rest of them.

The longer the war raged in Europe, the more the world was becoming increasingly appalled at Germany, and Edith's social circle were starting to feel the waves of disapproval. They complained of people's rudeness to them and dismissed it as ignorance of the true facts. Only last week, Edith herself was outraged because she was convinced she was being followed by the Gardaí. Otto had calmed her down, saying it was her imagination. They were not doing anything wrong, so why would the Irish police be following her? James believed Otto was right on this occasion – he was a nice man, who just wanted a quiet life and for the war to be over. James liked Otto, he'd been so kind and welcoming to him – only the company he kept was distasteful.

Edith had shrugged on hearing Juliet had joined up and had made no further reference to the subject. She never asked about Juliet anyway, a fact which hurt and confused him. To know he was the chosen twin didn't give him a sense of superiority over Juliet; if anything, it made him love and wish to defend her more. On the one occasion that he brought up her apparent lack of interest in her own daughter, his mother had been circumspect.

'James, my darling, Juliet has made her feelings towards me quite clear, as is her right. She wished to have nothing to do with me; I am simply complying with her request.'

The two women were similarly stubborn, if only they could see it.

Solange and his father, on the other hand, were living in constant terror that Juliet would be killed. They needed him around, now more than ever.

He still couldn't believe it, his sister working for the British war effort. He wished she'd confided in him earlier so he could have talked her out of it – but then, she was head over heels in love with this Ewan fellow, so probably she just wanted to be near him. James couldn't judge her too harshly; if the situation had been between him and Ingrid, he'd have done the exact same thing.

Still, it meant he needed to spend more time in Dunderrig, and it was wonderful that Ingrid was happy to come along. Helmut Clissman was a very understanding employer and seemed absolutely fine with Ingrid taking off to West Cork whenever she wanted to. In fact, it was often at his suggestion that she take the trip. The educational exchange was much quieter these days, he said, given the travel restrictions, so he could easily manage without her. James wasn't exactly sure what she did there anyway – she didn't seem to be a proper teacher, and Elizabeth took care of all of the paperwork. Perhaps Helmut was employing her as a favour to Otto – people always seemed happy to do favours for him, which wasn't surprising since Otto was such a genuinely nice character. James tried several times to find out what business Otto was in and eventually Edith told him that he was in gold and art – the buying and selling of it, apparently. James had no idea how that worked, but Otto must have been extremely good at it because judging by the lifestyle he and Edith enjoyed, business was booming.

Though some of Edith's friends were exactly as James imagined Nazis would be, it was virtually impossible to equate Otto and Helmut with the others. James thought being German must be a bit like being Irish. If you were from outside, you might imagine that every Irish person was fiercely, even violently nationalist and a member of the IRA, when in fact, what most people wanted was a quiet life to do what they wanted and not get involved in political struggles, armed or otherwise.

Ingrid always changed the subject whenever the progress of the war came up. When he told her about Juliet joining up, she just shrugged. 'Her boyfriend is in the airforce so naturally she wants to be somewhere she can see him, just like I go to Dunderrig to be with you. It is the curse of us girls, chasing boys all over the place.' The fact that his sister was now actively engaged in the effort to defeat Germany left her unperturbed.

'CAN WE JUST GO INTO the village on the way home?' she asked after their long day in the sun. She sat close to him in the car and stretched luxuriously. James fought hard to keep his eyes on the road.

'Of course, what do you want to get?'

'I wish to visit the post office. And I need a few personal things from the chemist.' She gazed out of the window.

James reddened then berated himself. He was a grown man in a proper relationship with a woman, yet the mention of women's things still embarrassed him. He was a doctor's son and brought up by a very liberal Frenchwoman so he should be more comfortable talking about anything intimate, but he wasn't. He couldn't even find the right words to tell her how much he loved her, how much he desired her. Whenever he tried, she just said, 'I know,' which put him at ease. He could never have imagined having a girlfriend as wonderful as Ingrid.

'Can I go to the post office for you while you get your...things...from the chemist? The post office closes at six and so does Miss Cunningham's so you won't make both – it's quarter to six now.'

'No, thanks. I'll make it. I just need to send something to Helmut, something I forgot to give him. It's all wrapped up, but I'm not sure how much it would be to post.'

'Sure don't be silly, I'll just put it on the Dunderrig account – is the address on it? And you can get whatever you need while I'm in there. What is it anyway?' James was pleased to be able to help.

Ingrid hesitated for a second, 'It's just a roll of film. He's putting a new brochure together of the school and wanted some beautiful landscape shots in it to entice prospective students. I told him there was nowhere more beautiful than Dunderrig.'

As they parked beside the green in the middle of Dunderrig village, it was five to six.

She rooted in her bag and eventually produced a small brown parcel addressed to Helmut.

'I can't imagine why women need such enormous handbags. Juliet and Solange are the same,' James joked. 'But then I never really know what women keep in handbags anyway – for all I know you could have old anchors or jars of jam or hand grenades in there.' Still chuckling, he kissed her on the cheek as they parted to opposite sides of the village square.

'Ah James Buckley, 'tis yourself back down from Dublin,' announced Mrs Kelly, the postmistress and local font of all gossip and scandal. James's father had insulted her only last week by remarking that her ability to proclaim what was abundantly obvious to everyone with a pair of eyes in their heads was truly staggering. He must have been fed up with her trying to pump him for medical information about the whole parish. Mrs Canty had looked thrilled as she regaled James with the story over breakfast the next morning; she and Mrs Kelly were old rivals. Apparently, Mrs Kelly had her eye on Eddie donkeys years ago.

'Hello, Mrs Kelly. How are you?' James was always polite. His father might be a bit short with people sometimes, God knows he had very little patience for what he termed 'idle gossip', but he'd always brought them up to be decent and kind. Richard Buckley was a lover of the plays of Sean O'Casey and would never have tolerated his children having 'notions of upperosity'.

'Ah sure, James, you know yourself, I'm a martyr to the corns. 'Tis being on my feet in here the whole time has me half crippled.' She added pointedly, 'Your father doesn't seem to be able to do much for me, so I think I might go into Skibb to Doctor O'Connor – he trained in Ireland, you see, not England, so he might have a better idea, no disrespect to Doctor Buckley...'

'Of course not, Mrs Kelly, I'm sure he just wants to see you back on your feet again. And you know, you're probably right, two very different animals, the Irish corn and the English corn. My father probably can only sort out the English variety. I'd say we'd have a different class of corn here altogether.'

Mrs Kelly looked at him sharply, unsure if he was making fun of her or not, then clearly decided against engaging in battle with two Buckleys in a week.

'Well, yes. Now did you want something?'

'I just want to get this in the post, please?'

James put the parcel on the counter with a huge smile.

'And what is it?' Mrs Kelly looked at the parcel and the name of Helmut Clissman on the front of it as if it were an unexploded bomb. 'We must ask, on account of the situation with the emergency, you see.' She smiled a sugary smile.

James was quite sure she had no jurisdiction over the contents of parcels posted within Ireland but decided it was easier to play along with her.

'It is camera film, for my girlfriend's employer, whose name you can see marked clearly there as Mr Helmut Clissman. He lives in Dublin.' James's voice betrayed none of his frustration.

'And that would be your *German* girlfriend, would it? Sending a parcel to her *German* employer?' Mrs Kelly was writing on a notepad.

'The very one.' James was struggling to remain civil. 'Though thankfully, Mr de Valera is keeping us neutral so that sort of thing doesn't matter, does it?' He never lost the cheery tone in his voice.

Mrs Kelly weighed the package and angrily affixed the necessary stamps. 'No harm to keep an eye out all the same. A very high-up member of the Gardaí was in here recently and made a point of asking me to note any unusual activity in the village, so I am perfectly within my rights. There were Special Branch men here too last week but obviously I can't discuss what they wanted. Will I put it on the Dunderrig account?' she replied, glad she'd shown James that she had the ear of the authorities.

'Yes please, Mrs Kelly, that would be marvellous if you could do that and my father will be happy to settle up with you. And I'm sure there isn't a secret service anywhere in the world with access to talents such as yours. I feel so much safer knowing you are keeping an eye on things.' James smiled innocently. Walking out of the post office, he saw Ingrid was waiting for him outside. In an uncharacteristic display of passion, he put his arms around her and kissed her for a long time, in full view of Mrs Kelly. Now, that would give her something else to wag her tongue about.

That evening at dinner, Ingrid was chatting with Richard and James about the history of shipping off the West Cork coast. Richard was regaling her with tales of wrecks, sunk when they hit one of the many hidden rocks in the bay. The West Cork coast was notoriously treacherous if you didn't know where you were going. Ingrid was explaining how all things nautical was a mystery to her. Solange watched her animated features as she held them enthralled. She really was a beautiful girl and so full of life and fun, and she did seem very fond of James. Solange felt guilty because although the girl had never given her a reason to dislike her, she just couldn't warm to Ingrid. She couldn't put her finger on it, but she just knew there was something about the younger woman that made her uneasy. James was utterly besotted and even Richard seemed to have really taken to her. Mrs Canty just kept saying how much she missed Juliet as if Ingrid's presence made her even more lonely for the girl.

Juliet. Solange had cried so many tears for her; she raged at her in private yet defended her when Richard called her irresponsible, flighty, and downright stupid. He was heartbroken that she had joined up, but he expressed that sorrow and pain as anger. The letter had read so unlike Juliet's normal communications – usually her sentences tumbled over each other, a stream of consciousness hopping from one subject to the next. This last letter had been well-constructed and written in measured tones, yet lacked any detailed information. Either Juliet was so anxious about telling them her news that she wrote and rewrote the letter before sending it, which was entirely plausible, or, she was lying. Something told Solange it was the latter.

If Juliet had really done as she said she had and joined the Women's Royal Air Force, then that was a frightening enough prospect. She would be living at a base, a base that Hitler would be targeting, and so she risked being blown to bits. Solange couldn't picture her doing a clerical job. Juliet was disorganised at the best of times. Perhaps, she was being trained as a mechanic or something practical. That was easier to imagine. However, if as Solange suspected, Juliet was telling them a lie, then where on earth was she and what was she doing? And why hadn't she at least told Solange in advance? No, there was something else going on, she just wished she knew what. She couldn't confide her fears to Richard; he was worried enough without imagining all sorts of other intangible possibilities. Jeremy had always teased her about her active imagination so perhaps that's all it was, but Solange feared for Juliet, and the feeling just wouldn't leave her.

Last night, with Mrs Canty gone to bed, she and James had been washing up after dinner. It had been nice to have him to herself, to speak in French.

'*T'as des nouvelles récentes de Juliet?*' she had asked.

'*Non, rien, et toi?*' he replied, turning to her with a smile. '*T'inquiète pas, elle m'a indiqué dans sa dernière lettre qu'ça pourrait être difficile...*'

'*Oui, oui, je sais bien, mais...*'

Richard had walked into the kitchen, putting a stop to any plans Solange had about cross-examining James to see what he knew. She would try again. The twins were completely loyal to each other, she knew that, but she was so worried she was determined to get it out of him if he knew anything. Juliet was impulsive enough to do anything. She was definitely gone from Belfast. Kitty had written to Richard saying how much she missed Juliet and that she was resigned now to go into an old people's home. Richard had written back, inviting her once more to Dunderrig but had as yet received no reply. She was not convinced that old bat Mrs Kelly in the post office wasn't delaying their post on purpose. Mrs Kelly had never liked anyone from the house since she and Mrs Canty fell out years ago, and Richard's caustic remarks the other day would have done nothing to help their cause. She wondered if Juliet had avoided writing the truth to her father for fear it would be steamed open by the nosy postmistress. Yet could she not have written to Solange, in French?

'Where is that book we had, Solange? You know, the one about the coast of West Cork? Ingrid wants to see it.' Richard's voice broke through her reverie.

'Pardon? Oh, excuse me, I was thinking of something else. That book is in the hall – remember Corny Davis asked to see it while he was waiting to see you last week. He was saying to anyone who'd listen that all that unprotected coastline was only asking to have the Germans invade us.'

Richard laughed. 'You're right. I knew I'd seen it somewhere odd recently. Poor Corny has been on about that for years. Sure he used to say back in the days of the troubles that we were completely exposed to a British invasion too, as if they would have any interest in invading us when they had their Tans and Auxies and G-men crawling all over the place. He's half-cracked, always was. His latest thing is that the Germans are in cahoots with the IRA. According to Corny, the Germans are going to give the six counties back to the Republic if the IRA helps them to defeat the British. It's bad enough having to deal with his imagined ailments without listening to that old guff every time, too. Best thing is just to agree with him, I've found.'

James grinned at Ingrid, pouring her another glass of wine. 'I'd like to see a German try to get past Mrs Kelly – he wouldn't be here five minutes, and she'd know what he had for his breakfast! You should've seen the fuss she made over me posting something for Ingrid earlier, trying to let on that the Special Branch were around the village and asked her to keep an eye out.'

Richard nodded. 'Well, there have been a lot of guards and even plainclothes fellows down from Dublin around in past weeks right enough. I suppose they are just cautious, and I doubt very much if they've chosen Mrs Kelly as their source of reliable information. That one always has something to say. In fact, she's been telling the parish how you two were making an exhibition of yourselves on the public street for all to see. She just happened to *mention* it to me when I was coming out of Molly Murphy's – her poor old mother's arthritis is bad at the moment. Mrs Kelly was watching out for me, I'm sure of it.'

James grinned unabashedly. 'See, what did I tell you? She's below now writing up a secret report on public displays of affection. I'd say the guards will be very interested in that all right.'

Ingrid didn't react to his joke. She was lost in thought. 'Hello...Ingrid,' James waved his hand in front of her face, 'you were miles away.'

'Sorry,' she replied recovering. 'I was just thinking about something else, what did you say?'

CHAPTER 30

'On the count of three.'

Juliet made eye contact with the young RAF flight sergeant who was shouting at her over the noise of the Lysander's engines. This was her fifth and final practice drop, a night-time one. She felt like a trussed-up chicken in her flying suit with the heavy parachute on her back. The earlier drops had been by day, and she'd been terrified enough but to voluntarily drop out the hole in the plane into pitch darkness was a whole other level of dread. Her instructions were to land safely, gather her parachute, and make her way back to Dunham House where she was billeted.

The move to Dunham had been the next stage

in the training. None of her fellow students from Wanborough had come with her, but whether that was because they weren't accepted for further training or had been sent somewhere else, she had no idea. She was simply told she had done satisfactorily after her time in Wanborough and to proceed to her next posting in Cheshire. Here she was to learn how to be dropped safely behind enemy lines.

Though they tried to teach safe landing techniques at the large hangar at the RAF Ringway Airfield – converted for that purpose using ropes and swings and an old plane with a hole cut in the fuselage – nothing prepared her for the sheer terror of the real thing. Some of the others she met at Dunham said they quite liked the sensation once they got the first one over, but for Juliet it was always nothing short of petrifying. She was determined not to put a foot wrong with this part of the training though, so she never voiced her fears to anyone.

Taking a deep breath, she jumped. Freefalling, within seconds she felt the familiar tug of the chute opening and she relaxed slightly. Now, to remember to keep her feet together and to fall sideways to minimise injury. The area was open fields, but she had been warned there was a chance of thickets of trees. It wasn't uncommon for a trainee parachutist to be found dangling, their chute caught in a tree. The instructors never saw the funny side of it, even though the sight of someone frantically kicking to release themselves several feet from the ground was often comical.

She could just make out the shapes of the landscape as it seemed to rush towards her. Toggling left and right as she had been trained to do, she aimed to land in the middle of a large field. Within seconds, she hit the ground. The speed of her descent seemed much faster than earlier drops, and she landed on the hard ground awkwardly, her hip taking her weight. The parachute silk billowed around her, threatening to pull her along the ground if she didn't get it gathered quickly. Ignoring the ache in her hip, she bundled the parachute into her backpack. Sitting in the dark field, she rooted in the side pocket for her torch, compass, and map. The torch wouldn't work; the impact must have broken it. She only had a rough idea where she was. The pain in her hip was bad but not debilitating so she knew nothing was broken. Walking to the ditch, she decided to follow it until she came to a gate and hopefully, a road. All of the signposts had been removed in England to confuse the Germans should they invade, so navigation was tricky. Juliet thought as she limped along that if she'd known what she was letting herself in for, she would never have signed up, but it was too late now. Solange and Daddy wouldn't believe their eyes if they could see her. She eventually found a gate and made her way over it, though her hip throbbed. She trudged in the darkness, navigating with her map and by the light of the moon down endless small country roads. Three hours later, soaking wet from the thunderstorm that had started an hour earlier and with every bone in her body aching, she turned up the avenue.

At 3:45 a.m., fifteen minutes ahead of schedule, Juliet arrived at Dunham House.

The side door opened as she approached. *'Bravo, Marine. Tout s'est bien passé?'* The officer in command spoke softly so as not to wake the whole house. Helping her out of her backpack and flying suit, he noticed she winced as she struggled to remove the tight-fitting suit.

'Etes-vous blessée?' he asked. She'd seen him around but as was usual, she didn't know his name.

'I think I bruised my hip on landing,' she replied in French, thinking how the months of training and speaking so little had made her so much more economical with words. The old Juliet would have been talking ceaselessly after such an ordeal, outlining and perhaps embellishing the tale of woe slightly. Living the life of a trainee saboteur had made her reticent and cautious, even when there was no danger as yet. She followed the man into the basement kitchen. There was a single pot on the stove being kept warm by a tiny flame.

'Best get it looked at. Hold on, I'll get someone. In the meantime, there's soup in the pot. Help yourself.'

Juliet was starving. She filled a bowl of soup and sat painfully at the table to eat it. It was watery and fairly tasteless, and she felt a pang of loneliness for the warm, welcoming kitchen at Dunderrig, with Mrs Canty's delicious homemade soup made from the bones of the previous day's joint and fresh vegetables dug by Eddie each day. She regularly thought about that smell of it and watching Mrs Canty swirling fresh cream on top and buttering slices of soda bread, fresh from the oven. She'd had nothing but awful margarine since she arrived in England and bread that tasted like sawdust. This soup was more like the water used to boil vegetables, only without the vegetables. The rationing and the terrible quality of the food they did have was something Juliet found hard to endure. She was used to the finest of fresh produce, cooked to perfection. At night in her sleep, she dreamed of Mrs Canty's floury mashed potatoes with a succulent roast, followed by apple tarts with pastry that melted on your tongue, made with the fruit from the gnarled old tree in the courtyard. Each morning as she scraped white margarine on thin slices of bread and drank the coloured water they called tea, she felt a pang for the sweet blackberry jam she loved, or the honey and brown sugar she poured liberally on her porridge every morning at home. Sugar was so rationed here, she couldn't remember the last time she had tasted something sweet. How she would love to be in the big warm kitchen of Dunderrig now, being minded by Solange and Mrs Canty while Daddy gave her something to help the pain in her hip. She was exhausted and sore, and she would give anything to be at home. Tears of loneliness and self-pity threatened to spill as she ate the horrible soup.

The officer came back with a sleepy-looking bear of a man. He was huge and the hairiest person she'd ever seen. He had an enormous reddish-grey beard and a shock of grey hair on his head. He was over six feet tall and must have weighed eighteen stone.

'Now so, what did you do to yourself?' he asked in the soft accent of West Cork. Hearing such a familiar accent brought further tears to Juliet's eyes. 'You'd better come with me, and we'll have a look at you.'

Following him into a room near the kitchen, she realised it had been turned into a makeshift surgery. It smelled so familiar, just like Daddy's surgery at home. Homesickness threatened to overcome her. She took a deep breath and closed her eyes. For just a moment, she was in Dunderrig and none of this was happening.

'Now so, your man outside said you hurt your hip. I suppose if you go throwing yourself out of aeroplanes in the middle of the night, you'll have that.' He smiled and patted her on the back. 'I'm Dr McCarthy, but everyone just calls me Mac. And who are you?'

Juliet looked at this kind man whose kind gruff manner reminded her of Eddie Canty. He probably even knew Daddy, but she had learned her lesson. It would have been lovely to tell him all about Dunderrig, that her father was a doctor too, about James and Solange and how she got to be here, it would have made them all feel a tiny bit closer, but she knew she couldn't.

'Marine,' she replied.

'Right-o, Marine,' he said, smiling at her. 'Let's have a look at this hip so, will we?'

There was the beginning of a large bruise on her hip bone. Gently he touched the area to ensure there was nothing broken. Juliet tried not to cry out as he pressed down on the point where she had landed. Tears came to her eyes, but she gritted her teeth.

'You gave yourself a nasty auld knock there then, but nothing's broken. 'Twill be very sore for a few days, though. I'll give you a few tablets to help you sleep. Rub this cream on it tonight and again in the morning, it'll bring down the swelling. Sure you'll be better before you're twice married.' He winked at her.

She smiled back. That's what Daddy always said to her and James when they got cuts and bruises as children.

'I don't want you doing anything much for a few days, do you hear me? Give that a chance to mend. Sure you could do with a rest anyhow – read a book, maybe?' He raised his enormous bushy eyebrows.

'I will. Thank you,' she answered, still in

French. It was the first time since she'd arrived in England that she felt like she was a real person and not just a project to be turned into something.

'*Tá fáilte romhat*, you're welcome.' he replied. She did not respond but that simple phrase in Irish made her feel a little less miserable.

'*ENTREZ*,' SHE CALLED AS she woke to the gentle knock on the bedroom door. Mrs Carnegie entered carrying a tray with tea and toast. A funny, busy Scots woman, she was the housekeeper at Dunham and seemed to run the whole place effortlessly, despite all its comings and goings. Her French was perfect though heavily accented with the long vowels of her native Argyle. She was kind to everyone, but she always had a special word for Juliet, who suspected that Mrs Carnegie was much more than just the housekeeper. She seemed to know everything about each one of the students that came to the house, despite the fact that they never discussed their personal lives. She referred once, while she and Juliet were alone in the kitchen, to Scotsmen making great husbands and as she said it, she gave Juliet a huge conspiratorial wink.

As she struggled to sit up, she winced.

'Now then, you are to rest in bed today, doctor's orders. I've brought you some writing paper also. Perhaps you would like to send a few letters. Needless to mention, they must be short and will be subject to the censor, so nothing specific, but if you'd like to let your family and your young man know you are all right, I'll see they get posted for you. I'll be back at lunchtime.'

She was brusque but gentle, and Juliet's heart soared at having permission to write home and to Ewan.

'You should continue to use the base at Brighton as your address,' Mrs Carnegie added as she straightened Juliet's bed clothes before she left. 'And if possible, we will try to have any replies forwarded to you from there.' She left, with a kind smile.

Happily, Juliet munched her toast, though the scrape of margarine on the gritty bread bore no resemblance whatsoever to the toast Mrs Canty made, dripping with real salty butter and chunky home-made marmalade. For the first time in ages, she felt content. Her hip hurt a lot, but it was worth the pain to get a day off and lie in bed. The training was so hard and when she finally achieved whatever awful task they set her, there wasn't a word of thanks or praise, just another horrible thing to have to do. The funny thing was, though, that the tougher the task, the more determined she became to succeed.

She finished her breakfast and used the tray to lean on to write. The thin airmail paper Mrs Carnegie had given her tore easily, so she had to be careful.

Dear Daddy, Solange, James, Eddie, and Mrs Canty,

I can only write one letter so you'll have to share! I'm fine and getting on well here. The food is horrible mostly, nothing like yours, Mrs C, and the work is exhausting, but I'm coping. I miss you all very, very much but please don't worry about me. I'm doing my bit to keep us all safe. I know you are cross with me, Daddy, but I'm doing something worthwhile, and I want you to be proud of me. Solange is taking care of everyone I know, so you are all fine I hope. I bet Dunderrig is looking beautiful now, it always does in autumn. James, I hope you're painting and still happy with Ingrid; don't get married without me! Solange, if a gorgeous Scotsman shows up looking for me, feed him and keep him there. Mrs C., I dream of your soda bread and roast leg of lamb. Eddie, I'm using lots of things you taught me. Daddy, please don't worry, though I know you will. I know you think I'm just a silly little girl but honestly I've grown up a lot, and I will come home safe and sound I promise.

I love you all with all my heart,
Juliet.

She carefully folded the letter but didn't seal it as it would have to be censored before it was posted. She hoped it didn't contain anything they would object to, but she could never tell with these faceless people.

She had written to Ewan regularly from Belfast and received lots of replies. He had always told her that he loved her and that he hoped it would all be over soon and they could be together again. She had written and told him that she was joining up just before she left Belfast but didn't know if he had received that information or not – it might have been censored before it reached him. Maybe he thought she was still in Belfast and was still writing to Kitty's address.

My darling Ewan,

They've only given me a tiny bit of paper, and I don't want to waste it so I'll keep it short. I'm in England at a training base; the address is on the top so please write and let me know you're okay and how you feel about, well, everything really. I look very different in uniform, though I doubt I'll ever be able to do my hair so no bits escape. I do wish I could see you, even for a few minutes, so if there is a chance of you getting leave then maybe we could meet up now that we are at least in the same country. If there was even a tiny chance, I would love that. In the meantime, please take care of yourself, my darling. I love you.

Your girl always,

Juliet.

She was deep in thought when the house-keeper returned, mid-morning. 'How are you feeling, dear?' she asked kindly.

'Better,' Juliet replied. 'I think a rest has made all the difference.'

'Well, enjoy it because you are moving to-morrow as far as I understand it. Someone will come to brief you later, I'm sure. Now let's get those letters posted for you, shall we?' Taking the letters and the tray, she left.

Later that afternoon, Juliet found herself once again alone in a strange room awaiting yet another unexplained conference with yet another uniden-tified person. With Mrs Carnegie's help, she'd managed to limp down the hall. The rest had made her hip stiff and walking was difficult. She longed to ask the housekeeper what the meeting was about but knew it would be pointless. She accepted such reticence would be necessary if she ever actu-ally got to France, but the secrecy with which everything was dealt with here, where there was no danger, really frustrated her. She knew very little about her future at any point in this whole process. No one spoke out of turn and though she longed to speculate with her fellow trainees, she knew that to do so would mean instant dismissal.

The fact that she was constantly being drawn into conversations by her superiors, often French men or women about seemingly random subjects made her sure they were checking her fluency. She was clearly being trained for some kind of clandestine work in France but what, she had no idea. She was both exhilarated and terrified at the prospect of being dropped behind enemy lines and having to pass herself off as French. So far, she could shoot, handle explosives, read maps, use a compass, find her way in the dark, and parachute from an aeroplane. What other skills was she going to have to master?

The door opened and an officer entered. His uniform jacket was emblazoned with insignia and his brass buttons shone. Though slight, he made an imposing figure. Under dark, bushy eyebrows, his eyes were bright and penetrating. He had a neatly clipped moustache and his thinning hair was combed back from a high forehead.

'*Marine, ça va?* I am Major General Colin Gubbins.'

'*Ça va bien, Monsieur.*' She was taken aback, partly that someone of so high a rank would be meeting with her at all, but also because no one had ever properly introduced themselves to her since she joined up. Juliet could never understand if this was a security measure, preparing them for life in the field where no unnecessary information should be given, or if it was a military thing. Perhaps that's how the armed forces worked – except for the job at hand, everything else was superfluous.

'You may speak in English now. I heard you took rather a tumble last night. How are you feeling?'

She hesitated for a moment. Was this another test? She decided to take him at his word. The enquiry was perfunctory, and the mischievous side of Juliet wondered if she did explain in detail how she felt, how he would react. But before she could say anything, he spoke again.

'You're Irish, I understand. Cork, I believe.' His tone was neutral.

'Yes, sir,' Juliet replied. 'West Cork.' The English words sounded strange coming from her mouth.

'Michael Collins country. I hear it's very

pretty. I spent some time in Kildare.' His accent was what she'd heard described as public school.

'Yes. It is, sir.' Juliet was unsure how to respond. A man of his rank could only have been in Ireland in one capacity, that of the forces of occupation before independence. The irony of this situation was not lost on her.

'Buckley. Hmm. An old colleague of mine, Colonel Maxwell served in Skibbereen. Is that anywhere near where you come from?' Though the question was delivered lightly, Juliet sensed this was not a general chat.

'Yes sir, it's the nearest big town to where I grew up.' Part of her was terrified about answering his questions – what if it was another test? But her instincts told her it wasn't.

'Does the name Maxwell mean anything to you?' His eyes never left hers.

'Yes sir, though I did not know him personally. I was very young when they, when he…left. I believe my father treated his son when he was a child.'

Major General Gubbins nodded. 'Yes, he mentioned something about that. He was very grateful to your father. Saved the boy's life, it seems.'

'Yes sir, I believe he did.' A surge of pride in

her father filled her. Referring to the British withdrawal from Ireland made her realise just how bizarre this situation in which she now found herself was. She and her entire country saw the British Army as the forces of subjugation in Ireland and their expulsion was a source of great pride. Yet here she was, on their side.

'I wanted to speak to you personally today. Normally, I don't get the opportunity to meet with all of our operatives. Presumably, you have some inkling of why you are here and why you are receiving this training?'

'Yes sir, I have a general idea though I don't know any specifics.'

'Indeed. I have a dilemma, Miss Buckley. Your instructors tell me that despite an earlier transgression, you are a determined and diligent student, brave and tenacious, and your French is good enough to pass as a native. But, I am concerned that your commitment to us is less than it should be.'

Juliet thought quickly, she had to convince this man she was committed. 'If you are asking me do I feel loyalty to the Allied cause, then I do. I am Irish, and of course, there is tension between our countries, but I believe, with every fibre of my being, that Hitler must be stopped. He just has to be, for *all* our sakes and if I can help to make that come about, then I want to do it. The history of our two countries is, at this point in time, irrelevant to me.'

He thought for a moment. 'How does your father feel about you joining up?'

Juliet knew that nothing short of total honesty was what he expected.

'He's not happy about it. Not because he is anti-British but because he is anti-war. He served with the Medical Corps the last time and was disgusted by what he saw – that, and of course, by what he witnessed at home during the troubles.'

Major General Gubbins gave a slight laconic smile at her reference to the War of Independence and the subsequent Civil War as 'troubles'.

'Your mother, she's married to a German now. And your brother is in a relationship with the man's niece.'

Juliet flinched. But of course they knew about Otto and Ingrid. Why wouldn't they? They knew everything else about her. Nobody had mentioned it before.

'I had been thinking that putting you back in Dublin, helping us that way, seeing the German community there from the inside, so to speak, might be helpful. We are fairly sure that all is not as it seems within that group, and the Irish police agree with us. Your mother and, it seems, your brother move in somewhat suspect circles, to say the least. A pair of eyes and ears there might prove most useful.'

Juliet couldn't believe her ears. After all that training, speaking French, parachute training and the rest, they wanted to send her to Dublin! To spy on her mother was unthinkable, not because she felt any loyalty to Edith, but simply because... And to suggest that James was involved was just preposterous. Her first instinct was to warn her brother, to get him away from Edith and Otto and whoever else he was mixing with these days. Quelling the urge to explode in indignation, she forced her voice to be calm and measured.

'My mother and I are estranged. We do not communicate at all. She is a bigamist as she is not divorced from my father, but yes, she is claiming to be married to a German, Otto Hugenberg. I only met him once, with my brother in Dublin in 1937, before the war. I will not go to Dublin and spy on her and her associates. She probably knows from James that I've joined up, and to sud-denly appear in Dublin pretending an affection we both know is false would be deeply suspicious.'

Gubbins seemed to consider her words but chose not to comment on them.

'And this Otto Hugenberg, what does he do in Ireland?'

'I have no idea. He is in some kind of business I think. As I said, I don't communicate with them.'

'But your brother James, he is in regular touch with them, and with your stepfather's niece, a young woman called…' he checked his notes, 'Ingrid Hugenberg. James is in close contact with a lot of people who are under observation by the Irish police and of whom we are highly suspicious. How does your twin brother feel about you being on our side, given his obvious pro-German leanings?'

Juliet felt a surge of temper, and she struggled to contain it. How dare he speak about James like that? Pro-German, for God's sake, what rubbish! Taking a deep breath, she replied with what she hoped was a dignified tone.

'My brother is not now, nor has he ever been "pro-German". He is in touch with our mother, he met Ingrid through Otto, and that's all there is to it. It's frankly ridiculous to suggest he is in some kind of Nazi circle. I can't speak for Edith or Otto, but I do know James would never be involved in anything pro-Nazi. He met and fell in love with Ingrid before any of this happened, and she and our mother are the only reasons he is associated with any Germans at all.' Juliet's outrage was palpable in the room.

Gubbins remained impassive.

'You must understand that it is vital from our perspective to ensure that our agents are one hundred percent committed to the Allied cause. You must surely understand that your background, being Irish, combined with the company your brother chooses to keep, gives us some cause for concern. Your father was decorated in the last war, and his loyalty was never in question for the duration of his time in uniform, but it seems he was rather less than helpful subsequently, defending criminals and terrorists of the IRA, during what you call the troubles, and refusing to give important information to the authorities, even when pressed. Perhaps, he was frightened of the consequences. The IRA were pretty ruthless.' He rubbed his moustache with his index finger, lost in thought.

Juliet held her tongue, while she seethed with rage. Who the hell did this man think he was? This typically supercilious attitude of the British military towards the Irish infuriated her. If this man knew anything about her father, he'd know that Richard Buckley had decided that he would help those who needed him whatever the colour of their politics as a doctor. The ability to keep a cool head no matter what the circumstances was part of her training; there was no place for hysterics in the field as they were constantly being reminded. With that in mind, she spoke quietly, smothering her inner fury.

'My father treated everyone equally, sir. Which side they were on, didn't matter to him. That is why he wouldn't tell the British authorities about those he had treated. You might be interested to note he told the IRA exactly the same thing when they asked him questions about any of the British soldiers who were patients of his.'

Major General Gubbins didn't react and began rubbing his moustache again – a sign he was thinking, she recognised.

'So, Miss Buckley, you feel your sudden arrival in Dublin would raise suspicions. I suspect you're right. Your loyalty has yet to be tested, but on balance, I think I am willing to send you on the next phase of training, which will deal with the more specific skills needed for clandestine work. I am speaking to you now to simply clarify our position. If you feel that you are compromised in any way, or if you even suspect that you are now or at any time in the future could feel conflicted with regards to loyalty, then I urge you, in the strongest possible way, to discontinue your association with this organisation instantly. It would spare all of us considerable inconvenience, to say the very least.'

Juliet's mind was in turmoil. Indignation welled up within her. After all they had put her through, all that she'd endured over the past months; they had the nerve to question her loyalty. She had done everything asked of her without a word of complaint and still she was being doubted. Pride tempted her to walk out then and there and have nothing further to do with these people. Yet living in England, in this environment, had made her realise how vitally important it was to defeat Hitler and the Nazis. The way they were treating the citizens of the countries they'd already invaded was disgusting, and the image of those Jewish children she and Ewan had seen in the station in Belfast was indelibly printed on her mind. If the Nazis came here or to Ireland, they would behave in exactly the same way. She thought of Dunderrig with jack-booted Germans in the post office or in the Dunderrig Inn, or of the Nazi swastika flying over the town hall in Skibbereen. She visualised them ordering everyone around, and she stiffened her resolve and swallowed her anger.

'I want to go, sir. I know you have to ask me these things, and I know why. I'm not English, nor do I have any desire to be. I'm Irish and proud of it, but I do want to help defeat Hitler, and I want that as much as you do. So if you send me, I promise I'll do my very best, whatever the cost to myself.'

He looked at her for a long minute and nodded. 'Very well, Miss Buckley. Let's see how Beaulieu suits you.'

Juliet hobbled slowly back towards her room, thinking about the conversation. In the hallway, the housekeeper intercepted her.

'There is some post for you, it seems. It's taken a while to get to you, but it got here in the end.' She handed Juliet a bundle of letters.

Tears filled her eyes as she recognised first the distinctive French handwriting of Solange, Daddy's scrawly scribble, two from James, and finally several from Ewan. They had been redirected from the RAF base in Brighton. It was like all her Christmases had come at once.

She rushed back to her room as fast as her aching hip would allow and sat on her bed devouring their words; she could almost hear their voices, all telling her of their news. James about Ingrid – even telling her they'd finally 'done it'. She smiled at the thought of James's blushes putting that down on paper, but she was glad he could confide in her. She'd written to him from Belfast telling him to go for it. Auntie Kitty's letter was all about her ankle and how she could get about now but that life wasn't the same without her darling great-niece. Daddy's letter was full of entreaties to take care of herself and not to do anything stupid; he loved her so much, she knew, but sometimes with him, concern came over a bit too much like 'giving out'. Solange's letter was full of stories of Dunderrig and the family.

Juliet kept Ewan's three letters till last. She'd not heard from him for a long time and was starting to think perhaps it was just a wartime romance – passionate, yet forgotten instantly once a new prospect appears.

Settling herself on the bed, she opened the first letter, dated in November, which had been forwarded from her aunt's address to Brighton.

My darling Juliet,

I'd heard nothing for weeks and then I got three letters from you together and was so relieved you hadn't forgotten me. Are you all right? I'm fine, getting on with things as you can imagine. I have that photo you gave me over my bed, and all the lads are mad about you, but I've told them you're all mine and they have no chance – although I was a bit worried when you seemed to have stopped writing! I see a fair bit of Dougie, which is great; he knows all about you and how I'm moving to Ireland after the war. I miss you and think about you every single day (and night). We will be in Dunderrig together. I promise.

All my love,

Ewan.

She folded it carefully and opened the next one.

My darling Juliet,

What on earth are you thinking? I've only just got your letter that you've joined up. Are you mad? I don't know how I feel. On the one hand, I could wring your beautiful, slender, kissable neck, and on the other, my heart is bursting with pride. I love you more every day, and I hate being apart from you, honest to God I do, but at least when I thought you were in relative safety, I didn't worry – but now? I'm out of my mind.

You asked me about leave, well I'm definitely due some but whether I will get it, is hard to say. I'm sorry for being vague, it's not how I feel, but I don't want to get our hopes up only to have them dashed. I would give my right arm for a night with you, my darling wee girl. You are the reason I know I'm going to come through this. We will be in Dunderrig together, I promise.

All my love always,
Ewan.

The last one was very short.

Darling Juliet,
I love you. I always will. Think of me tonight. Sorry it's not longer, but I've got to go. I just wanted to write to you first.

We will be in Dunderrig together, I promise.
Ewan.

This last one filled her with trepidation. Where was he going that he felt he had to write such a quick note? Fighting for the safety of the two remaining unoccupied islands of Ireland and England. She recalled Winston Churchill's speech to the House of Commons commending the bravery of the RAF: '*Never in the field of human conflict was so much owed by so many to so few.*' Ewan was one of the few, and she was proud and worried in equal measure.

Juliet read and reread all the letters and finally fell asleep with them underneath her pillow.

CHAPTER 31

*J*ames lay awake in his darkened bedroom. The moonlight streamed through the open curtains and the hooting of an owl was the only sound to break the stillness. He looked at his watch: 3:00 a.m. Ingrid was asleep across the hall. He'd heard his father go out about an hour ago, probably up to Paddy O'Sullivan – the poor man was in the final stages of cancer. Whenever he could, Richard was with his patients in their final moments. Earlier, in the kitchen, Richard had confided to James that sometimes, when nothing more could be done and the pain was too much for his patient to bear in their final hours, he would administer enough morphine to end the pain entirely, which in turn accelerated the shutting down of the body. While it was ethically questionable, it was the kindest thing to do.

He wondered why his father told him details like that. Was it to get his son to reconsider studying medicine or was he just unburdening himself about the difficulties of his job? It was hard to know sometimes, but there was a different feel to their relationship of late. It was as if they were more equals than father and son.

Richard was out of his mind with worry about Juliet of course, but having James and Ingrid around seemed to cheer him up. Whenever he got too upset about Juliet, usually after listening to the news, Ingrid managed to say the right thing – how the war would soon be over, and how quickly Juliet would be home safe. Richard was very fond of Ingrid, though James wondered how Solange felt about her. She was never anything but kind and friendly to his girlfriend, yet he suspected she found it hard to warm to a German woman. It was understandable given how much she'd lost at that nation's hands.

James longed for Ingrid as he lay in bed. He couldn't get the image of her beautiful body out of his mind. They loved Dunderrig, but the opportunities for privacy were much less frequent here than in Dublin. Edith and Otto were out a lot and, anyway, they knew he and Ingrid were lovers and didn't seem to mind a bit. Dunderrig was a lot more traditional. James wondered whether he should risk sneaking into Ingrid's room. Solange at least wouldn't mind, even if she did hear him – she was much more liberal in her views on that subject than his father or Mrs Canty.

He remembered an excruciatingly embarrassing conversation a few months ago when Solange realised things were getting serious with Ingrid. He had been painting in the garden when she approached him. Since they were alone, she spoke in French and got right to the point.

'James, *mon chéri*. I know you won't want to have this conversation with me, but I doubt your father has had it with you, so please hear me out, all right?' She was smiling in the afternoon sun. 'You and Ingrid are young, and you care a lot for each other, I can see. I don't know if you have made love yet, but I imagine you have or at least are wanting to, so that is what I want to talk to you about...'

'Solange, please. There's no need,' interrupted a mortified James. 'I understand all about it, so really...'

Solange smiled. 'Yes, of course you know all about it, that's not what I want to say.' Handing him a bulging envelope, Solange ruffled his hair.

'Now, I want you to take these and use them. People always say that women can only conceive at certain times in their cycle, but that belief is why Irish families have fifteen children, so unless you want to be a father before you are ready, you should use these.'

James looked incredulously inside the envelope, registering the contents.

'I know you hate this, it is embarrassing for you, but you are a normal healthy young man with normal healthy appetites. I am not trying to make you uncomfortable. It is because I love you and I want to protect you, both of you, from being forced into something before you are ready.'

Despite his embarrassment, James was relieved. It was something that was on his mind. In Dublin, Ingrid had access to condoms through a friend, who had brought them from Germany. Since they had come to West Cork, where condoms were considered illegal and immoral and, anyway, were impossible to get, they had been taking chances. When Ingrid had got her period, he'd breathed a sigh of relief. He couldn't imagine asking anyone in Dunderrig – his father would be sure to hear of it and be horrified. And now here was Solange telling him that she provided his father with these, to hand out to his patients. The world was so different from how he imagined it. What other secrets were his loved ones hiding from him? Muttering his thanks, he had stuffed the envelope into his pocket. Solange had promised not to mention their conversation to his father, but even her knowing what he and Ingrid were up to had made him blush.

The barn owl hooted once more. He could restrain himself no longer; he just had to make love to Ingrid. He knew she'd greet him enthusiastically. She really was the most incredible girl. She was happy for them to get up to all sorts anytime, anywhere. He often wondered what Juliet would think about it. Fiery and wild as his sister was, he doubted she was as adventurous as Ingrid – at least, he hoped she wasn't. He realised how hypocritical he was being, but he hoped this Ewan was treating her with respect.

Creeping across the carpeted landing, he was just about to place his hand on the door handle of Ingrid's bedroom when he heard a loud snore from his father's room. Yet he was sure his father had left the house – he had distinctly heard the front door close over an hour ago. Who else had a reason to steal out in the middle of the night? Maybe he just hadn't heard his father return.

Mystified and frustrated with desire, he returned to his own room. There was no way he'd risk spending the night with Ingrid with his father in the house.

The following morning was wet and cloudy. Over breakfast, as he buttered toast, James asked his father, 'Was there a call out last night?'

'No, thank God. I was delivering the latest O'-Driscoll above in Gleannrí the night before, so I was glad of an uninterrupted night's sleep. Why do you ask?'

Solange looked up from her coffee. 'I also thought you were on a call, Richard. I was woken at maybe two in the morning by the front door banging. Very strange. I'll ask Eddie to look at the lock, to see if the door could blow open and close again in the wind.'

Ingrid appeared in the kitchen, hair wet from her bath and glowing with radiant health. Kissing James on top of his head, she swiped a sausage from his plate.

'Mmm...Frau Canty, you make the best sausages in the world. When I go back to Germany, I will have to take some for my father. He loves sausage, but we have none as good as this. Though perhaps it is the way they are prepared. I fear they would not taste so well if I cooked them.'

The housekeeper coloured with pride. Mrs Canty was charmed by Ingrid and loved when she and James were in the house. She considered it a personal challenge to keep the standard of fare in Dunderrig as high as ever despite the rationing.

'Well, you have no look of a one that enjoys her food, Miss, there's not a pick on you, you're like our Juliet. She'd eat you out of house and home and never puts on an ounce. Though they're only half-feeding her over in England, the poor child says she's dreaming of home-cooked food.'

Solange and Richard exchanged a glance and smile. Mrs Canty had the whole village told of how Juliet was dreaming of her cooking.

'She is right. I don't know how she left this place. It is so beautiful, but James, perhaps it is time I returned to work. We have been here three months now, and I think Helmut will need me back for the new term.'

Ingrid was careful never to mention Edith or Otto, though James knew she thought he was making a big thing out of something trivial. Ingrid's attitude was nonchalant. His mother had remarried and now lived in Dublin with Ingrid's uncle. She didn't think Richard would even look up from the paper at such news, but she didn't know Richard as well as she thought she did. Richard never mentioned Edith, ever.

James's heart sank at Ingrid's suggestion. The thoughts of returning to Dublin and his mother and all that entailed filled him with dread. Perhaps he'll just let Ingrid go up alone this time. He had quite a few commissions now, so he could say with honesty that he needed to stay here and finish the pieces on order.

'Well, how about you go up and I stay down here this time? I'd go with you normally, but I have to get that landscape finished for the bank. They're having the centenary dinner on Saturday week, and I promised them the painting would be hung in time.'

Mrs Canty put in, 'Sure, Ingrid pet, your Hell-mutt is doing without you this long, won't you stay here altogether? I hate to think of either of ye going back up there. I know it was back last May, but them bloody Germans were not joking when they dropped bombs on Dublin, you know. Belfast is getting a right hammering. Poor Juliet is better off out of that, anyway, though God alone knows where the girl is now. I was only reading yesterday about how they don't let them say a blessed bit on the radio now over in England, or here either, or anything about the weather or anything like that for fear the Germans would hear about it. I don't know where it's all going to end. And, of course, herself down below in the post office is loving all of this, you'd swear she was in the Secret Service herself the way she goes on, with her notions! She thinks the Emergency gives her a right to stick her warty auld nose even further into people's business. Imagine, I went in there last week for stamps and there she was, large as life and twice as ugly, holding court about young people making exhibitions of themselves in public. I haven't a clue what she was rawmaishing on about, but you may be sure 'twas some slight on someone from this house, anyway.'

The fact that Ingrid was German didn't seem to occur to Mrs Canty at all. She considered her a member of Dunderrig and so someone who must be at all costs protected, from the Nazis or Mrs Kelly or any other adversaries.

James and Ingrid exchanged smiles.

After breakfast, they went for a walk in the chilly October air.

'I have to get this commission finished. You know that, don't you? It could mean big things for me. I might even have an exhibition next year. You do understand, don't you?'

Ingrid sighed. 'We both know the real reason, James. You could finish that painting in Dublin just as easily. You just don't want to be up there anymore. You hate lying to your father, so you avoid the situation.'

James shook his head. 'Of course, I hate lying to Dad and Solange, but it's more than that. I know we don't talk about it, but it's eating me up inside. Every day, we hear more of what Hitler is doing, and it's horrific, literally unthinkable, that he could be treating people that way. You read the news too, you must see it – and that's just what we do know. Can you imagine what's going on behind the scenes? I'm not comfortable sitting around with a bunch of awful Germans, many of whom openly support the Nazis, singing *Lili Marleen* and drinking *schnapps* and pretending everything is just fine.'

'And me? Am I just one of those awful Germans, too? Why are you bothering with me at all if I'm so dreadful? You knew who I was when you met me. If now my nationality and my patriotism are unpalatable to you, then there is nothing I can do. You are the one who is changing, James, not me. You must do what you want.'

James had never seen Ingrid so upset. She was normally so cool and collected. Yet he longed for her to rage against Hitler, to distance herself from the Nazis and the German social scene in Dublin. Surely, she couldn't condone the exploitation and mistreatment of people like that?

'I love you, you know that, but why don't you condemn what they're doing?' he said with angry sadness. 'You just skim over it and make out like there's fault on both sides.'

'Listen to yourself! Shocked by people who tell the truth and aren't afraid to speak out! And there you are running around behind your father's back like a little boy! You look like a man, James, but when are you going to start acting like one and tell him the truth about you and Edith? You're *pathetic.*' Ingrid spat the words venomously.

'It's a totally different thing...'

'So tell your father the truth.'

'You don't understand how it would hurt him and Solange.'

'Why would he care? And what does Solange matter, anyway? She's not part of your family.'

'Solange is a mother to me, you can't say she's isn't part of our family.' He was getting angry himself now.

Ingrid's eyes were flashing in temper.

'So, you tell lots of lies, and it is suddenly my fault? I am not the one who lives lies, that is you. You are happy to accept everything both your father and mother give you, and you get angry at me for telling you to be a man and tell the truth. You're not a man; you are a stupid little boy, afraid of his papa. At least your sister had the guts to do something with her life! You are in your twenties and yet you behave like a little child! For God's sake, James, we can't even have sex without you living in terror of being caught like a naughty schoolboy. I need an adult not a little boy. So yes, to answer your question, I do understand. Perfectly.'

Ingrid stormed off, and James sat on the stump of a tree, seething. Ingrid was so infuriating sometimes. She had no understanding of how complicated things were; she just saw what she wanted and took it. He also hated the way she spoke about Solange, like she was a servant or something. She was perfectly nice to her when they were together, but she never understood that Solange was so much more to him than just a nanny gone past her usefulness. The entire household of Dunderrig relied so much on Solange and despite all those years without their birth mother, he and Juliet had never wanted for love. Solange was always there. He missed Juliet so much; she would understand. She was braver than him, there was no doubt about that, but she wasn't like Ingrid, who saw no reason to consider others. The fact that she wouldn't condemn what Hitler was doing was taking its toll on their relationship. He had thought, in his innocence, that they could just ignore the war, but he realised now how foolish that notion had been.

Solange had watched the exchange between James and Ingrid from the landing window, her attention drawn by their raised voices after she had opened the casement to admire the garden's autumnal colours. She wondered what they were quarrelling about. Downstairs, the front door opened, and she heard someone run upstairs. A furious Ingrid almost collided with her.

'Ingrid, *ma chère*, are you all right?' Solange asked in concern.

'Yes, thank you. I would like to go to Skibbereen, please Solange, I'm returning to Dublin on the next train. Can you ask Eddie to take me in?' Ingrid spoke calmly though Solange could see the girl was upset and angry.

'Of course, if that is what you want. But perhaps if you had a cup of tea, maybe you would feel better?' Solange followed Ingrid into her room. She knew if the girl left like this, James would be heartbroken. She must try to get her to stay, at least until the young lovers both calmed down.

'No, thank you. I just want to go, now.' Ingrid's voice was cold as she threw her clothes and cosmetics into her suitcase.

'Ingrid, it's not my business, I know, but if you and James have had a row, then maybe you should talk about it. Once you are back in Dublin, you'll probably realise it was about a silly thing and then you are two hundred miles away.' Solange smiled kindly.

Ingrid stopped packing and looked squarely at Solange. 'You are absolutely right,' she said. 'It is not your business.'

She snapped her case closed and walked past Solange out of the bedroom.

IN THE WEEKS THAT followed, James painted furiously, throwing himself into his work. Solange knew he was hurting and longed to comfort him, but she also knew he didn't want her company – he wanted Ingrid. Occasionally, he wrote to Juliet – at least he had his sister to confide in.

Juliet had written several times since that letter telling them she had joined up but gave no real details about her life except to say she was fine and the work was hard yet she was coping. The censor removed sentences and words, which made the rest hard to figure out; yet every letter was read and reread by everyone in the house. Eddie wondered what things he'd taught her that might be useful to her now. Mrs Canty was trying to figure out a way of posting her some food, and Richard often just sat by the range at night when the house was asleep, holding the letters to his chest, as if by doing so, he could be closer to his daughter.

SOLANGE SAT AT HER desk by the window of her bedroom that overlooked the lawns of Dunderrig. The frost glistened on the bare branches, and the wind from the north was biting. She had called this bedroom home for over twenty years now, and she pondered the life she lived. It was a million miles from what she had envisaged as a young girl in Picardy, but it was a good life. She still missed Jeremy, even after all these years. Her man friend, as Juliet called him, was still around but while she liked him very much, she had no desire to make the arrangement more permanent. Solange often wondered if Richard knew of her relationship of sorts. She doubted it; and if he did guess, he probably didn't approve. She was not like him, though, happy to live a celibate life; she needed the comfort of a physical connection with someone, even if it was for only once every month or six weeks.

Her lover was a witty, handsome man who liked Solange enormously, who told her how beautiful and desirable she was, and who was no more in love with her than she was with him. He arrived in Cork on business every month or so and stayed in a hotel, where she joined him. They chatted about abstract issues, nothing personal; ate nice food, in so much as was possible these days with rationing, and they made love. Then she returned to Dunderrig and her life. She knew if people knew that side of her, they would be horrified – especially given her suspicions that he was a married man.

She'd never asked him if he had a wife, and he had never volunteered the information. If he was risking his marriage, she thought, that was his business. This last time, however, he had seemed edgy – possibly worried about being seen. Thinking about it now, she decided then and there to write to him and end the relationship. It had run its course. It was time for him to commit to his other life, whatever that was.

What life should *she* commit to?

She wondered if Richard ever thought about love, or romance or sex. Even with Edith all those years ago, they had slept separately; she was sure there had been no one since, but she would never ask him something so personal. They were such good friends, they advised and supported each other, and they were both grateful to the other for what they provided, but there was no intimacy in their relationship. Although warm and friendly, Richard kept his deeper emotions so tightly in check. She sometimes wanted to probe his inner thoughts, but she could never bring herself to do it; they discussed the twins, the patients, the house, the news, but rarely, if ever, conversed about feelings. She sometimes wished that they could, but it just wasn't in him.

Many women in the area tried flirting with him, but he seemed to be oblivious to it. He remarked only the other day that he couldn't figure out what was wrong with Marie Gallagher, a local widow in her forties. She came to see him every week with various complaints and insisted he examine her thoroughly each time. He'd run every test he could think of but could find nothing wrong.

Solange had laughed when he told her. 'Perhaps it is not the doctor's touch she wants but the man's touch?'

He threw his eyes to heaven. 'Would you go away out of that? You French, it's all ye ever think about.' Chuckling, he went back to the surgery.

He was in his surgery now, and Mrs Canty had gone to Cork on an 'emergency expedition' as she called it. She was having a difficult time gathering enough ingredients for the Christmas baking, and Solange had felt a tear come to her eye earlier when Mrs Canty claimed she wouldn't rest until she found glacé cherries because Juliet loved them in the plum pudding. Though there was no hope of it, everyone in Dunderrig had only one Christmas wish this year – to have Juliet home.

Pulling her writing pad from the drawer, Solange decided to write to her. They'd sent a parcel weeks ago with some little gifts for her in the hope that she would get them for Christmas. The infrequent letters were so welcome, but she wrote to the whole family together, probably due to restrictions, so Solange longed to talk to her alone. Eddie was bringing the tree in tonight if they were back from Cork on time. Solange thought sadly of the excitement of decorating the tree all those Christmases when the twins were small. She had all the decorations they had made over the years lovingly stored in tissue paper. If only they could turn the clock back to that time. Life was simple then.

Everything was different now. James was miserable without Ingrid, and Richard was very busy at this time of year as people battled winter coughs and colds. Medicine was increasingly difficult to come by and poor nutrition was taking its toll on the general population. The war seemed never ending. They had promised it would all be over by now, yet here they were facing 1942 and nowhere closer to victory. The shock of the Japanese attack on Pearl Harbour two weeks ago was still there, combined with a guilty sense of relief that now, at last, America would send troops. The might of the United States might just tip the balance and end this horrific war. Then they might get Juliet home.

My dearest darling Juliet,

How lovely to get your last letter. Papa says it's like a jigsaw puzzle by the time the censor is finished with it, though how your news could be a threat to allied security, I'll never understand. (I just realised this will probably be censored too!) Well, life in Dunderrig is uneventful, your papa is busy as always but now he is finding it very difficult to source medicines, everything is rationed so I am trying to come up with natural cures. I found a really old book in the drawing room shelf about herbal cures. Though he was a little reluctant at first, your papa is becoming more open to the idea. Now I walk purposefully around the countryside picking herbs, so it has now been confirmed to the people of Dunderrig what they always suspected, I am completely mad!

Ingrid and James are still arguing. It's been four months now, and they still don't speak. He is so sad, I know he misses you. We all do so much. Mrs Canty is trying, without much hope I suspect, to find cherries to put in the plum pudding for you (no currants though!).

I was in Cork about a month ago. I think that will be the last time; he is a nice man, but it is getting a bit complicated. Perhaps he is married, I'm not sure. Are you shocked, my darling? Anyway, I think I won't go again. He will be a little disappointed (I hope!) but not heartbroken, not like poor James. (I have just realised that because I am writing in English, I will have to post this in Skibbereen in case our local postmistress reads it – she is driving everyone mad asking even more questions. She says it is because of the war, but we all know she is just a nosey old frog! I know frog is wrong – I can't remember what animal you say a nosey person is.)

I don't know what is the best thing for James. Ingrid is a strange girl, I think. She seems so friendly, and she is really beautiful, but there is a coldness to her, I can't explain it. Perhaps, it is best if he finds someone else, someone warmer. Maybe that is just my opinion though, everyone else loves her. Perhaps, I am jealous that he loves a woman more than me!

You said in your last letter you'd heard from Ewan at last and he was well and fine and missing you and loving you. I am so pleased, and I can't wait to meet him when all of this is over. Is there a chance you can meet up when he gets leave? I hope so.

Another Christmas in Dunderrig will be lonely without you. I can't believe it's been over two years since you have been home. We also know you would come if you could. We love you and miss you more than words can say.

Write soon, my darling girl,
Solange.

JAMES TRIED HIS BEST to cheer up, but he had a pain in his chest over Ingrid. He now understood the term heartbroken. His heart felt broken in half. Solange and Mrs Canty tried cheering him up; Eddie even offered to take him fishing to his secret location, but nothing lifted the black cloud of misery that hung over him. His father surprised him though, taking him out for a pint one night to the Dunderrig Arms.

Richard took a long drink of his pint and sat back in the corner of the snug, looking at his son. 'Look James, I'm not great at this emotional stuff and God knows I'm not an expert on women, but I did want to say something to you. The thing is, well I know you're very upset over Ingrid, and we're worried about you. As you know, the workings of the female body are no bother to me but the workings of the female mind, now that's another story entirely.'

James smiled, for what felt like the first time in months.

'What I wanted to say was this. I loved your mother, I really did, but I thought I knew what was best for her. She never wanted to come down here, she certainly never wanted me to join up, but I just went ahead and did what I thought was the right thing. Look, maybe things would have gone wrong anyway, who knows? But I do know this – you won't keep someone by holding on too tight or insisting they do what you want. They'll go, anyway. Solange taught me that, too late for

Edith, but with Juliet it was the same. I wanted to make her stay here where she'd be safe, but Solange put me straight. If I held on too tight, she'd go anyway and maybe I'd lose her forever. I see you and Ingrid, and you remind me of when I was young, thinking I know best.'

James was moved to see his father being so honest; he knew how much it cost him to discuss his private life.

'The thing is, you should let her do what she wants. I know you love this place. We are the same, you and I, but Edith, Juliet, and even Ingrid are different to us – they need a bit of freedom to explore their own things. My advice is to let her off. If she loves you, and I'm sure she does, then she'll come back to you. And if she doesn't, then she was never yours to begin with, so you're as well off discovering that now.'

James looked at his father. 'Did you never want anyone else after Mammy left?' he asked.

Richard Buckley shook his head ruefully. 'Ah James – I'm a doctor, and a married man, and this is Dunderrig.'

Sensing that was the end of the conversation, James asked no further questions. But that night, he lay awake wishing things were different, for himself and for his father.

CHAPTER 32

The freezing French rain beat on Juliet's
back as she cycled up the winding hill,
and the skin on her face tingled painfully. Her
blond hair stuck to her neck, and her thin coat
and skirt were soaking. Hercule would not be
pleased with being kept waiting. She was expected at the farmhouse at three at the latest. No
matter how much she would love to stop and
rest, she had to keep going.

The safe house was deep in the countryside
outside Poitiers. Making this journey twice a
week didn't make it any easier. As the winter
wore on, the weather got colder and wetter. As
she climbed up the steepest section of the hill, she
heard a car behind her. Cycling on, she prayed it

was a local, though she knew it was not likely to be, given the petrol rationing.

The car slowed down and Juliet cycled on, glancing sideways to note the swastika flying merrily on the bonnet.

'Can we give you a lift? It's a nasty day for up-hill cycling.'

The German officer was smiling at her exertions. He was dark and looked more Spanish than German with his tanned skin and brown eyes. He had an infectious smile.

Juliet tried to appear calm. 'No, thank you, I'm almost there.'

'Please, I insist. Where are you going? My sergeant can put your bicycle in the back.' His French was accented but correct.

Juliet knew to resist further would draw suspicion. Why would someone not accept a lift in a car on such a miserable day? Anyway, when a German officer said, 'I insist', that's exactly what it meant, however charming the delivery.

'I'm going to Chauvigney.' She had just passed a signpost for the medieval village 'Delivering a prescription for a patient of my employer. He is quite ill, so I would be glad to get it to him sooner. Thank you.'

Settled into the car, she remained composed.

She was conscious of the water dripping from her hair and clothes all over the plush upholstery of the car. She had been trained in Beaulieu for such eventualities. *Calm down*, she told herself. Her cover story had held up before, and it would again. She had all the necessary papers to say she was a *'dame de compagnie'* for a doctor in Poitiers, helping in his surgery and taking care of his young sons. Her papers were regularly checked as she made her way around the city, possibly even more so than if she were in Paris since Poitiers was so close to the 'unoccupied zone' of Vichy France. The division of the country into two – one area ruled directly by the Germans and the other ostensibly by the Vichy French parliament in exile, but in reality by the Germans also – meant tensions ran high. The Germans were vigilant as they saw it as a hotbed of resistance.

Dr Blain's wife had died when the children were young. Juliet's story was that she was Marie-Louise Berniere from Amiens and had been educated in Belgium, which would account for any discrepancies in her accent. Just as the Italians were expert at spotting any inconsistencies in clothing, so could the French spot the tiniest nuance of accent. Often, it was not the Germans that were the real threat but the French themselves, some of whom were informers. The trouble was that one never knew, so she had to be convincing at all times and never drop her guard. She was twenty-two years of age and an orphan. Her parents had been killed in a car accident in 1925, which explained why she was educated in a Belgian convent. Her papers were *faux faux*, which meant they were produced in London, but they had been scrutinised many times, and so she was confident of them. Lise de Chambray, her contact in the city, explained that some agents used *vrais faux* papers, preferring them as they were real papers belonging to an actual person but which contained no photograph, so checking back with the Gestapo was impossible. Once London became adept at producing authentic papers however, *faux faux* were deemed safer. Before she left, her clothes were checked to ensure they were French – even the way the French sew on buttons was different to the English, so it was imperative to give nothing away. A kind lady from the Special Operations Executive went through everything on Juliet's last night in London. Nothing she wore or carried could mark her out as an enemy agent. She was parachuted in on the night of the fourteenth of February, 1942. She recalled the last words she heard in English, from the flight lieutenant of the Lysander that dropped her: 'Happy Valentine's.'

Dr Blain, her employer, was a jolly man and was kind to Juliet. The Special Operations executive had set her up in the Blain home but warned her never to deviate from her cover story, even with the doctor. If Hervé Blain suspected anything was unusual about his new assistant, he never remarked upon it. He asked her little about herself but constantly chatted about the weather and the perfect cheese to go with different wines. His children, Jean-Marc and Luc, were aged eight and six, and Juliet had come to love them. Juliet was a feature of the Rue de la Vincenderie surgery as the patients of Dr Blain came and went. Each day, she prepared breakfast, took the boys to school, and then did the paperwork for the medical practice.

Several times a week, a patient would pass her a note along with his or her prescription, containing instructions for a drop. She couriered information all over the city in her brassiere. She relayed messages between her circuit leader, Hercule, and an unnamed wireless operator who, Lise had told her, worked out of the attic of a shoe shop on Boulevard Chasseligne. She tried never to take the children with her on these missions, fearing she might implicate them or their father if she was caught, though once or twice she'd been forced to take them when the message was urgent.

Initially, it was terrifying; she was convinced she looked guilty. Now she was much more relaxed. Still wary, of course – her training taught her that – but she had confidence now. The first time she saw a German soldier, she was walking the boys to school. He brushed past her on the street, and she was sure he could hear the pounding of her heart. The Germans were so much a feature of city life now that people just adapted to them being there. The locals did not engage with them except when absolutely necessary, and people were very guarded in their conversations, but amazingly, for Juliet, life just went on.

Sitting on the back seat beside the man who wore the insignia of a *Hauptsturmführer*, which she recognised as being equivalent to a captain, she tried to appear relaxed. He was chatting happily, and she thought he looked very young to hold such an elevated rank; she guessed him to be no more than thirty. The *Scharführer* loaded the bicycle in the back and drove off in the direction of the village. Juliet would have to insist he let her out in the square as she had no appointment set up to deliver medicine – though she always carried a bottle of important-looking pills in her pocket in case she needed a cover story. The training at Beaulieu had drilled into her that it was vital at all times to have a plausible reason for being anywhere and doing anything.

'So, does your employer not have petrol for his car? It seems somehow cruel to have such a lovely young lady cycling in such weather.' The German officer seemed friendly, but Juliet knew not to relax her guard.

'As yes, but it is in short supply, so he saves it for emergencies. I don't mind really, I enjoy cycling – but yes, it is particularly chilly today.'

Reaching into a bag, he pulled out a hip flask and offered it to her.

'*Non, merci.*' She shook her head demurely. Though the warming whiskey or brandy would have been welcome, nicely brought-up French girls wouldn't accept a drink from a German like that.

'So, what is your name?' he asked pleasantly.

'Marie-Louise Berniere.'

'A beautiful name for a beautiful girl. I am Dieter Friedman, it is a pleasure to meet you, Mademoiselle Berniere.' Juliet noticed he didn't use his rank to introduce himself. 'And are you from Poitiers?' he asked.

'No, I am from Amiens, originally. I was educated in Belgium as a child. I'm working in Poitiers for Dr Blain, a general practitioner on Rue de la Vincenderie, helping in the surgery and taking care of his sons. He is a widower.' She felt she was chatty enough so as not to alert him. Also, she was anxious to steer the conversation to her current situation. While her cover story was good, and she had been drilled on it a thousand times before leaving England, she did not feel totally confident discussing Belgian convents or Picardy, considering she'd never set foot in either.

'A busy lady then. Do you ever have a day off? I hear the countryside of the Haute-Vienne is beautiful even in winter, but I have had no time to explore it. I am from Bavaria so the landscape is very different to what is here. Would you care to join me someday?'

Juliet knew that to refuse outright might offend him and cause him to question her further. The safest option seemed to be generally positive about the suggestion but to be non-specific.

'Oh, the scenery of the Haute-Vienne is really beautiful. You really should try to see it. Unfortunately, Dr Blain is very busy at the moment because his locum is away in Paris visiting his mother, and there is a nasty bug going around, so I will be working every day until he returns.' Juliet hoped she sounded genuinely disappointed. This was her first conversation of any length with a German, and she was anxious not to arouse his suspicion. She mustn't seem too enthusiastic – after all, a nice French girl should feel resentment of the occupying enemy – but she didn't want to antagonise him, either. Calm politeness was what was suggested when the question was raised during training.

'And when does he return, this other doctor?' he asked, smiling.

'I'm not sure. Probably not until after Christmas. His mother's health is failing.' They were approaching the village square. She needed to get out here without saying or doing anything that would make him think she was anything other than what she said she was.

'Does your patient live here in the village? Can we drop you to their door?'

Thinking quickly, Juliet said, 'The place is very hard to find, so I have been told to wait here in the square and one of the man's daughters is to collect the prescription from me. I can wait under that shelter. I am a little early, thanks to your generosity. Thank you so much for the lift.' She was praying he wouldn't insist she avoid the rain and wait in the car until the fictitious daughter arrived.

The driver pulled over to the kerb beside a makeshift shelter used during the weekly market. She made to open the door, but the officer leaned over her, covering the handle.

'Goodbye, Marie-Louise. We shall meet again, I hope.' He was very close to her, though not touching. He was clean-shaven and smelled of spice. She was terrified but maintained her composure. Checkpoints staffed by bored soldiers were one thing, but this was something very different. The sergeant opened the door for her and retrieved her bicycle. As the car turned into the square and drove back in the direction it had come, the captain waved from the back seat.

An old woman walked past her at the moment Juliet was returning his wave. She was hunched over and covered in a black cloak. She had several gaps where teeth should have been. 'Traîtresse,' she spat.

When she was sure the Germans were gone, Juliet once again mounted her bicycle and pedalled out into the countryside to meet her circuit leader. Hercule lived in a remote, tumbledown farmhouse perched on a hill, where he was surrounded by loyal volunteers who acted as his sentries. They were able to warn him of any unwelcome visitors long before they got there, by virtue of the building's vantage point over the surrounding farmland. There was a dense forest behind the farm, where several underground bunkers had already been dug for safety in the event of any Germans coming sniffing round.

Hercule was extremely grumpy – never a word of thanks, only sarcastic remarks and barking instructions. He seemed to regard Juliet as a silly little girl, who was utterly unsuited to this kind of work and was therefore a serious safety risk, though she'd never made a mistake in the ten months she'd worked for him. Once, on a previous visit, she had remarked about the weather, and he had looked at her as if she were simple in the head. Juliet was only slightly less terrified of him than she was of the Germans. Yet she was sure Hercule would be pleased with the message she was bringing him now. It was from the circuit's wireless operator and confirmed that there would be a drop of supplies the following night, providing the full moon was not obscured by cloud cover.

She knew the operator received many of his

messages through the medium of the BBC, delivered in code. But even listening to the BBC had become incredibly dangerous as the Germans now had mobile equipment that could intercept radio waves. Sometimes, operators had been captured and forced under torture to transmit messages that ultimately led to the capture of agents, so even within one's own circuit, safety was a very tenuous thing.

She debated telling Hercule about the encounter with the captain in the car. He might explode and berate her for even speaking to a German even though there had been no choice. Still, she had to tell him; it was too significant. She waited until he escorted her to the gate, handed her a message for London on a tiny scrap of paper, and turned to leave without saying goodbye.

'Hercule, there is something else you should know.' Her voice was halting. He paused and looked back at her impatiently. She felt tongue-tied and nervous. He really was a most unpleasant man even if his organisational skills made him invaluable to the Resistance. Lise had said he was English and that London trusted him implicitly. Juliet had no idea of his real name.

'What?' His French accent was Parisian.

'On the way here, I was given a lift by a German captain in his car. He insisted on putting my bike in the back and driving me to Chavigney. Well, actually, his sergeant drove – he sat in the back with me. I know how dangerous that was, but I had no choice. To refuse would have been suspicious. He asked me to go out with him. Of course, I said I was too busy...'

'What was his name, this German?' Hercule asked wearily, interrupting her explanation as if bored by her long-windedness.

'Dieter Friedman, and he had the insignia of a *Hauptsturmfürher* – so he was a captain,' said Juliet, pleased with her knowledge of insignia.

'Yes, clever you, a captain.' His voice dripped sarcasm. 'So, you've caught the eye of our local Nazi have you? You may not be as useless as you look.'

LATER THAT EVENING, JULIET railed against Hercule in Lise's dining room. Lise was second in command to Hercule in their circuit. She was gentle, quiet-spoken, and impossible to imagine as a secret agent. Her delicate features with pale blue eyes and blond hair made her look vulnerable and in need of protection, but Juliet knew that Lise was one of the toughest women she'd ever known. Her background was aristocratic yet she blended perfectly into all types of company. Despite the deprivations of occupied France, she always looked chic and smelled of freesias. She was cultured and well-read and had taken a liking to Juliet. Her cover story was that she was a Parisian widow, Madame Lise Chevalier, who was seeking refuge from the tension of life in the city. With a nonchalance that was her trademark, she lived in a ground floor apartment beside the Gestapo headquarters in the city.

'Marie-Louise, I know he can be a little condescending, but he really is very good at his job. I'm not sure he agrees with women in the military. But to give him his due, things are going very well in this region, and it's mainly due to him. Just bite your tongue if he says anything to rile you. He's all right really.' Lise soothed her, pouring each of them a glass of red wine, which she always seemed able to procure despite the restrictions.

'Now, tell me more about your German captain. What did you talk about?' she asked.

'Well, there's nothing much more to tell, really,' Juliet explained. 'He asked me out, I was noncommittal. I thought that was best. I think I handled it fairly well, to be honest. If you'd told me I was going to have to go through that in advance, I'd have been terrified but actually I was calm. He seemed nice enough, and it wasn't too hard just to chat with him.' Fearing she had made it sound like she enjoyed his company, she added, 'Of course, he's a German, I just meant...'

'I know exactly what you meant,' Lise interrupted. 'Not all of them are animals like our neighbour Klinker, that sadistic Gestapo pig. He is truly vile but at least you know what you're dealing with. The civilised ones are more dangerous in lots of ways. It's easier to forget who they are and why they're here.'

She spoke quietly, with the gramophone playing Schubert gently in the background. SOE had trained them to always obscure the sound when discussing matters of importance, in case of eavesdroppers.

'Perhaps, you should go on a date with your Captain Friedman. It would be very useful to have someone close to him. We know a recently arrived British agent was picked up in Poitiers a few days ago. We hope it was by an unlucky chance, but of course, there is always the worry that she was betrayed. Plus, we don't know exactly what she knew and might have told them. The fact that the captain sought you out creates the perfect opportunity for us – they are instantly suspicious of girls who flirt with them.'

Juliet was so shocked she couldn't speak. Was Lise serious? It could have been Juliet herself picked up just as easily. Not for the first time, the reality of what she was doing crashed over her like an icy wave. What had happened to that agent? Had she been tortured? Was she dead? And now Lise was suggesting that she put herself into an even more dangerous situation. Working as a courier was terrifying enough, but living a double life to deliberately get close to the enemy was a whole other level.

'I...I don't think I could do that. I mean, what if he suspected me...' She knew she sounded cowardly, but the thought of what Lise was suggesting made her almost want to vomit with fear.

Lise looked kindly at her young friend. 'What I'm suggesting is extremely dangerous. Of course, you shouldn't do it if you feel it would be too risky. You're probably right. Just say no and continue doing the excellent job you're doing. Please don't worry about it. Now, I've managed to get us some beef for our supper, just a little bit – but I miss meat, don't you?'

Lise chatted about life in general as she prepared a simple meal of meat and bread with some fried onions. Never again did Friedman come up in their conversation. It was simply a chat between two friends.

Lise deliberately had a lot of visitors, so that agents could come and go without causing suspicion from her Nazi neighbours. She had cleaning ladies, tutors of all kinds of things, charity workers – she was on several committees – and even a few gentleman callers. She even gave piano lessons. She called it 'hiding in plain sight' and claimed it was the safest way to live. The train station was just down the street, so there was always lots of hustle and bustle outside.

Juliet got up to leave at a quarter past eight. The curfew meant no one was allowed out after nine in the evening, and it was a twenty-minute walk to the doctor's house. She avoided public transport wherever possible as the buses were used by German soldiers. As she pulled on her coat, she asked, 'Do we know what happened to the British agent?'

'She's dead. They dumped her body in a field. She had been horribly tortured. Good night, my dear.' Juliet hugged her friend quickly at the door.

As she walked the streets of the ancient city, Juliet tried to absorb the horror of the agent's death. Despite it being close to Christmas, there was no air of festivity. Juliet wound her scarf tighter around her neck and held her coat closed against the biting wind. Who was that poor girl? How old had she been? The uncertainty of life in occupied France and the constant knowledge that the game could be up at any moment was exhausting. The idea that the agent had been betrayed filled her with panic. She tried to block it out, it didn't bear thinking about.

She wondered how she would cope if she was unmasked as a spy. It had all seemed so abstract in the various training schools in England and even, to a certain extent, here in France, but the events of recent weeks brought the reality of what she was facing into sharp focus. She coped with it by not thinking about the future if she was captured. Even the word *interrogation* made her nauseous. During her training, she had been left in no doubt as to what it meant. The methods used to extract information were many and varied, all of them unbearable. She thought of the tiny pill under the insole of her shoe. It was the final thing they gave you when leaving London. It guaranteed almost instant death in the case of being caught. Had the agent been able to take the poison before she broke down under torture? Juliet wondered if they had trained together. Had she been old or young? Had someone betrayed her? Had she in turn betrayed others? Did she know about Juliet? It was terrifying.

Letting herself into Dr Blain's house, she found Luc and Jean-Marc sitting on the stairs in their pyjamas, almost hidden behind a huge bouquet of flowers. As she entered, they charged at her, full of excitement.

'Marie-Louise! There was a man here, a German, looking for you. He gave us sweets! Papa told him you were out on an errand for him, but he asked us to give you these!'

All available land was being used to grow food, so flowers were a very rare sight indeed even in summer. Such an elaborate bouquet in the depths of winter was unheard of. Then, Nazis could get anything they wanted, everyone knew that. Dr Blain emerged from the kitchen and caught her eye over the heads of his sons. There was a message with the flowers, and Luc handed it to her, excited at such an unusual event. Juliet opened the envelope and inside was a small card.

I'll pick you up tomorrow at 11:00 a.m. The doctor agrees you work too hard! Dieter.

CHAPTER 33

$\mathcal{J}$ames sat in the café of the train station in Cork. People rushed on and off trains; rationing meant that they looked universally shabby – shoes were well-worn, coats were thin and frayed, and collars turned on shirts. A few men in uniform walked up and down belligerently, almost daring anyone to comment on the fact that they were fighting for the British.

She'd asked him to meet her at the little station in Skibbereen, but he'd wanted to intercept her journey here, away from all the prying eyes. He had been so happy to hear from her after over a year of nothing. At the start, he was sure the fight they'd had was just a little tiff and that it would all blow over, but when the days turned into weeks and he hadn't heard from her, he tried writing. He apologised for the fight and agreed with her that he should grow up. He knew that she received his letters – Edith had confirmed it when he rang her – but she didn't reply.

He hadn't visited his mother in months, but she'd been happy to receive his call. He was getting to know Edith; she wasn't one for recriminations or emotional blackmail. She was straightforward in that way. When he eventually went up to see her in March, she made no comment at the length of his absence. When he enquired after Ingrid, she merely said she wasn't there and that neither she nor Otto knew where she was. Clearly, if they did know, they weren't going to tell him. He wanted to ask straight out if they thought she was seeing someone else, but he couldn't bear to hear the answer. He returned to Dunderrig even more despondent than he'd left. Solange and Mrs Canty tried their best to cheer him up, but he had no interest.

He poured his misery into his art, painting all day every day, often into the early hours of the morning. By now, he had enough work for several exhibitions.

The sale of the six-foot-wide canvas of Castletownshend village to the Bank of Ireland last year had been lucrative and had placed him in the public eye. His paintings were in high demand and he worked tirelessly, not for the money but to try to fill the void left by Ingrid. He had an agent now, and there was talk of a large showing of his work in Dublin, but he was reluctant – that city held too many memories of when he and Ingrid had been happy and in love. He preferred the solitude of Dunderrig, where for the most part he was left alone.

He wondered if he should have brought flowers – or would that have been too much? Her letter had been warm but very short. He took it out and perused it for the hundredth time, trying to read between the lines.

Dear James,

I'm sorry I wasn't here when you came to Dublin. I missed you. I am going to come to Dunderrig, if that is all right. I'm not much for writing letters, as you know, so maybe we can just talk face to face. I always loved Christmas at Dunderrig. I'll get the first train down on the eighteenth and change at Cork. It's only a short wait, and you can meet me in Skibbereen. If you don't want to see me, can you ring Edith just to let me know?

With love,
Ingrid.

What did she mean, she missed him? Did she miss him in the gut-wrenching way he missed her, or was she saying she missed him by not being there when he came to Dublin? It must mean she was planning on staying over for Christmas though, which was a week away yet, so that was good news surely. He knew that whatever her terms, he would have her back in a heartbeat. He had tried going out with other girls in the past year, but no one came even close to her. He even spent a passionate weekend in a hotel in Killarney with an older woman whom he met at an exhibition in Cork and, while he enjoyed it and had certainly emerged from the experience a more worldly young man, she wasn't Ingrid.

The first train to leave Dublin would be into Cork in ten minutes. He walked along the platform and caught a glance of himself in the large mirror of the ladies' waiting room – someone had left the door open. His new navy Dunlap hat and coat made him look older and, he hoped, a little more distinguished. His blond hair was longer than when she'd seen him last; his Killarney companion had told him that he looked rakish and artistic that way, so he had let it curl over his collar. He swam every day in the sea – winter and summer – to relieve the stress on his body from painting and had bulked up a lot as a result. He hoped Ingrid liked what she saw in the new, older, and hopefully wiser James.

The train pulled in with puffs of smoke, the smell of burning peat permeating the air. There was no coal now for running the steam engine, so turf had to be used instead. The doors opened and people emerged onto the platform. James's eyes raked the platform for Ingrid, then noticed that someone was struggling to open one of the train doors from the inside and went to help. Time stood still as he realised the person he had freed was Ingrid. Her dark hair was shorter and she seemed less self-assured. James gazed into her face, unable to speak – until an outraged cry from the bundle in her arms distracted him, and his eyes were drawn in amazement to the tiny creature in her arms.

In a daze, he helped her off the train with her many bags, not trusting himself to speak. Around them, travellers dragged trunks and suitcases, people embraced, and the station buzzed with the commotion of the train's arrival, but James and Ingrid stood on the platform, oblivious to it all. Removing the blanket a little so James could see the baby more clearly, Ingrid spoke quietly.

'Hello, James. This is your daughter, Lili.'

The blood was pounding in his ears, Ingrid's words sinking in. *His daughter.* He couldn't take it in. Could this really be happening? Ingrid had become pregnant and then had never told him, then refused to answer his letters and wouldn't see him when he went up to Dublin. So that's why Edith and Otto had seemed so awkward when he had asked where she was. Suddenly, the mystery of Ingrid's disappearance was starting to make sense.

'Please say something, James.' Her voice was different – not as full of life as it once was.

He needed to be alone with her, with them, to figure this out. He couldn't discuss it in the middle of a train station. 'Let's go to the Metropole Hotel; we can talk there.' He barely recognised his own voice.

HE SAT ON THE chair while she lay on the bed, propped up on pillows, and settled the baby to her breast. He couldn't take his eyes off his child. 'How old is she?'

'Her birthday is on the first of May. She's seven months old. I know this must be a shock, and maybe I should have told you, but you were so young and so worried about everything. I knew I was pregnant that day in Dunderrig, and I was going to tell you when we got back to Dublin, but then we had that row and well...I realised it was too much for you. So I told Uncle Otto and Edith, but I made them promise not to tell you.'

'So, you don't tell me you're pregnant, then you make my own mother lie to me, you have my child, and you don't say a word about it, and now you just arrive off the train. Expecting what? What do you want? How could you have kept this from me?' James was shaking with emotion. How could she do this to him?

The baby stirred and Ingrid switched breasts. Settling her again, she said, 'If you are wondering if she's your child then the answer is yes. You are too polite to ask, but it's a logical question after all this time. You can check the dates if you like. Anyway, she has your green eyes – so vivid. As to your question, well, I don't know what you want, how you feel. I want us to try again. We were happy once, and we could be again. I want Lili to have a father who loves her and who will do right by her. But if that's not what you want, then you are perfectly within your rights to say no, and we'll return to Dublin by the next train.'

James sat and looked at them for the longest time. Ingrid sat Lili upon her knee, and the contented baby let out a loud belch, followed by a wide gummy smile. James's heart melted, all anger and resentment gone. As he looked at the smiling face of his little girl, he realised that everything he had ever wanted was there on that bed. All he had to do was take it. Ingrid was waiting for his response. He knew her well enough to know there would be no tears or pleading. She was offering him a life, a family, her love – and that's all he had ever wanted. Ingrid was right, he had been immature, but he had grown up a lot in the past year and now he felt ready. He walked over to the bed and lay down beside Ingrid, their daughter snuggled between them, and he kissed them both tenderly.

'Let's get married,' he whispered.

'We'd love that,' she replied. 'Wouldn't we, Lili?'

THE CAR APPROACHED THE station in Skibbereen as James and Ingrid stood waiting for it in the cold, Lili wrapped up in blankets in his arms. They had stayed overnight in Cork, and he had rung the house to ask to be collected at the station the following lunchtime. He had wondered if he should prepare them, to tell them about Lili in advance, but he'd decided against it. He hoped it was Eddie in the car, or better still, the young lad that helped out around the place now that Eddie was getting on a bit. Ideally, he wanted to tell his father himself, alone; that way if Richard said anything negative, it would be only to him and not to Ingrid. To his relief, it was the young fellow. He loaded all the bags into the car and drove them home without comment.

James brought his new family in by the front door. He could hear Solange in the kitchen with Mrs Canty, and the aromas emerging were mouth-watering. He showed Ingrid into the rarely used drawing room with Lili and asked her to wait. Then he crossed the hall and knocked on his father's surgery door. Richard had drilled into them since childhood that they were never to enter the surgery unannounced.

'Come in.' His father's voice sounded tired.

'Ah, James. You're back. Did you find the paints you needed?' The surgery was empty of patients, and his father was washing his hands in preparation for lunch. 'I'll tell you now, if I have to look at another bunion, I'll scream.' He smiled at his own joke. Sensing no reaction from his son, he turned around – and paled.

'What is it? Is it Juliet?'

'No Dad, it's nothing like that. I...I just need to talk to you about something.'

'James? Are you all right? Sit down.'

James inhaled deeply. He was a man, no longer a child, and he was bringing his family home.

'I'm fine, Dad, I just need to tell you that I didn't go to Cork for art supplies. I went to meet Ingrid. She wrote to me, you see, wanting to see me, and I've been so miserable...'

Richard patted his son's shoulder, his face flooded with relief. 'Thank God. I was sure it was something to do with your sister.'

'No. Well, anyway, I met Ingrid, and she...well, she had someone with her. A baby. My baby. Lili, a little girl. She's my daughter. She never told me, you see. I never knew until yesterday.'

Richard sat down slowly in his chair on the other side of his desk.

'I know it's a shock, and you are probably disgusted with me, but I do love her, and we are going to get married, be a proper family... I'm so sorry. I know people are going to talk.' He searched his father's face for a reaction to this news.

'So, you're a father and I'm a grandfather, is that it?' Richard was shaking his head in amazement. 'Well, truth be told, and as I well know from my life as a doctor, yourself and Ingrid are not the first young couple to do things upside down and back to front, nor will ye be the last. Sure, it's not the perfect way, to have the child before you get married, and there's plenty around here who'll have a field day with it, but to hell with them. This is nothing to do with them. If ye have decided to give it a go, and ye love each other, then I wish ye the best of luck. This world is full of terrible things happening all the time, people determined to blow each other to kingdom come at every opportunity. Your sister is out there doing God knows what, and us not knowing when we'll see her again. We have a new baby in the family and that's great news. Ingrid is a grand girl, and if ye want to get married, then I'm happy for ye both. Another Buckley of Dunderrig is just what we need. Is she here?'

James realised he wasn't surprised at his father's reaction. He just loved his children and of course he would love his grandchild. Juliet's absence had put everything else into perspective, and Richard was just happy to have his family around him.

'Yes, they're in the drawing room.' He was almost too choked up to speak.

'Jesus, do you want the pair of them down with pneumonia? 'Tis freezing in there. Let's go and bring them into the kitchen where they can sit by the range, and then Solange and Mrs Canty can have a look at this child, too.'

Putting his arm around his son's shoulders, they crossed the hall and opened the drawing-room door. Ingrid looked up in expectation, and Richard kissed her on the cheek and gave her a one-armed hug. He then took his granddaughter in his arms and studied her in delight, while she looked curiously at him. Her blond hair curled around her face, and she had exactly the same green eyes as James and himself.

'Well, now then, Miss Lili Buckley.' Richard spoke gently. 'You are very welcome to Dunderrig. I'm your granddad, and we are so happy you're here. Now, I think you've been a very good girl, so we'll have to make sure that Santa leaves something special for you under the tree. But first we must introduce you to Solange and Mrs

Canty, who'll be mad about you too and will spoil you rotten.'

Lili responded to her grandfather's words with one of her signature gummy smiles.

James put his arm around Ingrid as they walked after Richard and Lili across the hall. She nestled into him.

'I love you,' she whispered.

He replied, 'I love you too.'

Solange and Mrs Canty gazed open-mouthed as Richard announced, 'Ladies, let me introduce Lili Buckley, my granddaughter. Isn't she beautiful?' He stood in the middle of the kitchen as Solange and Mrs Canty stared in astonishment.

Solange had not expected to see Ingrid again, let alone this, and even Mrs Canty was uncharacteristically silenced.

Yet moments later, both women recovered their composure and drew close to the baby – and melted in instant adoration. Solange coaxed James and Ingrid out from behind Richard, and all five adults formed a circle of love around the newest Buckley of Dunderrig. Mrs Canty slapped James across the behind, like she'd done all his life.

'Aren't you a right divil now? Herself below in the post office is going to get great mileage out of this, so she will. I suppose 'tis only one more peculiar happening in Dunderrig. Sure without us to talk about t'would be a very dull village!' But the words were delivered with a chuckle, and James knew that his baby, Lili, was now one of the family.

CHAPTER 34

*J*uliet managed to get the boys to bed and as she was going to her room, Doctor Blain called her to the kitchen. A bottle of wine and two glasses sat on the table.

Pouring her a glass first, he handed it to her.

'I'm so sorry, Dr Blain, I had no idea he would just turn up here. I don't know what to do...'

'Marie-Louise, I don't know why you are here, I don't know what you're doing in France, and for mine and my children's safety, I do not want to know. But I do know some things. I know, for example, you're no more from Amiens than I am.'

Juliet looked at him in dismay. She'd been so careful – how could he have guessed?

'Don't worry. I just mentioned something a

while back – a large train crash that happened about five years ago in Amiens – and it didn't register with you.'

Juliet longed to confide in this kind doctor but her training was ingrained too deep. Also, as he'd said, the less this lovely family knew the better. So she said nothing.

'If you're going to see this man, and he seems to think that you will, then you must be extremely careful. I have been very happy with your work and my boys are very fond of you, but I cannot have German officers calling here, it is too dangerous, you understand. You are a very nice girl, well brought up, and I know you would never be a collaborator – so I assume you have other, better reasons, and I do want to help you. As you know, my boys lost their dear Maman, and I cannot risk making them orphans. So, what I propose is this, explain to your Nazi officer that life is difficult for girls who collaborate, so while you would like to spend time with him, he must be discreet. He seemed to be a reasonable man, for a German, so maybe this will work?'

'Perhaps,' Juliet replied. If only she could get to Lise before eleven in the morning, but she knew that she couldn't. It would be very dangerous for both of them if she made her way there now, after curfew. And Lise had said she was going to be away all day tomorrow. No, Juliet would just have to handle this on her own.

Dr Blain said good night, and Juliet sat alone in the small kitchen. The enormity of what faced her filled her with terror. How on earth had it come to this? She was Juliet Buckley, from Dunderrig, West Cork, and here she was, in a doctor's house in Poitiers, risking her life every day delivering information for the British under the noses of the Gestapo. Now, not only was she to do that, but she was to go on a date with a German officer who, if he found out who she really was, would have her interrogated, tortured, and shot. She wanted to be at home, in Dunderrig, sitting at the table with Mrs Canty making scones and Daddy reading the paper by the range and James painting somewhere in the garden. Instead, she was stranded in enemy-occupied France, and there was no way home.

She thought about just not being there when Friedman appeared in the morning, but she couldn't do that. It would put Dr Blain and the children in a very difficult position and, anyway, he'd probably just wait until she got back. She couldn't just disappear – where would she go?

Slowly and quietly, she crept to bed, hoping

not to wake the boys. She knew she wouldn't be able to sleep, and she wished she had something from home – a letter, a photograph, anything. She'd written letters to Daddy, Solange, James, and Ewan to be sent home in the event of her death. She had left them with Vera Atkins, the woman in charge of the French section of SOE. When writing them, it had all seemed so unreal, and – if she were honest – very romantic. She had none of those feelings now. This situation wasn't romantic or daring, it was deadly dangerous. She thought of her small suitcase back in England. All her personal things were in there – things that made her who she was – letters from home and from Ewan, the bracelet Daddy had given her on her eighteenth birthday, James's miniature painting of Dunderrig, the locket with a picture of Ewan inside. Here she was – not Juliet Buckley, girlfriend, daughter, sister – but a character the SOE had created for her to play in this potentially deadly game, with a fictitious past and very possibly no future.

All night long, she imagined scenarios. Perhaps, if she was silly or boring, he would have no interest in taking her out again. Maybe, if she just refused to go out with him on the grounds that she was a patriotic French girl, and she couldn't collaborate… Or maybe, she could engineer a huge row and slap his face, thus ending any potential romance.

She thought back to her final training course at Beaulieu. She tried to recall her classes – was there anything she had learned that she could use now? There she had learned how to live a clandestine life, how never to look suspicious, how to follow someone without being detected, and how to lose someone following you. She learned about invisible ink and one-time codes, how to pick locks and duplicate keys and how to think on her feet.

The part of the course that kept coming back to mind was how to withstand interrogation. One night, she was roughly pulled from her bed and shoved in her nightdress down the corridors of the house on the Beaulieu estate to a cold, damp-smelling basement. The men who took her were dressed in the uniforms of the Gestapo and spoke to her only in rough guttural German. There she was interrogated under bright lights and man-handled. They threatened her, they told her they knew all about her family and if she didn't tell them what they wanted to know, then her family would suffer. They shouted at her and whispered unspeakable threats in her ears. In her logical mind, she knew it was a trial run, not the real thing, but it was still a horrible experience. The next morning, when she was debriefed and told she'd done well, they told her that the real thing was much worse. The real Gestapo didn't just threaten to pull your fingernails out one by one, they did it. They used water to almost drown their victims, they beat them until they could no longer see, hear or feel – no type of torture was too brutal. As they described the way the Germans extracted information, she felt sick, wishing she had been left in ignorance. They told her it was vital she knew what she was getting herself into before finally signing up.

What had that poor British agent suffered?

By the time the sun rose, she had decided she was going to do it – she would go out with him and see what she could find out. If she was going to be caught and face the unthinkable consequences of that eventuality, at least it should be in the hope of achieving something. Perhaps the agent had indeed been deliberately betrayed, and she could find out who had done such a terrible thing.

She rose, washed, and dressed in her best dress. She pinned her hair loosely, leaving curling tendrils escape, and used cochineal from the doctor's larder to stain her lips red. She thought sadly of the doctor's widow and how she must have bought the food colouring for a cake before she died – and here she was using it to lure a German officer. Sitting on her bed at a quarter to eleven, she sent a mental note to Ewan, hoping that she could link telepathically with him in the skies over Europe.

My darling Ewan,

I can't write to you because I'm not me. I'm not where you think I am, and I'm not doing what you think I'm doing. In this web of lies that my life has become, one thing is true. I love you and I will, if at all possible, return to you. I'm about to go on a date today with a German officer. If you can hear me, sense me, please know that you are my man, and I am your girl. Nothing could ever change that.

We will be together in Dunderrig.

All my love,

Juliet.

Even thinking her own name felt dangerous. Her cover story had to be her; it was drilled into her from the moment she got it. She must act, think, and speak as Marie-Louise, even in her own head.

CHAPTER 35

'But what about Lili? Why can't you wait until next week? I'll have finished the Shelbourne commission by then, and we can all go up to Dublin together.' James was trying to keep the frustration out of his voice.

'No. I am going to Dublin, on my own, for a few days. Can't you just mind Lili here? Solange and Mrs Canty do most of the minding anyway, and it's only for a few days. Helmut needs me, and I can't let him down.' Ingrid was adamant.

'Look, Lili isn't the problem, you know that – sure, I love minding her, but I have to go up to Dublin next week, anyhow. The Gresham hung them in all wrong and then the manager complained to me about it. It's best if I'm there for the hanging myself. Can't Helmut wait for a few more days? It seems mad you going tomorrow and then me on Monday or Tuesday.'

James was trying to be reasonable, but Ingrid was the most stubborn person he'd ever met. Since they were married, she'd continued to work on and off for Helmut Clissman, which James found a little bewildering. She could never explain what she did for him – clerical things for the language school, she always said. But surely he could have got anyone for that? It was her decision to stay in Dunderrig – he'd have been happy to live anywhere, so long as he had Ingrid and Lili, but his new wife was determined to stay in West Cork. Richard had given them the cottage on Dunderrig land, which had been empty since the Cantys moved up to the main house – neither of them was getting any younger and Richard and Solange were happier knowing the aging couple were under their roof. The cottage was tucked away off the avenue up to the main house, and with the help of Solange, they'd made a beautiful little home. They were secluded enough to live their own lives but near enough to the big house for any help they might need.

Things were going very well for James with his art sales. The large painting he did for the bank had attracted attention from other financial institutions, as well as from hotels and country houses, and as a result he had commissions queuing up. He was easily in work for the next two years honouring those commitments alone. Lili was the light of his life, though now that she was running around, nothing was safe. He had come into the little room he used as a studio last week to find both the walls and his baby daughter covered in burnt sienna.

Ingrid had been extremely down lately, having miscarried two babies in eight months. The first time, she was only two months gone, and no one knew she was pregnant, not even James. She had told him once it was all over. The second one had been only a month ago – she had been three months pregnant and had miscarried in the hospital. She had refused to discuss it with him, and he didn't know what to say to help her. He was much more secure in their relationship than he had been before Lili arrived, but in loving Ingrid, he had to accept there was a part of her he would never know. All this trekking up and down to Dublin couldn't be helping her – she looked exhausted and had been very jumpy of late.

'It's only because I want to look after you, make things easy on you, that I'm saying it, you know?' he said, putting his arms around her. 'You look worn out, and I think maybe just taking it easy here is best, and when I'm going up to Dublin, we can go together. That way, I can do all the bag carrying and all that. You're not long out of hospital.'

He could feel her tense in his arms. 'James, you are my husband, not my keeper. I want to go tomorrow and so that is what I will do. Now can you look after Lili or not?'

'Of course I can,' he sighed.

Later that night, he walked up to the house. Ingrid had fallen asleep reading to Lili in German. He saw the light on in his father's study and tapped on the window so as not to wake the whole house.

Richard opened the French doors and James stepped in.

'Ah, James. Is everything all right? 'Tis late you're out and about.'

'They're all fine. Both fast asleep.' James looked at his father thinking how much he'd aged in recent years. There had been no word from Juliet since February of 1941 and the fear that she was dead or worse was a burden that Richard carried heavily. Her last letter was on his desk, read and reread.

'You know if she had been killed we'd have been told, Dad,' James said. 'She said she had given this address as her home address, and we were not to worry if we didn't hear from her. Bad news travels fast.'

It was true. The autumn of 1943 was fast becoming winter and still nothing. The war finally looked like it was turning in the Allied favour with the sinking of large numbers of U-boats. The Battle of the Atlantic was all but won, and there was a sense of optimism and hope that the end might be in sight.

'Where is she, James?' Richard looked broken. 'I got a letter a while back from that lad she was going out with. A Scotsman called Ewan McCrae. I wrote back saying we'd heard nothing, but we'd let him know if we did. Poor lad, I think he really loves her and is frantic to hear from her. I know how he feels.'

James hugged his father, wishing he could say something to console him. Juliet was always in his mind, and now that he was a father himself, he had a better understanding of the torture of not knowing where your child was, or if she was safe. James was glad that his little family was a distraction for his father. Richard's greatest joy was Lili. The baby had in no way replaced Juliet, but she was such a happy, funny little thing that she brought a sparkle to Dunderrig that would otherwise be crippled with worry and grief. Lili loved her 'Gandah' and Richard spent hours with her.

'Sure we are all in the same boat, but you know how close we are and I think I'd know, I'd feel something if she was dead, and I'm not just saying that. I've always felt that we were part of the same person...it's hard to explain. She's part of me and I'm part of her. She's all right, Dad, I know it. I haven't a clue where she is or what she's doing, but when this bloody war is over, she'll be home.'

'I hope you're right, I really do.' Turning to his desk, Richard took out a bottle of whiskey. Pouring two glasses, he handed one to James.

'Anyway, worrying won't solve anything, I suppose.' He gazed into the swirling amber liquid as he twirled the glass. 'Now, what has you wandering around in the middle of the night like a lost soul?'

James was never surprised when his father seemed to know instinctively what was going on. It was what made him a truly great doctor. He could see beyond the obvious, and he realised that pills were not what was needed in many cases, but a sympathetic ear.

'I'm worried about Ingrid. She won't talk about this last miscarriage. She shouted at Lili yesterday, which she never does, and now she is hell-bent on tearing up to Dublin to do some work for Helmut tomorrow. She's only out of hospital three weeks...' James downed some whiskey.

Richard thought about what to say next. He was reluctant to interfere in his son's marriage, but he could see James was trying his best and getting nowhere.

'Well, James, the thing is that for you, those miscarriages were sad, and you'd have loved to have a son or another daughter. At the same time, for us men, a baby isn't really a baby until we can see it in front of our eyes. For women, it's different – it's a baby from the moment she finds out she's pregnant; some say even from the moment of conception. We'll never understand it, but I will tell you this. Stay talking to her; don't let the silence build up between ye. I did that with your mother and looking back on it now, it must have been hard for her, stuck down here away from everything, all her friends. I was in France when she was expecting you two, so I was no help to her at all. She pushed me away, that's true, but I let her do it. I should have told her I loved her, tried to understand, but instead I left her alone – not deliberately, but in the absence of any better ideas. I should have tried harder, maybe given in a bit more. I know Mrs Canty would poison her if she ever saw her again, but you know, 't'wasn't all her doing, either. If I were a young man like you again, I'd do things very differently. I never knew what became of her but if I met her now, I think I'd owe her an apology. I came home destroyed after the war – I still am, I suppose – and I thought she'd just forgive me and move on. I never really tried to see things from her point of view. You know, James, the longer I live the more I realise we're all just trying to get along, trying to love and be loved. She gave me yourself and Juliet, and without ye, my life would have been mean- ingless. And for that, I'm eternally grateful to her.'

James knew that this was his chance to tell his father. If he let it go any longer, the lie would seem a lot worse. Richard had never spoken so openly about his marriage before – it was like they were not just father and son now, but friends. He knew he owed this man, who had reared them and loved them all his life, the truth.

'I see her, from time to time.' The words hung in the air between them. The clock ticked loudly on the mantelpiece. Eventually Richard spoke.

'I wondered, did you? But you never said and 't'wasn't my place to be asking. How is she?'

James was amazed how relaxed his father seemed at the news. 'She's well. She got married in Germany, before the war.'

Richard almost smiled. 'Did she now? The small matter of being still married to me didn't pose a problem then? Sure what harm, I suppose. What's he like? Did you meet him?'

James told his father the whole story, about the fireworks between himself and Juliet, about Otto and his connections, and of how he really met Ingrid.

Throughout the entire tale, Richard just sat and listened. And when James had finished, he sighed and shook his head.

'Well, I'm glad she's happy. I can well imagine the atmosphere between herself and Juliet – they never hit it off at all. You could have told me before, you know.' He smiled ruefully. 'But sure, then again maybe you couldn't. I can be a narky auld fecker sometimes, James, and 'tis worse I'm getting in my old age. If it wasn't for Solange, I'd have offended the whole parish by now. I don't know how she puts up with me herself. No wonder Edith was driven mad by me.'

'You're not old, and you're much more patient than I would ever have been with people's ailments. Everyone loves you, and they know you'll look after them when they need you.'

Taking another sip of whiskey, James thought about what Ingrid brought to his life – the love, the laughter, the wild uncontrollable passion, and felt a deep sadness for his father, who had missed out on a loving marriage. Richard was his father, a doctor, and the head of the household, but he was also a man.

'Was there any woman you even liked, back over the years?'

He had asked something like this before, and Richard had merely replied that he was a doctor, a married man, and this was Dunderrig. Now James put the question tentatively again. In the dimly lit study in the middle of the night, they were just two men drinking whiskey and talking. He could sense his father's hesitation, debating whether or not to confide in him. After several minutes, Richard spoke.

'You're not the only one with a secret, James. There was someone. *Is* someone, if I'm honest about it. She's been under my roof for the last twenty-five years, but she doesn't see me as anything other than a friend. She adored Jeremy – you should have seen the way she looked at him, like she wanted to crawl inside him. And he was mad about her, too. I think having yourself and Juliet to mind was the only thing that gave her a reason to keep going. Those early years, she used to walk around the gardens. I'd watch her from the surgery, the tears pouring down her face. I wanted to hold her and wipe the tears away, but I couldn't, and she wouldn't have wanted me to, anyway. Even if I could have won her, she could never have loved me as much as she once loved my best friend. And even after your mother left, how could I have offered her my heart when I could never offer her marriage?'

James was stunned. He had never imagined for a second that his father had feelings like that for Solange. He knew they were close friends and that he confided in her sometimes, but that he loved her as a woman was a revelation.

'Maybe you should say something...'

Richard frowned at his son. 'I will not.' His tone brooked no argument. 'This is her home as much as it's yours or mine or Juliet's, wherever the hell she is. If I started telling her anything like that at this stage of our lives, she'd feel like she couldn't stay here, I know she would. She doesn't feel the same about me, and I can live with that. What I couldn't live with is for her to leave Dunderrig. So she'll never know. You'll have to promise me that you'll never breathe a word about what I've told you to anyone – even Ingrid. Do you swear James?'

'Of course, I swear.'

'I'm only telling you about my marriage because I don't want you to make the same mistake I made. Talk to Ingrid, tell her you love her, try to understand that she's grieving. Please God, she'll have more children, but maybe she won't. She's a long way from home and if going up to Dublin and seeing her German friends makes it a bit easier to bear, then just let her off. Don't be breathing down her neck every minute. It must be hard for her, her whole family back in Germany. She doesn't even know what's happening to them. She loves you, you know that, and it's hard, I know, to find the right balance between not being too distant but also not too much on top of her. Give her a bit of time but don't withdraw – make sure she knows you're there whenever she needs you.'

James nodded. 'Thanks, Dad. You give great advice.'

'Don't I know it? I'm great at fixing other people's lives. Did you ever hear the phrase "Physician heal thyself?" It's from the Bible.' Richard drained his whiskey, and father and son sat in companionable silence, each lost in his own thoughts.

CHAPTER 36

*J*uliet lay wide awake listening to the sounds of the city waking up. Dieter's heavy arm held her close. His rhythmic breathing was peaceful. A dog started barking. Feeling him stir behind her, she breathed in deeply. The warm, musky scent of him was familiar.

'Good morning, beautiful.' His voice was still husky from sleep.

'Good morning,' she replied as he kissed her ear.

'I love you,' he whispered. She could feel his arousal as he ran his hands over her naked breasts. 'The sooner this bloody war is over the better, and we can live like normal people...' He nuzzled her neck.

She murmured, 'It's been going on so long. You think it will ever end?'

'It's only a matter of time...'

He made love to her quickly and passionately, and afterwards, as he washed and dressed, he called to her from the bathroom, 'I have emergency planning meetings all week. Go and buy yourself a pretty necklace for Sunday's dinner at Mueller's. He's planning a welcome party – Herman Spitz is in town. All the Gestapo, Wehrmacht and Abwehr top brass are invited, and I promised Mueller you'd play the piano for them, though why I let him drool over you like that I'll never know. Maybe it's because I know I'm the one who gets to take you home.' He approached the bed and kissed her cheek, thoughtfully. 'We'll live in Bavaria, when all this is over. You'll love it there.' He paused at the door. 'Don't repeat what I said about it being only a matter of time. People might think I am envisaging defeat.'

And he was gone.

Juliet got up and made a cup of coffee. The large fifth-floor apartment they shared had beautiful views over the medieval Poitiers, and she knew the city like the back of her hand. She would go to the couturier this morning to collect the new midnight-blue satin gown she'd had made. The restrictions that applied to the citizens of Poitiers did not apply to her. She had so many dresses and furs now that she hardly ever wore the same thing twice. Money was no object, and Dieter loved to indulge her. She would buy sapphires to go with the dress, and wear them to Mueller's. They would match her engagement ring. She looked down at her right hand again and felt the weight of the quarter-carat diamond encircled with sapphires that sparkled there. When Dieter proposed four months ago, the faces of the other French girls who had relationships with the Germans were green with envy. Dieter Friedman was the catch of them all – the perfect combination of funny, handsome, and powerful.

Today was her birthday – not Marie-Louise's birthday, but that of her other self, Juliet. It had been so long since she even thought about her. Juliet Buckley was like someone she knew in another life, which was in reality exactly how it was. She and James were twenty-four years old today. She felt more like eighty-four. In the beginning, living a lie had been difficult but as time passed, she found herself becoming Marie-Louise, so much so that she rarely thought of home now, of

Dunderrig, or even of Ewan. Dieter always said she was his mystery girl, so quiet and reserved – and indeed she was; it wasn't an act anymore. The bubbly, chatty girl from West Cork didn't exist, couldn't exist, in this world. Maybe she never would again.

If Dieter knew who she really was...if he met her family and heard the stories of her childhood from Solange and Mrs Canty... She could just picture him, sitting in the kitchen, delighted with the food and everything Dunderrig had to offer, charming her father. She shuddered and pressed her hand to her forehead. Strange imaginings. Dieter would never come to Dunderrig, and even if she ever made it back there alive herself, his name would never pass her lips in that house. She was here to spy on the top-ranking German officer, not to plan a future life with him. This was a man who was responsible for the deaths of so many. A man who had hunted down, tortured and murdered British agents and the French citizens who had helped them. A man who had sworn allegiance to Adolf Hitler – even if this morning he had admitted he was weary of this war.

Even if he was also the man who had cried in her arms when he heard about the death of his mother in an Allied bombing raid, the man who tried every day to make her happy, who in the darkness of the night held her in his arms as he told her of his fears, not just for his mortal body but for his eternal soul, when he was called to account for the crimes he had committed in the name of Germany.

That first time he'd picked her up from Dr Blain's house, she was so nervous she hardly spoke, but he coaxed her and charmed her and eventually she found herself laughing at one of his jokes. He brought her home that evening after a day driving around the beautiful Haute-Vienne. They had stopped for lunch in a little café where they ate *des escargots* with bread and rough red wine. Walking back to the car, he'd taken her hand. He was kind, sweet, and considerate – nothing like a man responsible for the torture and murder of British agents. She'd had to keep reminding herself: 'If he knew who you really were, he would have you shot.'

Emotionally drained, she sat silently in the passenger seat as he drove her home. Pulling up outside the doctor's house, he turned to her.

'You are such a restful person to be around, Marie-Louise. My world is full of people shouting and barking orders. My time with you was like an oasis of calm. Please say you'll let me take you out again?'

He had a way of leaning his head to one side as he smiled, his eyes full of enthusiasm, that she would have found endearing in another time and place. She knew Lise would be delighted that this top-ranking officer wished to pursue this relationship. At the same time, she had to consider the Blain family. She could not continue to fraternise with a German officer, for their sake.

He said, still smiling, 'I understand how this must be for you. But I really like you, Marie-Louise. I have done since I picked you up on the road, and today has been just wonderful. How about if next time, I meet you somewhere quiet and discreet – not as a German officer in uniform, but just as an ordinary man who wants to spend time with you?"

She tried not to allow her incredulity show on her face. Was he serious? Did he really want to start a real relationship with her as if there was no war on? Confused and frightened, she started to get out of the car.

He spoke again, detaining her with his hand on her arm, 'The terms are up to you – anytime, anywhere. I know you like me too. I can see it in your eyes. Just give me a chance, please.'

She would have to consult with her circuit leaders about her next move – but for now, she would have to give him something.

'Very well. Next Monday is my next day off. Meet me at the main cathedral door at noon.' He looked so eager, so delighted she was going to see him again, she almost smiled.

Lise and Hercule had been waiting for her at the farmhouse when she arrived that evening.

'Can you pull this off – yes or no?' Hercule snapped as he paced up and down in front of her. His torn jersey and baggy canvas trousers made him look very French. His jet-black hair and bushy eyebrows gave him a ferocious look. He sucked on his pipe constantly, and she wondered why he was always so aggressive. She hated the way he spoke at her rather than to her, like she was some silly schoolgirl who shouldn't be there.

'I think I can.' She spoke with a quiet determination she had not heard in her own voice before. She was sitting on an upturned box in the barn, Lise beside her.

Hercule addressed Lise as if Juliet wasn't even there. 'It would be vital that she did nothing to give the game away, no stupid slipup that would land not just her but all of us in it. I don't know, it's very risky. But to have someone on the inside, so connected, could be invaluable. What do you think?'

'If Marie-Louise says she can do this, I think she can. She's proved she is reliable and can hold her head in difficult situations. London has consulted her teachers at the training schools and has given the go-ahead, but ultimately, they are leaving the final word to you – and to Marie-Louise, of course.' She turned to Juliet, squeezed her hand and spoke intently to her. 'No one is forcing you to do anything, you must understand that. We can have you picked up and taken home on the next moon if that's what you want. If he's that keen, then you either have to go with it or get out of here. It's entirely up to you.'

'I want to do it.' Juliet was sure.

Lise smiled, clearly proud of her young friend, but then became deeply serious. 'What you are agreeing to, as I don't need to tell you, could lead to your discovery and subsequently ours if they torture you. I know you think you can withstand it, but most of us cannot, that is simply a fact. But if you could get close to Friedman, find out if he is using informers, find out his plans, then you could really influence the outcome of this war. Friedman is only twenty-nine, but already he has the rank of captain. He joined the Nazi party long before it was expedient to do so, and he is well connected to the cabinet in Berlin. His uncle is one of Hitler's advisors. He has been promoted over the heads of many men older and more experienced, not just because of his connections but because he is an excellent, intelligent, loyal soldier. Nor is he a psychopath or an active sadist – he leaves the dirty work to his underlings. But he doesn't question their methods. He is every bit as ruthless as the lowest of them, he just prefers to imagine himself as civilised.'

Juliet tried to equate the charming, handsome, young man of yesterday with the cold-blooded Nazi that Lise had described. It was very difficult – and terrifying. Then she thought about Ewan, about Auntie Kitty being bombed in Belfast, the girls in the Wrens, the devastation all over England, the children in the rail station, and the murdered agent, and she knew what she had to do.

'I understand the risks. And I'd be lying if I said I wasn't scared. But Hercule is right, it's a great opportunity. The Germans are wary of girls approaching them and flirting, but he is the one pursuing me, so it puts me beyond suspicion. He said nothing about his work today, but I think with time I can get him to trust me and with a bit of luck, confide in me. I know it is nearly impossible to withstand torture. I keep my L-pill in my shoe.' The idea that she could discuss her planned suicide by lethal pill in such a matter-of-fact way came as a surprise to her.

Hercule barked out a mirthless laugh and ran his hands through his messy dark hair in frustration. 'She thinks they'll give her the opportunity to rummage around in her shoe, the stupid girl! No, if she is to avoid putting the rest of us at risk, then she will have to see Mouret.'

Again Hercule was addressing Lise, ignoring Juliet. He really was the most horrible man, and clearly a misogynist. More than once, she had overheard him muttering about how women were more trouble than they were worth. He barely tolerated Lise and was bluntly obnoxious to Juliet. She had to keep reminding herself that she was doing this to help the war effort, and that it was nothing to do with this odious man.

'Mouret is a dentist we use,' Lise explained. 'He will insert the L-pill into a false tooth, in a glass capsule. In the event of your needing it, you can dislodge the tooth and crack the glass with your teeth. Death is almost instantaneous. If it comes dislodged any other way and you accidentally swallow it, you will be fine, just so long as the glass doesn't break.'

Juliet suppressed a shudder. She hated the dentist and had to be dragged there by Solange once a year. The idea of some French dentist extracting a tooth and replacing it with a false one – leaving aside that the new tooth contained a poisonous pill – filled her almost with more dread than the prospect of torture. Yet it would have to be done.

'When can he do it? Sooner rather than later would be best, I think.'

Hercule was thinking. 'The right approach is probably not to try too hard in the early days; don't initiate any discussions about the war or his work; just gain his trust. Don't be too keen, show reticence – it's a big issue for a well-brought-up French girl to take up with one of the Boche. Now, your cover story will need tightening up. It's fine for spot checks, but for a long-term relationship, you'll need something more substantial. I'll get London to work on something, in the meantime, try to steer the conversation away from yourself, or at least from your past.'

'Who will be my contact? If I hear anything I mean?' Juliet was trying not to be intimidated by his dismissive attitude, but everything she said sounded babyish and silly to her ears.

Lise said, 'It will be me. You can tell him that

I'm your piano teacher. You already play, I know, so if he asks you to perform you'll be able to.'

Juliet felt a huge relief that it wasn't to be Hercule or some stranger. Juliet trusted Lise and she looked up to her – her poise and courage were singular, and Juliet aspired to be like her. At least, a weekly visit to Lise would make her feel less alone.

SHE MET DIETER ON Monday as agreed, and then again, and again. They talked about art and music, they went to the cinema and for meals, and mostly, it was just as if there were no war on, and they were two young people getting to know each other. He called her his 'mouse' for being so quiet and retiring, and in time, because she clearly preferred to listen than talk about herself, he began to tell her of the problems he encountered in his job. She paid sympathetic attention, and he seemed happy that she was interested.

The romantic side of the relationship progressed easily and quickly, and while she never forgot the reason for their relationship, she admitted to Lise that it was not unpleasant. After a few months of going out, they moved into a beautiful apartment belonging to a family who had recently been sent to the camps for harbouring a Jewish relative. The first day she was there, she was almost forgetful of the reality of the situation as she chose fabrics for drapes and placed lamps and ornaments around. She was working busily until she opened a large box full of toys. The children who had owned these toys were now on their way to the camps, at the stroke of her boyfriend's pen.

Dieter had mentioned marriage, but she told him that she wanted to wait until after the war and have the proper, beautiful wedding she had always dreamed of in Bavaria. Other than that, she did everything required of a woman in love – she was supportive of him in every way. She cooked delicious meals for his superiors, she sang and played the piano, and she acquiesced to anything he asked of her. She would listen when he told her of how his colleagues and friends were harangued by their French girlfriends demanding this and that, insisting they spend more time with them, and always finished by saying how lucky he was to have found her. He was wildly in love with her and clearly confident that she was just as in love with him. His passion made him careless. His principal work was to liaise between the army and the Gestapo, and he was privy to everything that happened in the entire region. He held telephone conversations in front of her, and once or twice, left around letters from his superiors in Berlin. He loved to mock the bullish manners of Gestapo officers and often quoted their more grandiose statements to make her laugh.

She and Lise had built up a firm friendship. Dieter paid for her piano lessons – he adored music. As Juliet's fingers danced over the piano keys, she relayed to Lise every detail of her day, both important and trivial. Lise was right that the murdered agent had been betrayed. Juliet had discovered the source of the leak during the early weeks of the relationship – it was the daughter of a couple who were running a safe house. She had become besotted with a Wehrmacht private and had gossiped to him about a woman she had heard speaking in English. Juliet hated to think about the girl – she was shot by the Resistance, of course, just for being silly and in love.

She never saw Hercule. Lise told her he was very impressed by her work and had recommended her to London for a medal once the war was over, but she doubted he had ever actually expressed such a positive sentiment. Probably Lise was just encouraging her.

Still, she knew her efforts were important. The circuit knew in advance if anyone fell under suspicion and was able to get them out in time. She was able to relay to Lise conversations between Dieter and visiting Gestapo officers and knew a little of what was going on in the highest echelons of power thanks to Dieter's frequent correspondence with and occasional visit to Berlin.

In recent weeks, there had been growing reports of German losses. Stalingrad was holding out. The bombing of Germany by the RAF was having a devastating effect on war production as well as on morale. In France, the Resistance was gaining in numbers and becoming more organised by the week. London was sending leaders and supplies to them, arming and preparing them for the European invasion. Increasingly, she was sure that Germany would not prevail.

THAT NIGHT, DIETER ARRIVED home after midnight, tired and unshaven. She had waited up for him to show him her new dress and the necklace, but while he smiled, his mind was clearly on other things. While she rubbed his shoulders, he told her of how a Panzer division due to be sent to Italy had been destroyed in an RAF bombing raid – it was as if the British knew exactly where to target.

It was then he confided his worries about

Spitz, the Abwehr agent responsible for liaising between the various units stationed in France, who was coming to Poitiers that weekend. He feared the Spitz visit was a direct result of his own connections to an army officer in Berlin, who had fallen from grace.

'Just because my uncle was involved in some anti-Hitler plotting, I'm coming under attack. I knew nothing about it. And anyway, Canaris might be the head of Abwehr, but he's notoriously anti-Hitler himself – yet he is still sending this Spitz to keep an eye on me. It's a nuisance as well as unpleasant for me. There is a circuit operating here, and I'm close to breaking it down, but it's a delicate operation and needs careful handling. The Abwehr don't believe in subtlety. They will force me to arrest everyone in the region and torture them until they tell us something. I've tried explaining that in this uncertain climate, rounding up large groups of innocent people and interrogating them drives ever more of them into the Resistance, but they won't listen. I can find out everything I need to know without using those sledgehammer tactics; you just need to have the right people in the right places.'

She was usually careful never to question him,

but in this instance, she had to know more, and quickly.

'But surely it would be impossible to run any spy network here with so much military presence?' She kept her voice light.

'Hmm, you might think so but not really. The Resistance are very clever, and they're getting help from England, too. There's a wireless operation somewhere in the city, and we've been tracking the signal. The operator keeps the time very short, so we haven't got a fix on it yet, but we are piecing the information together, and we've narrowed it down to within a few streets. I want to take a few more days and be sure of him before we go in. Don't want to frighten him away as we seem to have done so many times before. Once we find him, or her, then they will certainly lead us to others.'

Juliet didn't flinch. The methods by which a loyal resistance worker could be forced to betray their fellow saboteurs remained unsaid. Dieter never spoke of the brutality that she knew he sanctioned.

She went to Lise's apartment early the next morning, and told her everything.

THAT EVENING, AS SHE and Dieter sipped cognac on the balcony after dinner, Juliet wondered what would happen to her if he ever found out who she really was. Lise had been very interested in learning of Spitz's impending visit and had told her to come to her again in two days' time for instructions on how to proceed.

Dieter reached over to touch her hand, and she glanced at him, startled. But he was smiling warmly.

'I love it here, at home with you, Marie-Louise. When we are together like this, it's as if there is no war.'

TWO DAYS LATER, JULIET was back in Lise's little sitting room. The wireless operations had been shifted to another location and now Lise had other things on her mind.

'Spitz is a big fish. He's been personally responsible for the arrest of even more agents than Canaris himself.'

'The welcoming dinner is tomorrow night.'

'The perfect opportunity. He loves his drink and beautiful women. He will be relaxed and vulnerable and off his guard.'

Juliet felt a myriad of emotions – resolve, fear. Evidently, the Resistance were planning to bomb the party. Of course, they would let her know the plan so she could discreetly withdraw to the bathroom at the appropriate time – still, what if something went wrong? But that wasn't what had sent the shiver up her spine…it was something else. Something she couldn't even admit to herself.

'It was bound to happen, you know,' said Lise.

'Of course,' Juliet replied. 'We can't let an opportunity like this slip by. It will do the cause great good. People will realise how powerful the Resistance is and feel emboldened to join us.'

'I didn't mean that.' Lise spoke quietly. 'I meant him. It was bound to happen that you would develop a certain affection for him. People are never all bad. You have hidden it well, but I know that there is a little voice in your head that says we don't know him like you do. That is true. No doubt he has a good side, and no doubt you have seen it. But, my dear friend, please remember – he is not your love, this is not your time, even you are not you. Your future is back where you come from, with your family and friends. Do not lose sight of that. You are not Marie-Louise, and it is she who has these feelings, not you. Sunday's events may test you in a way you never anticipated, but you must remember what he is and why you're here.'

Juliet took a long moment to look into her heart. For so long she'd been guarding her true feelings about everything, she wondered if she was even capable of knowing what they were anymore. Yet the more she thought about it, the more she had to accept that Lise was right. Although Dieter was everything she was here to fight against, there was a part of her that liked him, maybe even liked him very much. She raised her head and looked straight at her friend and mentor.

'I'll do what has to be done.'

They heard the front gate open and footsteps come up the path. Juliet immediately began to play the piano – hesitantly, as if she were being taught a piece. As usual, the score was open and both she and Lise were seated at the instrument.

A young girl whom Juliet had never seen before entered and gave a message to Lise. She looked about eighteen, and she was trying to appear confident. Juliet felt like she was looking back at herself when she first arrived. How long ago that seemed. The girl delivered her message and left quickly by the back door. Lise read it and instantly burned it in the fireplace.

She looked at Juliet as if debating how best to tell her the plan.

'Marie-Louise, this will be difficult for you.

You are to be picked up by plane tomorrow night, after the dinner. You...'

'That's ridiculous,' Juliet interrupted, alarmed. 'Totally excessive. There's no reason they would suspect me of being behind any bomb.'

'No, you don't understand.' Lise's tone changed. She took a deep breath and continued. 'There will be no bomb – that would be impossible. You are to attend and then invite Spitz back to the apartment with you and Friedman for a nightcap. Explain to Dieter in advance that you are going to charm him so that he'll be more predisposed towards the Poitiers office. When you get back to the apartment...' She paused. 'Your orders are to shoot both of them.'

Lise's words hung in the silence between them. After a few moments, the older woman knelt and lifted a floorboard under the table. She produced a pistol wrapped in a piece of cloth.

'A silenced Welrod MK1. London says you are an excellent marksman. I assume you're familiar with this make of gun?'

'Yes.'

The prospect of what faced her had rendered her almost speechless. Killing Spitz – that was within her capability. But Dieter?

Lise held her by both arms and stared intently

into her eyes. 'Marie-Louise, listen to me. You are a British agent, he is a Nazi officer. This is why you came here, why we are all here, to win this war. You must not hesitate, even for a second. No last words, you cannot give him time to react. You must offer them drinks, encourage Dieter to show Spitz the view, stand behind them, and then in quick succession shoot them both in the back of the head. Can you do that?'

She had to kill Dieter. Dieter, who loved her, who wanted to protect her from any harm, who wanted to marry her. Blood thundered in her ears, and sweat prickled her skin. She had to stop thinking of him as the charming, handsome man who had always made her laugh. She had to think of him as the man who would without a moment's hesitation torture and kill anyone he suspected of being an agent for the British. Dieter, who had happily moved them into the home of a family who were by now most likely dead.

'Yes,' she said. She didn't trust herself to say anything more.

'I know you can. I have no doubts about you. Once it's done, you leave immediately. There will be a vehicle to the right of the door. The driver will be expecting you. Get in the back and cover yourself with a blanket you'll find there. You'll be taken to the drop site. The Lysander will be on the ground no more than four minutes. Now go, don't think too much about it, just do it. Good luck, my dear friend. Perhaps we'll meet again.' Lise placed the gun in Juliet's bag under her music books then, kissing her on both cheeks, ushered her out of the door.

CHAPTER 37

*S*olange walked quickly from the kitchen door through the trees towards the little cottage. The dish she was holding burned her hands slightly through the tea towel. The stew was from Mrs Canty for Ingrid – convinced, as the old housekeeper was, that the reason the girl looked so pale and wan was down to not eating properly. It was true, Ingrid had lost a lot of weight and all her glossy vitality seemed to have faded. She rarely came up to the big house these days, and James seemed at a loss as to how to help her. She went to Dublin alone every week, leaving Lili in Dunderrig, but these trips seemed to give her no joy. Nothing did anymore.

Solange had advised James to be patient, but

in truth, she had no idea what was wrong with Ingrid. She seemed to love Lili, now two years old and full of mischief, but always appeared distant and distracted. Richard had suggested sending her to a gynaecologist in Cork after the second miscarriage, but she had refused. Reading between the lines from James, there was no chance of another pregnancy – that side of their lives was now non-existent. Though she was not very close to Ingrid, Solange loved James and Lili, and would do anything to secure their happiness.

Ingrid had apologised for the way she had spoken to Solange that day when she left, and Solange had assured her she completely understood. She really wanted to build a relationship with James's wife; she even made her the wedding dress. For a while at least, it looked like they were becoming friends. Yet in recent months, it was as if the girl had something on her mind. Solange was reluctant to interfere, but the little family seemed so unhappy. Perhaps the miscarriages were the problem, or maybe it was something else. Ingrid had no family except her uncle in Dublin. Solange knew what it was like to be young and far from everything you knew and understood, so she resolved to try to help. If only she could get Ingrid to talk, to tell her what the problem was, then maybe a solution could be found.

James had gone to a gallery opening in Cork, so she knew Ingrid and Lili would be alone in the house, and Mrs Canty's stew was the perfect excuse.

As she approached the cottage through the woods, she saw Ingrid in the little back garden talking to – no, arguing with – someone. Richard was in surgery, and the Cantys were busy in the house. Whoever Ingrid was addressing was hidden from view by the shed; she was gesticulating wildly, clearly upset. Lili was crying inside the house. Solange stood watching, unsure what she should do. Ingrid finished the conversation and went back inside. 'I'm coming, Lili!' Her voice was close to hysterical.

Solange opened the little gate at the bottom of the garden. She passed the shed, but there was no one standing there. Ingrid's unseen companion must have walked around the side of the house and left by the front gate. She knocked on the open back door.

'Hello, Ingrid? It's Solange. Can I come in?'

'Solange…yes, yes, of course.' Ingrid seemed startled to see her. Her hair was standing on end, and her whole appearance was uncharacteristically dishevelled. She was as white as a sheet, and her eyes were red-rimmed as if she'd been crying. Solange decided just to act normally until she calmed down.

'Mrs Canty made a stew for your dinner. She's convinced you're not eating enough! Don't worry, she does the same with everyone. She won't be happy until we are all waddling around Dunderrig like fat little ducks.' Solange tried to keep the conversation light. Looking around, she could see the cottage was badly in need of being cleaned. Used cutlery and delph were scattered on every surface and in the corner, a bin overflowed.

'I'm sorry about the mess, I…I just haven't had time…' Ingrid tried to make space for Solange to sit down.

Solange decided that she would say something. The poor girl was so miserable, and now this strange visitor in the garden. She was certain it wasn't a romantic entanglement, because Ingrid, who always made time to ensure she looked her best, was wearing no makeup and hadn't even washed her hair.

'Ingrid, what's wrong?' Solange asked kindly. She took Lili in her arms and led Ingrid to the couch. Placing Lili between them, she gave her a doll to play with. 'Please tell me and I promise you, it won't go any further – not to James or Richard or anyone. We are all so worried about you, especially James, he loves you so very much, and little Lili needs her happy mother back.'

Ingrid looked like she might cry and, clearly not trusting herself to speak, she simply shook her head.

'Is it the babies? The miscarriages?' Solange guessed Ingrid wouldn't volunteer anything so she had to try to guess. She was determined not to let this moment pass; she didn't want Ingrid to close down again and insist everything was fine.

Ingrid hunched her shoulders. She looked small and defeated.

'Ingrid? I'm sure, whatever it is, we can work it out together.'

'I am in trouble, Solange. If I tell you something, you have to swear to me, on Lili's life, that you won't say anything. James always says that when he and Juliet confided in you, you always kept their secrets.'

'I promise,' Solange agreed.

'Oh, God! How did it come to this? It's all ruined, everything. My life is over, and James and Lili, I just can't, I can't Solange.' Ingrid was shaking now.

541

'Just take your time, tell me everything. What can't you do?' Solange was rubbing the younger woman's back as giant sobs racked her body.

'My boss in Dublin, Helmut Clissman, he...he isn't just a school manager. He works for the Abwehr.'

Solange tried to absorb this information. 'The German secret service? How did you find out? That must have been such a shock to you – you've known him and his wife for so long.'

Ingrid half-smiled through her tears. 'Solange, I always knew. Edith, Otto, all of them, they're all in the Nazi party. Otto sells artwork and jewellery confiscated from the Jews, that's why he's so rich. He has contacts all over the world, since before the war. He sells the stuff, pays a significant portion to the party and keeps the rest himself. James thought they were just Germans sitting out the war in Dublin but that's not the case. The Clissmans work directly for Hitler. The others...well, they're all involved.'

Solange was struggling, trying to process this information. Richard had told her about James and Edith so her name didn't come as a surprise...but that they were working for the Nazis? It was too much to take in.

'But, if you knew, why did you work for them

in the school, continue to see them, lie to James about it? I don't understand, Ingrid.'

'Solange, don't you see?' Ingrid was anguished. 'I work for them too, not as a secretary. They, we, are involved with some things that...I thought I could handle it, but I can't. The lies, the danger to you all, I can't take it anymore. In Dublin, it was different, I wasn't alone, but down here, I never realised...'

Solange thought quickly. She had to get Ingrid to tell her the full story. What danger were they in? The need to protect her family surged through Solange.

'Ingrid, tell me everything. I promise I'll help you, there must be a way out of this.'

Ingrid looked up into Solange's face, like a child. Sadly, she shook her head. 'There's no way out of it.'

'Ingrid, look at Lili. Do you want her to grow up in a world where Hitler makes the rules? Tell me what's going on. When I was approaching the garden, you were speaking to someone. Who was that?'

Ingrid looked at Solange with fear in her eyes.

'I don't know his name. I think he's from the IRA. They've been involved from the start. Apparently, we are going to give them back the

North when we win the war. He's here to ensure I'm doing my part. I think Helmut sent him. He's worried about me.' She barked out a joyless laugh. 'Well, not about me as such – worried I won't do what I'm supposed to do.'

'And what's that?' Solange spoke gently, trying to control the panic rising within her. Ingrid seemed strange, slightly manic.

'There's a boat coming into the cove at Castletownshend tonight. There's someone on it, someone important. I don't know who. I'm to meet him and help him ashore and put him up until it's safe to move on. I also have a package of maps and photographs from Helmut to deliver to the man rowing the boat, to go back to Germany.'

Solange felt her heart race. What on earth had the girl got herself into?

'But Ingrid, how are you supposed to do that? It's impossible. You would be seen, and where would you bring him?'

Ingrid spoke then, more confidently. 'Solange, did it never occur to you why I was so interested in the coastline, taking photographs constantly? I've helped four agents get into Ireland on their way to England. I put them in the barn behind the old ploughs that don't get used anymore since Eddie got the tractor. Mrs Canty never notices if food is missing, it was easy really. Dunderrig has played host to many Germans since I came here. At the start, well it was fun, exciting. I didn't have Lili to worry about. But now, I just think of the danger to her... It paralyses me.'

'And James, is that why you went out with him, married him? So you'd have a legitimate reason to be here?' Solange could hardly contain her anger at how this girl had used her family.

'At the beginning, yes, and that's the truth. But then after Lili was born, I became slowly disillusioned with everything – Helmut and all he stands for – and I did fall in love with James. And now, I can't tell him. He'd never forgive me for putting all of you in such danger, for using Dunderrig. I'm scared, Solange.'

The clock ticked on the dresser and silence descended on the cottage. Lili sat playing with the doll on the rug as Solange tried to decide what to do.

'You have every reason to be scared.' The deep voice came from behind them. Solange whipped around to see a man standing in the doorway of the little cottage, his arm outstretched and a pistol pointing at the baby. He was tall and broad and spoke with a West Cork accent. 'Helmut was right about you, Ingrid. All talk but no action. Get the package.'

Ingrid looked frozen. 'I...I ...it's upstairs.'

'Well, go and get it then.' His voice dripped with sarcasm. He kicked the back door closed with his heel.

'Please, don't hurt the baby,' Solange begged as Ingrid ran up the narrow staircase.

'Shut up!' he roared at her.

Lili burst out crying with the shock of the loud noise. Solange knelt and cradled her, shaking. Ingrid appeared downstairs with a brown-paper parcel. He took it and checked through its contents, then pointed the pistol at Ingrid's head.

'Now, listen carefully. You're going to lead me to the beach and signal the boat that it is safe to come ashore, then hand this package over exactly as you are supposed to do. I will be watching you every step of the way and if it doesn't go exactly as it should, then I will kill your daughter. Do you understand me?'

Ingrid cried, 'Please, let Solange take her, I promise I'll do whatever you say, just let her take my baby away to somewhere safe.'

He grinned. 'So she can go squealing to the guards? No, Fraülein Ingrid. We all wait here until it's time to go, so make yourselves comfortable.' He made her sit down and stood over them all with the gun. 'Now, aren't we an international little bunch? A German, a French lady and a patriotic Irishman. And of course, a sweet little Irish girl.'

Solange had heard the political gossip that there were links between the German government and the IRA, united by the common enemy, but she had always assumed it was just that – gossip and idle speculation. Now it seemed as if it were true. And either way, one thing was sure: this man did not intend to leave two witnesses. It was certain he intended to kill them once he'd forced Ingrid to carry out her part.

She sat in silence, wracking her brain for an idea to get them out of this terrifying situation. The cottage was hidden even from the avenue up to the main house, and there were few visitors. James was staying overnight in Cork so he wouldn't be home to rescue them. Richard was going to be busy all day – he had told her that he intended to pay a house call to a new mother between afternoon and evening surgery. He wouldn't have a moment to stop and wonder where Solange had gone. Mrs Canty might notice her absence... No, Solange had told her this morning she was going to spend the day with Ingrid.

The man's voice interrupted her thoughts.

'So, how is the traitor doctor these days? Busy polishing his British war medals, I suppose.'

Was he talking about Richard? She was sure she never met this man before, yet he evidently knew something about their household. 'I don't know what you mean.'

'Ah, you do of course. The lovely shiny medals he got for betraying his country and being a good boy for the English king. Sure you know all about his wartime heroics, didn't he bring you back as the ultimate prize? I heard ye drove his poor missus out with the antics of the pair of ye! Oh, he's a dark horse, all right. He doesn't look like much of a ladies' man, but he certainly knows how to pick 'em all right.' He sat sneering suggestively.

She decided to ignore him and say nothing further, rather than rise to his bait. Lili became fractious and reluctantly the man allowed Ingrid to fetch her some food from the little kitchen. The two women fed and changed her. Lili slept, and the time crawled slowly by. Darkness fell, and the man announced it was time to go.

'Now, you two are going to put the child in

the pram and walk to the arranged meeting place. If you meet anyone just say she was unsettled, and you're trying to get her off to sleep. I'll be following you, so don't try anything stupid. Do you understand? If I suspect you of anything, I'll shoot her. Don't think that's an idle threat. Now sit her up nicely against the pillows so I can see her.' The words were deadly but delivered in sweet baby talk as he patted Lili's head. She giggled, delighted with the attention.

Solange and Ingrid wrapped up the little girl warmly against the winter chill. Ingrid's hands were shaking uncontrollably as she tried to button her daughter's coat. Lili smiled and chatted through the whole experience. They pushed her pram along the path and then down the avenue. The lights were on in the house. Surely Mrs Canty would have noticed Solange's absence by now.

They trod the moonlit road in silence as Lili prattled with delight over such an unusual occurrence – a walk in the dark! The man shadowed them, an occasional twig cracking under his feet. They walked for over an hour in silence. Just before Castletownshend, Ingrid indicated they should turn off into the woods. The terrain was too rough for the pram, so they took Lili out and carried her. By now she was fast asleep, and the move didn't wake her. Solange made a sling from one of the sheets – at two, the child was heavy and the going underfoot was treacherous. The moonlight was obscured by the canopy of trees, and roots protruded across the path. Solange felt her way along in Ingrid's wake, carrying the child and praying for a miracle as she listened for the man behind her. He stumbled over a root and cursed softly. Solange was sure her thumping heart would burst. Lili nestled close, blissfully unaware of the danger. Ingrid forged on, and Solange could hear the gentle lapping of the ocean up ahead.

Eventually, they emerged from the woods onto a tiny beach with rocky outcrops on either side. Solange could see why Ingrid had recommended this spot to her German masters. It was the perfect meeting place – unreachable by road and hidden from the village by a narrow headland. From her bag, Ingrid extracted a bicycle light, which she switched on. She was shaking, but she went about her job diligently, almost ignoring Solange and Lili. She sent a series of flashes across the dark water. Within minutes, they could hear the sound of a creaking boat as it was rowed in their direction. The night was now inky black with only a shadow of moon peeking through the dense cloud.

Ingrid ran to the water's edge to help pull the little boat up onto the beach. With a splash, a figure jumped out into the shallow water and the high cry of surprise at the iciness of the sea surprised Solange – clearly, the agent was a girl. Low voices whispered in German as Ingrid and the person remaining in the boat conversed hurriedly. She handed over the package and once more the creaking sound of oars came floating over the water as the boat made its way back out into the inky sea.

Suddenly, the entire beach was lit up by powerful searchlights, and a male voice roared through a megaphone: 'Put down your weapons and raise your hands. You are surrounded, so do not attempt to resist arrest.'

The German agent swore and opened fire with her pistol. More shots came from the direction of the rowboat. Solange dived behind a rock for cover with Lili, who was now crying lustily having been woken from her sleep. The IRA man ran onto the beach, firing behind him as he came. Uniformed men came running out of the woods, heading for the seashore and the boat. Dogs were barking. Solange covered Lili with her body as bullets flew in every direction. Through the noise and shouting, she heard her name being called.

It was Richard, ducking his head and racing in her direction. He threw himself down beside her. 'Are you all right? Are you hurt? You've got Lili, thank God. Where's Ingrid?'

'I have you now, you British bastard.' The IRA man was standing over them, aiming his gun at first one, then another of them. 'You and your French whore and that traitor's brat...'

'*Lili!*' Ingrid was screaming, racing towards them. '*Lili!*' She threw herself between the man and her daughter and at that very moment, he fired his gun. For a moment, Ingrid's beautiful face registered stunned surprise, and then her body slumped, her arms around her child. The IRA man laughed and turned his gun on Richard, but it was too late. Two policemen in uniform grabbed him from behind, handcuffed him, and dragged him roughly away.

The German agent was lying in the sand, wounded but alive. A plainclothes policeman stood over her, his gun trained at her head while two other officers handcuffed her. The rowing boat was being dragged up onto the shore; the boatman was slumped over his oars – obviously dead.

Richard rolled Ingrid's limp body gently away from her daughter and onto her back. He searched for a pulse. There was none to find. He closed her eyes and arranged her hair. Handing the baby, who was sobbing by now, to Solange, he put his arms around both of them.

Declan Quinlan, the local Garda sergeant, approached them. He removed his hat at the sight of Ingrid's body. 'I'll leave ye for a few minutes and then send them down with the stretcher for her. I'm sorry for your loss, Richard, Solange.' He nodded respectfully and walked away.

'This is a nightmare.' Solange whispered. 'Ingrid, the poor girl. She died saving Lili. If she'd stayed where she was, the child would be dead...'

'And so might we. She loved that little girl with all her heart, whatever else about her. Jesus, James will be heartbroken. How will we tell him? How can this have happened? I just don't understand, and now...' Richard couldn't take his eyes off Ingrid's lifeless body.

Solange said, her voice choked with emotion, 'She'll be known as a criminal, but she just got caught up in something that spiralled out of control. She was so sorry, Richard. She'd got herself in too deep to get out, and it wasn't just her – Edith and Otto, they were a part of it, too. She only went out with James to give her an excuse to spend time in West Cork in the beginning. But after Lili... In the end, she really did love them both. She was so miserable; she hated putting her family in such danger.'

Richard and Solange knelt beside their daughter-in-law. As Solange held Ingrid's cold hand, Richard bent low and whispered a prayer in her ear. *'O God, by Whose mercy the faithful departed find rest, send Your holy angel to watch over this girl's soul, through Christ our Lord. Amen.* Goodbye, Ingrid, don't worry about anything. It's all over now. We'll look after Lili and James for you. They know how much you loved them, and Lili will grow up always knowing how her Mammy saved her life. Rest in peace.'

They kissed her forehead and withdrew. Two uniformed guards lifted her body onto a stretcher and carried her away up the beach.

Richard took Lili from Solange and stood gazing after the small procession. The child was not crying now but was silent and wide-eyed. Solange was at his side.

'How did the guards know, Richard? When did they tell you?'

He looked down at her, over the child's head. 'It was I who told them. I knew something was wrong when I spotted Patrick O'Riordan at our gate last night and then again this morning on the path to the cottage. I recognised him from when I treated him once, years ago, when he was a young fellow back during the troubles. He cursed me for wearing a British uniform as I was pulling a bullet out of his leg. To be honest, my first assumption was that Ingrid was seeing someone behind James's back, so I planned to confront her today. Then Mrs Canty said you were gone over there, so I thought maybe your approach would be better, more diplomatic. When you never came back, I was worried, and I decided to walk over. I was surprised to find the back door closed. Then I saw Ingrid at the window. She mouthed the word 'Help'. I crept around the front and saw your man sitting in the chair, the gun pointed at you and Lili. I swear to God, Solange, I nearly had a heart attack. I couldn't risk storming in there; he could have shot you or the baby, so I raced down to Declan. Apparently, the Special Branch had warned the local Gardaí to be alert to any IRA activity in the area, since it was known they were assisting German agents. I told him he was out of his head if he thought just because Ingrid was German that she'd be involved in anything like that. I still thought it was some sort of a love affair gone horribly wrong. But he got on the phone, and they were here like a shot – uniformed guards and the Special Branch, even G2, the intelligence services of the army. I nearly got myself arrested, roaring at them to go in and get ye out straight away. But they said it was too dangerous and besides, they had been tracking Ingrid's boss, Helmut Clissman, for ages and thought this was their chance to trap him and collect themselves a couple of German agents at the same time. I never put down such a long day in all my life.'

Solange was trying to take it all in. 'So, all the time, when I thought I was alone and going to die and would never see you or Dunderrig again, you were watching over me?'

'I was in despair that you might be killed in front of my eyes. And in the end, I couldn't save poor Ingrid.' He sat down on the rock; his voice became anguished. 'How did it get to this, Solange? Didn't we see enough of it the first time? I thought if I came back home, I could keep myself and the people I love away from all the mindless death and destruction, but I couldn't, no one can, it'll find you. Now I have to break my son's heart and tell him this news and little Lili will grow up without a mother. And where the hell is my own little girl? I don't even know if she's alive or dead.'

His shoulders shook and Solange realised he was crying. In all the years she had known him, she'd never seen him break down like this. Dawn was creeping across the sky as she took Lili from him and set her down in the sand, where the child immediately set about happily digging a hole with her hands. She put her arms around him. After a while, his shaking stopped, and she sat beside him, still with one of his hands in hers. When he spoke, his voice had returned to normal, but there was something different about him.

'I just want you all to be safe and away from all of this, but I can't protect ye. When I thought something might happen to you today, Solange, I nearly went out of my mind. I swore to myself if we came out of this alive, I'd tell you the truth. Please don't think what I'm about to say will change anything, but I just need to get it off my chest. I love you, Solange, not just as a friend. In fact, I've always loved you. But I knew you could never love me as you loved Jeremy, so I never said anything. All these years I was so grateful to have you, for me and the twins. I knew you didn't feel the same way about me, so I just left it alone. But tonight, when I thought I'd lose you, I couldn't bear it, Solange, honest to God I couldn't. You don't have to say anything. I know how you feel, and please, I beg you, don't leave Dunderrig because of what I've just said. I don't expect anything from you, but I just couldn't have one of us die without saying that I love you with all my heart and I always have and always will.'

Solange was silent as they sat together on that rock, the water gently lapped on the sandy beach, and the little girl played happily on the sand. Lili was going to need them even more now. James would recover from Ingrid's death, but it would take time. She and Richard were going to have to be strong in the months and years ahead. Solange already thought of Lili as her granddaughter and James and Juliet as her children. What would be so bad about loving this good, kind man, and having him love her? It had been so long since she'd been loved like that. Jeremy was from another life, and while she would always cherish the memory of him, that's all he was now, a memory. Now, sitting here, the thought of living out her days with Richard, feeling loved and loving him in return, was very appealing. Already he confided in her and trusted her implicitly, and she realised she felt the same way about him. He had rescued her after Jeremy's death; she had held him together in the aftermath of Edith's departure. Together they endured the torture of not knowing what had happened to Juliet. The horrific events of the past few hours only confirmed what she had always known: Dunderrig and the Buckleys were her life.

She reached up her hand and turned his face towards her. His once sandy hair was now silver, and his skin was weather-beaten from a lifetime of exposure to the wild vagaries of the West Cork climate. His once narrow frame had filled out, due to years of culinary warfare by Mrs Canty. Yet he still had the vivid green eyes of his children. Leaning towards him, she kissed him and wrapped her arms around his neck. He responded, holding her close. When they finally drew apart, she whispered, 'I love you too.'

CHAPTER 38

The dinner was interminable. All the members of the Poitiers Gestapo, along with high-ranking army officers and their French girlfriends, ate, drank, and sang with such gusto it was hard to imagine there was a war on at all, let alone one they might very conceivably lose. Juliet studied the over made-up faces of the women and feared for them. She would not like to be in their shoes when the liberation finally came. The local people, after suffering years of deprivation and abuse, saw them as unpatriotic whores – 'horizontal collaborators' was the term used. When the time came, these women would pay dearly.

Spitz was holding court, swilling claret, a

scantily-clad girl balancing drunkenly on his knee. He was an incredibly unattractive man, with small piggy eyes and a hooked nose. He was balding but in an effort to hide this, had combed a long, greasy piece of hair across his shiny scalp. His companion had managed to dislodge it as she caressed him, so it now hung crookedly down over his ear. He was well below average height and was rail-thin. When he had shaken her hand earlier, it had felt clammy and limp and she'd had to suppress a shudder. Watching him now, she kept thinking of the weasel in Kenneth Grahame's *Wind in the Willows*, a book that Daddy used to read to her and James when they were small.

Dieter was beside her; he kept squeezing her hand under the table, catching her eye as if to say how much he despised this drunken company and wished to be alone with her.

'I think we should invite Spitz back for a nightcap,' she murmured in his ear.

He looked horrified, whispering, 'God no. Bad enough we have to put up with him here. I've had him all day in the office going over every single file, I can't take another second of him.'

Around them, the company burst into a lusty chorus of 'Lili Marlene', and Juliet had to nudge her German lover to remind him to take part. It would be no good to her if Dieter displeased Spitz.

Later, she drew him out onto the balcony and offered him a cigarette. The warm August breeze lifted her beautifully coiffed hair. He wound a stray tendril around his finger. Slipping her arm around his waist, she cuddled up to him.

'If we have him back for a drink, I'll play the piano and sing and flirt a little with him – look how he is with that trollop on his knee. He loves female attention. If I can charm him, then he's going to give you a much more favourable report, don't you think?'

Dieter sighed as he played with her hair. He spoke so quietly she had to strain to hear. 'That's so kind of you, darling, I really appreciate you trying, but he won't be saying anything good about me or the way I run things here. No, it's the Russian front for me. Apparently, I have the wrong friends in Berlin and so, I'm guilty by association.' He reached around her to crush out his cigarette on the railing. He murmured in her ear, 'Spitz keeps telling me how Klaus Barbie is doing such an excellent job in Lyon and asked why did I not adopt his techniques, as they were obviously more effective. I tried to explain that by keeping investigations more targeted, and not being seen by the local population as a butcher like Barbie, that I was stemming the flow of recruits into the Resistance. But he wasn't interested.' He sighed. 'How can I leave you, my darling Marie-Louise? I love you so much, more than you can ever know. I want to tell you now, no matter what happens to me, I will come back and find you when all this madness is over – if you'll wait for me?'

He looked so sad she wanted to hold him and promise to wait for him. Instead she said, 'Look Dieter, you of all people shouldn't underestimate my powers of persuasion. I don't want you going to Russia, or you might never come back to me. Let me at least try. All it will cost is a little whiskey and half an hour of our time. Surely it's worth that. If he leaves with the same opinion of you, then we've lost nothing. He's a fool, and in the early days of this war, no one like him would be in such a high position. Let's see if he can't be convinced to spare you.'

He smiled at her and wrapped her in his arms.

'All right, if you think so, but he is not to put a hand on you. I'll kill him myself if he does, the lecherous pig. If he suggests anything, he'll be wishing he was freezing his ass off on the Eastern Front.'

She buried her face in his neck to smell the familiar musky scent. Perhaps the fate that awaited him was preferable to what his superiors had in mind for him. The thought gave her a little comfort.

Spitz accepted her invitation to join them for something better than the rough red wine to which the party was now reduced. Juliet promised him a twenty-five-year-old single malt Scotch that Dieter had acquired months ago, and was flirty and amorous in her invitation. The Abwehr officer's companion of earlier was slumped on a chair, makeup smeared all over her face, clearly of no further use. Though not completely intoxicated, Spitz was too drunk to suspect anything untoward in Juliet's motives. He was clearly arrogant and deluded enough to think she might be attracted to him. He leered at her in the car as they sped across the city to their apartment.

They greeted the soldier on the door as Spitz stumbled up the steps. Entering the large foyer of the apartment, she asked Dieter to take him into the lounge, pour him a whiskey and show him the view, while she slipped into something more comfortable. Turning right into the bathroom, she locked the door. Standing on the toilet she reached up into the cistern, extracting the gun she had placed there earlier. She fitted the silencer while she ran the tap to drown out any noise.

Heart thumping, she gazed at her reflection in the mirror over the sink. 'This is not you; this is not your life. Your life is in Dunderrig with Daddy and Solange and James and the Cantys and hopefully with Ewan. None of this is who you are; it's just what has to be done so we can all live in peace. Goodbye Marie-Louise.'

She was Juliet Buckley from Dunderrig, and she was going home.

As she entered the lounge, both Dieter and Spitz were gazing out of the large bay windows overlooking the city. She shot Spitz first. The muffled cough from the silenced pistol made Dieter turn. Registering the shock on his face, she aimed and squeezed the trigger. The bullet penetrated his skull directly between his eyes. Death was instant.

THE LYSANDER WAS WAITING on the makeshift runway, its huge engine ticking over. The journey through the empty streets of Poitiers had gone without a hitch, though it had seemed to take hours. She didn't communicate with the driver and just lay under the blanket as Lise instructed. There was no reason for the authorities to suspect anything until neither Dieter nor Spitz turned up for work in the morning.

She felt the car bump over rough ground and realised they must have reached the landing field. Taking off the blanket, she saw the torches shining out in the darkness. Her driver got out and opened the door. Looking at him for the first time, she was surprised to see a face she recognised.

'I normally don't do this, but I just wanted to make sure you were gone,' Hercule smiled, something she'd never seen him do before. 'Seriously, well done. You have shown remarkable bravery. You should be very proud of yourself.' He thrust forward a calloused hand and shook hers briefly but firmly. Juliet was nonplussed. Hercule had never been anything but horrible to her, yet here he was risking his own safety to drive her to the plane.

'Thank you, Hercule.' Not sure what else to say, she leaned over and gave him a peck on the cheek. 'Keep safe.'

She sprinted towards the plane. Every moment on the ground was dangerous, and she knew the pilot would be anxious to take off. She was hoisted up by another crew member, and within seconds, they were airborne.

The pilot shouted at her over the din of the engines. 'Nice work! Glad we could get you out without too much drama!' She didn't know what to say in reply – she hadn't heard English in so long, and it felt strange to be allowed to speak it now. The pilot turned to smile at her.

This time, she found her voice. *'Ewan?'*

'It's a pleasure to meet you at last, Juliet. I've heard a lot about you, and I've seen your photograph. I'm Dougie McCrae, and I believe you know my brother?'

CHAPTER 39

*J*uliet felt sick. She decided to walk rather than take the bus to meet him. The fresh spring air might help to clear her head. London was destroyed; it seemed more buildings were in ruins or boarded up than were still standing. The SOE were putting her up in Baker Street at their house there. The debriefing was arduous with repeated interviews that had taken place over three weeks, but now she was free to go.

She had met Major General Gubbins again, and he'd been charming. Apparently, she was to be decorated for her services. At last, she could understand why her father never wanted to talk about the war or his medals. She felt the same.

She would do it again if she had to, but what she had accomplished in France wasn't something she wished to celebrate. It had to be done and she did it, that was all there was to it.

Walking quickly towards the Dorchester, she tried once again to practice what she was going to say to Ewan. Her excitement at seeing him again was overwhelmed by fear at how he would feel when she told him everything. She wanted so much for things to return to the way they were, but she would have to tell him about Dieter. There was no way of their relationship pro-gressing if this huge secret existed between them – yet how could she explain her feelings towards the German officer? If she were honest, she couldn't even explain them to herself.

It would be so easy to paint Dieter as a man who had exploited her but that wouldn't be hon-est. The fun they'd had, the interest in music they'd shared – she had to tell Ewan the whole story and in doing so face the real possibility that he would walk away from her. Dieter was a Nazi, and he had done terrible things. Often she had listened in horror as Lise told her of his latest tactic to crush the Resistance, and couldn't rec-oncile this knowledge with the way he was with her. Still, when it came to it, she had done what was necessary. Perhaps that would convince Ewan.

The elegant doorman greeted her as she stepped into the sumptuous foyer. The Dorchester was reputed to be the safest building in London since its construction of reinforced concrete the previous decade. Ewan joked in his letter that they'd better meet somewhere safe as it would be a disaster to survive the war this far and be killed by a falling wall in London.

She was early, so she went to the ladies to check her makeup. Thankfully the room was empty, and she gazed at her reflection. Did she look different? Her makeup was perfect – Chanel liquid foundation and lipstick. For most women, these treats hadn't been seen for years, but she'd had access to anything she had wanted through Dieter. She brought the more expensive jewellery with her in a little bag – including the sapphire engagement ring he'd given her – and given it to the debriefing team with the wish that they sell it and give the money to charities helping refugees. There had been so many beautiful things, all got through someone else's misery – silk stockings, beautiful clothes, handmade shoes. She wondered what had become of the rest of her wardrobe in the apartment in Poitiers.

SOE were reticent as always when she asked if her actions and sudden departure had any repercussions. They couldn't or wouldn't tell her, simply saying that the deaths of Spitz and Friedman were a major coup for the Resistance and her role had been invaluable. She thought of Lise and Hercule and prayed they were not paying for her actions.

Taking one last look at her reflection, she went back to the bar. He was sitting there now, facing the door. As she entered, he jumped up and covered the distance between them in three huge strides. Drawing her close, they said nothing, just stood clinging to each other. Eventually, he drew back, looked into her face, and kissed her gently.

His once dark hair was greying now at the temples, and the crow's feet around his eyes were deeper. Other than that, he was the same handsome Ewan. Then she noticed a livid scar running from his ear down his neck. Tentatively, she touched it.

'What happened?' she whispered.

'Bit of flying fuselage one night over the channel. Missed the jugular though, so no real harm done. You look...amazing. I thought I'd never see you again. Oh, Juliet...I can't believe you're here.' He buried his face in her hair, breathing her in.

Leading them to a table, a waiter took their order. They just sat and stared, drinking each other in.

'When the letters stopped coming, I nearly went out of my mind. I even wrote to your father asking if he'd heard from you, but he hadn't. In the end, Dougie found out you'd been recruited to SOE but could tell me nothing more, he shouldn't even have told me that. Your father and Solange have been going out of their minds too, they write every so often to know if I've heard anything. I couldn't tell them where you were because Dougie would get into serious trouble, and anyway, it would only have made them worry more. I was going out of my mind until...'

'The night he picked me up. For a moment I thought he was you.' Her voice, speaking in English, still sounded strange to her ears.

'He drove to my base right away, as soon as he had brought you back. He wasn't supposed to tell anyone, but he knew how I was about you...' Ewan's voice was thick with emotion. 'What had you been doing all that time?'

'Look, I can't say too much here.' Glancing around the room, she didn't think anyone was eavesdropping, but she was trained to be careful. The old Juliet was impetuous and carefree, but she was a different person now. She wondered if she would ever be the same again. 'Let's finish these, and we can go for a walk. I'll tell you every-thing then. What about you?' She sipped her tea.

'I'm in bomber command. Over Germany, mostly.'

'It can't look worse than here,' she said ruefully.

'Oh, it does, darling, it really does. We've flat-tened most of it and will continue to do so until he surrenders.' Ewan's voice held no note of tri-umph but steely determination.

'It must be terrifying.'

'Aye, well we have them on the back foot now. But yeah, every night you wonder if this is your last. So many of the chaps I knew are gone. I sup-pose you just get on with it; try not to think about it too much. Just do your job.'

Juliet nodded. She knew exactly what he meant. They finished their drinks as he told her of his life since they'd last seen each other. Then they left the hotel and walked hand in hand to-wards Hyde Park. It was full of servicemen and women enjoying the fresh air.

Ewan said softly, 'It's a miracle we've found

each other again. When Dougie told me he had seen you, I...well, let's just say my reaction wasn't very manly. I can't ever remember crying as an adult until then. I was sure you were dead, you see.'

'I couldn't contact you in any way. Even thinking about the real me was dangerous. I had to be who they made me. But sometimes, when I felt scared or alone, I would write to you in my mind, and imagine you, maybe even flying over France, over me. And I prayed you would hear it. I never stopped loving you, Ewan.' She spoke quietly. She wanted him to understand that before she told him the rest of it.

He stopped and pulled her down beside him onto a bench. 'Nor me you. I'm never letting you go. They won't send you back again, will they?' he asked, suddenly anxious.

'No. I thought they might, and I'd have been willing to go, but it would be too dangerous. They know who I am, you see.'

Ewan looked at her incredulously. 'Who do? The Nazis?'

'Yes, I did something, fairly...fairly high profile, I suppose. So yes, the Nazis, Gestapo, Abwehr, know who I am – or more, who I was.'

Ewan was trying to take it in. 'And who were you?'

Juliet took a deep breath. Her whole future happiness would be decided in the next few minutes. She prayed he'd understand.

'My name was Marie-Louise. I started out as a receptionist for a doctor in Poitiers. I was also a nanny for his children. They were lovely boys. I used to deliver messages between various agents operating in the area.'

'Right under their noses? You are one plucky lady, Juliet Buckley.'

'Not really. As you said, you have a job to do and you just do it. Anyway, one day I was cycling to meet someone with an important message. It was freezing and pelting rain and the road was uphill. A German officer stopped his car.' She paused.

Ewan said, 'Go on.'

'He offered me a lift, and I had to take it. To do anything else would be suspicious. Then he asked me out, and I was terrified. Anyway, he wouldn't take no for an answer, and my superiors decided that I should accept. They suspected there had been a leak, you see, and they needed to find out the identity of the informer. If I got close to a German officer, I could find out things.'

She spoke slowly, looking straight ahead, not daring to check for his reaction. When Ewan said nothing, she continued.

'His name was Dieter Friedman, and he was a captain of the Wehrmacht. We moved into an apartment together, and I was his girlfriend. He was fairly high up and used to go to Berlin regularly, and he trusted me. I fed information to the Resistance. The information I found out was often very useful, but it was vital not to blow my cover. He never suspected a thing. Last month, a senior Abwehr officer came to Poitiers to meet with Dieter. My orders were to kill them both. So I did.'

The sounds of children playing and birds singing in the trees seemed incongruous with the weight of silence between her and Ewan. She longed for him to say something. She could hear him breathing beside her, and she turned to look at him for the first time since she began speaking. It was impossible to know what he was thinking.

'That's it then,' he said.

She felt panic rising in her chest. He was going to walk away. She wanted to beg, to explain but before she could form the words, he spoke again.

'We all do things in wartime that we would

never normally do. I don't like to think about the innocent women and children I kill every night, and I know I do kill them. It's not just military targets we sometimes need to take out, but installations in the middle of built-up areas. No one will emerge from this with clean hands. I don't need to know any more than what you've just told me. I love you, and I want to marry you if you'll have me. You did an incredible thing, and I'm so proud of you.'

Juliet finally allowed the tears to flow down her cheeks. She could now let go the emotions held so closely in check all this time.

Ewan held her as she cried and when she had no more tears, he wiped her face with his handkerchief and said, 'Well, the first time I proposed, I roared at you, and now when I do it, you won't stop crying! Are we getting married or what?'

'Yes. Yes please.' She giggled through her tears.

EPILOGUE

*S*pring 1943

Lili played on the grass as Richard and Solange sat on a rug in the garden in the early sunshine. She leaned her back against him, and he stroked her hair.

Mrs Canty had made them laugh earlier by announcing they were 'like a pair of young wans, always pawing each other.' They put up with her good-natured teasing because they both knew that she was secretly thrilled. The realisation that they loved each other was blissfully easy in the end. Though they could never marry, as Richard was already married, neither of them cared. They were married in everything but name and

Richard had even taken to calling Solange Mrs Buckley whenever he could.

James was slowly coming to terms with his wife's death. He had a long way to go but the initial outpouring of grief had abated. For the first few weeks, they never left him out of their sights. They had buried Ingrid in Dunderrig, and James went to the grave most days. Eddie had planted some flowers and they often took Lili there with her little watering can. The whole village came out for the funeral, which surprised Solange.

Richard had explained, 'Ingrid was James's wife, and James is one of their own. No matter what she did or didn't do, she was one of the Buckleys of Dunderrig and that means something around here.'

JAMES SAT BY THE sea at Barleycove, remembering the times he had laughed and talked here with Ingrid. He took her last letter out and unfolded it carefully. He'd read it so often, it was tearing on the creases.

My dear James,

If you are reading this, I am no longer here. I want to tell you that I'm sorry for everything, for lying to you, for using you and your beautiful home, and for putting you all in such danger. I never intended it to turn out this way. As I'm writing, Lili is asleep on our

579

bed beside me and if I could have one wish, it would be that I could be a good mother to her and a good wife to you. You deserve so much more than me, but no matter what happens, please know that I love you and I love Lili more than anyone or anything in this whole messed-up world. I know you will be a wonderful father to her, and between Solange and Richard and the Cantys, she will have a lovely life here in Dunderrig.

Goodbye, my precious James.

Your loving wife, Ingrid.

He could never reconcile the woman he loved with her treachery, and his father had advised him not to try. He told him to remember her as she was with him and with Lili and forget the rest. 'We adapt to our environments,' he said, 'and people do things in extreme circumstances that they would never normally do. Ingrid got caught up in something, and she paid the ultimate price. Let her rest in peace.'

He was taking his father's advice these days on most things, and though it was very hard and some days he struggled to get up, he knew that it was due to Solange and his father and the ever-present Cantys that he could keep going.

His father and Solange were so close these days, and James was happy for them.

Juliet's room was dusted and aired, and the sheets regularly changed, ready for when she came home. Mrs Canty still refused to put currants in the buns because Juliet hated currants, even though everyone else liked them. The possibility that Juliet might never see Dunderrig again was not one any of them gave voice to. Though he had no reason to think so other than his intuition, he was sure she wasn't dead and everyone around him clung to his belief. He missed her in a way no one could understand but going through everything in the past few years without her, had made him stronger in lots of ways. He'd always been led by Juliet but now he was a different person. He wanted to tell her that she had been right about Edith.

Edith came down for Ingrid's funeral, and everyone remained very dignified though Mrs Kelly nearly did herself an injury trying to get a look at her at the top of the church. Even Mrs Canty remained stoic in the face of her old adversary. He was so proud of Solange and his father that day. They shook hands with Edith and thanked her for coming. As James watched his mother get into Otto's car after the funeral, he knew for certain he would never see her again. Otto was in prison, awaiting trial, as was most of their circle. To his surprise, seeing her go, all he felt was relief.

As he looked out over the azure sea, he knew he was getting better. A part of him would always love Ingrid, but he knew he would survive.

He drove back to Dunderrig wanting to be in time to bathe Lili and read her a story before bed-time. They had moved back into the big house as the cottage held too many memories, and besides, it was easier with Lili. He had converted one of the outhouses into a studio and kept himself very busy with commissions. Lili loved Dunderrig and ran everyone ragged. Her delighted cries of, 'Daddy, come home!' whenever he walked in were the high point of his day.

Passing through the village, he saw the Cork bus offloading passengers and produce for the shops. As the bus pulled away, two figures were left standing. The woman was pointing some-thing out to the man and he had his arm protec-tively around her shoulders.

James turned the car and pulled up alongside them.

'Do ye need a lift?'

SOLANGE AND RICHARD HAD convinced the Cantys to sit down outside and have a cup of tea, though neither of them was comfortable doing so. Despite being in their late seventies, they both worked all day every day. Richard and Solange tried everything to get them to take a holiday, or even a day off, but they always resisted. Eventually, Solange realised that Dunderrig was their home and the care of the Buckleys their purpose as they saw it, and to make them leave it, even for a few days, would only upset them. Eventually, she stopped trying. Instead, she employed a young lad from the village to help Eddie with the heavy work, and a lady came twice a week to help out with the laundry and the cleaning. Mrs Canty grumbled that it wasn't done properly but everyone, including herself, knew she needed the extra pair of hands.

They turned to look up the avenue at the sound of an approaching car.

'Ah good, James is back, I'll just get another cup.' Mrs Canty went to get up.

'God almighty, woman, will you sit down! He's big and hairy enough to get his own bloody cup, not have you running around after him like he's three years old,' bellowed Richard, mock annoyed.

Solange was pouring milk into a small tumbler for Lili, who was happily munching on a freshly baked bun. No one noticed that James had two passengers in the car until he pulled up in front of the door and shouted out the window, 'There better not be currants in those buns!'

The car door opened, and Richard and Solange turned at the same time to see her standing there in the sunshine – beautiful and radiant and beaming from ear to ear. Beside her, in RAF blues, was a tall, good-looking man.

Richard ran to her, scooping her up in his arms as if she were a child again.

'My darling girl...you came home. I was so worried...I thought we'd lost you.'

When her father finally let her go, Solange held Juliet so tight she nearly choked her, tears pouring down her cheeks. Mrs Canty was as giddy as a two-year-old, fussing about food and sheets, while James held Lili in his arms. Richard pumped Ewan's hand, 'Thank you, thank you for bringing her home to us.'

'No problem, sir,' replied Ewan. 'I always promised her we'd be together in Dunderrig, but we just got a bit delayed.'

'Who dat, Ganda?' Lili asked Richard, pointing shyly at Juliet.

'That, Lili,' Richard told her as he picked her up in his arms, 'is your Auntie Juliet. She's a very bold girl for going off and not telling her Daddy where she went.' He squeezed his daughter with his free arm. 'She has spent her life putting grey hairs on my head, but I've never been so happy to see anyone.'

Eddie waited his turn as the family crowded around Juliet, all talking at the same time. Eventually, she spotted him and went to stand beside him. Everyone was fussing about cups and glasses for the champagne that Solange had miraculously produced.

'What was it I taught you that was so useful?' he asked quietly, the question was still on his mind since the last letter two years earlier. 'Was there much call for gardening where you were?'

Juliet put her arms around the man she always saw as her granddad and whispered in his ear. 'Not gardening, no, but I was glad you taught me to shoot.'

The End

AFTERWORD

If you enjoyed this book, and I sincerely hope that you did, you might consider writing a review on Amazon.com. It is a wonderful way for me to connect with readers and feedback is always welcome and very much appreciated.
If you would like a free novel, just go to www. jeangrainger.com and join my readers club, membership is totally free and always will be.

PREVIEW OF SHADOW OF A
CENTURY - CHAPTER 1

*S*carlett set the alarm on her new cream Mini Cooper. It emitted a satisfying beep as she crossed the underground parking lot of the *Examiner* Building. She felt a surge of pure joy. For the first time in her whole life, everything was perfect. She looked great, an expensive new wardrobe saw to that, and she knew that she was unrecognisable from the insecure girl she had once been. The elevator doors opened and she stepped in. The young cub reporter from the sports desk nodded, and then stared at the floor. She smiled to herself. She didn't intend to be intimidating but she was now senior staff so the kid probably didn't know what to say to her.

As the elevator ascended to the fourteenth

floor and the editorial suite, she had to remind herself once more that this was really happening. Her years slaving for Artie on the *Yonkers Express* were behind her and here she was, a senior political correspondent for the *Examiner*, one of the biggest nationals in the country.

She glanced at her iPhone. It was odd that Charlie hadn't texted; he usually did, to check that she had gotten up. He was always gone by 5 a.m. on the nights he could stay, but last night he couldn't make it. She understood. In his position, his time was rarely his own. She smiled as she thought of the private messages he was sending her on Facebook last night while he was supposed to be deep in discussion with the representative of a powerful lobby group for tax reform on a video conference call. Ron Waters was a crashing bore according to Charlie, and a Republican through and through, so he was never going to vote for Charlie or his party anyway, but he had to be seen to show willingness. He promised he was trying to get her some face time with the guy, though, for another high profile *Examiner* piece.

The elevator door opened and the bright, modern, busy Newsroom buzzed in front of her. Hundreds of screens flashed images, and lots of reporters, IT people and administration staff seemed to teem constantly from all directions. She breathed deeply, almost inhaling the atmosphere and didn't miss Artie and his chain-smoking ways one little bit. She made her way with enthusiasm to the office of Carol Steinberg, the editor in chief.

Scarlett could hardly believe she was heading into her eighth month of working here, the time had flown by and her star was definitely on the rise. The piece she had done on the extremist Islamic mullah on the Lower East Side was garnering a lot of attention. Her pieces on Charlie were also getting her a lot of column inches, much to the chagrin of many of the other journalists in the city. Carol's text saying 'Get here ASAP' had come through when she was driving into the office anyway. She was looking forward to the meeting. The urgency of the text suggested some exciting development. Scarlett knew that Carol had a reputation as ball-breaker, that she intimidated almost all of the staff, but Scarlett admired her. She had to be tough to get where she was and one day Scarlett intended to hold a similar position.

Was she imagining it or did the noise in the office, usually so deafening, suddenly drop to a murmur? The political team were standing to-gether at their corner by the bank of flat screen plasma TVs. She wasn't imagining it; they had all stopped talking and were staring at her. They must be really ticked off about the mullah story, she thought.

She pushed open the opaque glass door of Carol's office and entered the sumptuous sur-roundings. The TV beside her desk was live paused, and Scarlett instantly recognised Char-lie's handsome features, stilled in mid-sentence.

'I'm assuming you've seen this?' Carol's voice was quiet but lacked her usual warmth.

Scarlett was nonplussed, 'No, is this from to-day? I haven't seen...'

Carol interrupted her by pressing play on the remote. Charlie was unshaven and tired looking. He looked as if he'd slept in his shirt. His familiar voice filled the office.

'Words can't express my regret. I have of-fended my party, the good people of this city who elected me, and most painfully of all, I have let my family down. I feel deep shame and embar-rassment at my reckless and unprofessional be-havior, and though I don't deserve any special favours, I would ask you, ladies and gentlemen of the press, to restrict your interest to me and to leave my family out of this. They are innocents in this whole thing and are suffering enough at this time. Thank you.'

Charlie turned away and went back into the offices behind him in a hail of questions and flashing cameras.

'I don't understand.' Scarlett's voice cracked. 'What happened?'

Carol gazed at her with thinly veiled fury.

'Last night Charlie Morgan was in a video conference meeting with Ron Waters, the Republican senator. Morgan was sending him some data to support a point he was making, but he inadvertently sent him a message of an explicit sexual nature, clearly intended for someone else. The message also mentioned *this* newspaper by name. To add insult to injury, the message went on to outline how boring and stupid Morgan thought Waters was. Waters immediately reacted and exposed Morgan, who has, about an hour ago, admitted that he is having an affair with a journalist, the person for whom the message was intended. In addition, he has told the world who that journalist is.'

Scarlett felt nauseous. Blood thundered in her ears. This wasn't happening, it couldn't be.

Charlie would never do anything like that to her. He couldn't, he loved her.

'I took a chance on you, Scarlett. You are only twenty-six, very young to hold the position you did.' Scarlett heard her use of the past tense and every fibre of her being prayed that this wasn't happening.

Carol went on, her voice icy, 'I appointed you over others who have more experience, and who felt they deserved it more than you. I thought you had something, that's why I convinced the board to take you on. I'm at a loss for words. How could you throw everything away, everything you've worked for, and more to the point, how could you have dragged us into this mess with you? We pride ourselves on the highest standards of journalistic integrity here at the *Examiner*. You have let us down, very badly. To have an affair with a politician for someone in your position is to relinquish all moral and professional authority.'

Carol's tone conveyed nothing but disgust. 'Your in-depth interviews with him that we printed have made us look as foolish and corrupt as you are. But to be involved with a married politician, especially one whose unique selling point is his position as a family man, something you wrote about with such empathy... words escape me, Scarlett. I'm so disappointed in you. I thought you were so much better than this. Get your things now, rather than coming back for them, and try to get away without the gathering press outside seeing you leave, though they are already circling the wagons.'

She paused, and then added coldly, 'And Scarlett, if you give any interviews about this I'll drag you through every court in the country. Do I make myself clear?'

Carol got up and without a backward glance left the room.

There she is! Scarlett! Scarlett, over here! Just turn around! C'mon Scarlett ...'

Scarlett emerged from the car and pushed her way up the steps to the front door of her brownstone, blinded by the incessant flashing of cameras as she pushed through the heaving mass of bodies. Every hack in New York was out in force, circling like vultures. News anchors smugly did their pieces on camera down the street. The fact that the target was one of their own had obviously made it even more tantalising for them. Many of them resented her growing profile, and felt she was too young and had come out of nowhere, so they were thrilled to see her crumble. No such thing as loyalty in this business, she thought, while trying to keep her face immobile.

She fumbled for her keys in the bottom of her new Prada handbag as the reporters jostled and pushed to get closer to her. Her red hair was escaping from the chignon she had hastily tied in the car, and she could feel the make-up slide from her face as she began to sweat. Despite her best efforts to look calm and collected, she was cracking. She couldn't find the damn key, and her hands began to shake badly as she gritted her teeth, determined not to cry, refusing to show any weakness. They'd love that. Not that anything could make this situation any worse, but to have her tear stained face splashed all over every tabloid and gossip show in town would be the final straw.

'Come on Scarlett, just one shot. At least this way you get to look good!' There was a collective cackle.

Would she have been any different if it was one of them? If she was to be honest, probably not, except that salacious sex scandals were not really her thing. Mercifully, she finally found the key, and despite her shaking hands, managed on the third attempt to get it into the lock. She quickly slipped inside and slammed the heavy door shut, leaning her back against it, adjusting her eyes to the relative gloom of the hallway. Relief flooded through her. Everything was as she'd left it this morning. The highly polished mahogany staircase gleamed, its snow white carpet runner fluffily breaking the austerity of the architecture. The house smelled exactly as it had done, of lilies and cleanliness, an oasis of serenity.

She went into the kitchen at the end of the hallway and immediately shut the blinds. Alone, in her new beautiful home, she disintegrated into wracking sobs. The strength that held her together for the past two hours suddenly drained out of her. The paintings, mirrors and everything else she had gathered so lovingly over the years were invisible to her now. That was it, it was all over. Her life was over. This just couldn't be happening. That press conference playing over and over in her head.

How could Charlie have hung her out to dry like that?

Dreading what she was about to see, she typed 'Charlie Morgan confesses all' into YouTube. She watched in horror as he explained that he was a weak, foolish man who loved his family, and he deeply regretted his inappropriate liaison with the political correspondent Scarlett O'Hara.

Facebook, Twitter and bloggers were already on the puns. Torturing herself, she scrolled through, "Charlie's Scarlett Woman," "Morgan really has Gone with the Wind," "Frankly my dear." It went on and on and on.

Scarlett hated her name. She used to dread meeting new people and enduring their shocked expressions, the attempts to hide a smirk, or the all too common 'did you know there was a movie...?' When she met Charlie, he told her he wanted to be her Rhett Butler. She felt a sharp stab of pain at the memory. Normally anyone who would have said such a thing would have felt the sharp end of her tongue, but he was different. Even though he constantly joked and teased her about it, she forgave him. She forgave him everything, and then he betrayed her.

CHAPTER 2

Scarlett sat on her Roche-Dobois oatmeal sofa that had cost almost a month's salary. She fought back the panic at the thought of her mortgage and credit card bills now that she was unemployed. She could hear the raucous laughter of the journalists outside the door. She longed for someone to help her, somewhere to go, but she realised that in recent years she had had no time to keep up friendships. She avoided her mother, and she had no other family. Charlie took up any spare time she had, waiting for him to call, or grasping precious moments with him. Without him and her job she had nothing, absolutely nothing. A feeling of hopelessness, something she had not felt for so long, came creeping back.

She was drawn back to another time, another sofa, in a dingy run-down apartment in Yonkers. The familiar feelings of terror threatened to choke her as she remembered sitting on her mother's lap, in the calm after the cops had picked her father up yet again. She could only have been four or five, trying with her little hands to stem the blood from a cut on her mother's face or holding frozen peas to a swelling injury. She would say prayers to the many Catholic saints represented on the damp walls of the room, that her mother wouldn't die. Lorena took her faith seriously, and the only thing that equalled her faith was her love of movies. She would tell Scarlett how she was named after the most beautiful woman in the world, and then, when she knew it was safe, her mother would draw out her old cookie tin from under the table and show her the pictures from her old movie magazines. To Scarlett, the names of Vivien Leigh, Fred Astaire and James Dean were as real as her mother and father. It was one of the many things about his wife that drove Dan O'Hara mad, and when he was mad he was terrifying.

She remembered the titters from the other

children and the outrage from Sister Teresita in St. Peter and Paul's Elementary when she announced that she was not, as was Catholic tradition, named after a saint, but instead after the most beautiful woman in the world.

As she became a teenager, though, she learned to hate her name. The childhood innocence was laughed out of existence by bullies and teachers who jeered and mocked. She tried several times to shorten it and did everything she could to get a nickname, but nothing would stick. She was born Scarlett O'Hara and Scarlett O'Hara she was going to stay. She was teased mercilessly.

Dan O'Hara, Scarlett's father, was regularly to be seen staggering drunk around the streets of Yonkers, bellowing abuse at passers-by and scaring kids. He was from County Mayo in Ireland and had come over to the United States as a young man full of dreams and ambition. Life was going well for a time, and he met and married Lorena, a fragile hot house flower from Georgia, whose southern charm beguiled the young Irishman. But things soon turned sour. Dan was a charmer, good looking and smart, but work-shy. He always wanted to make a fast buck but never did any actual work. He had a friend who worked in construction who offered him job after job, but Dan would scoff, claiming that manual labour was for 'fellas too thick to do anything else.' He always had a scheme going, some kind of a scam to get rich quick. He convinced several people to invest in his so-called business opportunities, and to a man they lost their shirts on them. Eventually, he was untouchable and started drinking. He was unwelcome in the more respectable establishments, so he hung out in grotty, smelly bars, and over time, he was even barred from them.

The blame for his failure was never his own. No, it was Lorena and Scarlett's fault. They were holding him back, he used to snarl. If he didn't have them hanging on to him, he'd be making a fortune out west. His disappointment with life was expressed by using his beautiful young wife as a punch-bag. Scarlett had hated him.

When Lorena opened the door to the police, the winter Scarlett was fifteen, they told her Dan had walked in front of a truck. She tried her best to compose her face into that of a grief-stricken widow. Scarlett remembered Sergeant Kane, who'd been coming to arrest Dan for all sorts of offences over the years, not the least battering his family, sending the other officer to wait in the car. He sat down in the tiny living room and said,

'That's it Lorena. You and Scarlett are safe now. It's over.'

Lorena looked as if a huge weight had been removed from her, though she was in a daze of disbelief. Scarlett remembered Sergeant Kane explaining how her father had been killed instantly; he would have known no pain. Witnesses said he seemed to be very unsteady on his feet as the truck approached.

'What kind of truck was it?' she asked, only mildly curious.

The sergeant tried his best to remain composed, professional, but he'd known this misfortunate family a long time. Though he normally hated bringing news of this nature, in this case it was a blessing. Fighting a smile, he said, 'A Guinness truck.'

Scarlett's abiding memory of her father's untimely death was of her mother and Sergeant Kane weeping with uncontrolled gales of laughter.

Life got much easier after that, in lots of ways. Lorena, who was becoming even more zealous about her Catholic faith as the years progressed, gave the teenage Scarlett enough freedom to do as she wished. Lorena had been raised Baptist, but Catholicism appealed to her dramatic nature, so she had converted when she married Dan. She loved all the pomp and ceremony, and every spare wall of her house was adorned with icons and statues and holy pictures. She had a particular love of the more gruesome ones. In the hallway there was one of St. Stephen being stoned to death that really used to freak Scarlett out. The house was a source of cringing embarrassment, but since she wasn't that close to anyone anyway, she didn't have to endure kids from school seeing the macabre décor of her home.

School was fine. She loved English and had a great teacher who inspired her to think for herself. He often lent her books or printed out articles for her to read about world events. She wished she had blonde hair and tanned skin. Failing that, she would have really liked to look like Gloria Estefan, but her Irish heritage gave her flame red hair, alabaster skin and emerald green eyes. Boys tended to steer clear, their parents warning them off because of Dan, so she kept herself to herself. One guy had asked her to the prom, but she declined. He was good looking and seemed nice, but there was no way she was having him come to the house. Scarlett remembered her mother's disappointment when she said she wouldn't be going. Lorena had bought her a dress, but Scarlett couldn't face going, nor could she explain to her mother why, so she sat in her room and read instead. She loved travel books, especially the books by the *BBC World News* Editor, John Simpson. He wrote with empathy and intelligence about places Scarlett could only dream of, Afghanistan, Iraq, Russia. She devoured his books and dreamed of one day visiting those places.

In her final year at school, she signed up for a trip with her political science class to hear a Bostonian congressman who was touring high schools in the tougher areas of New York. He was a noted self-server, and it looked good for the electorate that he cared about those less well off. He was part of a National Education Taskforce that was allegedly asking the students what they thought should be done to improve educational standards in disadvantaged school districts. He was a pompous ass, as she recalled, and patronised and flirted with the girls in her class. He tried to flatter her during the coffee break, asking her questions while all the time ogling her breasts. He repulsed her. At the end, the girls were given an opportunity to ask him any questions. The teacher, Miss Fletcher, was obviously a fan of the congressman and giggled and fawned whenever he addressed her. She'd prepared a long list of sycophantic questions and distributed them among the students, giving him ample opportunity to explain just how wonderful he was and how marvellous it was that he would ask their lowly opinions.

For no reason other than to knock him off his stupid perch, Scarlett raised her hand to ask a question. It was not the one on the card distributed by Miss Fletcher.

'Where do you stand on the subject of Gay rights?'

It was 2007 and the St Patrick's Day parade in the city was drawing the usual controversy by continuing to ban the Gay, Lesbian, Bisexual and Transgender groups from marching. She had read about it in the paper that morning over breakfast. Miss Fletcher went pink and stammered, 'I...I'm sorry Congressman Bailey. That was not an authorised question...' she glared with unconcealed horror at Scarlett.

The congressman gave a slimy grin and said, 'That's quite alright Deanna... I mean Miss Fletcher.' The teacher had blushed and giggled again. 'I'm sure this little lady didn't mean any offence.'

He turned towards Scarlett. 'Now then my dear, a nicely brought up girl such as yourself need not concern herself with such things. I'm sure that nobody at St. Peter and Paul's wants its young ladies discussing a matter that is, after all, a mortal sin. The church is very clear on its position on that subject, and as a devout Catholic I would vote with my conscience.' His smug self-satisfied smile made Scarlett want to punch him in his stupid fat face.

That was the day the Scarlett decided she would be a journalist.

CHAPTER 3

She walked into her beautifully decorated bedroom. The kingsize bed dominated the sunny space, and dust mites danced in the shaft of sunlight that streamed through the glass doors that led to a small balcony. She caught a glimpse of her reflection in the full length mirror that formed the doors to her walk in closet. She looked awful, pale and dishevelled, eyes red from crying. Though the room overlooked the little communal garden at the back, she quickly closed the blinds in case one of the hacks managed to get in and perch himself in a tree, waiting for the perfect shot with his long range lens. She sat on her bed, and held a pillow up to her face. It smelled of him, of his faintly spicy cologne. How often had she gone to sleep in his arms, only to wake alone. Always the same story. She was transported back to the early days of their relationship, before she became used to his early morning disappearances.

Scarlett recalled vividly how the alarm of his cell phone cut through the darkness. She stirred, wrapping her legs around him, willing the piercing ringtone to stop, her face buried in the back of his neck, her arm around his chest.

Charlie groaned and gently removed her arm. 'I have to go.' He kissed her palm as he tucked her arm under the sheet.

'But it's only...' Scarlett picked up her phone, '2 a.m... for God's sake.'

Charlie ran his hand through his tousled brown curls. 'I know but I said I'd take C.J. to school. First day and all that. I can't just rock up at 7 a.m. You know that.'

'What will you say?' her voice was steady, betraying none of what she felt.

'Oh, a meeting ran on, something like that. Don't worry about it. I'll try to call later.' He padded into the shower, washing all traces of her and her house from his skin. He asked her not to wear perfume in case Julia smelled it on his clothes, even the shower gel she bought was fragrance free.

Feigning sleep, she heard him slip out. He'd walk the two blocks to the subway and take a cab from there. Despite his passionate nature, Charlie Morgan was very careful. She tortured herself imagining him slipping into bed with Julia, she all concerned that he worked so hard. Then she'd wake in the morning, looking fresh as a daisy and prepare their two adorable children for school. She was beautiful in a really natural way, no botox or plastic surgery. Her hair was naturally blonde and her skin tanned to a golden brown since she played often on the beach with the kids. She was on several worthy committees and was always in the papers. The perfect politician's wife.

Scarlett lay down on the bed and pulled the cover over herself, glad of the warmth. Though filled with self-loathing, she tried think. It wasn't all her fault. She had never intended for things to turn out like this. She was doing a profile piece on him in the run up to the election and had met him and Julia at home. Carol was amazed and delighted she had managed to secure a feature piece on him. He was notoriously private about his family, and Scarlett knew it was a really good mark for her, especially since she had only been

with the *Examiner* a few short months. He repeatedly explained to the media that his children and
his wife did not run for election, and so he
wanted them to have as normal a life as possible.
This 'family comes first' attitude had won him
lots of votes in a world where most politicians
used their kids to further their own campaigns.

During the interview, the Morgan children,
then aged five and seven, played angelically with
educational and sustainable wooden toys while
munching happily on carrot sticks and hummus.
Julia sat on their large comfortable sofa beside
her husband. If you had to draw the perfect
American family, the Morgans were as close as
you could get. The perception was that Charlie
Morgan was a powerful man, unafraid to do what
was right, but despite that, an all-round good guy.
Scarlett was terrified but managed to hide her
nerves as she asked intelligent and pertinent
questions. Artie had set the interview up for her,
but made her promise to take the credit. Her old
editor was more like a father figure to her, and
though he made out like he was insulted that she
had left him and got the job at the *Examiner*, she
knew that really he was proud of her. He knew
Charlie Morgan's father from years ago, so pulled
in a favour.

The interview was wide ranging, sounding Charlie Morgan out on issues from abortion to gun control, and he presented a compassionate yet realistic case for everything. Broadminded, liberal, he appeared to have his feet very firmly planted in the realpolitik of twenty first century America.

So impressed was she with him, that she wrote an uncharacteristically flattering piece on him, admitting that she had been looking for flaws but there just didn't seem to be any cracks in the image he presented to the world. All really was as it seemed. Of solid New England stock, he had graduated from Harvard and chose to leave the family business to his brothers and entered politics. Julia was his childhood sweetheart and they seemed happy. As he sat in the sunny living room of his Montauk home, he looked handsome and relaxed. Not slimy or aggressive or sexist or any of the other traits she'd come to associate with politicians. His brown, slightly curly hair was well cut to look casual, and the light blue linen shirt and Levi 501s fitted him perfectly. His skin was tanned dark brown from a summer sail-boarding with his children.

It was at moments like this that it struck her how far she'd come from the cowering kid of a crazy alcoholic Irishman and poor old Lorena. She had kept her promise to herself and studied hard for her last year at school and graduated, then went to the local community college to study journalism. There was no way Lorena could have afforded to send her to one of the big colleges.

She did well and managed to get a job on a local Yonkers newspaper, writing about local charities and reporting on town council meetings. Artie Schwitz, the editor, was a small old Jew who liked the spark he saw in Scarlett. He remembered Dan from his days drinking and roaring around the streets and decided to give his daughter a chance. She was tenacious and dogged in her pursuit of stories, often scooping the bigger publications, and it was through her persistence she managed to increase the circulation of the *Yonkers Express* to record numbers. The interview she had done with the mullah from a radical Islamist mosque on the Lower East Side, who had refused all interviews before, plucked her from obscurity. In a letter that she was sure was correct, written in his native tongue, she'd told the old man from Iraq how she had gone to night school to learn Arabic. He agreed to talk to her and explained the despair and fear in Moslems in

New York in the wake of 9/11. It was an unimaginable scoop for their small paper and led to a huge surge in circulation.

Her coverage of 9/11 continued to be very well received, and when she wrote a feature on the reaction of the Islamic community of the city to the terrorist attacks one year on, with the blessing of the mullah, she won the prestigious Carter award for journalism, the youngest ever recipient. She knew she was on the rise, and when she saw Carol Steinberg at a press event, she approached her and asked her for a job. Carol had smiled politely and suggested that she email her resume to the *Examiner* office. Two weeks later she had an interview. Life since then was a whirlwind. She bought a small house, a car and a whole new wardrobe on the strength of her new salary and the money she had saved over the years working for Artie. She was on top of the world.

Charlie made no reference to the fact that his father had asked him to do the interview as a favour to Artie, and she was grateful to him for that. In the months that followed, they would meet at events and they were always friendly. Then one night in Atlantic City, after a Democrat campaign meeting, they found themselves staying at the same hotel. He invited her for a nightcap in the small residents' bar, and not realising his staff had gone for the night, she agreed.

They talked and laughed until the early hours, and she found herself telling him about her father. Not used to drinking, she poured her heart out, about the violence and fear that overshadowed her childhood. Her anger at her mother for not leaving, for not keeping them safe from him, and her anger at Lorena for giving her such a stupid name, it all came out. Charlie said he loved that she was called Scarlett O'Hara and that she was every bit as hot as Vivien Leigh.

He listened without judging and congratulated her sincerely on how far she'd come. Undoubtedly the whiskey played a part, for she had never told anyone about her past, but Charlie was easy to talk to. She felt she could trust him. They met a few more times after that night, both knowing an affair was inevitable. And so it began, she was his mistress, the other woman. She looked at herself in the mirror some mornings and said that to herself, but those sordid, dirty little words just couldn't be applied to what she and Charlie had. With him, it was honest, it was love.

She tried to block out Julia and his children,

the eldest now about to start middle school. If the relationship was good, he wouldn't be seeing Scarlett. That's what she told herself. He never gave her any of the standard lines, that his wife didn't understand him, that he was only staying for the sake of the kids, that they'd be together properly when the kids left school. He simply never discussed it. His life with Julia was one thing, his life with Scarlett something else completely and never the twain shall meet.

She pretended that it suited her, that she was so taken up with her career that a full-time relationship would be just too restrictive. But as the months went on, she knew she was lying, to him and to herself. She never raised the subject with him, probably, she told herself, because she wasn't at all sure of what his reaction would be. He told her all the time that he loved her, that she was not like anyone he'd ever met, that she was gorgeous, but still she was not convinced. If he had to choose, would she be the one? He used to joke that she was his Vivien Leigh and always signed his texts 'Rhett' or just 'R'. She always thought it was cute, though she wished he could have chosen something other than her ridiculous name to make jokes about. In the cold reality of what had happened, she realised that he wrote R in case anyone found the texts. Charlie was protecting himself.

And now, the worst possible thing had happened. She'd destroyed everything she'd worked so hard to build.

Available at most online retailers.

ACKNOWLEDGMENTS

To finish a book, you have to be selfish. As a mother of four with a full-time job, opportunities for selfishness are few and far between unless you are lucky enough to have someone else to do the endless driving, collecting, feeding, cooking, shopping, funding, and conflict resolution, which is part of everyday life in our house. I am that lucky. Without Diarmuid's endless patience, love and support, both moral and practical, there would be no books.

I would also like to thank my friends whose encouragement to a man (and woman) has been invaluable. You never doubted me, even when you probably should have. Ye mean the world to me and ye know who ye are.

Thanks to my family, who are always on hand to cheer the victories and give each other courage in the darker days. The Ewan McGregor story is true, by the way.

To my editor Helen Falconer I owe a huge

debt. Through her talent and wit, she manages to turn what could, and possibly should, be a difficult process of carving up your first draft into something fun. Her observations regularly have us both in fits of laughter. Thanks Helen, you are wonderful. To my colleagues and friends Beth-Anne and Cecille for fixing my French, *merci beaucoup*!

Finally, to Conor, Sórcha, Éadaoin, and Siobhán, my proudest achievements yet.

ALSO BY JEAN GRAINGER

To get a free novel and to join my readers club (100% free and always will be)

Go to www.jeangrainger.com

The Tour Series

The Tour

Safe at the Edge of the World

The Story of Grenville King

The Homecoming of Bubbles O'Leary

Finding Billie Romano

Kayla's Trick

The Carmel Sheehan Story

Letters of Freedom

The Future's Not Ours To See

What Will Be

The Robinswood Story

What Once Was True

Return To Robinswood

Trials and Tribulations

The Star and the Shamrock Series

The Star and the Shamrock

The Emerald Horizon

The Hard Way Home

The World Starts Anew

The Queenstown Series

Last Port of Call

The West's Awake

The Harp and the Rose

Roaring Liberty

Standalone Books

So Much Owed

Shadow of a Century

Under Heaven's Shining Stars

Catriona's War

Sisters of the Southern Cross

Made in United States
North Haven, CT
17 October 2023

42863746R00375